THE PRESIDENT'S DAUGHTER

BOOK TWO: TRIAL BY ICE

Copyright © 2025 Micky O'Brady
Cover Design: www.KimG-Design.com
Interior Format: Dorothy Dreyer

Published by Snowy Wings Publishing
PO Box 1035, Turner, OR 97392

Paperback ISBN: 978-1-963870-19-0
eBook ISBN: 978-1-963870-18-3

THE PRESIDENT'S DAUGHTER

BOOK TWO: TRIAL BY ICE

MICKY O'BRADY

Table of Contents

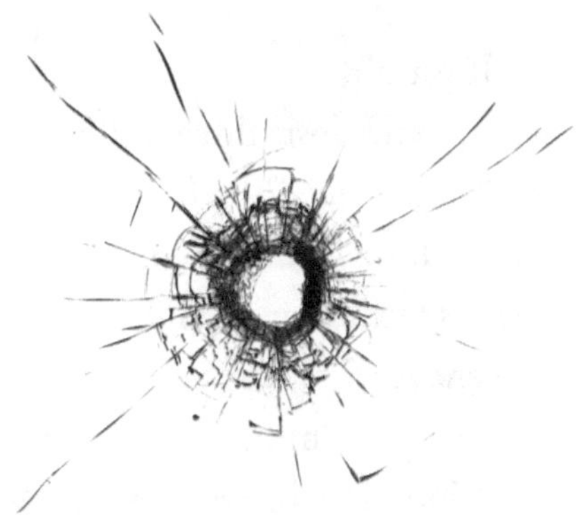

CHAPTER ONE
Smack in the Middle

"Keep your steps light. If we set off the motion detectors, they're gonna come running." My tour guide's voice is no more than a whisper before he waves for me to follow him around the last bend in this empty and sterile hallway.

Not a problem, but not because I'm super sneaky—I'm not. My thumping heart alone would set off the motion detectors, if Ian hadn't disabled them.

Sorry, Megatech United. You may house the target of my mission, the MU Titan, MU's top-of-the-line electronic brain, but your security is lacking.

Like your data protection.

Megatech United recently snagged a contract for Government Cyber Security thanks to bargain rates and a couple of Democrats siding with the Republicans in thinking outsourcing Government Cyber Security to save tax dollars would be the right way to go.

Yeah. Surprise. It wasn't.

Two months in, MU lost three million Social Security records last week. *Ouch.* The FBI's Cyber Counterintelligence Unit scoured MU for leaks and breaches but came up empty. Neither they nor MU's technicians could explain what happened to the data. It just went *poof.*

And that would be why I'm here for this historic mission—the first official collaboration between a sitting president and PRICS.

Drumroll, please.

My tour guide—Stephen, I think—glances over his shoulder at me. "Right there." He nods to a set of imposing double doors ahead. "You'll love this. Fifty trillion calculations per second. Connected via high-speed optical network. Wooo!" He pumps one fist in the air.

Well, good thing we also killed audio.

"Can't wait," I hiss-whisper back and give him a thumbs-up. Never been gladder to be a geek and science nerd.

Of course the president would show his genius-level daughter America's premier computer lab.

Of course she'd get her own private tour, while her father got one by CEO Masterson himself.

Of course she'd sweet-talk her guide to show her the Titan, and *of course* she'd get close enough to plant a bug. We don't like data to go *poof,* especially ours, and especially confidential data.

I brush my thumb over the ring on my fourth finger. Ready.

Stephen stops in front of the double doors. They scream security—warning signs, a palm scanner, triple-camera coverage. No angle uncovered, no shot missed.

Stephen throws a nervous glance at the ceiling. "They're at lunch. They only check the footage if something else triggers."

Like motion. Like sound. Which we took care of.

Shh—the video is gone too, they just don't know it.

And they'll never find out.

Stephen swipes his card and presses his palm to the scanner, forcing a daredevil grin that looks more queasy, actually. He's not the type to sneak into the Titan without permission, but resistance was futile: a fellow geek plus the president's daughter? *I have my ways.*

The five locks on the double doors disengage in sequence.

And we're in.

I stroke the ring's blue stone—housing a supercharged electromagnetic pulse emitter coupled to a high-frequency bundle brancher. All I need is a couple of seconds within fifteen centimeters of the Titan, and Ian's newest creation, a self-embedding surveillance program named Sneaker, will do its magic.

Not even Titan's power brain will know what hit it: within point-oh-oh-three seconds, the EPS emitter plus brancher will drill a peephole for Sneaker to get through and piggyback itself into the Titan's system, no matter its firewall or defenses—mission accomplished.

With a scratching squeak the double doors slide open in front of us, and I hold back from cranking my neck and shaking out my arms. Would be too obvious, right?

Showtime.

Stephen takes me by the elbow and across the threshold, and I stumble over my feet, because this… This is *whoa.*

I knew the Titan was massive—there's a reason for that name, presumably—but this… This spans a football field. Two stories of pristine white walls, white floors and white ceiling, crossed by a catwalk. Pure sci-fi, bathed in eye-searing light.

And it holds the biggest electronic brain I've ever seen.

No beginning, no end: Twenty-plus rows of over one-hundred man-high racks hold the tech making the Titan a supercomputer legend. A faint blue hue emanates from all of them, and I'm in geek heaven. This machine was thought infallible—until it lost the social security data, that is.

Stephen bows. "Voila, the heart of the company: the mighty Titan." He pushes his glasses back up his nose.

I take a couple of steps into the room.

Breathtaking.

Like a metallic giant the Titan's frame ascends until it nearly grazes the walkway connecting the two second-floor doors. Despite its imposing presence, it runs so quietly, our footsteps echo off the surfaces. Something so massive, engineered to run on a whisper, not a roar. Truly fascinating.

I play with the ring, giving the little stone a half-turn to the right until I feel a slight vibration: activated. Now I only need to get closer to *somewhere* on this ginormous thing to release Sneaker.

I turn to Stephen. "It's incredible. I never imagined… wow. Look at it!" I layer wonder into my voice, while I step closer to the Titan.

Fifteen centimeters away from a main drive. Looking at the size of this thing, I should be good anywhere here.

Stephen rocks back and forth on his heels, beaming like an excited school kid. "You've heard all the specifics of course but let me tell you this little goodie: We've got quantum-hardened neural barriers thicker than the Great Wall of China, zero-day defense matrices working alongside our autonomous code-healing protocols. Our distributed blockchain verification runs through military-grade quantum encryption. Titan is not just a super-computer—it's a self-evolving digital fortress with the most advanced cognitive architecture you'll find world-wide. Smartest artificial brain. Period."

I nod. I know. But the very brightest *organic* brain works for us and is about to have me unleash his surveillance program onto the Titan.

My footsteps echo as I approach one of the monolithic server towers, its black surface gleaming under the glaring bright lights. I stretch my hand out—just one touch and it should be enough to release the bundle brancher and—

"Stop!"

The command cracks like a whip through the processor-lined corridor.

The command slices through the humming silence. Every muscle in my body seizes, my hand frozen mid-reach.

"Hands where I can see them! Don't. Move. A. Muscle!"

Iron authority rings in each syllable. I swallow hard. Crap. Not as I planned this mission to go.

"Now slowly turn around! Slowly!" Metal-soled boots whisper-click against the raised floor. The sound echoes off the server walls, making it impossible to pinpoint its source.

From somewhere behind me, Stephen's control splinters. His breathing comes in short, panicked bursts: "Oh shit, oh shit, oh shit," each repetition higher than the last.

Double-crap. I bite back a curse. We're in deep. A guard— an actual guard. Our intel had promised empty corridors. There wasn't supposed to be a guard! I close my eyes and silently groan in frustration. So close, I was *so close*.

My PRICS-training kicks in. Deep breath. Analyze and act accordingly. What can I—

I turn around and look straight into the barrel of a gun aimed right at my head.

"Whoa!" The word breaks free in a pathetic squeak. "Easy there!"

My body betrays me with an instinctive step backward, courtesy of slight PTSD when it comes to guns. Happens when a sniper was out to kill your dad.

My sudden movement makes the gunman shift his stance, but his aim doesn't waver. If anything, the barrel rises with practiced precision.

Oh, shoot. No pun intended.

This isn't a rent-a-cop with a weekend-certification. Everything about him screams military: The way he fills out the black uniform, like it's tactical gear, how his body is coiled like a predator, the hair buzzed to near invisibility. Oh, and his neck is as wide as my thigh.

That guy means business.

And he keeps the gun aimed right between my eyes.

I swallow dry. Triple-crap.

A little whimper comes from Stephen. He shakes like a leaf— so much that his glasses have made their way down his nose. Not helping, bro.

Soldier makes a small movement with the barrel of the gun. "Over there. Move! On your knees! No one gets near this baby here." He nods his head toward the Titan.

I check where Soldier is pointing the gun.

Yeah, no.

Out of the question. There's no hard drive anywhere close to it. It's the farthest away from any part of the Titan, which is probably his point. Still, it won't work for me.

So I pull myself together and clear my throat, although it does nothing to calm my racing heart. "Listen, I'm pretty sure you don't want to point that gun at me. Why don't—"

"I said *move* and *kneel*," he barks at me. "No talking!"

Geez. "Okay, okay," I say, yet I'm not moving, because I really, really need Sneaker released. "But actually, this is a misunderstanding. My dad is—"

Soldier growls. "Three seconds to get away from that computer and hit the ground, or your leg gets a new hole. One!"

Adrenaline surges through my system, bringing a tsunami wave of nausea. "*What?* Are you insane? Do you know who I am?"

"I don't give a damn! Two!"

Three weeks. Three weeks of meticulous planning, and this muscle-bound zealot is about to wreck everything.

The program still isn't installed.

He's bluffing.

I'm a harmless teen girl accompanied by a geek with the company's ID dangling from his lanyard—what kind of threat am I? None! I mean, yes, I am a threat, but soldier doesn't know that!

I inch closer to the Titan. "No, please, I'm the President's—"

"Three," he counts and drops the aim of his gun down at my leg.

Shit.

In retrospect, maybe I miscalculated. I punch both of my palms out, as if that could stop him, panic lacing through my voice. "Stop! You can't shoot me! I'm—"

"Alix!" Dad's voice crashes through the room like thunderclap.

The soldier's composure cracks for a split-second, while Stephen squeaks like a mouse.

I look up and breathe a sigh of relief. The bridge spanning across Titan's massive frame has transformed into a gathering of

Washington's elite. Dad's there with his usual power circle: Oliver Brooks, his best friend and ever-present Chief of Staff; Brandon Lee, wearing his National Security Advisor authority like a cloak, and Megatech United's CEO, looking distinctly uncomfortable. Even Floyd Waterhouse, PRICS' overlord and FBI Cyber Counterintelligence Director, is there, with the usual scowl on his face.

But they're window dressing compared to the real show: Seven Secret Service agents, weapons drawn, lined up along the railing like angels of death, their guns aimed at the soldier in front of me.

Aww.

The cavalry is here.

And that means I better use the second chance I've been given.

I push my lower lip forward and add a tremble, for emphasis. "Daddy!"

And Dad has absolutely no problem playing along. After all, taking control is in his job description. "Mr. Masterson, call back your security guard!" His voice booms through the room—and it's the presidential one, layered with authority and command. Oh, and anger. "My agents will not hesitate to shoot, and I assure you, they're better trained than your guard. *Now*, Mr. Masterson!"

Yup, he's definitely angry, although I'm pretty sure it's not at me, but at the situation I'm in. And yes, I'm also not too thrilled about the curveball soldier threw at me. But I still have a chance to complete the mission.

Dad glares back at Masterson, but it's not Megatech's CEO who steps forward, but Waterhouse. He nods down to the soldier and makes a dismissive motion with his hand.

Wait, why does Waterhouse—

Soldier gives one crisp nod, bends forward at a snail's pace, and lays the gun on the floor. His face is red as a beet. Clearly, he didn't expect this specific turn of events.

Well, I was trying to tell him.

But anyway: I don't need an invitation to take this opportunity.

Initiating acting 1-0-1. I let a sob burst from my throat as I edge toward the right bank of computers. "Dad! He had a gun! Stephen wanted to show me… and then… he had a gun!" My voice cracks perfectly, and yes, after almost a year of PRICS I'm *that* good.

The CEO blanches white as a sheet. "I'm so sorry, I didn't know…! Since the incident we increased security. Oh my god, I'm so sorry!"

Dad ignores the CEO's groveling, switching to concerned-father mode. "Honey, are you okay? What are you doing down there? I missed you during the tour."

Laying it on thick, maybe, but nobody will notice. And he's handed me the perfect opening.

I sniffle, stepping closer to the bridge and one of Titan's massive towers. A calculated stumble lets me lean against it for, uhh, *support,* while looking up at Dad. Needless to say I'm still keeping up the strategic quiver in my voice.

"I w-wanted to see the Titan. Stephen was s-so nice and told me it would be o-okay. And this… this man came, and the gun, and…" *Sniffle, sniffle.*

Come on, Sneaker, do your thing, work your magic…!

The ring on my right hand vibrates.

Yes!

I hide a satisfied grin and meet Dad's gaze. "And my leg hurts.

I think I'm going to call it a day."

Dad gives a curt nod, and only because I know him really well do I see the flicker of relief, satisfaction, and pride flash across his face. He knows the code: Sneaker is in.

Mission accomplished.

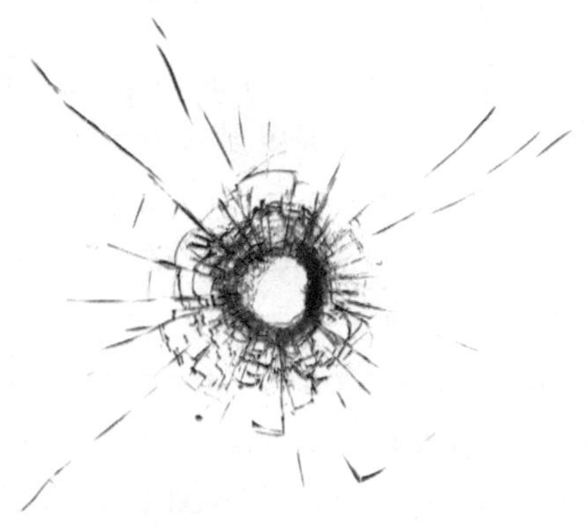

CHAPTER TWO
Debrief

We ride back to the airport and Air Force One in silence—well, at least Dad and I do. Oliver on the other hand, seated right across from Dad and riding backwards in the Limo, is in a pretty chatty mood. Here and there, Dad grunts out a reply, but that's it. I'm wondering if Oliver is overlooking Dad's nervous tapping of his fingers on one of the infamous water bottles, or if he's rather talking over it in an attempt to get Dad to relax.

Har, har, good one.

We both know Dad isn't happy. The tension in his jaw is yet another give-away.

The moment Limo One comes to a stop at the airfield in front of Air Force One, a Marine opens our doors. Dad all but jumps out and up the gangway.

Once we're on the plane, he turns toward me, one eyebrow up, lips pressed into a thin line. "Alix?"

Uhh, yeah. I cringe. Him calling me to his office might be part of our debrief, but I know this tone of voice. Granted, finding your daughter at gunpoint is a good reason to be… frustrated, but too fresh is the memory of a time where all we did was fight, where I could do no right.

Needless to say, it doesn't take me much effort to play along.

I drop my gaze to the floor and bite my lower lip, deflated like I knew I was going to get chewed out by Dad for getting myself in trouble back at MU. Letting go of a deep sigh, I follow him to his office, and the reactions of his staff couldn't be any more different.

Oliver shoots me a reassuring small smile. He's been on the receiving end of Dad's rants before. Happens when you're the Chief of Staff to the president and one of his best friends, I guess. I get a supportive pat on my shoulder when I pass him.

Waterhouse on the other hand… His stare burns a hole into my back.

Ugh.

I wouldn't say we're besties at this point, not after Fourth of July and his mismanagement of the situation. If it hadn't been for Ian and me, two-thirds of the Forrester family could be six feet under at this point.

Anyway. Instead of letting that man get to me, I focus on Brandon Lane. Him I like, with his short brown hair and dimples when he smiles. While he's still pretty new on the job, he's had a distinguished carrier as a diplomat in several foreign countries over the last two decades. Plus, he survived an abduction and several months in captivity during his last position. Not bad for a desk jockey in his mid-forties.

Even though Lane hasn't been privy to many dad-daughter interactions between Dad and me so far, he understands. He whispers at me, "Stay strong!", and gives me a small wink.

I nod, let my head hang even lower, and follow Dad through the moderately narrow hallway of AF-1. The second he closes the office door behind us and we're alone, he lets go of a big breath. "Way too close a call." He turns around and pulls me into a tight hug.

Must. Not. Tear. Up.

Seriously.

But *dang*, it still feels good to be hugged by Dad. We've gone way too long without it.

He breaks the embrace after a couple of seconds. "No, seriously. It scared the—well, you know. When I saw that gun pointed at you…" He shakes his head and squeezes my shoulders.

No need for him to finish that sentence. I know. He's had a rough time with how I nearly died to protect him. Coupled with the guilt he carries from the accident that injured my spine in the first place… We've both had our burden to carry for the last two years.

"Dad, I don't think he would've shot. It was to scare—"

"Well, it worked." He lets go of my shoulders and walks around his desk. Both of us fall into our respective chairs, one in front of the desk, one behind it.

"I want to get Mr. Miller informed. And I'd like him to tell me how you ended up with a gun to your head."

He pushes the intercom button harder than strictly necessary. "Send in Mr. Miller, please."

We wait in silence for a couple of seconds. The good thing about AF-1 is that it's bigger than a normal aircraft, but not too big. It doesn't take long for Ian to arrive. He knocks crisply and enters once Dad calls for him to come in.

"Mr. President. Alix." Ian nods from one of us to the other.

I can't help but smile. He is one of the most easy-going guys I know, but the second my dad is anywhere near, he turns into the embodiment of professionalism and respect. I'm not quite sure if it is because he's talking to the president, or my dad, or if it's a combination thereof. Probably the latter, garnished with a sprinkle of better-safe-than-sorry: Dad tends to give him a hard time. Paternal overprotection.

My heart does a familiar little dance when he comes in, followed immediately by a stab of guilt. Sam is literally three rooms away, and here my stomach flutters when I lay eyes on Ian. But then, Ian always affects me like this. We vibe at the same frequency, period. I mean, it helps he's cute, no matter he still wears his naturally blond hair dyed black. I even like the goatee he grew for his work with PRICS. But the kicker is his eyes. Emerald green, framed by thick, long lashes. And when he looks at me, like he does now...

Cue the inevitable blush.

Pull yourself together, Alix. We're *not* going there. Plus, if Sam could peek into my head right now, it would spark another argument I'd rather avoid.

But... it doesn't change that sometimes, when Ian looks extra smart like now, I feel weirdly proud of him. And I say weirdly, because it's odd to be proud of somebody a couple of years older than you, but hey: This is one of the smartest guys in the Secret Service, and he's working for my dad and together with me. Yes, I'm the luckiest little geek alive.

"Mr. Miller, thank you for coming. I'd like to discuss Alix's class work." Dad using Ian's alias name and talking about school is nothing more than an opening line. It means we're not secured yet and could be listened to. You never know, not even aboard the AF-1 in Dad's main office.

Ian fishes a little pen out of his pocket. "Of course, Mr. President. In case Alix hasn't told you yet, we were thinking of starting her on Latin to get her a better footing with her scientific papers." He doesn't even pay attention to Dad, but twists the little pen's top, until a red light on it begins to blink and then turns into a steady glow.

Ian meets Dad's gaze. "We have five minutes, sir."

Dad nods. "Thank you, Ian. First things first, Alix did great. Sneaker is released."

Only once we're completely safe from eavesdroppers, like now with Ian's radial soundwave blocker activated, does Dad call Ian by his true first name. Otherwise, it's Mr. Miller, or maybe Jason, but really mostly Mr. Miller.

Ian breaks into a grin. "I knew it! Good job, Alix!" His enthusiasm makes me feel all warm and fuzzy inside. The supernova that is my face probably says it all.

Dad sighs and rubs his eyes. "Well, yes. There's just the small matter of the unexpected security guard who had her at gunpoint." He fixes Ian with a pointed look.

Ian's smile vanishes faster than the Social Security data from MU. "A... *what*? A security guard had her at *gunpoint*? That's impossible, we triple-checked the facility's security schedule. I need details. What exactly happened?"

Typical Ian. Facts are data, and data helps him get to a solution.

Dad waves off the question. "Turns out it wasn't facility security at all. Waterhouse had extra FBI agents patrolling off-books. He was the one who called off the guard." He takes a measured sip of coffee. One perk of being president is the endless supply of perfectly heated brew. "What I want to know, is why neither of us knew about the FBI's increased presence at

Megatech United. I don't appreciate surprises, especially ones that put my daughter in crosshairs." The glance he gives Ian would petrify lesser men, but Ian is used to Dad's borderline rude attitude toward him. Unfortunately. I wish he'd drop it, but for Ian, the standards have been raised to impossibly high, after all, he's taking care of Dad's only daughter.

Ian claims the chair beside me, a whiff of his typical spring soap scent accompanying him. "Sir, Waterhouse should have followed protocol. If he didn't, there must be a reason, though I wasn't informed."

No surprise there—things have been tense since Dad gave PRICS more autonomy from Waterhouse's droopy eyes. I'd say it hasn't exactly made him like me more than before.

Dad keeps his accusing eyebrow up, so Ian continues. "I'm confident he wasn't aware of our operation, mainly because the information about it never left PRICS and the Oval Office. This wasn't sabotage, sir, just poor timing. We'll ensure it never happens again."

"I agree," I say and sit up straighter. "And look at what we pulled off together. Great teamwork with a good outcome for both sides." Dad couldn't have gotten Sneaker installed and MU surveyed without me, and I wouldn't have been successful without him. Teamwork.

Ian's pen blinks. "Two minutes, sir. To wrap it up, since Alix did implant Sneaker, I'd like to debrief her now and then start to gather information on MU. It might be a while until we find something, *if* there is anything to find—as we discussed, sir."

Dad stares hard into his coffee, lips pressed into a thin line. "All right then. Let's take this as a learning experience. Keep me updated on what Sneaker discovers."

Dismissed.

Ian all but jumps to his feet. "Of course, Mr. President. Alix?" He indicates the door with his chin.

I get up. That could've gone over worse. "See you later, Dad." I wave goodbye and follow Ian.

Back at the door, Ian holds up the pen so we both can see it and twists it counterclockwise, until the flashing light stops.

Break is over.

The show is back on.

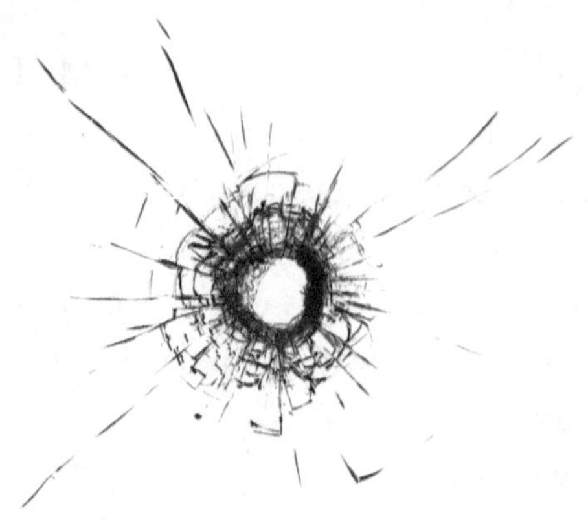

CHAPTER THREE
New Light

I follow Ian through the bowels of Air Force One until we're in our assigned classroom. Obviously this room wasn't used for school work before Dad became president, but just another boring conference room. Since they have a clear abundance of those on board the AF-1, it was re-designed into a classroom once it became clear the president's daughter would probably accompany her father on the occasional interesting trip—aka a PRICS mission.

And when I say "redesigned into a classroom," I mean that Ian and Dimitri got their hands on a few details, like updating safety features, soundproofing it, and adding a couple of handy inventions courtesy of Ian's genius to it to make life on board AF-1 easier for a PRICS agent like Ian or myself. Or Dimitri, for that matter.

Speaking of: Dimitri waits for us in front of our classroom. He opens the narrow door, and even though it's always difficult to tell whether he looks at me or not—thank you, extra-dark sunglasses—I still give him a little wave. The corners of his mouth turn upwards the slightest bit. Dimitri and I, we get along just fine.

I close the door behind me and—

Ian takes me by the shoulder and backs me against the wall. Before I even have time to understand what's happening, he has me caged in, one hand planted next to my head, the other on my chin, tilting my head up at him.

Uhh…?

Nothing more than a sheet of paper would fit between our bodies. Goosebumps erupt down my arms and neck. A chill runs down my spine, and my heart does a weird fluttering thing that doesn't exactly improve my situation. With the exception of training Krav Maga, this is the closest we've been since… since those fateful five seconds.

Five seconds was all I got.

Five seconds was all *we* got.

Ian's gaze bores into me from such short distance all I see is green with little specks of brown. Everything around me vanishes in that instant. Everything. Amazing how that happens.

I suck in a little gasp.

Mistake.

Spring soap. I—

Ian cups my chin and lifts my face to his. Something inside my stomach decides it's a good time to flutter up.

He narrows his eyes. "At gunpoint? You were at *gunpoint*? Again? That can't become a habit, Alix! Tell me exactly what happened!"

I swallow dry. I'm trapped between Ian and the wall, and the minuscule distance between us… Focus, Forrester. *Focus.*

"Uhh…" Speech as a concept left me the moment that *something* fluttered up inside my belly.

Ian sighs, and even that soft sound tugs on a heartstring.

He closes his eyes and leans forward, so close that I can feel the warmth radiating from his forehead on my skin. Only a bit more, and we'd be touching, like on that wonderful, fateful, awful Fourth of July.

He exhales and opens his eyes. "I can't have you at risk like that. I can't. You were in the line of fire once, Trouble. I think that's way enough. No mission is worth getting shot for. If that ever happens again, you abort, no matter what. Is that clear, or do I need to make it an order?" His voice sounds rough. Deeper than normal.

It's all I can do to squeak out a reply. "Okay. Abort." I force down the driest swallow ever. How in the world am I supposed to focus on anything, when Ian's gaze drills into mine with *this* intensity—this blazing look that shoots down right to my core? The one where I *want* to look away because it's too much, while all I *can* do is sink deeper into the quicksand trying to drown me?

Something deep flares between us, something that I haven't allowed to surface for months, because every time it does, it burns me from the inside out.

And I don't look away.

But neither does he.

I let myself feel how close he is, how any movement in any direction would bring me to touch him. How his breathing is faster than it should be in a resting position. How he swallows once. Flicks his tongue out over his lips—

A small gasp escapes me, and it breaks the spell.

Ian closes his eyes for an eternal second, and when he opens them again, he pushes off the wall and releases me.

I let go of a breath I didn't know I held.

Easy there, heart. Easy. Skipping beats is *so* not healthy.

"Come on." His voice is rough as he walks over to our couch under the small oval windows. "Give me a report. Be thorough, and don't leave anything out."

It takes me a good thirty seconds to regain my composure, and I use that time to carefully and thoroughly tie my shoelaces.

Not that they technically needed tying, but I needed a moment to get myself back into business mode.

Professionalism.

That stuff's tough when the hormones come out.

Once I feel sufficiently calm, I stand up, brush my palms over my thighs and let myself fall into the couch, pulling both legs in to sit crisscross applesauce. Such a small move, yet it would've been impossible a few months ago. Now with the need for pretense out the window and the splint off, moving the way I want to is a luxury I'm not taking for granted. If I hadn't met Ian, if he hadn't invented my chip, I'd still be in my brace and on crutches. As it is, Mom still isn't over the miraculous recovery of my nerves. Tickled her diagnostic senses, but when the MRI only showed what we expected, a healed spinal cord, she accepted our luck and moved on. Good for me, because one, I don't like to be under her scrutiny, medical or otherwise, and two, I remember Ian's frustration when he deleted the chip from the MRI-scan. We have a technology able to help so many people, and yet we're keeping it secret. It irks him to the n-th degree, which is why we both have been talking to the higher-ups to make the technology available to others.

Soon, hopefully.

Ian pours a cup of chai and hands it to me. Exactly what I need. Bringing him up to speed means going through a report so thorough it doesn't leave out a sneeze.

He raises his cup. "To a successful mission."

"And many more." Our cups meet with a gentle clink before I take a sip.

Seriously. This has become my life. When one mission is over, I can't wait for the next, and even if there's none, or if they're easy-peasy, there's always more training. More learning.

And there's *tons* I can still learn from Ian. Since he started working on Sneaker, he's cranked up my programming and coding lessons: No better way to let me know I'm still the student in our combo here, IQ of 160 or not. Watching his fingers dance across the keyboard while crafting that extraction program was like watching a virtuoso at work.

I cradle the cup between my hands, enjoying its warmth. For whatever reason, AF-1 is always freezing cold. I sink deeper into the cushions, trying to escape the A.C.'s arctic blast. Ian mirrors my position, but twists his body sideways, so that he's propped up with one elbow on the couch's headrest, one leg angled up on the cushion, his knee touching mine.

"Okay, Trouble, tell me what you learned from this mission." He taps his finger on my leg twice.

That IQ of 160 re-routes all processing power to his fingers on my knee and his knee touching mine. Darn distractions. Darn hormones. No matter Ian behaves like Fourth of July never happened, the same can't be said of my body. It *insists* on remembering. Vividly.

I clear my throat. "Uh, well, first, I will try to not get shot at. Always a plus. That means, I will abort missions that become too dangerous. Second, improvisation is important, and third, so is a good team for backup." Right? I blow into my tea to cool it. And myself, let's not kid anybody here.

Ian nods and gives me the thumbs up. "Good. I'd like to emphasize the point where you don't get shot at." He gives me a stern look. "But change of topic. Once we're back home, we can start analyzing Sneaker's data feeds and look for hack patterns. I want you to do most of the work there. My goal is to get you to a point where you can look at a source code like Sneaker's and tell me what I could do better."

Hah! A challenge I can do—not like Dimitri's Krav Maga challenges a là *who can kick a heavy bag the farthest?* Spoiler alert: It ain't me.

A grin spreads over my face. "So that's when the Padawan becomes a Jedi?"

Ian's smile widens as he drops his voice into character. "Much to learn you still have, my young padawan."

I hoot. "Your best Yoda yet!" He's really nailing that croaky voice and twisted syntax. And yes, I've heard his full repertoire, from Darth Vader to a surprisingly convincing R2.

We share a knowing grin and tap cups again.

Ian leans over to the coffee table, swapping his mug for a DUTI-pad that flickers to live under his palm. "Check this out, Trouble." He motions me to come closer.

"After MU lost the Social Security data, all major Government facilities improved their cyber security. Look at this though." He pinches a graphic on his DUTI-pad and twists it, making it pop up enlarged dead center on the screen. "Hacking attacks on Government sites have skyrocketed, we're talking double or triple the normal rates over the past two months. And we now have somebody claiming the fame for it."

"We do?" That should be good. Makes our life easier.

"Yup. Don't get too excited, it doesn't make our life easier, unfortunately."

Whoa. Mindreader. "Why not?"

"Because the Dark Unit is behind it, and we don't have a clue what they want."

I groan. "The Dark Unit?" The international hacker organization with the most cliché name in cyber-crime history? They've been popping up in many of our recent briefings, but so far they've been all bark and no bite.

Ian nods. "Those guys. The last two hours you were gone were busy for them, or rather, for me. It's official now, the Dark Unit hacked MU. They're in possession of the Social Security data."

I cringe. "Ouch. That's not good."

"Depending on. Here's the twist: They claim they don't intend to use it."

Now, that's odd. "Why not? You steal something and then don't use it? Why hack it in the first place?"

"That's a very good question, Trouble. And it gets worse: They've since hacked into two more Government sites, the DMV and the INR, all hosted by Megatech United. Crashed the servers for hours. But as far as we can tell, no data was damaged or stolen this time."

I scrunch up my nose and forehead. That doesn't make sense. "They crashed it? That's it? Why would they go through all that trouble plus the risk of getting tracked and found out, just to temporarily knock some sites offline?" Hackers *always* want something, even if it is only to prove they can, otherwise, they don't need the hack.

Ian nods and double-taps something on his DUTI-pad. "Don't get me wrong, they did get something out of it. Both websites displayed this image for over two hours nationwide until we finally managed to take over the system again."

He turns the pad around, showing a screenshot of a regular browser window with the DMV logo and URL. Business as usual, if it wasn't for the overlay of a poem written in red and bold:

Humpty Dumpty sat on a wall,
Humpty Dumpty had a great fall,
all of the president's horses and all of his men,
couldn't put Humpty together again.

Under the text is a small picture of a computer mouse, its black tail encircling the rhyme—the logo of the Dark Unit.

I hand the pad back to Ian. "It looks harmless at first glance, but I assume I'm missing something, if you're worried about it."

Ian sighs. "Well, right you are, I'm definitely worried. Alas, I seem to be the only one." He catches my quizzical look and continues. "You know, the FBI's Cyber Counterintelligence thinks this is another dumb hack, nothing more. Not quite as dumb as the hundreds of other almost-hacks we have every month, but still probably the work of someone in the Dark Unit who wants to see if they can get in, and then have his or her five minutes of fame displaying their message. A power play." He draws a circle around the rhyme with his finger. "My problem with this is twofold: first, why update the rhyme to say 'president'? This is a message until proven otherwise. Second, why Humpty Dumpty?"

"Also a message until proven otherwise?" I raise one eyebrow.

"Given that they purposefully altered it and chose this rhyme from how many hundreds?"

Ian looks up to the ceiling and lifts both palms. "Yes! Thank you for following my train of thought! Nobody else would find this remarkable." He lowers his hands for a high five I hit. "Do you know where the Humpty Dumpty story comes from?"

I blow out a puff of air. "Well, I thought it was about an egg, but given your question I assume it's not." Can't say nursery rhymes are my area of expertise. I bet Mom read to me from her medical journals when she brought me to bed. A nonsense-rhyme? What a waste of a golden teaching opportunity.

Ian smiles. "The egg is a common misconception. The probably more truthful story is that Humpty Dumpty was actually the nickname of a huge cannon mounted on a church wall in Colchester, England during the civil war. It was used to support King Charles and fight off the Parliamentarian forces, but when the wall was destroyed, the cannon crashed to the ground, and, well, all the king's horses and all the king's men couldn't put Humpty together again. Meaning, they couldn't get it back onto the wall, a major blow to their defense. So, what do you make out of that?" He gives me *that* look, the one that tells me to get my brain in gear.

Okay, wait, History, English Civil War—*oh.*

If Ian is right, this is a biggie.

I blink twice. "So in translation, the uprising forces destroyed the government's weapon.

So… what? The Dark Unit is going to quote-unquote *break our weapon*? What does that even mean?" It's not as if we had enemies we're holding at a figurative or literal gunpoint with some kind of weapon. "It must be something cyber-related, but why not just do it, but tease about it?"

"That's what I don't know," Ian says. "I think we need to investigate this further, find out who in the Dark Unit is behind it, including their motives, etc. It's too hot to let it sit unsolved. They got into our system twice already, at MU and now at the DMV and INR, and it's bugging me. Something is going on within the Dark Unit, and I don't like it."

Neither do I. "So what's Waterhouse's problem? Or rather, what does he not see as a problem?"

"Your pick. This is just an attention grab by the Dark Unit, if they had any real power, they'd have taken data or done damage. We can't spare resources, after all, we have more concrete threats than nursery rhymes. And, of course, I shouldn't suspect a complex conspiracy behind a minor hack."

I blow out a puff of air. "He calls hacking MU, the DMV and INR a minor hack?"

"Apparently. I wish Waterhouse and his team would take the Dark Unit more seriously. It's going to be tough digging deeper with only you and me."

I huff. "You know he won't."

"Won't what?"

"Take anything serious that you or I say. One, he's still a sore loser he had to hire you to train me, two, he's an even worse sore loser since Dad gave us more independence. I mean, we know he isn't your biggest fan"—Ian shudders in agreement—"but I feel Waterhouse isn't on Team Alix either. Take today, it was almost like he was working against us."

Ian cocks an eyebrow at me. "Ouch, Trouble."

"Ugh. I don't mean it like that." I deflate. "I'm not accusing him of working against us, I'm just saying that he isn't the least supportive. Geez, even Brandon Lee is telling me to let him know if I need something, and he's never been in with the secret service." Granted, that might mean he thinks we're playing around most of the time, but given that we had to throw everything about PRICS at him out of the blue, he handled it well.

Ian works a hand through his hair. "I know what you're getting at. Waterhouse is very difficult to get along with. I trained with him when I was first recruited, and he brought me this close to quitting."

I stare at him. "*You* almost quit?" That doesn't sound like Ian.

He makes a face. "*Almost.* Quitting… wasn't really an option."

No kidding. For Ian quitting is never an option.

"Believe me, Trouble. I'm sure it is nothing personal with Waterhouse. He has a difficult personality—"

"I've noticed." I roll my eyes.

"But he's really good at his job, and he definitely didn't put a guard into the computer room at MU to make life more difficult for us. Remember, our mission was top secret, and only us and your father knew about it. Knowing about PRICS doesn't equal knowing about every mission we run, especially now that we're more independent."

And being mad at us doesn't equal screwing those missions up for us, I know that. "Okay, okay, I get it." I wave my hand. "Anyway, what are we going to do about the Dark Unit?" That's our job, that's *my* job, and I'm not going to ignore any possible threat against Dad, no matter if Waterhouse takes it seriously or not. Ian does, and that's all I need to know.

Ian taps on something on his DUTI-pad. "We'll develop a little counter program using some bleeding-edge tech. Check this out, young padawan."

I take the pad from him and scroll through the code.

And stop.

And go back up.

And again.

No, wait, that can't be what I'm seeing.

I look up at Ian and back at the code. "It looks like… don't get me wrong, but this programming seems to be using some kind of quantum-neural architecture? The patterns are almost… organic." The code structure is unlike anything I've seen in current AI models, it almost looks like it's… *alive*, somehow. It seems to adapt and evolve in real time, predicting and countering security measures before they even activate.

Ian shrugs. "Sort of. It's a hybrid quantum-classical system using something called adversarial reinforcement learning. But it sounds less impressive when you hear what teenage-me named it." His cheeks take on a reddish hue. "Torpedo. You know, unstoppable, precise… In my defense, I wrote the first version of this in high school. Been refining this architecture for years, staying ahead of the publicly available AI models." He shrugs again, like, no biggie, sure, that's what every teenager does.

That moment at MU, when I thought to myself the smartest organic brain was working for us? Heck, I was *so* right! My mouth drops open. "Ian…! You wrote that in *high school?*" And I thought I was advanced!

"An early version of this, nothing spec—"

"An early version that's probably still more sophisticated than what I can access right now via the web! And given that A.I. made huge leaps forward over the last years…" I shake my head. Unbelievable. I'm going to stay a padawan forever. Looks like I'm way behind the curve already.

Ian rubs his neck. "Oh well. I was focused more on programming than actual school. And to be honest, had I had any common sense back then, I should've come up with one system, not two. Sneaker handles intrusion detection and real-time threat analysis, nice, and then Torpedo can adapt to and bypass pretty much any security system once it's fully optimized. Two programs… So inelegant."

A laugh bursts from my throat. "Yeah, very offensive." I lean forward and punch him in the shoulder, lightly, of course.

Ian chuckles. "Unless of course I'll come up with some more programming and turn this into swarm intelligence. Maybe that would redeem my reputation." He taps his index finger against my temple. "Either way, for now we both work on Torpedo. Look at the code. Understand it. Once we're both happy with it, we're going to release that baby onto the Dark Unit and see what we can get, while Sneaker keeps an eye on MU." He drops the DUTI-pad onto my lap. "Your mission, Trouble. Go for it."

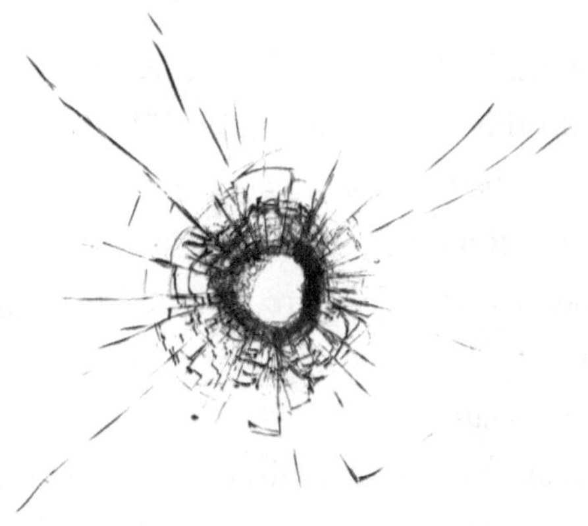

CHAPTER FOUR
Invite

It takes me thirty minutes alone to get a rough—and I mean very, *very* rough—understanding of how Torpedo works, and the moment I feel like I at least kind of get it, the wall clock hanging above the door begins to flash in a bright red light.

I groan. I was just getting the hang of—

Brooks, Sam'mear, Intern.

Oh, never mind.

The evacuation plan-turned-monitor next to the door springs into life and displays the aisle leading to our classroom, a red circle around the face I know as well as my own.

"Visitor." Ian sighs.

What happens next is a quiet dance we've performed far too often over the last couple of months. Ian powers down his DUTI-pad and turns it into an inconspicuous sheet of foil, shoves it behind a cushion on the couch and picks up a math book from behind that same cushion.

Simultaneously, he scoots farther away from me and opens the book. I do the same with my DUTI-pad, only I grab a pen and a pad from behind my cushion, opening it to a page with several formulas scribbled down already.

We're like a perfectly choreographed team making sure we don't get caught.

Two seconds later there's a knock on the door and Sam peeks in, handsome as always in his suit, the light brown wavy hair a bit shorter since he got promoted from junior intern to full-fledged intern once he turned eighteen over the summer. The moment his gaze falls onto me, he gives me a smile. I wish it came with that adorable twinkle in his eyes, but oh well. Long day.

"Hey, Sam, come on in." Ian waves Sam into the room.

"Hey, Jason. Hey, Alix." Sam hovers in the doorway after closing it behind him, unsure where to settle. On the couch, Ian and I have some room between us, but it's not much.

Not much at all.

Sam's gaze drops from me to that small space, and something flickers across his face as his jaw tightens.

I know exactly what he's thinking. It's happened enough times now, those comments about how much time I spend with Jason. At first, they were subtle hints dropped into the conversation, but over time and especially lately they've become more frequent. Predictable. Like a slow drip wearing away at stone.

The worst part is, it's a symptom of a larger issue. Sam and I... we're stuck in this strange limbo. Sometimes it feels like we're dancing around each other, never quite in sync. He keeps his distance—emotionally and physically—as if he's got one foot on the gas and one foot on the brake. Every time I try to get closer he pulls back a little bit more, and ugh, it's so, so frustrating.

Blech.

Ian talks over the slight awkwardness. "Thanks for dropping by. There's only so much Number Theory I can stomach per day. What's going on?"

Sam shoves his hands into his pockets. "I was wondering, Jason, if you don't mind…? Can I talk to Alix for a second?"

I'm already on my feet before Ian can respond. This is rare enough—Sam seeking me out—that I'm not about to waste the opportunity.

He sighs again and waves dismissively. "It's been decided for me. But hurry up guys, we have to work through that problem involving modular arithmetic before we hit Washington DC."

I take a quick couple of steps toward Sam, get up on my toes, and kiss him gently on the cheek. We try to stay somewhat professional while at work. "Hi," I whisper.

He captures my hands and holds me exactly where I am.

"Hi." His voice is so low and tender it's barely audible. He squeezes my hands and kisses me on the nose.

I close my eyes and inhale his butterscotch-Sam scent. "What's up?" Sam rarely interrupts class—usually only if something's brewing.

He brings my hands up to his lips and presses a kiss against my knuckles. "I was wondering if you'd have dinner with me tonight? Back home, around seven?"

I raise an eyebrow. "Of course." Sam's become a regular fixture at our family dinners over the last couple of months. Sure, it's under parental supervision, but I can't exactly just waltz into a restaurant, being the president's daughter and all. That would take tons of preparation and Secret Service agents in every corner, and there goes peace and quiet.

Sam's gaze flicks to Ian. "No urgent assignments, no

homework…?"

Uhh, no. Don't think so, although PRICS isn't really a guarantor for predictable evenings. I shake my head. "Nope. Pretty sure I'm all clear."

He forces a smile. "Good. I thought we could try something different. Night picnic in the White House Gardens. I'll prep us a basket. And, most importantly…" His eyes light up. "…I'll bring the telescope. It's the Hutchinson Meteor Shower tonight, remember?" Another kiss lands on my nose.

Ian clears his throat, but the wave of joy and excitement hitting me drowns out the sound. A picnic! How sweet is that? Not only did Sam remember I wanted to see those meteors—no, he's also asking me out on a beautiful romantic date with a picnic, blankets, probably hot tea or hot chocolate, and a telescope! Count me in!

"It sounds perfect." I mean it. It does. I couldn't imagine a better date with Sam. Especially because I'm always freezing, and I'll end up snuggling in his arms eventually. Under the starry sky. Oh yes, that's more than perfect to speed things up between us. Next level, here I come. No more holding back, Sammy-boy!

Sam releases my hands to cradle my face. I wrap my arms around his waist as his lips touch mine and—

Ian's pager splits the air with an ear-piercing screech. He launches off the couch as if bitten by a mutated spider. "Excuse me guys, excuse me, coming through." He wedges himself between us on his way to the phone, effectively killing our moment.

Sam squeezes my hand once and steps back. "See you at seven, Alix." That sounded like a promise, if I ever heard one.

Squee! "See you at seven." I wiggle my fingers at him as he leaves without saying goodbye to Ian—who's punching numbers into the phone on the desk as if it was his enemy.

As soon as the door closes behind Sam, Ian hangs up the phone and grunts. "Wrong number, how annoying."

Right.

How annoying, indeed—and happening with suspicious frequency lately. In fact, Ian's beeper has interrupted quite a few of Sam's visits. Too often to be a coincidence.

But speaking of...

I cross the small room toward the teacher-and-student-desk combo crammed in here, the one we rarely use, because the couch is much nicer to sit on. Like he always does in our classroom back at the White House, Ian sits on top of his desk, so I slide behind mine.

Deep breath.

"Hey, Ian?"

"Huh?" He looks up from his pager.

Here goes nothing. "I was wondering... you know, it's been almost a year with me in PRICS. I would..." Oh heck, I have to spit it out, but it doesn't get easier the more I ask it. "I would like to bring Sam in."

There we go. That wasn't too difficult. I breathe out slowly, waiting for a response.

Ian's mouth opens and closes, then opens again. "Alix..."

Disappointment crashes over me. I know that tone. This isn't the first time we've had this conversation.

Ian massages his neck, then drops his hand. "We can't bring Sam in. Telling him about PRICS is against the rules. Your father was an exception, because he figured most of it out on his own, and Brandon Lee was a must thereafter because of the position he holds. But we can *not* bring Sam in. The more people know about us, the more dangerous it becomes for us and them, and the less we will be able to fulfill our mission undisturbed. There's no way I can get clearance for that."

He slides off his desk, walks over to the coffee table, and grabs our cups. He hands me mine and sits back down on the desk with his.

I take a sip of my tea. The little bit of warmth left in it doesn't do squat to chase away the chill settling in my bones. "I know, *I know*. But it's hardly fair. After Dad was brought in, he got to update Brandon Lane, because it's important for his work. I need to bring in Sam because it's important for my *life*."

Maybe it's not the best comparison, and intellectually, I understand why I can't let Sam know about me and PRICS, but I need to try. My quote-unquote *school work* is a constant source for discussions between Sam and me, and none of them are fun to go through.

Thing is, I can't really fault him. There were so many situations where I couldn't explain why I wasn't where he expected me to be, and so many situations where I behaved odd without a reason.

Sam is one of the smartest guys I know, not quite as smart as Ian, but still acing every test he ever took, and taking law classes online besides working over twelve hours per day for Dad. Sam knows something is off. He knows I'm hiding something from him, and I don't want to be doing that. I want him to know.

I want to be honest with him.

Keeping my gaze glued to the scratches on my desk I trace them with my finger. "It's *Sam*, Ian. He'll understand. He works for the president. He knows how things are handled around here. I... I don't want PRICS to be between us, you know?"

Can't look Ian in the eye. Never can when talking about Sam.

Ian takes a deep breath and releases it slowly. "I know,

Trouble, I know. It's... Our team has already had more exceptions than any other before us. Even with good reasoning, I doubt they'd approve Sam as another exception. I mean, not even your mother knows."

True, but also beside the point. If I had the choice between bringing in Sam or Mom, it would be Sam. Without a doubt.

Ian gives me a sad smile and shrug, and we both stay silent for a moment.

Well, nobody said life as a spy was easy.

After what feels like eons, Ian sighs once more and gives me a small nod. "I'll see what I can do."

It sounds good, but the underlying message is clear: Don't hold your breath.

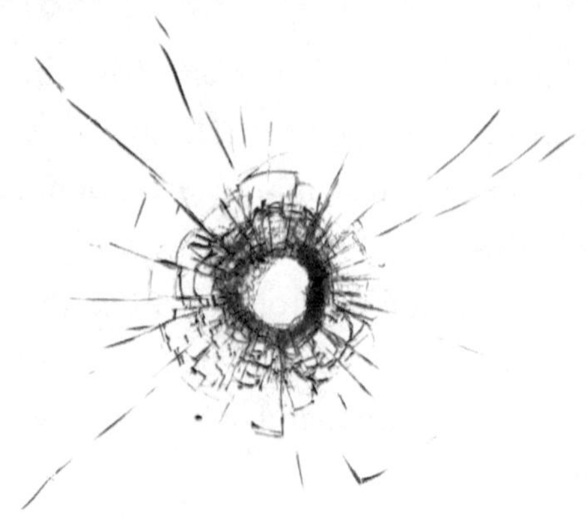

CHAPTER FIVE
Over and Out

The rest of the day flies by in a breeze.

As soon as we arrive in Washington D.C., everybody scurries off for work, and that includes me.

Thing is, an impeding night-time picnic with Sam is a pretty good distraction from Ian's class, especially because Torpedo is on hold while we go over the Threat-Level Report for the rest of the afternoon.

Yes, I know, we're having another rise in cyber-attacks worldwide. No, we don't always know who it was, although the Dark Unit is pretty high up on the list. Yes, several groups are threatening Dad to do… something I didn't really listen to, or they will continue their cyber terrorism. No, nothing else is going on.

After what feels like an eternity, we finish for the day. By that time, my mind's basically fried from the effort to focus on class and not let my thoughts drift off to Sam.

Maybe tonight's the night we're going to move our relationship one step along. A little step at least. A *tiny* one, and I'd be happy, as long as he doesn't throw on the brakes again. And heck, I don't mean that in a pushy way. We can go as slow as he wants or needs, but…

I suck in my lower lip and chew on it.

The problem isn't that he wants to take things slow.

The problem is I feel he doesn't want to go faster—with me.

And that thought is just… vexing. Weird. Confusing.

When we just got together and Sam visited me in the medical wing, we had a hard time keeping our hands off each other. To a degree, it's still the medical wing, but he wanted to touch me, and now… I don't know. He still does, but it feels different.

Or maybe that's all in my head because I'm feeling bad I have to lie to him.

Double-sigh.

I push those thoughts away once I hit the residence and spend a ridiculous hour agonizing over what to wear—which is so not like me and also very much pointless, since everything's going under a winter coat and blankets anyway, given that it's freezing outside.

In the end, I go with my trusted comfort-combo: favorite jeans and a black turtleneck. Sorry, not a girlie-girl. I plop down at my desk, tapping my foot on the floor. What? No, I'm not nervous. Why would I be? Sam's surely taking his time though. I force my foot to stay still, but that anticipation needs to have an outlet apparently, so I fidget with Sneaker on my finger instead. Leave it to Ian to invent and design a ring that's both functional and beautiful. When there's finally a knock on the door my heart jumps—but it's only Mom.

"Sweetie, there is an *adorable* young man here waiting for you with a picnic basket." She winks, knowing Sam is picking me up and that we're *going out* tonight. "And if I'm not mistaken, he can't wait to get you out of here, so hurry up, sweetie, hurry up." She waves for me to get off my chair.

"*Mo-om*!" Borderline embarrassing—and it gets even worse. Like, when she leads me out into the hallway and smiles up at Sam.

"Why don't you stand next to Alix for a moment, Sam?"

And—*click*—she's taken out her cell and snapped a picture of us. Ugh. That's gonna come out great. Don't know about Sam, but I looked like a deer caught in headlights.

I roll my eyes and groan. "Mom, really?"

"Oh come on, Alix, be a good sport. A mother is allowed to cherish her daughter going out on her first date." Mom shoves her phone into her pocket and brings on her best I'm-so-happy-for-you-smile.

Oh gosh, somebody save me. I was nervous before, but in a good, anticipating way. Now that Mom is blowing this way out of proportion—first date! Pictures!—I feel completely underprepared.

Is this our first date? Yes, it's the first time of us going out, but we've had dinner together before. Did that not count? We've been kissing for months now—admittedly not much more than that, but still. It counts, doesn't it?

How confusing.

I shake it off, grab hold of Sam's hand and yank him toward the door. "Let's go before the meteors are gone. Bye, Mom. It'll be late, but I've got Dimitri, so no worries and don't stay up for me." Meaning: don't come checking how and what we're doing. It's something she might do. She is surprisingly thick sometimes.

Sam mumbles a hasty goodbye to Mom before trailing after

me. Two overstuffed picnic baskets wait outside the residence, practically bursting with enough food to survive an apocalypse.

"Sorry 'bout that." I point my thumb over my shoulder. "You know how she is…"

"No worries, let her do her thing if she wants to." Sam lifts and drops his shoulders as if to say 'who cares'.

Nice of him, but she never wanted to do *her thing* before, and I was completely fine with that. I reach for the smaller basket, ready to get this show on the road, but before I can even straighten up, Sam clamps his hand down on my arm.

"Nope. I'll take it."

"You've already got the monster basket. I'll handle the small one." No need for him to schlep both around like a donkey on its way to the mill.

Sam's already prying my fingers off the handle. "No, no. It's fine. You'll shake it too much or break something."

Seriously? The eye roll practically hurts from holding it back. What's in there that's so precious? Motion-sensitive explosives? Geez…!

Alas, I swallow my frustration. Maybe he really has something fragile in there. A cake? I love cake, so maybe that's it.

I hereby firmly choose to believe cake is the reason. So, I paste on a somewhat fake smile and let go of the basket. "Sure, here you go."

Sam, totally blind to my annoyance, brightens. "I set up the telescope already," he says, taking the lead.

Dimitri falls into his usual shadow-routine behind us, keeping that careful giving-you-privacy distance. It's the most I'll get after the stunt I pulled on him on Fourth of July.

Sam's chosen spot sits far from the White House flood lights, close to the little forest on the grounds. He has no idea the area hides the emergency exits from the PRICS' and VP's secret catacombs, but to me it's kind of funny he chose this spot.

That being said, the location is perfect: sheltered from prying eyes, but with an unobstructed view of the stars above. A thick blanket is spread across the ground, and as promised, the telescope is up and aiming at the stars. Sam sets the basket down and opens his arms. Finally.

I melt into his embrace. Even through our winter layers—my thick jacket, his heavy coat—his familiar butterscotch scent wraps around me like an olfactory hug.

"I missed you," I whisper in his ear.

He tightens his arms around me. "I missed you too. The evening couldn't come fast enough." He kisses my forehead.

My heart swells. I love to hear that.

More kisses follow, each one softer than the last, trailing down to my nose, tickling along the way. When his lips graze the corner of my mouth, I freeze—though my heart turns into a jackhammer inside my chest.

Then, gentle as a whisper, his lips meet mine.

Whoa.

That slow brush… it makes my world spin. Everything about it is perfect. His soft, full lips, that hint of butterscotch, the slight roughness of his stubble against my skin…

I part my lips, and Sam accepts the invitation. This kiss… this is the real thing. He isn't holding back this time, nu-uh. He presses his hands into my back, bringing us so close, only our winter layers keep us from becoming one person. I forget to breathe, because who needs air if Sam's kissing you? My heart thunders, my stomach does Olympic-level gymnastics, and my knees feel like jelly.

This is exactly what I dreamed this picnic would be.

Note to self: Less talking, more kissing. Definitely more kissing.

The kiss could've lasted seconds or hours—who's counting when your mind can't form a coherent thought? When Sam finally pulls back, we're both breathless.

"Dinner time," he whispers, stealing one last quick kiss before releasing me to unpack our feast.

Sam has outdone himself: Finger food, steaming soup, sandwiches, fruit, a thermos full of hot cocoa, chocolate—everything I could possibly want.

Nothing's missing as we eat, talk, and laugh.

Nothing's missing when we spot the meteorite shower through the telescope.

And definitely nothing's missing when he grips my hips, turns me around, and pulls me into his lap, my back against his chest, wrapped in is warmth.

"Ready for dessert?" Sam smiles down at me and reaches for the picnic basket.

"Always." I was born ready for dessert.

He digs through the basket until he finds the chocolates. The moment he lifts the lid the scent of dark, rich chocolate fills the air. *So* good. I spot my favorite and reach for it, but Sam playfully slaps my hand away.

"Ah-ah. Who said you get to pick? Lean back. Relax. Don't move, or they'll all end up on the ground. I got you, Alix."

Oh, *ooookay*…

I bite my lower lip. He's only trying to make it more romantic.

Peeling off his thin wool gloves, he points to a chocolate. "This one?"

I nod. Of course it's the exact one I wanted. He knows me

too well, and just like that, I forgive the hand-slapping.

Sam takes the chocolate and holds it out for me to bite. His fingers brush my lips, leaving burning, beautiful sparks.

Before he can pull it away, I catch his wrist. Not so fast.

With one bite, the candy is gone. It melts on my tongue, divine, but I'm not done with his hand, candy or not. Priorities. His fingers are warm, only the tips slightly chilled from the night air.

As soon as I've swallowed the candy, I purse my lips and gently blow on his fingertips to warm them, then take his bare hand between my two gloved ones and rub it, warming it up. And because the darkness and this heady mix of Sam and chocolate is kind of intoxicating, I push things further. Someone has to.

I draw his fingers to my mouth and nibble on his pinky. It's barely a touch, but the moment my tongue meets his skin, Sam's breathing changes.

Not quite so calm anymore, are we?

Good.

Each finger gets the same treatment. Feather-light kisses. Gentle nibbles. Tiny tastes.

My pulse pounds so loudly in my ears, I can barely hear anything besides Sam's ragged breathing.

So yeah, I take the next step.

I take his index finger into my mouth, like a lollipop.

Sam's sharp intake of breath and tensing body tells me everything I need to know.

I give his finger one careful bite. A swirl with my tongue. A little suck.

His moan vibrates through me, hitting something primal and deep in the center of my core.

One more lick and—

In one fluid motion, Sam lifts me off his lap and shifts aside. Without letting me release his finger, he guides me onto my back, his burning gaze locked to mine.

We roll to face each other, him propped up on his elbow, me rolled to my side, gazes locked. The intensity between us is on a whole new level, which is great—fantastic, actually—but I'm beyond glad it's dark. In daylight my courage would wither away, I know that much.

Sam leans his forehead against mine. His breath comes out in little gasps, warming my face. The darkness acts like a cocoon around us. Nothing else matters between Sam and—

He sweeps his finger across my tongue, exploring, and that sudden spike in adrenaline close to gives me a heart attack before he slides his finger free, tracing my lips.

I hear him swallow before he reaches for my hand, brings it to his mouth, catching my glove between his teeth to tug it off.

Heck, I can help with that.

The moment my right hand is freed, he covers it with soft kisses, while fumbling to take off my other glove. My heart's beating like it's going to explode, but weirdly my brain still isn't getting enough oxygen. Woozy. Totally.

Finally, the left glove comes off and Sam takes my hand—

He freezes.

Like a ginormous red light had lit up, everything comes to a screeching halt.

He drops my right hand onto the blanket.

Takes my left between both of his.

Complete and utter silence.

And then it hits me like a fist to the gut.

Sneaker.

The ring. I'm still wearing the ring.

Ian's ring.

I want to scream. How could I be so stupid? An hour obsessing about clothes and I forgot about the damn ring?

Sam doesn't move.

Doesn't speak.

Just stares at my ring and the blue stone catching in the moonlight.

"From your parents?" He presses his lips into a hard line.

I open my mouth—and close it again. The lie is right there, gift-wrapped in his question.

But I don't want to lie anymore.

Yeah, tough luck, because I also can't tell him about PRICS either.

Sam reads my silence like a book. "So it is from *him.*" His voice is flat. Flat and quiet, barely a whisper.

And it scares me.

It scares me that Sam made the deduction so easily.

It scares me that I didn't take the ring off.

Most of all it scares me that he called Ian *him.*

"It... well, no... yes, but it's not... it's... It doesn't matter, Sam." Shoot. I doubt that made it better.

Sam turns my hand over in his. Not looking at me, just the ring, and he's still oh-so-quiet. The silence before the storm.

"He has no right to give you a ring. He's your teacher, and nothing more." He twists the ring on my finger. "But you, Alix. Why are you wearing his ring? Why are you out on a date with me, wearing a ring *he* gave you?"

That's when he finally looks into my eyes and I wish he hadn't.

Sadness.

Disappointment.

Pain.

The apple in his throat moves up and down hard. "Are you in love with him?"

I jerk back. What? In love with Ian? Where did that come from? Did I slip up? Give away anything about PRICS—

Sam drops my hand and sits up straight.

The gap between us is more than just physical now.

"That's what I thought."

What?

"No, Sam, no. Listen." I reach for his hand, but he pulls away.

His gaze hardens. "I don't know, Alix. Why would I? I knew something wasn't right these past months. I knew it. Every time I asked you about school, or when you were late, or when you cancelled—it never felt right." Anger blazes in his eyes. "Tell me I'm jumping to conclusions. You spend more and more time with Jason, you behave weird, and now you're wearing a ring from him? A ring your *teacher* gave you? What the hell am I supposed to think?? Obviously something's going on between you two, and honestly, I don't want any part of it. Hell, I don't even want to know what it is. It's sick!"

His last word hits me like a slap to the face.

Sick.

"No, Sam, there's nothing going on. I—Jason is my teacher, and—the ring… it's for completing a really hard assignment." The words taste like ash—technically true, but yet another lie.

My eyes water up, and I blink. "It's nothing, Sam. I'll get rid of it right now. Look." I tug on the ring, but Sam shoots out his hand, stopping me.

"Don't bother. Keep it. Who cares? When you're ready to tell me what's really going on, let me know." He gets up, gathers his gloves, brushes off his coat, and… walks away from me.

Just like that.

He walks away.

In that moment, time stops.

I can't process the last five minutes, can't comprehend how everything shattered so quickly.

How Sam is walking away from me.

I leap to my feet. "Sam!"

He hesitates for a heartbeat, but doesn't turn. Instead, he shoves his hands deeper in his pockets and keeps going until the dark swallows him.

Gone.

I'm left alone on the picnic blanket that was supposed to be our first official date.

A single tear, hot and wet, runs down my face, before I wipe that stupid hot lava off my cheek.

Maybe deep down I always knew this day would come, and that it had been coming for a while. The day Sam would stop loving me.

I just never thought it would come so soon, or for a reason that's both the most obvious truth and the biggest lie of all.

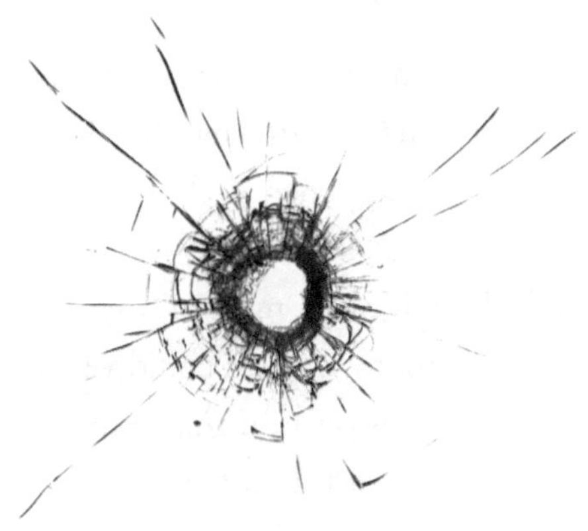

CHAPTER SIX

Rollercoaster

When my alarm goes off the next morning I feel like I've been hit by a truck.

Sleep didn't come easy, or at all. I kept jerking awake, feeling for Sneaker on my finger—falling back into a weird mix of half-sleep and alertness a second after I realize I really had taken it off this time and dropped it on my desk.

Still, none of the last few hours were fun.

I don't know how I survived the night.

I don't even know if I slept at all, but probably not.

I *do* know that whatever I did, I did it with Sam on my mind. Sam.

After hours of contemplating, thinking, and brooding, my stomach hurts, because I'm mad.

Mad, mad, *mad*.

Mad for doing the unforgivable and leaving Sneaker on my

finger. Mad for not thinking quicker on my feet and coming up with a different explanation during the picnic. Mad, because none of this would've happened if I'd been allowed to tell Sam about PRICS.

Most of all though, I'm mad at myself for screwing up completely and on so many levels. I could've paid more attention to Sam and not cancelled on him that often, but that would've meant less time working with Ian. I could've kept my head more in the game when I was with him, but I was distracted thinking about… Ian. I could've been more conscientious about taking off Sneaker, but then it came from Ian, so…

And that's my problem right there: Ian.

I'm *not* together with Ian.

I *am* together with Sam.

Was, probably. But still.

Over the last months, I did so much better. Less googly-eyes at Ian. Less caving to the hormones flooding my system every time he was close. Less of my pathetic school-girl behavior.

And still, subconsciously, I prioritized him over Sam.

What the heck is wrong with me?

Ian hasn't given me a single sign that things could be different between us, and he had plenty of opportunities. No hugs. No innocent touches that lingered maybe a tad longer than strictly necessary. *Nothing* to kindle that spark we had before—and on— July 4th.

Nothing besides those pitiful five seconds.

I rub both palms across my eyes.

And Sam… Sam hasn't been giving me much more either. Some hugging, some kissing, maybe a shy second base. It's all great when it happens, but *something* is keeping us from getting closer, from truly moving on, from truly connecting.

Yeah.

That *something* is probably me.

I press those palms into my eyes until I see stars.

Sam is my forever-crush. Smart. Cute. Dedicated. Dad's best friend's son. Primed for success and a perfect match for the president's daughter, according to Dad.

Ian... is different.

He's the onslaught of emotions I didn't plan for—I *couldn't* plan for. Ian gets me when nobody else gets me. We vibe on the same frequency. Nerdy jokes, geeky comments, it doesn't matter. He knows and understands me like nobody else does, and I trust him with my life.

But Ian is forbidden.

I sit up from my bed and rest my head on my knees.

Four years older.

My teacher. Well, boss. Or whatever.

And, most importantly, not favored by Dad.

Sometimes... sometimes I get the feeling that Sam and I, while we've obviously liked each other forever, are more a by-product of our dads' relationship. They're both thrilled about us, and how could they not? The president's daughter and the Chief of Staff's son. They try to hide it, but whenever they see us together, they can't help but let the pride shine through: their kids. Together.

Yeah, one could say there's a bit of pressure on Sam and me, and I'm not sure it helped us.

With an effort close to moving a mountain, I lift my head off my knees and blink.

So, what am I saying? That I made the wrong choice on Fourth of July? That I should've listened to my heart, and not my history with Sam, or Dad, ignored reason, and seen where it would take me with Ian?

Right.

Ridiculous.

What if I had? If I had been so crazy to go against Dad, against years of crushing on Sam, against all *freaking common sense*?

Easy: I would have had to hide our relationship. Lie even more. Always fear discovery. And if Dad caught us, there'd have been hell to pay. Boarding school for me, dishonorable discharge from the Secret Service for Ian. No doubt about it.

Besides, who says Ian would have even wanted that? He seems to be doing a fine job separating work and emotions. Who am I to assume he would've chosen me over his career, his life's work? Would I have even had any right to push for it?

I know the answer, and it's a no. And over the last months, he has kept his distance. Yesterday in the AF-1 was one of the few times he breached the professional barrier between student and teacher, and I blame that on me being held at gunpoint.

Other than that, Ian has recovered well from those fateful *five seconds* back on Fourth of July.

Better than me, it appears.

I reach over to my desk to grab Sneaker. I hurt Sam. Badly. I hurt myself too, but that's par for the course.

Worst is, I don't know where to go from here.

I drop Sneaker back onto my desk like a poisonous snake, and then I do what I always do. What I do best.

I go to class.

The moment I enter the classroom Ian knows something is off.

Whether it's because Dimitri gave him a heads-up or because I look like crap is anybody's guess, but he's especially cheerful this morning. Not even a second after I sit down Ian brings over my obligatory cup of chai.

"How ya doin' today?" he asks in his best Southern drawl imitation, maybe even adding a little additional jolliness into that, for good measure. Oh, he *definitely* knows something is off today.

I rub my eyes. "Fine. Didn't sleep much. You?" Nothing I want to talk about. I'd like to be distracted and think of something else but Sam and my screw-up, thank you very much.

Ian holds up a finger. "All good here. Am excited about today's class, but more on that later. Let's get started with a Threat Level Report. Today, we actually do have a little more than the last couple of weeks." He grabs his DUTI-pad and activates it.

We have something more? I cringe. I mean, I like the distraction, but… "You know, I'm not quite sure if that's good or bad. No news is good news, and any news around here means that something or someone is bad news for Dad's safety."

Ian takes a sip from his tea and clears his throat. "Relax. Cyber-security, or rather, the lack thereof. Another hack by the Dark Unit, the way it looks. This time, they took down the Alcohol, Tobacco, Firearms and Explosives-Bureau website and left us another message. At least from my point of view." He pinches and drags the picture on the pad to enlarge it, then turns it around for me to see.

Like the last time, the website is all whited out, with an overlay of yet another children's nursery rhyme displayed in the middle. To be fair, the overlay's happy and colorful font improves the boring and grey previous design, but I keep that comment to myself. The moment I read the title, I cock an eye brow. "*Twenty little monkeys?*" I scroll down all the way past the at least fifteen or twenty verses to the sign of the Dark Unit on the very bottom: a computer mouse with curly tail, looking all innocent and cute.

"Weird." I hand the pad back over to Ian. "Twenty little monkeys jumping on the bed…"

"…one fell off and hit his head. Mama called the doctor and the doctor said: 'no more monkeys jumping on the bed'," says Ian, finishing the first verse.

"So you think this is another threat because it's the same style as the old one, a nursery rhyme. I don't think they changed much besides the number? Twenty monkeys instead of ten." I only glanced at most of the rhyme and didn't scan it word for word, but that seems to be the main issue.

Ian scrunches up his face. "I agree, it is not as clear-cut as the other one. I always thought there was five monkeys, you thought ten, so clearly there is some variance to the rhyme, but whatever. It looks like"—he scans through pages on the pad—"it looks like the FBI's Cyber Counterintelligence Unit called it a friendly hack, because nothing was damaged or stolen. The Dark Unit blocked the site for a couple of hours, and then our guys got in and removed the bug."

I raise an eyebrow. The FBI. That means my special friend Waterhouse. "What do you think?" I trust Ian twenty times more than that man.

He sighs. "I'm not sure. We need to step it up, and we need to get that computer code finished to protect our sites—so that's your job for the afternoon: Torpedo. Nothing better than an intelligent program to defend our networks. I don't like anybody hacking their way into government sites. As for this one… I don't know. It seems to be an attention getter, but who knows."

I agree with him. Who knows? If I've learned one thing over the last months, it's that rarely anything is what it seems in politics.

Ian slides off his desk. "But that's for later this afternoon. Now it's time to go down to the Eagle's Lair." He claps his hands like an eager entertainer.

Ugh. Three million steps that suck, no matter I got rid of the brace on my leg. "I don't mind if I work on Torpedo up here. I can get started right away." Without being out of breath.

Ian shakes his head and palms open the holographic wall behind the fireplace. "Nu-uh, Trouble. Special task for you. Down there." He points a finger down the stairway and I groan.

A special task.

That can only mean one thing.

I'm going to be so sore.

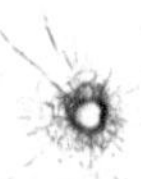

All three hundred fifty-five billion steps down to the lair, I'm in a bad mood. I don't want to go through a Krav Maga torture session. I want to curl up somewhere and be miserable. I want to cry and think about how I can fix things with Sam—*if* it's fixable. Getting punched and kicked is not on my to-do list for today.

I'm so lost in thought I don't even wonder why Ian and Dimitri are quiet the whole way down.

I also don't pick up on the glance they exchange before Ian opens the holographic entrance to the Eagle's Lair.

Only when the wall vanishes and everything behind it is pitch black instead of bathed into the artificial bright light of twenty-five ceiling lights do I snap out of it.

"Crap," Ian says. "The power's out. Careful where you step, I'll check the fuse box." And with that, he disappears into the darkness.

Great.

Now the power is out, fantas— Oh, maybe that means no Krav, so maybe it's a good thing. Yay?

Dimitri nudges me forward, and I oblige with a grunt. Would've been fine waiting in the fake janitor's closet, but sure, let's all step into the dark—the *complete* dark, once the wall comes back to life behind us.

I just hope Dimitri won't come up with some kind of weird night drill, to not *let this opportunity go to waste*. Please, no.

After stumbling through the dark and banging his shins multiple times by the sound of it, Ian's rustling stops. "Lights," he announces, and BAM, the office lights flare into existence, blinding me.

"And sound!"

I slam my hands over my ears as Queen's *We are the Champions* explodes from every direction at maximum volume. "What the—?"

"Surprise!" Ian yells from across the room.

Wait, what?

I squint against the bright light, and—

What in the actual…?

Ian stands next to the coffee table, grinning like a maniac and wearing a party hat on his head.

"Congratulations?" I read off it. What the what?

But that's just the start: he holds a bunch of balloons in his hands that look like they raided a rainbow, there's a two-story cake on the coffee table, drowning in pink sprinkles, but mostly, there is Dimitri.

OMG, Dimitri. Standing behind Ian like a statue in a suit, face completely blank, holding exactly one bright pink balloon and a party blowout with all the enthusiasm of somebody filing taxes.

I burst out laughing. "What even is this? How come I didn't get the invite?" I make my way to the coffee table, still laughing.

Ian toots his party blowout in perfect sync to Queen while I approach. When I'm close enough, he drapes one arm around my shoulders and makes this dramatic conductor gesture. Instantly, the music drops down to ear-friendly levels. Leave it to Ian to have gesture control for music. Sweet.

Ian squeezes my shoulder, radiating pride. "Congratulations, Alix! It's my pleasure as your Commanding Officer to be the first to congratulate you on passing your basic training with flying colors. Well done!" He squeezes my shoulder once more before he releases me.

Wait. What? I passed my basic training? Already? I thought I had months left. A slow grin creeps across my face. "I'm done with basic training? I graduated? Does that mean I can finally ditch languages and start specializing?"

Ian hangs his head in mock despair. "Yes, yes, you can abandon languages, though you really should keep them up. Good balance for all those science-heavy grad courses. And yes, you graduated: fastest basic training since PRICS was founded. Very well done, Trouble!"

I blush and bite my lower lip. Damn, I'm a sucker for his compliments. "Uhh, thank you." I brush a strand of hair behind my ear. "I don't think I could have done it without the two of you, so thank you. Really, thank you." It's true. Ian pushed me harder than anyone ever has and Dimitri… well, Dimitri kept me grounded, in more than one aspect.

Even Dimitri's stone face shows something akin to a smile. Before it gets awkward or too touchy-feely, Ian yanks open a drawer and pulls out a cake knife and… a syringe?

"Let's not get too emotional. Cake's coming, but first: the tracker." He holds up the syringe like he's presenting it on late-night TV. It's not huge, but that needle? Definitely thicker than I'd prefer.

"Tracker?" My voice betrays me with a crack. Nobody mentioned a tracker before, and why can't I wear it?

Ian nods as he checks the syringe and grabs some antiseptic wipes from the drawer. "Yep, tracker. All official PRICS members get one, and congrats, you are official-official now. No dodging this. It's incredibly useful, and, uh…" He drops his gaze to the floor. "Let's just say last July would've gone differently had you had one."

That's all I need to hear. I've kicked myself a million times for letting Gary overhear me—and to kidnap me right after. The Evil Lair was no fun at all. With a tracker like this, Ian could've found me. "I'm all yours. Seriously, bring it on. How does it work?"

Ian lights up like a Christmas tree. Nothing gets him going like talking tech. "It's subcutaneous, so under your skin, and practically undetectable. A specific frequency only we can track. It's my technology, and we're the only ones using it and the only ones who know how to read the signal. Completely undetectable, because no one else would know what they were looking for or recognize what it was if they came across it accidentally."

Nice. "So only PRICS can access my location data? Past and present?" Not that I'm planning anything sketchy, but hey, I'd like to know my options.

Ian flashes a thumbs up. "Exactly. And we don't look, unless we have to. Plus, when your father is done with his term or terms, we take it out. Minor procedure, barely leaves a mark."

Ian grabs his supplies and comes over to me. "Sit down. This one stings."

I shrug, but plop my butt onto the couch. "I don't mind. Not the biggest fan of needles, but Mom made me give myself the tetanus booster when I was eleven."

Ian snorts out a laugh. "Seriously?"

"Seriously. Builds skills and character, she said." Other mother-daughter-duos braid their hair together, or whatnot. We vaccinate together.

Oh well, could be worse.

Ian chuckles, then takes my arm and pushes up my sleeve, feeling over my deltoid. Goosebumps pop up on my arm, spreading all the way down my spine. If he notices, he doesn't let it on, and I'm thankful for it. He uses an alcohol pad to disinfect my arm.

"Did you see your name on the cake?" Ian grips my arm like a vise.

I whip my head toward the cake. "Oh, that's nic—OW!" Pain explodes in my deltoid. "What the—"

Ian cringes. "Sorry, Trouble. Warned you this one would sting." He withdraws the needle. "All done."

Most of the throbbing subsides, but the pulsating stabbing sensation is still there. I sink into the pillow with a groan. "Worth it. Now you can find me anywhere?"

Ian looks up from his cleanup, his mouth set in a determined line. "Anytime and anywhere, Trouble. No more guessing games."

Good. That's all I need.

Ian pats my thigh twice. "Cake time! You earned it—

graduating top of class."

Right. Easy when you're the only student.

He eyes my hand rubbing my shoulder. "And for braving the tracker implant, of course."

No argument there.

Ian cuts the cake like a sushi chef on amphetamines. Within seconds we're all holding slices of raspberry-vanilla heaven. Even Dimitri pulls up a chair to join us.

I love this.

Exactly what my bruised soul needed.

We eat in comfortable silence, the kind that feels natural when it's just us three. After a few bites, Ian sets down his plate and dabs his mouth with his napkin.

"I almost forgot." He heads to his desk, opens a drawer and pulls out a little something with a bow on top. "Catch!"

It lands perfectly in my hands, more because of Ian's precision throw than my talent when it comes to catching things.

"And a present, too? Awesome." A grin splits my face. Unlikely as it was, but this day has gotten better. I look at what I caught, a small jewelry box—

A... *jewelry box?*

My jaw drops.

Before my brain can short-circuit, Ian cuts in. "Not what you're thinking. Open it."

Not what I'm thinking? What *was* I even thinking? A jewelry box—

Inside sits a tiny pink folded paper.

I glance at Ian. He nods encouragingly, so I take the paper out and unfold it.

One word in his handwriting: *Yes.*

Yes... to what?

"Yes?"

Ian's smile turns wistful as he settles back. "*Yes* for what, you want to know? Well, that's easy. I spent ages thinking about your graduation gift. Something you'd like, something PRICS-related, ideally both. But the one thing you really wanted, that's what the yes is for." He leans forward, hands clasped.

"I went all the way up the food chain, Alix. I broke a few rules and stepped on a few toes, but I know how much this means to you, and… I want you to be happy. So I pushed until I got permission: Yes, you can tell Sam about you and PRICS. It's approved."

A wave of emotion crashes over me, so suffocating and complex, I don't know how to react.

Ian got me permission.

The one thing he said was impossible, but knew I needed most. He got it for me.

He must've moved mountains for this authorization. This single *yes* is the most thoughtful gift I've ever received. Something swells in my heart, filling it to the brim until it overflows with warmth—that special kind of warmth that only comes from someone's genuine caring, from their lo—

I suck in a short breath.

The paper trembles in my hand.

I blink hard.

Ian misreads my silence. "You were right, Alix. You need Sam in your corner. I keep forgetting you're only seventeen, cut off from everybody else your age, and carrying the weight of protecting the president. It's not healthy to only have me. You need him."

Oh.

I blink again, harder. That tender warmth curls in on itself, retreating to the darkest corner of my soul, leaving nothing but cold.

I need *him*.

Right.

Ian's thoughtful, well-meant gift is good for nothing. It's too late. Pretty sure Sam broke up with me last night. Or at least hit pause. Either way, it's not looking good.

From the corner of my eye I see Ian tilt his head. "Alix…?" His voice is soft. Careful.

A weird strangulated half-sob breaks from my throat, so embarrassing I slap a palm over my mouth.

Within a heartbeat Ian's beside me on the couch. "Trouble." He reaches for my shoulder, hesitating for a short, but noticeable second, before he lays his palm on my shoulder and squeezes it. "Hey. What's going on?" He moves his thumb in soothing circles, tearing a hole into my walls.

I'm not going to cry, I'm not going to cry…! But to be safe, I bury my face in my hands. Yes, Ian has seen me cry. No, we don't need a repeat performance. My body shakes from the willpower it takes me to suppress all the crappy emotions hell-bent on taking over. I won't let them.

"Trouble. Hey. Shh…" He pauses the mesmerizing circling of his thumb—and then slides his hand across my back toward my opposite shoulder. One gentle tug pulls me against him as he rocks us slowly. His goatee brushes my cheek and ear as he leans in. That overwhelming flutter-pain inside my chest and stomach flares again, making it hard to breathe.

Pathetic.

Ian pulls me closer, a little helpless sigh escaping him. "Whatever it is, you can tell me. I'm all yours."

All mine.

Except he's not. Not even close. If he were, I'd have thrown my arms around him the moment he sat down. I'd have buried my face in the crook of his neck and drenched his shirt with my tears. Ignored the invisible lines.

I curse it all. Laws. Regulations. Waterhouse. Even Dad. Everybody who ever stood between Ian and me with their precious rules about *fraternization*—Dad and Waterhouse's favorite word.

But even if that weren't an issue, I still couldn't give in: Sam left because I'm too close to Ian. If I want any chance with him— even friendship—that can't happen again.

But do I want that chance?

Is Sam my first thought in the morning? My lst before sleep? The one my mind circles around every waking second?

The answer is easy: No. He isn't.

That honor belongs to somebody else.

Somebody who crept into my heart and made a home there. Who's only dug deeper with each passing day, allowed to or not.

I suck in a harsh breath filled with Ian's spring soap scent, and it brings back those *five seconds*.

Uber-pathetic.

I jerk upright. Need space. Need distance, or… I'll never manage any at all. Ian and I make a great team, nothing more. Couldn't be anything else, even if we wanted it. Which we don't. He doesn't see me that way anymore, and I can't complain: I chose Sam.

I brought both onto myself: Sam leaving me. Ian's distance.

Congratulations, Forrester. Well played.

I sniffle and wipe my nose with my sleeve. And so classy, too.

Ian reaches under the table for some tissues. "Just in case. Ready when you are."

Not that I have much dignity left. I take a tissue, blow my nose like an elephant with flu, and take a deep breath. "Picnic didn't go well."

Ian arches an eyebrow at my crumbled tissue. "You don't say."

"Well, it started out okay, but—" I wince. Who calls a super-romantic picnic with their boyfriend just *okay*? Thanks, brain, for that clarity. "I forgot to take off Sneaker. Sam saw it and… he concluded it was from you."

Ian's eyes go wide. "Oh. *Ohh…*"

Okay. Only slightly embarrassing. "Yeah. I told him it was a reward for work, but… he was still mad, Ian. Everything came out—every missed date, every weird excuse, and he… he broke up with me." Saying it out loud hurts. I deserve it, though.

"Ouch." Ian winces.

"Yeah."

Silence hovers.

Ian sighs, rubs his eyes, then snatches his plate. He takes a bite before shoving a big piece of cake into my mouth. "Eat. Cake always helps."

I close my lips around the fork as he pulls it away. Crap. That cake, it comes with an extra serving of pheromones.

He drops the plate back on the table. "I'd offer to talk to Sam, but I'm afraid it wouldn't improve the situation."

"Wouldn't," I mumble around cake. It would just confirm Sam's fear about Ian and me being too close.

More silence.

"You can still bring him in. Tell him about PRICS. Maybe that'll change things. Help him understand all the strange stuff from the last few months. Sam's smart. Reasonable."

I open my mouth, but nothing comes out. True. I could

explain everything. Maybe he'd see things differently. But do I want that? We had something good, but was it great? Was it—

Dimitri's deep voice cuts through my existential crisis. "If he loves you, he will give you a chance. If he hurts you… You know where to find me." He raises an eyebrow and cracks his knuckles.

God. I burst out laughing, and… it feels amazing. "Thanks, Dimitri. I hope that won't be necessary."

He gives me one sharp nod before retreating to his usual spot in the corner. His support means a lot. It's not part of his job description.

Ian's soft chuckle follows. "Dimitri is right. Go to Sam tonight after his shift. Bring him in. Explain what we do, and why we do it. Don't lose him over miscommunication." He takes the plate and lifts another forkful of cake to my mouth. "Never give up on someone you love. Never. You talk, you fight, you wait for the right moment, but you don't give up. You always give them another chance." *Something* swings in his voice, and that something makes my hands clammy and my knees weak.

Ian wipes his hands on his thighs and claps them twice. "Right. That's settled then. Back to action. Alix, finish your cake. Dimitri, get everything you can on the Dark Unit. I'll start on counter surveillance. Alix, join me when you're done. It's a busy day, and I need your brain to get this one right."

He launches off the couch, crossing to his desk in three strides. Dimitri grabs a DUTI-pad probably diving into FBI-files on the Dark Unit. In seconds, we're buzzing like a hive, all purpose and focused.

I take my plate and cake, grateful for a moment to breathe. I bet this wasn't Ian's plan for today. The only reason he's starting work on the Dark Unit now is to keep me distracted until Sam comes off duty tonight. Nothing distracts me better than a problem to solve. Same for him.

We're so alike.

My gaze follows him as he juggles two DUTI-pads and his laptop.

So alike.

Yet so far apart.

I wipe my mouth with my sleeve and drag myself off the couch.

Time to work.

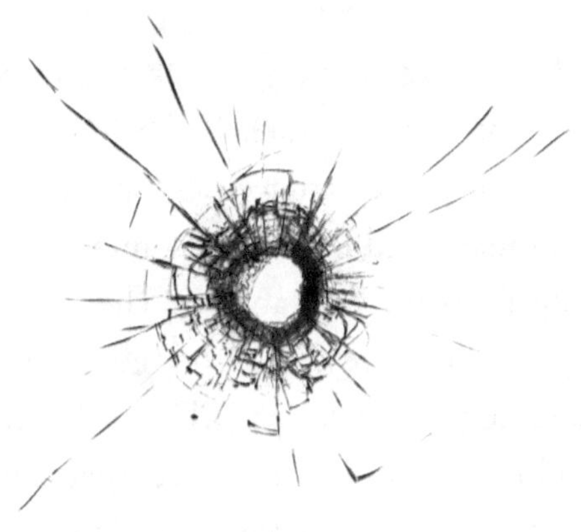

CHAPTER SEVEN
Revelations

My mood improves as the morning stretches on. It's a bit scary how diving into PRICS projects makes me feel better. Might also be a bit pathetic, too, but well, that's me.

After our lunch, we move upstairs to the classroom instead of staying down in the Lair. If we don't want people to notice our absences, we have to keep up appearances.

Even though we're fresh and rested from our break, it takes us several hours to make at least a little bit of progress. The Dark Unit is proving harder to track than we thought. Ian's having trouble breaking into their systems, and so far, we're coming up empty. To be honest, we failed so epically, I allowed my mind to drift here and there. It takes way too much willpower to keep it from going back to Sam.

My plan to fix things sounds easy: find Sam at the end of the day, get him alone, and, well, bring him in. Then he'll have to understand. Maybe we won't get back together—and I'm not even sure I'd want that anymore. But being honest and staying friends, that'd be nice. No hard feelings, that kinda thing. A sharp pain hits my stomach and I sit up straighter.

Ian gets up from his desk and stretches. "The Dark Unit is keeping busy. Two more hacks on government sites. Both followed the same pattern as the MU attack, only this time we were able to block them. Fool me once, shame on you, fool me twice, shame on me." He unscrews his thermos and pours more tea.

Capping it again, he frowns. "I don't know what to make of these attacks. They're good, but looking at their programming, I think they could do better, and I wonder why they don't. Or what's up with those hidden threats. Or maybe I'm overreacting and this is nothing, like Waterhouse said."

I roll my eyes. "Let's not go that far. When in doubt, I'd rather play it safe, thank you very much." One barely-missed bullet to Dad's head was enough.

"True. At least besides this Dark Unit headache, things are quiet. Oh, by the way, the Secret Service only bumped us up one security level for your father's Europe trip tomorrow. Should be an uneventful trip to the G20 summit." Ian knocks on the wooden desk, not tempting fate.

The Anatomical Chart Monitor by the door chimes. "*Black, Christopher. Mail Delivery,*" appears in text around the face on screen as the nervous system diagram switches to a hallway view. Dimitri's back is in clear view, and so is a young man on his way to our classroom.

Ian sighs. "No peace and quiet here," he mutters.

A moment later, Dimitri opens the door and the guy from the monitor steps in. "Sorry to interrupt, but I have mail for...

Jason Miller?"

Ian raises his hand. "That would be me."

Mail Guy comes over, throwing me an apologetic look. "Really sorry about this. I'd have left it in the mailbox, but it's marked urgent, personal delivery." He shrugs.

I shake my head. "No problem." Urgent personal delivery, that's a first.

Ian takes the envelope. "Thanks, man."

Mail Guy nods and scurries off as Ian studies the envelope before tearing it open. I turn back to my DUTI-pad and the programming code, figuring I should at least try to be productive.

Then, I notice the silence.

After a couple of seconds, I pick up on the complete silence. That's odd—

I look up from my work and drop my pad the moment I lay eyes on Ian.

Ian is white as a sheet.

His eyes are locked on the letter, expression frozen in a mixture of panic, horror, and sadness. His hands are shaking so badly, I doubt he can even read the words anymore.

"Ian?" Something is wrong. Something is very, very wrong.

He doesn't respond. He's completely checked out.

My stomach twists. "Ian? What's going on?" This isn't like him. Ian doesn't freeze. He attacks problems head-on. His mind works faster than anyone I know.

He finally looks up and stares at me, but no kidding, he's looking right through me. The letter drops to his lap. He closes his eyes, swallows hard, and lets out a shaky breath. When he speaks it's barely a whisper. "Lair. Now."

He slides off the desk, abandoning the tea and his DUTI-pad as he heads to the holographic wall.

That's when real fear hits me. Ian doesn't leave PRICS material lying around. *Never.* Ignoring the pad means that he considers it getting found not as important as what's in the letter, and that thought scares me more than anything I've been through with PRICS over the last year, including the assassination attempt. Even then, I knew that I had Ian to fall back on, and he would be able to fix it.

Seeing him like this… it's the most unsettling sensation I've ever had, like impending doom, only I don't know what kind of doom. I grab both our pads, stuff them in my schoolbag, and hurry after Ian.

Dimitri catches up with us a second later, as always.

Neither of us says a word as we descend the zig-zagging stairway and enter the Eagle's Lair. Ian palms open the holographic wall, walks straight to his chair next to the coffee table and falls into it, clinging to the letter like a lifeline. He's even paler than before, and his mind is far, far away.

So. Not. Good.

I sink into my usual corner in the couch and drop my backpack next to the coffee table.

Silence fills the room like thick fog.

Ian rubs his eyes, then buries his face in his hands and leans forward, the very picture of despair.

"Ian… what is it?" I'm amazed how steady I keep my voice.

Ian releases a big breath. "Dimitri, sit with us." His voice is so flat and quiet I'm surprised Dimitri heard him. But he does, settling on the other end of the couch next to me.

Seriously: So. Not. Good.

Ian takes the letter out of the envelope and hands it to me. "We have a problem. Well, *I* have a problem."

It's not a letter—it's a printed photo. At first glance, nothing seems wrong: just a farmer's market I don't recognize. Shoppers browsing stalls loaded with fruits and veggies. The photo centers on an elderly couple, probably in their early sixties. The woman's arm is linked through her husband's while he carries their shopping basket. They're completely unaware they're being photographed. Something about the man looks familiar, but I can't quite place him.

There's *nothing* scary about this picture at all, and if it wasn't for the thick, black marker words printed across the bottom: *Get out or they're dead.*

Wait, what, who? The elderly couple? We get dozens of threats like this every day, and it's never—

Click.

Oh, crap. Double-crap.

That's why the man looks vaguely familiar. For the first time since Ian's meltdown in the classroom true fear explodes in my stomach.

I swallow dry. "They… they're your parents, aren't they?"

The corners of his mouth twitch up by a millimeter, acknowledging my deduction, but that's it. No praise, no change in those lifeless eyes. I pass the photo over to Dimitri, who scans over it and drops it back onto the table.

Ian leans forward, elbows on his legs, hands clasped behind his neck like he's bracing for an emergency landing. It's not enough to hide the emotions sliding over his face: Longing. Fear. Shock. Worry. All tangled together.

"Yes. My parents."

He opens the coffee table drawer and takes out the Radial Sound Wave Blocker pen, the one that keeps unwanted ears from listening. He twists the top and waits for the red light to come on. Oh, holy everything. Ian activating the RSWB-pen ranks pretty highly on the oh-shit-scale. We're safe down here in the Lair. I *think*. We've never needed any special precautions against eavesdroppers before.

Ian stares at the pen like hypnotized, blinks hard, then tears his gaze away. "Here's the deal. We have a photo of my parents and a pretty clear blackmail attempt. *Get out or they're dead.* I assume whoever sent this wants me to leave PRICS, or they'll kill my parents."

Something feels wrong. Actually, all of it does. I shake my head. "Why assume it means you have to leave PRICS? It could mean anything. Dad gets tons of these every day, and usually demands like this are about military stuff. Get-out-of-whatever-country. Free-these-political prisoners. Yes, they're using you and your parents—"

"Which is exactly the problem. The real problem, no pun intended." He holds up the envelope. "It's addressed to Jason Miller. To *fake* Jason Miller, whose *fake* parents died when he was sixteen, and who has no living relatives. Again: Jason Miller has no parents. But somebody out there knows Jason Miller is Ian Donckers, and that somebody knows where I work, how to get to me, who my parents are, and how to track them down." His mouth tightens. "This isn't just a threat to me and my parents—it's a threat to *all* of us. We have a breach. Someone is leaking top secret information, and we don't know how much, or to whom. This," he flattens his palm against the envelope, "*this* could kill us all."

I gape at Ian as his words sink in. Stare at Ian open-mouthed. A cold shiver ripples down my spine.

Holy cow, that—

He's right.

He's absolutely right, but there has to be something else, some other explanation—

I cross my arms tight in front of my chest and sink deeper into the cushions, but the chill that gripped me won't let go. "Not good," I mumble. I was right. So. Not. Good.

Ian lets out a dry chuckle. "Nope. On several levels, and you don't even know the best of it." His laugh is bitter and razor-sharp.

"What do you mean?" The best? More like the worst, judging by his tone, but—

His gaze locks into mine. "Alix, my parents don't know I work for the Government. The last time I saw them was the day I joined."

"Wait—seriously?" My jaw drops. Yeah, he said things around him were pretty secret, but *that* secret?

Another harsh laugh. "Yeah. And I can one-up it."

Oh dear. At this point I'm scared to even to ask.

His gaze clings to mine like I'm his last anchor to reality. "I can't warn my parents without blowing my cover, Trouble. Because officially, I'm dead." He takes one more deep breath. "Ian Donckers was sixteen years old when he died in a car accident."

What. The. F—

"You're kidding." I shake my head. No. This can't be. Can't be true. Secret Service, Government, Top Secret—whatever. Nobody fakes somebody's death for recruitment. This isn't some spy-movie.

"I wish." Ian's voice is as lifeless as his expression. *Beaten.* "The last time I saw my parents was the day I 'died' to join the

Secret Service. I haven't seen a picture of them for years. I mean, I kind of keep track, sort of… my dad retired, he… It's not important. This"—he holds up the photo—"this complicates things."

No shit, Sherlock.

I lean forward, pulling my legs under my butt criss-cross-applesauce and try to wrap my mind around the bomb Ian just sprang on me. I'm not sure I can. "You died? *Died?* What the heck, Ian?"

Bitterness creeps into his voice. "Yeah, right? What can I say—I was young. It made sense at that time. They told me I'd be involved in projects with the highest clearance level there is. Anyone who knew the Secret Service had snatched the genius kid about to present his holographic projector at a national science fair was going to be a security risk. Military applications and all that. They said I'd put my parents at risk. Extortion. Blackmail. So yeah, I signed a confidentiality agreement… and then I died. So to speak."

Silence fills the room.

I stare at him open-mouthed. What do I even say to that? He was sixteen! A year younger than I'm now! He left his parents and faked his death, and they don't know. They *still* don't know.

"How can that be legal?" My family problems seem so insignificant in comparison. So egoistic.

"It's a grey zone." There's that bitter edge again.

"Grey zone. I've heard that explanation before." For my own recruitment into PRICS.

"Yeah. They really like the grey zones."

I throw up my arms. "But how can something like that be a *grey* zone? It's a big, fat, red, no-go-zone! I can't believe the FBI did that."

He waves his hand. "Well, let's just say it was teamwork. The NSA—"

Ugh. "NSA. Of course." Now it makes sense.

"Yes, the NSA. They came up with the plan, and all the clandestine services benefitted from me joining. I'm a *big, multi-partisan collaboration and investment into the future of undercover agencies in America.*"

"Sounds like a recruitment flyer, but the kind you should've ripped up."

"Not when you're sixteen and the big league is interested in you. It's what they said when they scooped me off on the way to school one day and gave me their spiel. And I loved it."

Whoa. Like something straight out of a movie, although I'm not quite sure it's one I'd like to watch. *Scooped him off on the way to school*—a sixteen-year old! Man… "How did you… How did you handle it?" I'm trying the best to keep the pity from my eyes, but it's hard. *Sixteen.*

Ian gives me this sad smile that's so pretend-devil-don't-care even I can spot it as fake from a mile away. "Wasn't easy at first, but it got better. Saved up quite a bit of money, which is surprisingly easy when you're in a well-paid government position and officially non-existent… and never go out. Made up a lottery they had 'won' so I could give them money without rising suspicion. It boosted their retirement fund nicely and they never found out which one of them had forgotten they had entered a lottery." A wistful smile plays around his lips. "Plus, work keeps me busy, so I don't think about them much. The Secret Service recruited me as their inventor-on-call for all things computer and military before Waterhouse promoted me to work with you. Not much time for guil—for much else."

Not much time for guilt.

"But I don't get it. Why can't they know?" Tell them a cover story, done.

"Like I said, all I was told is, it was too dangerous. For other recruits, the Secret Service would've vetted their parents and given them a clearance level, but in my case, the risk was too high. Not only if they let something slip, or my cover being blown when I met with them. They were a liability."

I narrow my brows. "That sounds like overkill, no pun intended."

Ian sighs. "With a few years of Secret Service experience under my belt, I agree. But, Alix, I was the first. No teen had ever been recruited like this, as a high-value asset. The holographic projector… it's one of a kind. It gives our military a huge advantage. And it's complicated. Like, *really* complicated and complex. That's why everything about me is Top Secret." He runs a hand through his hair. "When I signed my life over to the NSA and their multi-partisan collaboration, all my files about it had to be destroyed for security reasons. Nothing was left. The only hard drive with the data on it was here." He taps his temple. "That made me very valuable. And a liability." He holds up the picture of his parents.

Still: How cruel. "I can't believe they did that to you."

"Sometimes I can't either. But, it's a done deal. I knew what I was getting into." The dimness in his eyes calls him a liar, but I'm not about to point that out.

Ian heaves a deep breath, raking both hands through his hair until it's even messier than before. "But let's focus on what matters right now. We're in deep. One, somebody's blackmailing me into leaving PRICS, and we don't know who. Two, I can't warn my parents without blowing my cover. Three, and that's the kicker that I don't like at all, the blackmailer knows where I work, so they know about you, Alix."

About me as in *Agent Forrester*, not as the civilian president's daughter. "Oops."

"Oops, indeed. Oh, wait, I have one more: Four, we have absolutely no clue who the blackmailer could be, and what they really want. What's their motive? Why make me leave PRICS? What's their angle?" He shakes his head. "To be honest… I don't know what our next move should be. I can't run this alone. I'm too close, too biased, and too scared something is going to happen to my parents, or to you, Alix. I need help on this one."

For a moment, the sadness in his eyes softens into something warmer, something so intense it makes my cheeks burn.

And it shakes something loose inside of me.

"You're not alone in this, Ian. You've got me. You've got Dimitri. We'll handle this together. We're a team, remember?" I lean forward, trying to channel Ian's usual confidence.

We can do this. We have about a thousand IQ-points between us. We can figure this out.

We're not going to let anybody blackmail or threaten us.

"Let's think this through. First question: How do you know it is a current picture and they have a current location on your parents?" I don't know what Ian's parents looked like several years ago, so it's difficult for me to tell whether it's a newer, or rather an older picture.

"Easy," Ian says, perking up a little, "billboard in the background. Announces a movie coming out next week."

Oh, okay. In my defense, I didn't look that closely.

I nod to Ian, acknowledging what he said. "Right. Next. Who knows about you and your history? Where could the leak be? For sure all of us three, plus my dad. Who else?"

Ian answers without hesitation. "NSA. FBI. Secret Service. Heads of departments and training facilities. Lane, Waterhouse, obviously, some others. Only people who met me, recruited me, or are ranked high enough to have access to both, the confidential PRICS and undercover files, such as mine."

"No one else? No other agency I don't know about, no cross referencing, no sharing data bases with anyone?" Gotta make sure.

"Nothing." He shakes his head.

"Okay. That narrows our possibilities. Next question: Why get you out of PRICS? Why now? Any idea? Any enemies you can think of, either from your old life or your new one?"

Ian takes a few moments to consider. "None. I was the premature high school geek with one friend, and the guy no one would remember in a yearbook."

No way. That's exactly how I would've described my high school experience. Two peas—

I push that thought aside and focus on Ian again.

He sighs. "There're always people who don't like you or whom you don't like, but I haven't had any real conflicts here at the FBI or PRICS. Nothing that would lead to this"—he gestures at the picture—"rather than throwing rotten eggs at me or spitting in my coffee."

I nod once. "Dead end then, all right. Let's try another angle. What are you working on that someone might want to stop?" If it's not personal, maybe it's professional.

"Nothing unusual. I'm not working on any inventions right now, military or paramilitary, no weapons, no treatments—nothing. All I've been doing is PRICS and training you for the last couple of months. Nothing more and nothing less."

His eyes widen, and so do mine.

We're reaching the same conclusion at the same time.

"Nu-uh." I shake my head. "That's ridiculous. This isn't

about separating us, it's obviously aimed at you and your parents." Even if the leak knows about PRICS and my training. Seriously—that's not some elaborate plot to get me separated from Ian. Way too complicated.

Ian collapses back into his chair. He runs a hand over his face, covers his eyes, and lets out a heavy breath. "But what if it is, Alix? What if they're after you? There isn't always logic behind a crazy person's actions. They might think this is the best way to get to you. *You* are the only thing that stands out in my life for the last year. Nothing else. Training you and getting you field ready has been my biggest accomplishment since inventing the chip that made you walk again."

He jumps up and starts pacing back and forth through the office, hands behind his back, gaze fixed on the floor. "If I left the White House… went into hiding until this term is over… get Waterhouse to take over, maybe… yeah, it could work."

I only catch half of his muttering, but it's enough.

Oh, hell to the no.

I stand and plant myself straight into Ian's path. "Stop, Ian. *Stop*. Nobody is going anywhere." I throw my arms up, practically catching him as he paces past, his mind so far away he doesn't see me coming. "Listen to me: Nobody is leaving. We'll find another way. Nobody. Is. Leaving."

I don't know where this certainty is coming from, but it's as clear as daylight to me how we need to handle this.

Maybe because this time the mission is not about me, but about Ian.

Maybe because he's losing it—afraid for his parents, me, for himself—and I need to be the one who keeps it together for once.

Maybe because I graduated basic training and got a ginormous ego-boost.

And… maybe because I also received a reality check I dare to do what Waterhouse and Dad explicitly forbade: I rise on my tippy toes and wrap both arms around Ian's neck.

Every muscle in his body goes rigid, and I try to ignore the sting his reaction brings. "Hey. We'll figure it out. We *will*." I squeeze tighter for emphasis. "You're not alone. We're stronger as a team. Promise me, you won't do anything rash. Don't leave, Ian. You can't leave, you hear this? Don't leave." I can't bear the thought of him disappearing, without me, without us knowing where he is. I just lost Sam, I can't lose Ian too.

The tension drains from his body little by little. Slowly, deliberately, he brings one arm up to return my hug, then the other. He digs his fingers into my shirt as if he needed to hold on for dear life. His breath comes out in uneven little puffs, against my hair.

"Ian. I've got you. Please don't leave."

A nod, so tantalizing close to my face, my stomach muscles contract.

"I promise," he whispers near my ear.

Neither of us moves.

We hold each other for a long time, until we both feel strong enough to stand on our own again.

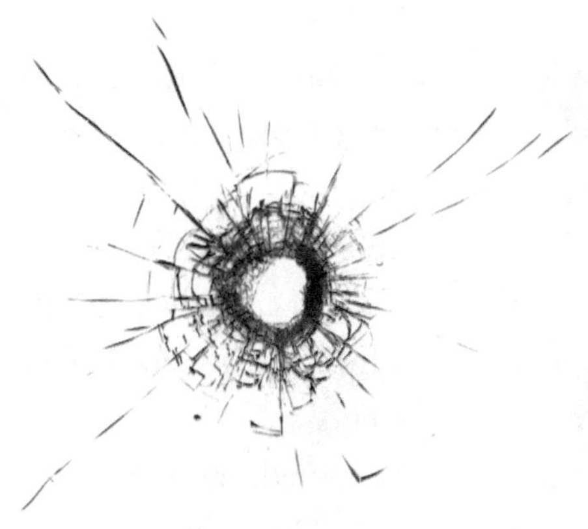

CHAPTER EIGHT

In and Out

Time's running short before my quote-unquote school day officially ends, but we make good use of it.

We tackle everything possible: Ian fortifies the Eagle Lair's security, making sure no one can eavesdrop or access our cameras without triggering an alert. We search for DNA traces and prints on the picture and envelope, run spectrographic analysis on the ink and paper to analyze for brands or origins, and scrutinize every square-millimeter of the photo for clues—reflections in glasses or windows that could timestamp the image for cross-referencing with street cameras.

When that leads nowhere, we tap into the public camera feeds around Ian's hometown, hunting for an angle that might have caught the photographer in action, but it's useless. Whoever did this, they covered their tracks well.

Ian calms down considerably during that time. The activity

helps him, at least he hasn't taken off running yet in a misguided attempt to protect me. But knowing him, that thought is still lurking in the back of his mind.

I steal glances at him between searches. His eyes are puffy and red, though I never caught him actually crying. Talking to him is like chatting with an android—his voice is flat, his attempts at smiles just empty movements.

This picture shattered something in him.

My heart aches for him. The worry about his parents. About what this means for us. For PRICS. I can't even imagine what he must be going through. He never talked much about his parents, and now I know why: The guilt for leaving them the way he did, letting them think he was *dead*.

How the Government could come up with a brain fart like that is beyond me.

Everything makes sense now. Why he's always working. Always here. Never mentions anything about his family or any social life.

What. The. Heck. Did. They. Do. To. Him.

Even his nightmares make sense now—those mornings every few weeks when Ian looks exactly like he does today: defeated. Hollow. Like life landed a sucker punch. Those are days when he didn't sleep thanks to nightmares, I knew that much.

For the first time, I can imagine what haunts him—heart-wrenching guilt about abandoning his parents, about making them grieve their son's death. And with the high-clearance level slapped onto his case, it's not as if he could go and see a shrink about it.

Screw Waterhouse.

That man is evil.

I stick my tongue out to him-slash-fate and focus on

analyzing the letter one more time. We'll figure it out. I won't let Ian down.

"Trouble?"

"Huh?" I snap my head up to meet his gaze.

"It's six." He taps his left wrist, offering a shadow of his usual smile.

Oh. Whoops. I blush. "That… went by fast." And I nearly forgot. Or at least, I didn't pay attention. Another example of me putting Ian before Sam, although this time I can at least blame it on a mission.

I shut down my DUTI-pad. So weird and surreal. Here I am, dealing with a blackmail attempt of epic proportions, and my next step is a make-up-slash-beg-for-friendship session with my ex-boyfriend. My life is split in two distinct halves, agent-me and teenage-me.

Before I leave, I rest my hand on Ian's shoulder. "Hey."

He turns and fails miserably to hide the worry in his eyes.

"First thing tomorrow morning we're back on this, okay? Don't do anything crazy tonight. Please. Text me if you want. And if I wake up tomorrow morning and you're gone, I swear we'll hunt you down. I'm the president's daughter. I've got resources. You got that?" I punch his arm playfully, and his ghost-smile inches up the tiniest bit.

I'll take it.

"Don't worry. I won't take off. I don't know what I'm going to do… but it'll have to wait until tomorrow. Thanks for today, Trouble. Thanks for being there." His voice cracks, and something inside of me does too.

Screw Waterhouse.

He looks so young, so *lost*, I pull him into the second tight hug within a few hours, bringing us chest to chest.

Like earlier, Ian stiffens. "Troub—"

"Relax." I keep my hands on his upper back. "The alarm would warn us if anyone came." As if that justified what I'm doing. Getting advance notice doesn't change it's still wrong. I shouldn't hug Ian. A supportive pat on the back and encouraging words? Sure. A hug? No. Students don't comfort teachers. Dad and Waterhouse would have a fit. But we've never really been student and teacher. We've always been Alix and Ian.

And right now, he needs me.

His breath falls in waves against my neck. "Thank you." He draws me closer, resting his head against mine, careful and gentle.

That's sick, Sam's voice echoes in my mind.

No.

No, no, *no*.

This is Ian and me. *Nothing* about us is sick.

I hold on even tighter, until Ian clears his throat.

We separate in silence, pack up, and head out, the mood heavy.

After he closes the door, Ian holds up something silver in his hand. "Before I forget. You might want to use this tonight." He hands me the RSWB-pen.

For my meeting with Sam. "Thank you."

Ian nods once and walks down the hallway and around a bend to the right. Wait a second—

"Dang," I whisper to myself, "so much for knowing him." I look at Dimitri next to me. "Where does Ian live?" Because I honestly have no clue. In my defense, the topic never came up.

"In the Lair, downstairs. We both do. We have rooms there." He straightens. "We also have fake apartments in D.C., but they're impractical. To keep up appearances we enter and exit through the White House main entrance like regular employees, then take a secret elevator back down to the Lair."

That. Explains. So. Much. "You are always on duty."

"It works best that way." He lifts an eyebrow with a slight nod.

It really does. And how convenient. I touch his forearm. "Dimitri, will you do me a favor? Check in on him tonight? I'm pretty sure he won't do anything stupid, but… it's Ian. Who knows what that mind of his might cook up."

Dimitri nods. "I will."

A weight the size of a boulder falls off my shoulder. That's all I need to hear. Dimitri is keeping an eye on Ian. Good.

We move through the White House in silence, making our way to the West Wing and the Oval Office, or rather, the Front Office, where Sam and Mrs. Houser have their desks.

For the first time since ditching them I actually miss my crutches. My knees feel like jelly and I'm out of breath after walking the short distance from our classroom to the West Wing. It's not poor fitness, it's pure nerves. Pretty sad my body's flooding with fight-or-flight adrenaline when I'm just aiming for a calm conversation.

My heart cramps inside my chest.

I know what I need to do, even if it won't be easy.

Time to find some courage.

Like always, I knock on the door frame, but don't wait for a response before entering. At least now I'm not worried about Dad kicking me out of the Oval Office anymore.

Yeah, those were the days.

Mrs. Houser sits at her desk, backed by the windows overlooking the White House Gardens. She's in the middle of a headset phone conversation, but manages to wave hello with a smile, without missing a beat of her endless sentence. That woman could out-multitask anyone.

I wave before turning toward Sam's desk. There's a good chance I'll start hyperventilating the moment I look at him, depending on how it goes. I'm not entirely sure what I'm trying to salvage here tonight, but at the minimum our friendship.

I clasp my hands behind my back, digging my fingernails into my palms. The pain grounds me, like an old friend.

Sam's at his desk, buried in paperwork. He looks gorgeous as ever, and the only reason I know yesterday's falling out affected him is the stubble. He forgot to shave.

Maybe there's still hope.

I mentally kick myself into action. "Hey, Sam."

His gaze flicks up to me from his papers, and while I think there's a little spark, I might be imagining it. His face stays carefully neutral.

Blank.

"Hey." And just like that he's back to his papers, not gracing me with more of his attention than strictly necessary to acknowledge my presence. The wall he erected between us is almost tangible.

My fingernails carve crescents into my sweaty palms. "Sam… Can we go out to the gardens for a couple of minutes? Please?" I fight to keep my voice steady, despite my heart hammering up in my throat.

Sam pauses, but doesn't look up.

I hate that he isn't immediately saying yes. What's there to consider? It's after hours, and we *need* to talk, no matter what—wait, is there a chance he's not even going to give me a chance to explain?

Two of my fingernails are definitely drawing blood now.

Oh my goodness, judging by how well this is going, the

amount of self-mutilation I will need to keep my mind firmly grounded in reality is going to be immense.

After what seems like forever, Sam gives a curt nod. "Let's go." He pushes off his chair and desk. "We're stepping out for a while, Mrs. Houser."

The Chief Secretary waves acknowledgement, still focused on her phone call.

Sam grabs his coat from behind the door, and we exit through the terrace door by Mrs. Houser's desk.

"Trouble and Timber Wolf moving, Trouble and Timber Wolf moving," the stationed Secret Service agent announces my make-up date with Sam to the Secret Service community. Sigh. Privacy is *so* out the window.

Dimitri follows, nodding to his colleague while maintaining respectful distance between us. Thank you, Dimitri.

It's freezing out, though mainly from the cold radiating off Sam in waves. I zip my jacket up to my chin and bury my hands deep into my pockets. "Let's go to the bench at the Kennedy Garden." Nobody will be there at this time of day. We need whatever privacy we can get, for multiple reasons.

Sam follows silently. Our breath clouds in the air, but as we leave the bright White House lights, it melts into darkness.

After another way too long silent minute, we reach the bench and sit. While Sam's not quite at the opposite end, he's leaving way more space than usual.

I close my eyes for a second and take a deep breath. My fault.

And now I need to fix it.

Focus, Alix. Focus.

I look straight at Sam, who's completely absorbed in studying his folded hands. "Could you do me a favor and please listen to me without storming off? What I need to tell you is…

complicated, and I need you to hear me out, Sam. Can you do that, please?"

There's no good way to start this. He needs to hear everything—I'm bringing him in. He'll be one of only a handful of people to know about PRICS. Ian briefed me on what to say, and thank goodness he did, because I surely wouldn't have ticked the boxes.

Sam glances up briefly and nods, but that's it.

Great.

I unzip my jacket enough to fish out Ian's super pen, then zip up against the cold.

The pen's top is stubborn with gloves on, but the little light glows red after my second try. We're now secured against listening devices within a ten-meter radius, although I'm sure there's no one else around besides Dimitri. He would've spotted an invasion to our privacy.

Here comes the tricky part.

"Sam, under Paragraph 352a, section thirteen, subsection twenty-three, this conversation is and must remain secret and confidential. You cannot discuss what you hear today with anyone except U.S. government employees with a clearance level of 6a or higher about what you will hear here today. Any breach of this is a felony, punishable by jail time and immediate dismissal from Government service."

I pause for a second.

Well, I definitely have his attention now.

The stubborn look and defiant posture vanish. He leans back against the bench, arms crossed in front of his chest, but body angled toward me. And—hurray—there's a hint of curiosity in his eyes.

"Do you understand what I have told you?" I need to hear his confirmation. It's part of the protocol, Ian said.

Sam nods. "Yes."

Good. And hey, he's still here. Hasn't gotten up and walked away already.

I chew on my lower lip. Finding the right words is crucial, but no pressure. "Sam… I know I need to apologize and explain… Things got complicated after Dad's inauguration last year. I… I was recruited. By the Secret Service." Ugh. My ability for complete sentences has evaporated.

I backtrack. "On Inauguration Day, I was introduced to a secret branch of the Secret Service. Their mission is to add an extra layer of protection for the President of the United States, and I'm part of this additional security given my unique relationship to the president, meaning, being his daughter. This past year I've been trained and gone on a couple of missions already since then. I know it sounds insane and completely unrealistic, but I promise you, it's true. Only a select few know about this division. It's top secret. Not even Dad knew about it at first. He figured part of it out after I saved him from that bullet on Fourth of July."

Sam's eyes widen and he sits up straighter. "That was *you*?"

Right, Sam doesn't know half of it, only the modified truth.

I nod. If I'm coming clean, might as well go all in. "Yes. DiBiaso kidnapped me and tried to kill me. I escaped, and barely made it in time to tackle Dad before the sniper took him out. Best tackle of my life." My attempt at humor falls flat.

Sam's brows furrow. "So, you're telling me that for the last year you've been part of a secret branch of the Secret Service to protect the president?"

"Yes. I know what it sounds like, Sam, but Jason told me—"

Mistake. No, *big* mistake. I should've used Ian's real name from the start, but I'm so used to the alias now—

A muscle in Sam's jaw ticks. "Jason. Yeah, tell me. *Please*. About time *his* name comes up. How does *he* fit in? Does *he* know? Are you telling me your fucking *teacher* knew about this, but your boyfriend didn't?" He practically spits out the word 'teacher.'

Crap.

I swallow hard. No way to soften this. "Actually… He's not my teacher, at least not the way people are supposed to think. Jason Miller's real name is Ian Donckers, and he is my Commanding Officer. He recruited me and trains me."

Sam pinches his lips together as he kicks a pebble in front of the bench. "So all those times you were late, all the cancelled dinners, all of that plus all day long during school or whatever you want to call it, you were with *him*?"

Crap, crap! Not going the way I want it! I shift uncomfortably. "Yes and no. Ian oversees every mission. There aren't many people in this branch. Please don't misinterpret this, Sam. I was gone because of the job, not because of Ian." Technically. My cheeks flush.

Sam shakes his head and blows out a noisy breath. "I can't believe it. I thought I knew you better than anyone. You've been lying to me for almost a year—*deceiving* me for almost a year, and I never figured it out. I don't know what's more shocking, that you're in some secret-Secret Service undercover branch, or that you lied so easily and well that I never caught on. How could you do this to me? How could you lie to me every single day? Was there anything real between us, or was I just an alibi boyfriend?"

The last sentence is so loud, not even the sound-blocking pen will cover it up.

Alibi boyfriend.

And now comes the hard part. Pressure builds in my chest, the kind that comes from guilt. "You were my crush for forever, Sam. I—"

His head snaps back. "Were?"

Crap. "Uhh—" Freudian slip. It wasn't supposed to come out that way! "No, I mean—"

Sam straightens, towering beside me, shoulders rigid, eyes blazing. "*Were?*" he grinds out through clenched teeth. "Are you telling me what I think? That you used me? That you had this exciting, secret life going on, and I was nothing but your beard?"

Every single words stings like a whiplash. I shake my head so hard my ponytail slaps my cheeks. "No, Sam! No! That's not true. I... I really crushed bad on you, and—"

"Past tense. Again."

Anger surges through me. "Well, yeah! Because in case you missed it, things haven't exactly been great these past few months!"

"Tell me about it, Mrs. Super Spy." His sarcasm slaps me across the face, but I refuse to turn the other cheek.

"It wasn't all me, Sam! Yes, I was busy! Yes, I should've invested more! Guilty as charged, but come on, don't pretend you were all in, because it surely didn't feel that way!" I cross my arms in front of my chest, the pen tugged under my armpit. I hope it's still working.

Sam opens his mouth, then closes it, pressing his lips into a tight line.

I try again, calmer. "All I'm saying is that we both—"

"What about the ring?" Sam nods at my hidden hand. "Why did he give it to you?"

Damn it.

I'm not getting through to him, I can feel it. The pen vibrates against my skin. Our protected time is running out. Crap, crap, *crap*.

"It's a surveillance program with a software-releasing tool integrated in the stone. I used it during a mission at Megatech United in the morning and I forgot to take it off. That's all." I keep my voice as level as I can.

Sam clenches and unclenches his hands. He leans forward, turning to face me. "I can't believe you lied to me for almost a year." His nostrils flare.

Gah! I'm getting nowhere! "I was under orders, Sam, I—"

"You could have said *something*. Given me a hint."

"You work for the president. You know it doesn't work that way."

"I can't believe you let Jason, Ian, whatever his name is, talk you into this. What a garbage idea! Do you honestly think the Secret Service needs *you*? That there's anything they don't already have a hundred people for?" He throws his hands up in the air. "They don't need *you* for anything, Alix! I don't know what game he's playing, but I don't like it."

I recoil as if he's slapped me. What— "Excuse me? What are you saying? That I'm useless? That I can't do my job? In case you forgot, *I* was the one who saved Dad from that bullet!" How dare he—what does he think I am, some non-functioning Barbie doll?

Sam makes a dismissive sound. "Yeah right. I don't care what *he* tells you or what you think you're doing, if they expect you to take a bullet, this is crap! You need to get out of there, and *he* needs to get as far away from you as possible. If he's making you think you could be a spy, then he's dangerous for you." Anger hardens his features as he glares at me like I'm the enemy.

I'm speechless. How did we end up here?

We are *not* enemies.

We are—were—boyfriend and girlfriend. At the very least friends.

My anger dissolves into nothing. I don't want his rage. I don't want this fight. "Sam, please. Let's talk about this, and don't be mad at me—"

He cuts me off. "Not be mad at you? Are you insane? The whole last year was one big lie! I don't even know you. Everything I thought I knew—"

He stands, jamming his hands in his pockets. "I'm going back inside. Don't call me. Don't text me. The only time I want to hear from you is when you stop working with *him*. And if that doesn't happen…" He pauses and turns away from me. "Then the White House is big enough that I never have to see you again."

And then, for the second time in less than twenty-four hours, Sam walks away from me.

He's ended everything—not only on our relationship, but worse, our friendship.

I stay frozen to the bench.

Speechless.

Motionless.

How did everything go so horribly wrong?

My mind is blank. Completely empty.

Sam disappears into the darkness like last night, but this time I don't even have tears left. Something broke, and I don't know if I can fix it anymore.

I hear the terrace doors open and close. Still I don't move.

The pen in my hand goes dark.

We would've had a little longer. I didn't even get to say half of what I needed to say.

And while part of me understands this is *bad*, I feel nothing.

Nothing.

Absolutely nothing.

After a while, footsteps approach from behind. Dimitri.

He rests his large hand on my shoulder. "Come on inside. You're freezing." Only because my mind is too numb to come up with a different idea, I stand up and follow him inside.

This is what *alone* feels like.

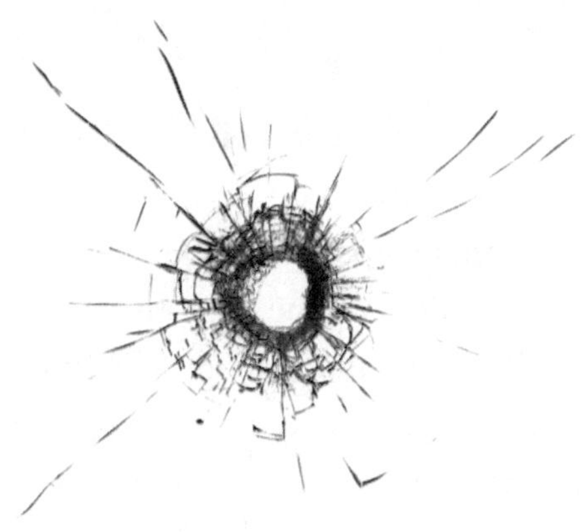

CHAPTER NINE
Digesting

The numbness lasts and won't go away.

Trying to act normal at the dinner table is a spectacular failure. I can tell, because Dad keeps steering the conversation away from me. Mom doesn't notice a thing, as usual. How typical mother-daughter-pairs pick up on every little mood shift in each other is beyond me; it never worked for us.

The chef has prepared an amazing pasta dish, and normally, I'd be all over it. Not today. I push the noodles around my plate, managing an occasionally bite, but that's about it. My body is here at dinner, but my heart and soul are withering away under a park bench in the Kennedy Garden like Lord Voldemort at Union Station.

Everything's mechanical. The last half hour has morphed into a suffocating blanket of undefined feelings and thoughts. My mind has slowed to the bare minimum needed for breathing and eating.

An increasingly persistent noise finally breaks through—Mom's nagging from my left.

"—or at least tell me about the food, if you don't want to spill any secrets, Alix." Mom eyes me expectantly.

Secrets? Wait, secrets and... food? What foo—

Oh. Yeah. Food. *The* picnic. It has dropped quite a bit on the ladder of important events over the last twenty-four hours.

Dad sets down his fork and dabs his napkin against his mouth. "Go easy on her, Bethany. Remember how you hated your mom quizzing you after our first dates? Let her keep that one for herself." He winks at me, but it's forced. He knows me too well.

Mom narrows her eyes with an exaggerated sigh. "Well, yes, yes, I don't need every detail. A summary will do. You didn't give me a chance to ask her. You've been talking all dinner long." She shoots Dad a mock glare. She's right, he has been talking more than usual, but I think I know why. Just more proof Dad and I sync better than Mom and I ever will.

But I won't shake her when she's in investigation mode. Better give her something and get it over with. I abandon my spoon on my plate—not like I'll be eating the rest of my meal anyway. One more sip of water buys me another second to think.

Setting down my glass, I fake a shy smile. "Dad's right, Mom. Don't pry. Great food, great shooting stars—that's all you get." Thank you, Ian, for showing me how to answer indirectly without lying.

I take another sip of water. *Drop the topic, drop the topic, drop—*

"Aww," she squeals at a pitch that hurts. "What did you do after?"

Dang. My mom's a terrier locked into the mailman's ankle.

"Bethany." Dad gives her *that* look.

"Oh, come on. She won't tell me if she doesn't want to. Give me a little something, Alix! Your first date, I'm so excited for you!"

I snort out a sarcastic chuckle. Of all things and days, *this* must be the one Mom picks for mother-daughter bonding.

If I have to discuss anything Sam-related with a parent, I'd choose Dad. I fake a cough into my elbow for time, then look straight at him. "So, after the picnic? I brought Sam in."

My parents' reactions couldn't be more different, though neither notices the other's.

While Dad masks his surprise and shock, Mom rolls her eyes. "Well, honey, I figured that, it was freezing outside." She's not satisfied with my one-liner, but that's fine, I got more.

I raise an eyebrow at Dad. "Yeah, right, I thought so too, but seems like Sam would've preferred to stay out in the cold." *Unless I stop working with Ian.*

Dad... he gets it perfectly: I told Sam about PRICS, but it went badly.

A flash of disappointment crosses his face before settling into sympathy. I wish dinner was over so he could hug me. No, I'm not getting too old for that. Not on days like today.

Before Mom can protest my vague answer, there's a knock on the door. That's the thing about living and working in the White House—you're never truly off.

"Come in," Dad calls. The door opens and who walks in, of all people in the whole, wide world?

Yup.

Sam.

He steps into the dining room, carefully avoiding looking in my direction.

And it hurts, because I caused it. Well, most of it.

"Sorry to interrupt dinner, sir, but you're needed in the Situation Room, if you don't mind." His voice perfectly controlled. The picture-perfect textbook definition of professionalism.

And it makes me mad.

So he can to do his job, but I can't? Because I'm a girl? Because I'm geeky little me? Because I am—was—his girlfriend?

My dad drops his napkin onto the table but stops behind me on his way out.

One kiss to the top of my head.

A reassuring squeeze of my shoulder.

Yeah. He understood exactly what transpired between Sam and me.

Gratitude washes over me. He's not just showing he is here for me, it's also a message to Sam. A sign that I come first.

Between Sam and me, Dad chooses me. Not that it should come as a surprise, but given the ups and downs of our last year, especially the downs, it's not guaranteed.

"Don't wait for me. I will probably be late," Dad tells Mom before closing the door behind him on the way out.

Mom sighs. "Again. I feel like he makes them call him down whenever he's traveling, and I end up packing his suitcase." She stabs at her noodles, most of which evade their fate.

"What traveling?"

She tries and fails to keep a straight face. "Honey, you just told me more about your date with Sam with that one sentence than you have all night. If you didn't hear a single word your father has been droning on about all evening, then it was a *perfect* date."

I disagree. "Well… uhh, yes, it's hard to not think about it. So, where's he going?"

She swallows some pasta, washing it down with water. I don't think my parents have touched wine or beer for dinner since the inauguration. Both prefer staying clear-headed to begin with, and neither wants to risk having alcohol in their system when duty calls, which could be anytime.

"The G20 Summit in Berlin, Germany, sweetie. Your father leaves tomorrow with the whole team, including Sam." She winks. "Better prepare yourself for a couple of days without your man. They'll be gone a while."

Right, the G20. I nearly forgot. It's been huge these last two or three weeks, with major economic problems in most participating countries, plus increased terrorism and cyber terrorism. Dad's been swamped. I feel awful for forgetting, but I've been too wrapped up in my own drama. Bad spy and daughter I am.

Bad spy, bad daughter, and really, really bad—ex—girlfriend and friend.

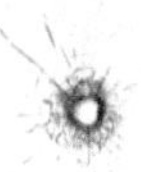

Not even two minutes later, I excuse myself from the table and retreat to my room.

Leaving the lights off, I fall back onto my bed, staring at the ceiling. Amazing how life can change in a day. Yesterday at this time, we were having our picnic, and everything felt okay.

Now The Dark Unit is hacking us left and right, somebody's blackmailing Ian and threatening to kill his parents, and Sam and I… are over.

Time-turner, anyone?

I reach over and grab Sneaker from my nightstand. Moonlight catches its blue stone, casting turquoise rays across my skin.

"Hey, trouble-maker," I whisper to the ring. Such a tiny thing, such a massive impact.

I understand two of Sam's three problems with me being a Secret Service Agent: First, I lied to him. True. I hated it, but I still did it. Guilty as charged.

Second, I spend tons of time with Ian. Also true, and Sam's closer to the mark than I'd like. No, nothing's going on with Ian. Nothing will. But honestly? I've never stopped hoping.

I led Sam along without even realizing it. Again, guilty.

Third problem of his—and this one I can't and won't accept—that I shouldn't be a Secret Service agent, period.

I've got to admit, that one hurts worst of all.

How dare he say, or even *think*, I can't do this? Since we started dating, he's treated me like a child. He never did that before we became a couple. It's like he's trying to mold me to some image in his head. It drives me crazy, but not in a good way.

Him telling me I can't handle PRICS?

That's crossing a line.

Maybe that's what broke when he left me on that bench. He can't cherry-pick which part of me to accept. I come with all my geekiness and dorkiness, but if he likes that part of me, he gets the rest too—the part that learned to fight, to decode, to hold my own. I refuse to go back to being the shy and insecure girl I was a year ago.

Sneaker catches moonbeam in its center, casting a blue shadow across my hand as I turn it. When Ian recruited me, I never imagined becoming the agent I am today. I'm proud of my growth. I love that I help Dad be the best president possible, and

I wouldn't give up PRICS for anything.

A glint catches my eye—an engraving on the inside of the ring I never noticed. It's hard to make out in the dark, but I don't want to break my cocoon of darkness. I hold Sneaker close until I can read the tiny letters:

GG d- !a !Br!_ct C+++ t+++ kya++++

No way.

A smile spreads until it splits my face. My pulse drums in my ears, thundering through my body.

Ian wanted to give me a graduation gift I needed, and he gave me the *yes* to talk to Sam. Well, that part crashed and burned, but this—*this* is better. This tells me everything I need to know. A perfect description of how Ian sees me. in Geek Code. Meaningless to most, but everything to people like me who can read it.

In the spur of the moment, I slip the ring on. This is my real graduation gift from Ian—the perfect reminder of who I am and how fragile everything can be. After all, this ring ended things with Sam.

Sneaker fits like it's always belonged there.

I curl onto my side, not caring about brushing my teeth or changing into my PJs. All I need is sleep.

For a while, I hover between waking and sleeping, the Geek Code repeating in my mind until I drift off completely.

GG d- !a !Br!_ct C+++ t+++ kya++++ — Geek of Government, dressed in jeans and t-shirt, her age is none of your business, she is really brainy but cute, a computer expert who loves Star Trek, and she can kick your ass from here to the moon.

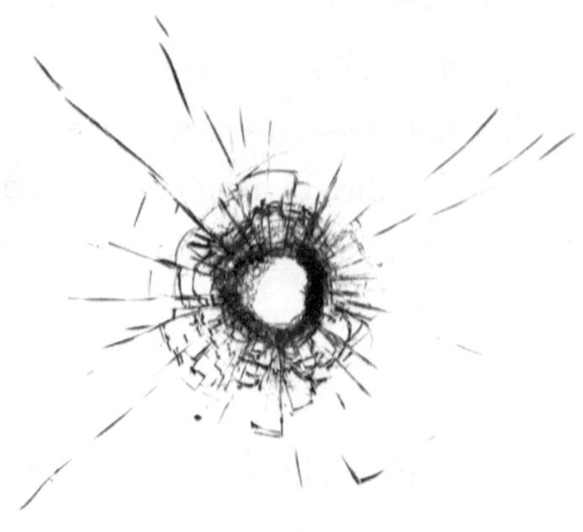

CHAPTER TEN
Results

The next morning I grab my backpack and leave the residence a little earlier than usual. I woke up earlier as well, but my mind was done resting. Today's going to be a big day. An important day. I have several new ideas how to tackle the blackmailing, no matter if Sam thinks—

My stomach lurches.

No.

I'm guilty as charged in lying and spending time with Ian.

But Sam's guilty being a misogynistic ass.

I lift my chin up higher and open the door, Sneaker's blue stone on my hand sparkling under the artificial light.

Dimitri waits for me in front of the residence, as always.

We exchange silent nods and head for the stairs. Something's off about him, but I can't quite put my finger on it—maybe I'm not the only one losing sleep.

Speaking of.

At the bottom of the stairs, far enough from any eavesdropping bodyguards, I stop him.

"How was he last night?" I hope Dimitri kept his promise to watch Ian.

Dimitri quirks an eyebrow. "Good. Took him sparring. He did well."

My jaw drops. He did *what*? Taking Ian sparring wasn't exactly what I meant when I asked him to keep an eye on him! "You took him sparring?" I echo.

Dimitri's eyebrow inches higher. "Yes. He needed an outlet. Sparring provided one."

A surprised laugh escapes me. Okay then. I mean, I didn't expect them to have a movie night and paint each other's toenails, but sparring—

That's what's different!

I let out a low whistle. "He got you good. Nice shiner."

The swelling around Dimitri's left eye is subtle behind his sunglasses, but once you see it, it can't be un-seen. And judging by the stiff way he walks, he's got a couple of other bruises too.

Dimitri grunts. "Like I said, he needed an outlet." He strides ahead toward class. Conversation over, apparently.

I stifle a laugh.

Guys.

"Today is the day we tackle all problems, solve them, and move forward." I hold my teacup out for Ian. Mission Optimism: launched.

His expression softens. "Thanks, Trouble." He clonks his cup against mine, and we sip. While I'm glad he appreciates the idea, Mission Optimism is as much for me. I know all the ways this could go wrong.

Ian could bail and leave me.

The blackmailer could kill his parents.

The Dark Unit could cripple the government.

Sam could hate me forever—

—nope, can't go there. So yeah, Mission Optimism is more Mission Fake-It-Until-You-Make-It.

We set our cups down.

Ian cocks his head at me. "How did bringing in Sam—"

A shrill whistle cuts through the air from his DUTI-pad. One glance at the screen is all it takes to drain all color from his face.

To turn him ghost white.

And to curse at the top of his lungs. "Crap!"

He clicks his keychain, and—*boom*—we go into active mode: windows tinting for privacy, lights dimming, hallway sounds fading into silence.

Ookay, what—

Ian presses another button, and Dimitri comes in, closes the door behind him and walks up to us in fast, long strides.

I sit up straighter, the tea forgotten in my hands.

Dimitri and Ian exchange a loaded look.

My gaze bounces between them. "What is it?" Throw me a bone here!

Ian lifts a finger to his mouth. *Shush.*

Oh, heck. Not again.

Adrenaline floods my system. What is it? Another leak? The Dark Unit? Something else?

Whatever Ian saw, it's bad enough to warrant maximum security. He takes out the pen I gave him back right when I arrived and twists its top. We have at least three layers of anti-listening devices active right now, and I really hope they don't cancel each other out. To top things off, Ian presses another combination on his key chain, and all lights turn off, plunging us into near-darkness, only faint light filtering through the tinted windows.

This is new.

Ian and Dimitri drag chairs to my desk, their faces lost in shadow. Ian sits close, stopping me with a hand on my knee when I try to make room.

"Stay put. We need to be close." His voice is quiet and controlled, but there is a hint of… panic seeping through.

I don't like this at all.

Dimitri settles across from us.

Ian takes a deep breath and releases it in a heavy sigh. "This is bad. Beyond bad, actually."

He rakes his free hand through his hair. "We have first results from Megatech United. Sneaker found something."

That should be good news, right? Sneaker's working, protecting MU and informing us of the hack so we can track the intruder. This could be our first breakthrough against the Dark Unit.

Ian's grip burns through my jeans. "Another hack-attempt. Sneaker barely blocked it. The source code it sent back…" He pauses. "I didn't need to analyze it. I know this code. I wrote it. In High School."

Holy cow…! "Torpedo?" If Torpedo is in the hands of a hacker, we're screwed. A self-thinking counter-measure evading program in a hacker's hands…

Now I get the lockdown. If that code is out there, it could have made its way anywhere—anywhere, where Sneaker wasn't there to catch it.

Ian's grip on my knee gets stronger. "Yes. Torpedo. From scanning over it, seems like they barely modified it—"

"They? The Dark Unit?" It would fit their pattern, hacking into systems.

"Maybe. No rhyme, no threat, just an almost-successful hack at MU for unknown reasons. But that's not even the worst part."

Dimitri stiffens. So do I.

I should've known a hack, even with Ian's code, wouldn't trigger this level of security.

Ian bites his lip. "Torpedo shouldn't exist outside my head. It burned in the same car I 'died' in almost four years ago."

Boom.

His words hit like a bomb.

If Torpedo is back, then… "Are you sure it was destroyed? Couldn't it have—"

"Survived the crash?" He laugh is hollow. "Maybe. But even if that happened, we're still screwed."

His grip on my knee becomes vise-like. Most wouldn't notice, but Ian is about to pop an aneurysm. I cover his hand with mine, gently prying it off. He latches onto my fingers instead, holding like a lifeline.

"I'll explain, but it's complicated. After joining the Secret Service, we planned my death. A car wreck with a burned, unidentifiable body seemed simplest. I'd just gotten my license— perfect cover. The planning was surreal. Choosing clothes that wouldn't burn completely, for identification, sparing them a fake autopsy. I chose my favorite leather jacket, the one my mom had given me for my birthday the year before. I knew they would recognize it immediately, even charred."

His voice cracks and he pauses. My heart aches. I couldn't

have made those choices at his age—heck, or at my current age! I stroke his hand with my thumb, and he squeezes my hand back in response.

"We planned everything thoroughly. The NSA dictated and organized everything. Implanted a radio-controlled driver unit into my car, told me what to pack, what to leave, where to stop, where they would take over. I took all my computer gear. Told my parents I was going to a computer club meeting in the neighborhood county. The Secret Service had me join that club exactly for this purpose two months earlier. I packed everything—and I mean *everything*—that ever had data on it and I hadn't already destroyed. Every hard drive, every old laptop. Everything. After my *demise,* there couldn't be any trace of my source programs, or my inventions. They all belonged to the Secret Service now. All they allowed me to take needed to be in my head." He taps his temple.

For anyone else this would be impossible, but Ian's memory is perfect.

"That night, I said goodbye to my parents for the last time. Dad had just finished a long shift at the police station. He worked as an officer at the local police station, and no way I'd risk him responding to my accident. Being cruel enough to join the FBI was one thing, but that would have crossed a line. So… I said goodbye and got in my car, like I had done a hundred times before. I drove to the meeting point in the middle of nowhere— rural Washington, you know—and got out. The Secret Service team remotely crashed it into a tree and torched it. They used undetectable accelerant to reach the temperatures we needed to burn 'me' and the drives to a crisp. They gave me a wig, sunglasses, threw me in the back of their nondescript Mercedes, and Ian Donckers was gone."

He turns his head to look at me, eyes darker than normal and full of sorrow. All the guilt he had over the years is coming up again, as fresh as on the first day.

I curl my free hand into a fist.

Waterhouse.

But, the government's insanity isn't the point right now. Everything seems to have gone as planned. "Could you have missed something at home? Maybe in a different room? Left anything with a friend?" These hackers got his code *somehow.*

He shakes his head. "No. I was always pretty OCD about my stuff and security. I had everything in alarm secured boxes." He chuckles dryly. "I even gave my parents cutting-edge security—fingerprint reader at doorknobs, windows, facial recognition… I was already paranoid then."

Classic Ian, indeed. "So either the drives survived, or somebody from the Secret Service with clearance to know enough stole Torpedo and is using it against us."

He traces over my fingers with his thumb, pausing when he hits Sneaker. "Bull's eye, Trouble," he whispers. "That's why I went into full lockdown mode. Whoever leaked my identity could've leaked Torpedo."

Oh, hell.

Our enemy could be deeper inside than we thought.

"But here's the thing. This is the original code from high school. Which means—"

"It's from the wreck," I whisper. "How—"

"Everything went to the Little Springs police evidence locker," Ian says. "Every burned-to-a-crisp hard drive, CD, or whatever." He shifts. "Alix, I need to go to Washington and figure out what happened to the evidence in that police locker. I need to find out what happened—who could've taken one of the burned drives—or I won't be able to piece things together."

He pauses. "That means I'll have to resign from PRICS."

It takes me an embarrassingly long second to understand what he just said. My anger on the other hand flares up in no time. "Oh, *hell* no!" I crush his hand in mine. "Are you insane? You're not going there alone! You said it yourself, it could be connected! Somebody leaks your identity, threatens to harm your parents if you don't leave PRICS, and your code vanishing from a police safety locker? If this is the same person, you're going in with a full team, or not at all!"

I glare at him through the darkness. The nerve of him—

He sighs. "Alix… Trouble, think. Yes, there might be a connection is possible, but I don't know enough. If I'm right with my first theory and the blackmailer wants easier access to you by getting me out of the way, I'm not about to hand you over on a silver platter and make it easy for them. I promised you after the VP incident I'd watch out for you, and taking you out of the White House and into an unknown situation does *not* meet that definition."

He covers our joined hands with his free one, playing with Sneaker. His touch sets off a distracting pull inside my stomach that I force myself to ignore.

None of Ian's reasons matter. He can't go alone. Even if we monitor from here, what if… what if… There are way too many what-ifs for my taste.

"Ian, you need backup. *You* taught me how important backup is." I want to shake sense into him.

Dimitri's deep baritone startles me. "Alix is right. Too many unknowns. Blackmail, leak, possible theft from a police station. This is too big for one person, it's a team effort."

My heart lifts. Two against one, although that *one* could

technically overrule us.

Ian groans. "I can't take Alix, Dimitri! Besides exposing her to danger, travelling with the President's daughter kills stealth! The Secret Service is going to be monitoring us the second her ID gets swiped at the airport! And obviously, I can't take you either, because you have to—I repeat—*have to* stick with Alix. So yes, this is a one-man mission."

He lets go of me and plants both of his hands firmly on the table.

Crap. I hadn't even thought about my name being a problem. Of course I can't travel as freely as I used to—almost everybody knows my face and my name, first as the poor presidential candidate's daughter in this bad accident, now as the president's daughter. Everybody knows my face. With me tagging along, the stealth approach is definitely out of the window.

Dimitri adjusts his sunglasses. "That's why we have fake IDs and undercover training."

Fake ID?

Ian groans. "You had to bring it up, didn't you? Couldn't give it a rest and let me do my thing?"

"You have a good team. Alix graduated. We have the tools for success. As a team."

Did I mention I loved Dimitri? Can't fault his logic. I press on. "If you leave alone, we will track you down. That's way more dangerous than going in together, and with a plan." I'm not above manipulating his sense of responsibility and duty.

Ian folds his arms on the table and drops his head on them. "I surrender. Apparently, I can't win this. Okay. It's a team effort. But I'm warning you—we know whom or what we're facing. We'll need to be careful, and one step ahead."

He looks up again, serious. "And one more thing, and this is a requirement. We're going to tell your father what we're doing and ask for permission for you to go. I'm not taking the Commander in Chief's daughter on an outside mission without approval."

A grin spreads over my face. *Yes!* I hold my knuckles out to Dimitri, and somehow, despite semi-darkness and sunglasses, he bumps them.

We are *on!*

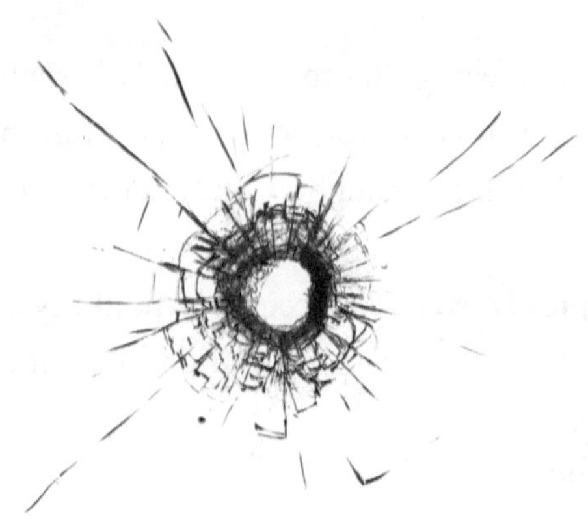

CHAPTER ELEVEN
Permission

This is when the real work starts.

We lift the lockdown and head down to the Lair. Dimitri handles security prep for the trip, while Ian and I tackle tech.

Ian hands me a small plastic card. "Behold, my criminal masterpiece." He clutches his chest, mock-serious.

It's an ID—my ID. Or rather, not. "Kira Sanderson?" I read. Twenty-one, a California address, dark hair and... and a nose piercing. "A piercing."

Really.

I cock an eyebrow. Dad's going to love that.

"What?" Ian makes innocent puppy dog eyes at me. "It'll suit you, and—ow!" He laughs, the first real laugh in a while, and rubs his arm where I punched him. "But kidding aside, it's a fake stud, obviously. So, yes, this is your government-approved fake

ID for traveling. Kira Sanderson has the advantage of being twenty-one already, so no underage problems. She also comes with a clean background check, in case anybody ever wanted to dig deeper into her."

Sounds legit. "What about you and Dimitri?"

Ian produces two more IDs from the same drawer. "Hi there, I'm Elliott Nowlin, and this"—he hands me Dimitri's ID—"is my friend Elroy McMonahan."

Glad to see I'm not the only one who looks like she could be playing in a rock band. Both fake-Ian and fake-Dimitri sport black hair and piercings. Punk-y.

Ian leans forward hands clasped. In an instant the atmosphere shifts from joking to serious. "I'll have to ask you once again. Are you sure? Last chance. Yes, you've been trained, but…" He looks down onto his hands. "But real-life missions have unexpected twists."

I know. Like the guard at MU we didn't expect. "I'm sure. You're not going alone. We got this."

He manages a faint smile. "That's what I thought. Thank you for that. The whole thing with my parents…" He leaves the sentence open.

"I know. We'll find who's behind all that. They'll be safe." Strange being the reassuring one.

Ian nods. "And speaking of. Let's get your father's permission. In terms of a cover story for your mother and Sam—"

My heart twists. "Sam won't need one."

Ian flinches. "He won't—"

That's right. We hadn't gotten to that part yet. "No. He decided that me working for PRICS must be the dumbest idea ever." I cross my arms in front of my chest. Wish it didn't sting so much.

Ian opens his mouth, and closes it. He sighs. "I'm sorry, Trouble. That sucks."

I brush it off. "Whatever. I won't change who I am to please him." Doesn't mean it doesn't hurt though, because it does. It throbs. It burns. It eats at me during every second since it happened. Somewhere deep down I still think this must be a ginormous misunderstanding, a mix-up of epic proportions, but I know better.

It had been coming for a while.

And at this point, with his reaction, I need to let it go.

I force down a hard swallow. "Anyway, we should talk to Dad now." I push up from the couch. Talk to Dad, pack, prep, get an early-morning start. Done.

And neither Dad nor Sam can stop me.

Around this time of day the halls of the West Wing aren't that busy anymore, and the closer Ian and I get to the Oval Office, the more nervous I become.

Sounds like a typical me-thing to assume Dad is going to say yes, forgetting he is history's most protective dad. The kind who would fake-hate me for a year if it meant it kept me safe.

I'm still surprised he let me continue with PRICS—with Ian—although to be fair, I kind of blackmailed him into that. Guilty as charged. Here's hoping by now he trusts I know what I'm doing. But yeah—there's a very real chance he's going to say no after all. And what am I going to do then? Beg? Can't very well take off without his permission. That's not an option being the president's daughter. Dad needs to let me go, and I need to play this smart.

I hold Ian back from entering the front office and lower my voice. "If he says no—"

"Then you stay, Trouble," Ian whispers. His jaw sets to match the determined look in his face. "It's the Commander in Chief's call. Your *father's* decision."

Grr. Commander in Chief or not. Technically, he's neither our boss nor authorized to give us orders, but I see where Ian's coming from.

I sigh and knock on the doorframe. Luckily, the only person in the office is Mrs. Houser, typing away on her keyboard. Don't know what it says about me, but I'm glad Sam isn't here. "Hey, Mrs. Houser. Can we go in and talk to Dad for a second?"

She offers an apologetic smile. "Sorry, Alix. He's in a meeting, and then off to the airport afterwards. The G20. Sam is off to pack." She winks.

Of course she'd assume I'd like to know my boyfriend's whereabouts, only that I don't. And I'm pretty sure Sam's going to welcome an ocean between us.

Mrs. Houser glances at the clock. "Give him a call when he's on the Air Force One. That might be easiest." She smiles at me again and returns to her typing.

Crap. Right, he's leaving soon. If we don't get him now… We can't very well explain my plan to him via phone, especially not with leaks around. The Oval Office is the one place I can talk to Dad without compromising safety.

I exchange a glance with Ian and get a short nod: *Go for it.*

Switching tactics, I hold up my laptop. "I know, Mrs. Houser, but he told me to come by before he left. School project and," I lower my voice conspiratorially, "Mom's gift."

Surprise flickers across her face—but she picks up the phone.

Exactly what we were going for when coming up with the emergency code: Happy wife, happy life—and happy wife equals a happy president in this case.

And lo and behold, thirty seconds later, Dad opens the door to the Oval Office, beaming at me. "Alix. Mr. Miller." Ian gets a nod.

Funny how I'm still relieved he's not kicking me out. Guess that wound will take a while to heal.

Dad hugs me and shakes hands with Ian before he makes room for us to enter the Oval Office.

The Oval Office never fails to give me chills. The sheer history of what happened in here over the years, the stories those walls could tell…

Dad's presidential desk commands the far corner by the window, facing out into the room. The massive Presidential Seal woven into the carpet—eagle's gaze fixed to the right—and the plush, cushy couches arranged around a coffee table all breathe an air of legacy and power.

Unfortunately, two of the chairs around said coffee table are currently taken by Brandon Lane… and my special friend, Floyd Waterhouse.

Talk about polar opposites. Brandon seems genuinely pleased to see us, while Waterhouse turns an even more annoying shade of pale-beige, garnished with a badly hidden scowl.

I groan inwardly. Rookie's mistake. Should've asked first whom Dad was meeting.

Ian recovers faster than me, as usual. "Mr. Waterhouse. Mr. Lane. Excuse the interruption, we will only need a minute."

Dad leads us over to the desk. "Yes. Gentlemen, excuse us for a second, will you please?" Ever the professional, he positions himself with his back toward Waterhouse and Lane, just as Ian taught us. Nobody should be able to read the president's lips. He drops his voice. "What's going on?"

Ian stands at attention. "Sir, I would like to ask permission to take Alix on an outside mission." Following Dad's lead, he keeps his voice low and his face hidden from the coffee table crew. Nobody should be able to read his lips either.

Dad tilts his head. "Outside mission?"

"Yes, sir. Washington State. My hometown."

Dad's eyebrows shoot up. "Your hometown."

Ian's cheeks flush. "Yes. It's… a recent development." He squares his shoulders. "The reason why I'm asking for permission is, because strictly speaking it's not a straightforward PRICS-mission. We—"

"Then the answer is no."

Gah! Ian! Not the way to handle my dad. I step half in front of Ian—partly, to cut him off, partly to be hidden from the coffee table. "Dad. Listen. It's not that simple. Here are the facts. Somebody's trying to blackmail Ian out of PRICS. Plus, we got a lead on the MU incident. Sneaker found something, looks like an old code Ian wrote in high school that should've gotten destroyed when he joined the Secret Service. Someone got their hands on it and is using it against us."

I clasp my hands behind my back. Dad's expression is pure politician. I can't read him at all. "The reason why Ian said it's not a straight PRICS-mission, is because we don't know if the blackmail and the stolen code are connected, but it's a possibility. Our plan is to get to Washington State and start investigating."

Still no interruption, no dismissal. Deep breath. "I'd appreciate if I could go, Dad. Ian wanted to handle this solo, but it's not a one-person job. I trained for this, and—"

Dad tugs on his sleeve. "What kind of blackmail?"

Some of the tension leaves my shoulders. That's not a no.

Ian jumps in before I can. "A picture of my parents—recent. Caption said 'get out or they die' under it. Nothing else."

Dad flinches. "I'm sorry to hear that, Ian. That must be tough."

Not as tough as leaving your parents at sixteen, and *leaving* is a euphemism here.

"Thank you, sir. And yes, it is." Ian maintains his professional mask. I'm beginning to hate that word. "As you know, my parents aren't aware about PRICS, so—"

Wait, what? My gaze locks with Dad's. "You knew? That Ian's parents think he's dead? You—"

At least Dad has the decency to look uncomfortable. "I did. But remember—" He holds up a hand. "Remember this isn't my doing. As you love to point out, Alix, PRICS is off presidential access."

I snap my mouth shut. Point taken. A battle for another time. "Okay, well, anyway. It's a basic search and recover operation. Low-risk. Go in, get the intel, get out. Dimitri is going to be with me at all times. We'll be disguised. Please, Dad." I'm not above begging on my knees, but I'd prefer if it wasn't in front of Waterhouse and Lane.

Dad gives a slight nod but stays quiet. The wheels are still turning.

One last shot. I look straight up at him. My heart hammers so hard it might just sprint to Washington without me. "Dad, I'm prepared for this. I want to help. Besides the blackmail, we have to uncover who took the code, what they're planning, and how to stop whatever they're doing. It's a matter of national cyber security. This is my wheelhouse. You know I'll be careful. Plus, I'll have the guys. Please, Dad. I'm ready for this." Knee fall coming up in three, two—

Dad fiddles with his tie. "Alix, we talked about that. If I had my way—"

Oh no, we're not going down that route again! "If I had mine, you wouldn't have run for president. Still, you chose to run and won. I chose PRICS because that's where my skills matter most, and you know it."

Ian shifts uncomfortably, caught in the crossfire. "Sir—"

"Dad. I know you're having a tough time with the whole letting-go thing, but I'm seventeen. Almost eighteen. You know the guys. It's not as if I'm on spring break in Cancun with a bunch of people you've never met."

Dad's jaw tightens.

Oops. Maybe I shouldn't have mentioned the guys and Cancun in one sentence.

"I'm not reopening the PRICS-conversation. I'm okay with you serving as long as it adheres to certain guidelines, but this…" His mouth tightens. He closes his eyes briefly, then sighs. "You. Dimitri. And… you?" His look at Ian could melt steel.

Ian's face goes super nova. "Correct, sir. But—"

Dad looks straight at me. "Sam?"

"Huh?" What does Sam have to—

"What happened with Sam?" He tilts his head, waiting. Unfortunately, there's not much I want to discuss less than my breakup with Sam—other than talking about Sam with Ian standing *right next to me*. Low-blow, Dad. "It doesn't matter what happened with Sam. Completely irrelevant for the mission. I—"

Ian's gentle hand on my shoulder stops me before I say something I might regret. "Sir, Alix's help would be invaluable. She graduated PRICS as one of our top agents. Her wanting to help means everything, but…" He pauses. "I completely understand if you withhold permission."

I whirl around. "Are you kidding—" Not cool, Ian! Not cool at all!

Ian ignores me. "That said, her safety will be our absolute priority, and I agree that her cyber security expertise is crucial here."

Dad deflates, massaging the bridge of his nose. "Search and recover. Nothing else."

"Nothing else, sir." Ian shakes his head.

"Cover story for the White House? Why are my daughter and her teacher absent?"

Hope floods me like a tsunami. He's asking about cover stories—does that mean—

"I thought we'd call it a field excursion to strengthen her leg. After all, we just took her splint off and are working on *regaining full strength*." He uses air quotes. "Gradual recuperation and increase of her physical therapy goals should work and will also serve us well as a prep."

"Reasonable." Dad straightens his suit jacket. "Assuming I approve this, who's your home base backup? I'll be away for a couple of days, and Alix only goes if this is airtight."

Uhh, backup? As in—

"We'll brief Waterhouse, sir." Ian nods toward the beagle-eyed man behind Dad. "We want to keep this quiet, given the possibility of leaks within our circles."

"Within our circles?" Dad's brows pull down into a V. "Not what I want to hear. But correct. The two men behind me have the highest clearance level in the government besides myself. They're my personal advisors, thoroughly vetted. Waterhouse and Lane already know about PRICS, so you're minimizing spread."

I suppress an eye roll and groan, but only barely. Seriously—Waterhouse? I don't mind Lane, but Waterhouse?

But, being Dad's daughter has taught me one thing: I know when to stop negotiating. Take what you got and leave while you can.

If getting permission means dealing with Waterhouse, I'd probably even kiss—well, or not.

"Reasonable," Ian says.

My dad lays both hands on my shoulders. And there's that weight again, quite literally. "Don't make me regret this, Alix. I'm trusting you on multiple levels here." His pointed look says it all. "Now, brief Waterhouse and Lane while I discuss… parameters of this mission with Ian." He pats my shoulders twice before stepping aside. "Gentlemen, a short break from the situation in Switzerland. Alix would like to inform you of an upcoming PRICS mission."

Oh, I do?

"Go," Ian mouths, making a shooing motion.

Okay. Sure. Let me brief the head of PRICS and several other Secret Service departments, and the National Security Advisor. No big deal. I do that every day.

I throw Ian one last glance as I approach the coffee table. Dad's got his arms crossed, wearing his boss-man expression. Ian keeps a distance—

"This better be good, Agent Forrester," Waterhouse growls.

"I hope so, sir." Look at me, all polite and professional, although there *is* a cup of coffee on the table that I *could* throw into his face. Won't though. So mature.

I settle onto the couch across from them and clear my throat. Here we go, short version—although I don't get far before Waterhouse barks at me. "How is this the first I'm hearing about any of this? The PRICS division's standards are clearly—"

"Easy, Mr. Waterhouse." Brandon Lane raises his palms. "Let's focus on the mission. I'm assuming you need home base backup while your father's away?"

Thank you, Brandon. A true diplomat, which is why I direct my response only at him. "Yes. Dad made it a requirement." I want to make sure they know it wasn't our idea. We can run our own missions, thanks.

Lane chuckles. "Your father is a wise man. Always have backup. Now, given my limited military background, walk me through what we might need to do."

Whether it's his calm tone or his ambassador experience, Lane bridges the gulf between me and Waterhouse perfectly— and I'm thankful for it. We hash out the details until both men seem satisfied with the backup plan.

Waterhouse's pessimism is no fun at all though. "You're on a wild goose chase, agent. Doubt you'll find anything, but by all means, go and waste government resources."

Awesome pep talk, really.

He jabs a finger at my laptop. "Show me that letter." A *please* wouldn't kill him, but I open the laptop and pull up the file anyway. Whatever gets him off my case.

Waterhouse clicks around, lips pressed tight. "You went through analysis?"

"Of course." We're not amateurs.

"May I?" Lane leans in, and from my spot across from them, I catch Waterhouse's quick eye roll.

"Of course," he says, tone suggesting anything but.

Brandon takes the laptop and studies the letter intently, brows furrowed in concentration.

Ian and Dad rejoin us, neither of them looking pleased. Ian's actually looking a bit green.

"I assume everything's set?" Dad checks in first with Waterhouse, then with Lane.

Brandon shakes his head. "I'm trying to look at the—what did you do to it?" He tilts the screen toward Waterhouse.

This time, the eye roll is obvious. "Nothing, Brandon. Stick to diplomacy and leave this to me." He hits some keys and the letter pops up again.

"Ah. Well." Lane grimaces as he looks over the letter. "Nasty business, but solid plan. Smart to look for connections." He returns my laptop with a smile, while Waterhouse just harrumphs. But hey, who cares. We got permission. All that counts.

Dad walks us to the door. "See you in a few days, Alix. Check in with Waterhouse and Lane for any changes or if you need help, and please, *please* stay safe. Can you do that?" He grips my shoulders once more, holding on tight. Ian barely gets another glance, but I guess they've discussed everything earlier.

"I'll be careful. You know me, Dad. I think before I act. Thanks for trusting me," I whisper and move in for a hug. We embrace, and it hits me how weird this is—me leaving for a mission while he heads to the G20 summit. Other father-daughter couples hug goodbye going to work and school, or something like that.

Dad opens the door. "Have fun on your school trip, sweetie. Mr. Miller."

Mrs. Houser lifts her eyes off the computer for a second and smiles at me—but it's the choked sound from the left that stops me cold, making Ian crash into my back.

"Ouch, Alix." He wraps his hand around my upper arms and guides me forward. "What—"

One look into the front office, and he *knows*.

Sam.

The Oval Office door clicks shut behind us, leaving no excuse to not look at him—or for him not to look at us. At Ian. At Ian's hand on my arm.

Sam rises from his desk, face hard as stone. "A school trip?" The question drips with implications.

"Yes." What else can I say? It's my cover, and Mrs. Houser is right there.

Sam's jaw clenches. "I see."

Silence.

"And of course you're going too, *Jason*?"

I jump in before Ian can respond. Maybe I should appreciate Sam's keeping up appearances. But as it is, I'm still mad at him. At me too, for a billion reasons, but also at him. "Of course Jason is coming, Sam. It's a *school* trip, and one I wouldn't want to miss for the world." I lift my chin, spine straight.

Sam radiates anger in waves of silence.

Finally, he breaks it. "So that's it then." He balls his hands into fists, then relaxes them. "You're going on this trip. That's it."

I hear the real message: I leave, we're done.

This is my last chance. My last chance to fix things with Sam.

Screw you, last chance. We've been done for a while.

"Yeah. That's it." I take one final look—one last look at the boy I fell for, the boy I had a crush on since, like, forever.

The boy who doesn't believe in me.

I give him that one last look, and then I walk out of the Oval Office, Ian's footsteps behind me.

Sam and I are over.

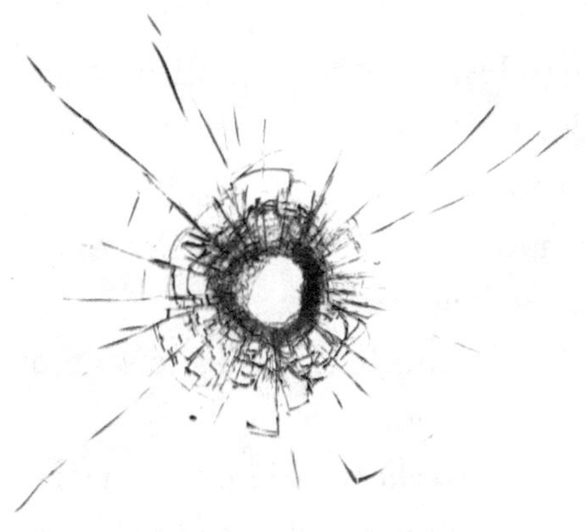

CHAPTER TWELVE
Baby Steps

While Ian heads down to the Lair to pack, I do the same up in the residence.

I'm waiting for that wave of sadness, that gut punch of loss—but nothing.

Somehow I feel… better. Better? Yeah. A tad.

Free.

Broken and hurt, sure. But free.

Guilty, too. But *free*.

Even after I'm packed and in the Lair, sadness is MIA. A certain void and emptiness, yes—but nothing even close to the devastation I felt right after Sam stormed off during the picnic. Maybe I should evaluate my time with him a bit more closely. First breakup and all, but I'm pretty sure it should hurt more. Unless… unless the amount of emotion invested wasn't what I thought. Maybe our break-up had been a long time coming.

Let's face it, I wasn't exactly girlfriend of the year.

But I still *loved* Sam.

I cringe. Past tense.

I suck in and bite my lower lip. Thorough self-eval coming up, but not now. Not the time.

I settle onto the couch, expecting to wait for a while, but Ian arrives a mere minute after me.

"You're early. Excellent." He closes the door to the hallway behind him, waves Dimitri over, and points to three cardboard boxes on the couch table. "Grab the one with your name on it and let's get this party going. Wheels up in a couple of hours." He hands me my box. Heavy.

I set it down onto the couch next to me and peek inside. Black Jeans, black shirts and sweaters, black boots… classic Kira Sanderson gear. I dig deeper and—

Yowza.

Black lace panties and bras.

Holy cows dancing in heaven.

Ian bought me underwear.

Ian. Bought. Me. Underwear.

That thought is equal parts mortifying and… something else entirely.

I check the label. Victoria's Secret—and panties and bras are exactly my size. That makes it even worse. Or better, I don't know. How does he know my size? How did he pick these out? Did he—

"Everything okay back there?" Ian's voice floats over, all innocence.

My face burns crimson.

Never have I been more grateful to have my back to Ian. "Uhh, yeah. Fine. Right size."

"Glad to hear that."

I swear there's a grin in his voice, but when I check from underneath my lashes, he's all focused on his own supplies.

Okay. Moving on. I drop the underwear and keep on rummaging through the box. Better than dwelling on… whatever that was. Nothing happened. Dimitri probably got matching boxers. Part of our cover.

I pull out a box of hair dye. Oh. Another thing I forgot about. "Anybody done this before?" I hold up *#54, Black Soul.* Both guys give me that where-did-you-grow-up-look and nod. Ian points to his considerably darker-than-natural hair, part of his disguise as Jason Miller.

Right, forgot.

Hi, I'm Alix. Apparently the only teen who's never dyed her hair.

Ian rubs his hands. "I'll help you, Trouble. Rather not have you look like a first-timer—which you obviously are." He grabs our hair dyes and heads for the hallway. "Come on."

I follow, stat. Am really hoping mission prep isn't part of my eval. Not my strongest start.

We take a corridor close to the gym to a bright-white door Ian palms open.

"Voila, my humble abode. Excuse the mess—busy day." He flips on the lights.

Ian's apartment.

Why do I feel like I just got knighted?

Crossing that threshold feels… significant. Like a big step. A personal one.

This is Ian's home.

And surprise, it's spotless. We're nine or ten stories underground, so no windows. The space is small: kitchenette in one corner, couch and coffee table in another. Two doors likely lead to bedroom and bathroom. Books fill floor-to-ceiling shelves on almost every wall, making the lone bare wall look strangely naked.

Ian grabs a DUTI-pad from the coffee table. "How rude of me, let's get some light." One swipe and the white wall transforms into a window overlooking the White House Gardens, just like from my room.

My mouth drops. "Whoa." That 3D-projection is incredible! I crane my neck. "Wait, where's the projector?"

Ian beams. "Like it? Old invention of mine. I was going nuts down here without a window, so I went for 3D back projection, no 3D-glasses needed. Had to have at least the illusion of a window. Check this out." He swipes the pad again.

The gardens vanish, replaced by sunrise over a beach. Waves crash, sea birds call— "There's sound?" Coming right from the wall, no visible speakers.

"Yep. A little side project." He wiggles his eyebrows. "But wait—I've got something that you'll like even more."

Okay. Now I'm curious.

He opens the left door and gestures me in.

That, uhh, *that* would be his bedroom.

It's tiny, just enough for a queen-sized bed and a couple of cabinets and shelves. Everything's black: walls, linens, ceiling. The only color comes from a shelf of Star Trek memorabilia. There's the Enterprise—Kirk's Enterprise—and DS9 right next to—

Ian takes me by the shoulders and guides me backwards until my knees hit the mattress. They buckle, and suddenly I'm sitting on Ian's bed.

Repeat: I'm sitting on Ian's bed.

"Uhh…"

He towers above me, face lit with excitement. "Surprise in three, two…" He conducts an invisible orchestra. "One."

Darkness falls completely.

Then something magical happens.

Earth rises above me.

Earth rises with the moon in its far corner. Continents peek through as clouds shift above them, the subtle movement making it hyper realistic.

"Wow," I breathe.

The mattress dips as Ian sits beside me. But despite his leg touching mine, I can't take my eyes off the scene above my head. "It's unbelievable. Like we're actually in space." I stare at the ceiling and the room around me. The illusion is perfect, three-dimensional, almost tangible.

"It's even better when you're not dislocating your neck, Trouble. Lie down." Ian guides me back, and I let him.

The view rivals anything from the ISS or a space shuttle.

"Can you do Saturn and its rings?" I whisper in awe.

Ian chuckles softly. "Only Earth," he whispers as he shifts, his shoulder pressing against mine. We're both flat on our backs, gazing up at our planet.

And… I'm lying on *Ian's bed*.

Next to him.

In the dark.

My mind wanders to places so right and so wrong at the same time—

I suck a harsh breath in, but the assault of his spring soap doesn't exactly help.

Gosh, it's ridiculous. We've been literally on top of each other during Krav Maga ground training, and this shouldn't be any—

Ian sighs deeply. "Trouble?"

My heart hammers a drum rhythm. "Yeah?"

"Thanks for coming on this mission with me. The whole thing… maybe having to leave you and the agency, my parents in danger, someone stealing my code…" He swallows audibly. "It hits too close to home. Literally. Thanks for having my back."

He trails his hand down my arm until he finds my hand and slides his fingers in-between mine.

Holy freakin' cow.

He brushes his thumb over my wrist, and I'm sure there must be something wrong with me. A simple touch like this, one that we've had dozens of times before… it shouldn't make me feel this way, but damned if it didn't.

My stomach flutters and aches, the intensity catching me off guard.

I fight to keep my voice steady. "Of course. Anytime, you know that." I squeeze his hand, and the ache intensifies when he squeezes back.

Movement next to me.

"I know," Ian whispers, so close to my ear his lips gently brush over it.

Heaven help me.

A shiver runs down my spine, clenching my stomach.

"Thank you," he breathes against my ear.

Really, I should respond, I really should, but the power for speech has left me.

He shifts—and presses his lips against my temple.

Time slows down.

And freezes.

Nothing exists besides Ian's lips on my skin.

Nothing.

It can't last longer than a second or two, yet it feels eternal when he pulls away.

Ian just kissed me.

Ian. Just. Kissed. Me.

And I want more.

A hunger, a need, a yearning so intense it shakes me to the core—how can all of that be there, when I just broke up with Sam? When I thought I made the right choice on that fateful Fourth of July?

I shouldn't feel any of this, but… I do. Ian pulls me in like a magnet, always has, and I don't want to resist that pull anymore. I can't fear these feelings anymore, consequences be damned.

I want to turn and kiss him properly. Want to feel his lips on mine, not only my temple. Run my fingers through his hair. Feel the muscles under his shirt.

And I want his hands on me.

A craving settles next to the fluttering and ache and pushes me over the edge.

I'm going to make my move, like I should've done all those months ago, no matter the stupid old men trying to control us.

I gather all my courage and—

Ian releases my hand and sits up. "Break's over. Time to dye your hair, Trouble."

He claps twice. The lights flare as Earth vanishes.

I throw my arm across my face, only partially against the brightness.

Mostly to hide my humiliation.

Because I was about to kiss him—while he clearly wasn't thinking the same thing. What guy passes up the perfect set up with a girl on his *bed* in the *dark*, if he's even slightly interested?

The sting of rejection pierces my heart. No, even worse, it's not a rejection. It's just… nothing.

I'm the seventeen-year-old president's daughter. The forbidden one.

Legal issues. Fraternization.

Seventeen versus twenty-one.

No more questions, your honor.

Four months ago, during those fateful five seconds, maybe—*maybe*—something could've developed between us. Now?

Apparently not anymore.

Ian tugs my pants leg. "Up, up, Trouble. I need you focused."

Focused. Not crushing on your teacher.

Message received.

Not even forty-five minutes later, we're airport-bound in our agency-issued car. Dimitri drives, Ian rides shotgun, and me, I'm… trying my best to wrangle my hormones into submission.

Seriously, Forrester. Get a grip.

Of all the bizarre PRICS situations, tonight wins. Me, kneeling at Ian's bathtub while he stood over me, dyeing my hair.

Shirtless, his own hair soaking in dye.

Yeah.

I sink deeper into my seat, grateful for the darkness only broken by streetlights.

We drive in silence, but Dimitri keeps checking on me in the rear mirror every couple of minutes. Maybe it's my new look—black hair, a nose stud, cartilage rings, all black clothing. It'll take some getting used to.

Still. "What?" I snap, probably too sharp, but come on, at this point I'm half convinced my shirt is inside out.

Dimitri's gaze snaps back to the road. "Nothing."

He doesn't look again until we reach the airport.

Boy, am I glad it's early. Or late, depending on the point of view—because Dimitri… Dimitri looks scary. In the Lair, he was already in the car when I got changed, so I only saw Ian in his new outfit, and Ian's change wasn't too far off the beaten path: Hair a bit spiked up, a couple of piercings, black clothing.

But Dimitri? He's scary enough in a suit and shades, but in black leather pants and combat boots… he's terrifying. The shaved head—barely different from his buzzcut—somehow makes it more intense. Add piercings, and nobody's sitting near him.

Despite our looks, we have absolutely no problems boarding, and after that, it's smooth sailing. We land about fifteen minutes ahead of schedule.

Once we pick up our rental SUV, things become interesting again.

The guys treat it like an enemy operative, scanning bumper to bumper for bugs and installing a Radial Sound Wave Blocker-clone.

And once that's done and we're on our way again, Ian gets quiet.

Dead quiet.

The closer we get to Little Springs, Washington, the more jittery he becomes, and when we pass the sign that says "Little Springs, Washington. Population 22,000", he melts into his seat.

"Five years," he whispers so softly it wasn't meant for anybody but himself.

I reach forward and squeeze his shoulder. "It's okay to freak out. I would."

He turns, eyes huge and dark. Miserable. Am I glad we didn't send him here alone. The mission he can handle—Little Springs he can't.

Eventually Dimitri pulls up to our hotel. We slip into character, less polite, more world-weary. Fits our current moods well. We get our keycards and make it up to our room.

True to his Secret Service training, Ian chose a corner room with fire stairs in front of the window, secure but escapable. It looks nice, with its dark red carpet and light-yellow walls. The window is big, the walls rather nicely decorated with modern pictures, and the two Queen-sized beds to the right of the entrance promise a comfy night.

Two beds.

Oops.

I count again. Still only two beds. The guys don't seem to notice or care. They're all business, silent until the RSW-Blocker is activated. Even then, it's nothing more than short commands from Ian to Dimitri. They're dividing up the room between them as they sweep and scan every square inch even more thoroughly than the car.

Ten minutes later, both are satisfied. Ian falls backward on the bed closer to the window.

"Dibs," he says, breathing out heavily like he's run a marathon.

Dimitri drops his suitcase on the other bed.

Right. Dibs are implied.

That leaves me kind of bed-less.

Ian reads my mind. He pats the mattress without looking. "Trouble."

I sit down next to him. Second time today we're sharing a bed. Yay me.

"Don't worry," he says, eyes closed. "We'll condemn Dimitri to the couch or I'll share a bed with him. Meh, couch it is for him. We shared a bed once, and he kicks in his sleep. Too dangerous for me." He uses my arm to pull himself up. "And you get the bathroom first."

I snort. "I'll take it." And I'll add it to the list of things I didn't think of when volunteering for this mission. Sharing a room. Bed. Bathroom.

We take turns and freshen. It's weird sharing a room with two guys, but at the same time less awkward than I would've guessed.

That being said, in retrospect, I understand Dad's insistence about Dimitri staying close at all times.

Once we're all done, Ian pulls up a map of Little Springs. We left our DUTI-pads at home, bringing just one laptop. Feels low-tech, considering our usual standards. Ian scowls at it as if it somehow offended him. "This is our location." He points. "Police station, my parents' house, the farmers' market where the picture was taken." Point, point, point.

"Our main priority is finding out what happened to Torpedo, and who got their hands on it. If we get leads on the blackmail, fine, but that's personal and therefore secondary. Torpedo has absolute priority. It's a matter of National Cyber Security—me being blackmailed not. I know you all want to help me with that one, and I appreciate it, but the rules must be clear. Main mission first."

He waits for our nods. It's about the fiftieth time he emphasizes it, so message received.

I'm still hoping we can check on his parents.

Ian points to one of the red dots. "We start at the Police Station, as discussed. That's going to be you, Alix. You got your cover down?" He shoots me a questioningly look.

Easy stuff. I flash a fake grin and wave. "Hi there, I'm Kira.

I'm writing a piece for the college newspaper, you know, drinking and driving and teenage deaths. Could I interview a police officer about it?"

Seemed the simplest approach. Ian can't go himself, and Dimitri... looking at Dimitri screams intimidation. Especially in his current outfit, the police would be more likely to arrest him than help him.

I on the other hand am right in the sweet spot. Young, female, and not too punk-y despite my black outfit. Since Ian's car crash was big news and no teenager has died on the streets around Little Springs, Washington, since then, we're hoping to get the information we need.

Ian gives me the thumbs up. "Good. Remember, improvisation is key. We don't know whom you'll meet or what they will ask you in return. React like I told you. Stay as close to the truth as you can, and let them fill the holes in your story themselves. In case it's something specific, I'll guide you through it. Speaking of."

He reaches into his bag for a tiny box containing a couple of skin-colored Band-Aids and what looks like tiny clear jelly beans.

"Your ears and mic. It's a three-way communication system. Alix, we'll be hearing everything you say and vice versa. Try to not get distracted by our voices, but pay attention to our instructions."

Okay. That part doesn't worry me. Multitasking I can do, improvising... well, I'm getting better, so maybe there's hope for this mission after all.

I trace a line between our hotel and then the police station on the map. "I can walk from here. Dimitri is trailing me?" Of course he is. No way he's going to let the president's daughter walk an unsecured street by herself.

Dimitri responds with his trademark nod. Not a man of many words.

I turn back to Ian. "And you're on getaway car duty, right?" I really hope we won't need one, but it never hurts to have an escape route set up.

"Yup. I'll be stationed here." He points to a spot central to all our marked locations. "I'm your backup. If anything goes wrong, you abort, you get out, I get you. That counts for both of you. Clear?" His is the most serious I've ever seen it.

"Crystal." We're not taking any chances with this one. I swallow dry.

"Okay then." Ian holds out a fist for Dimitri and me. "To a successful mission."

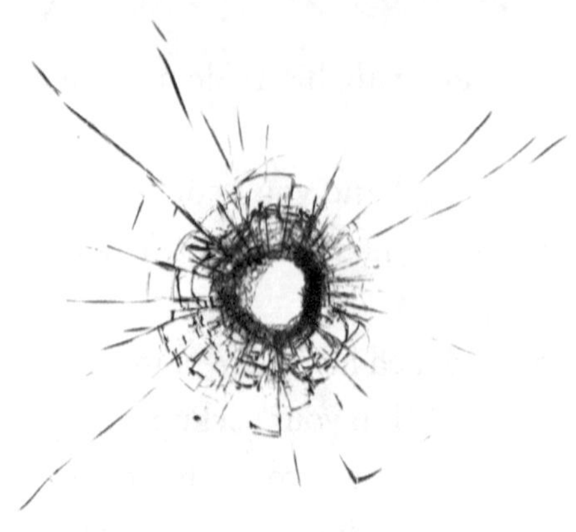

CHAPTER THIRTEEN
Police

I step out of the hotel, and into my identity as Kira Sanderson. Easy-peasy. I stuff my hands into my pockets, pop in some gum, and walk with more of a purpose—which, coming to think about it, isn't even an act. This is *my* mission, and I'm more than motivated and determined enough to make it successful. Ian is counting on me and my skills. So yeah, walking with a purpose comes easy.

Little Springs, Washington is picture-perfect. Everything's within walking distance and the streets are well-kept. The buildings sport cheerful colors, and thanks to some kind of local ordinance, there's not a neon sign in sight.

It makes a world of a difference. Even the Starbucks' logo looks classier in carved wood than in glowing LED and plastic.

Every few blocks, I pause to study a storefront, giving Dimitri time to maintain his position. I can't see him—and I know better than to look around and check for him—but of course he's close by. I can feel him stare holes into my back. That man's been on edge since the mission started. Maybe it's taking his protégée out in the open.

I stop at a toy store, clearly family-owned rather than part of a chain "Mayson's Toys," I murmur.

Ian's voice crackles in my ear. "Mayson's! I *loved* that place as a kid. Is the Bubble Bear still above the door?" I glance up, and sure enough, there's a three-foot plastic teddy bear mounted on the ledge, holding a bubble wand. Though it's not moving now, the scratches around its right arm suggest it can move the wand between the bubble bottle and its mouth.

"Cute," I comment, as if to myself. The streets are quiet on this late Thursday morning, and I can't exactly hold a conversation with thin air—without a visible Bluetooth headset or phone, anyway.

Not even three minutes later, the police station comes into view.

Showtime.

The moment I step into the lobby, I realize I've never been inside a police station before. Probably a good thing.

It's sparse—just a few chairs arranged in pairs facing a large counter and desk. Since nobody else is here I ignore the *WAIT— Respect Privacy* sign and approach the officer behind the counter.

"Hello." I add a little wave, and then inwardly cringe. Kira wouldn't wave.

The officer looks up with mild annoyance. "How can I help you?" Not unfriendly, just unenthusiastic.

No reason to get disheartened.

"My name is Kira, and I'm with the Bears News. I'm writing about teenage driving, trying to promote responsibility, you know? No drunk driving, wearing seatbelts, all that. I was wondering if I could maybe talk to you or one of your colleagues about it? Get the authority perspective, you know?"

I flash my most earnest smile.

The officer stays quiet, eyebrows furrowed.

Ian nervously smacks his lips, and it sounds weird in my ear.

I'm about to launch into another explanation, when the officer's expression softens. "Great project, love it. Got just the right person for you." He picks up the phone, mutters a couple of words into the receiver, then turns back to me. "One moment, okay?"

I keep my enthusiastic smile up. "Thank you so much, sir. Really appreciate it."

Phew. I'm getting a real person to talk to, not just a couple of brochures. That was a distinct possibility.

"Good job," Ian whispers in my ear. As much as I appreciate it, the real work is about to begin. My body knows it, too. I've been antsy for the last five minutes or so.

Another door behind the front desk opens, and a younger police officer in the standard black uniform enters.

"There you are," my older officer says. "This young lady is writing about teens and car accidents. Thought that topic was close to your heart. Go ahead and take her back and help her out, will ya?"

The younger officer gives his superior a crisp nod. "Of course, sir. Ma'am, if you'd please follow me?"

Ian takes a sharp breath in. *Ouch.* Loud.

I nod at the older officer. "Thank you again, sir." Never hurts to leave a good impression.

The younger officer holds the door and leads me through the station to what looks like a conference room—white board, oval table, several chairs.

"Have a seat, Ma'am." He gestures to a chair. Another sharp breath from Ian. "So, you're writing for your paper? About teens and car accidents?"

I nod. "Yes. It's worse in other counties, but it's crucial to raise awareness. Most of my friends think alcohol is the number one killer, but it's actually unsafe speed, ignoring right of way, or improper turns. Especially here in this county with all those woods around us, speed can be lethal." I mentally congratulate myself for delivering my cover story.

The officer's face darkens and he drops his gaze down to the table. "You're right about that. Especially around here. Trees are not very forgiving when you crash into them."

I nod. "Exactly. I was hoping we could discuss calls this station's had involving teen accidents. I want to get the word out, and I want to make it clear cut and impactful, maybe even with photos." Because that would surely include Ian's wreck. "People need to see the ugly truth, or the message won't sink in."

The officer taps a slow rhythm on the table. "You're right. Sometimes, shock value works best. When I was younger, that's what got through to me. I lost my best friend to a car accident."

I nearly jump when Ian curses in my ear. "Fuck!"

What the—

The officer meets my gaze. He can't be that much older than me, probably fresh from the academy, early twenties, at most.

Okay. *Focus.* I clear my throat. "I'm sorry to hear that. What was it? Speed?"

"Yep. Burned out completely." His tapping quickens as his gaze drifts around in the room.

"Alix," Ian's voice trembles, "what's the officer's name?"

Really? How am I supposed work *that* into the conversation

naturally? Can't read his name tag with the ceiling light reflecting on it, and even if it didn't, I can't just blurt out the name without looking like an imbecile.

I suppress an annoyed grunt at Ian, and modify my approach. Thinking on your feet? Check.

I lean forward, covering my mouth in shock. "Oh, no. That's horrible, officer…?!"

"Walters," he supplies with a light smile.

Two things happen simultaneously.

"Paul," Ian whispers in horror, as Officer Walters extends his hand. "But call me Paul, I'm not that much older than you."

Paul Walters.

Whose *best friend* burned in a car wreck, when *Ian* quote-unquote burned in a car wreck—Ian, who had *one friend* in high school, as he told me.

The connection isn't hard to make.

Fate delivered me the one person with the best possible insider knowledge—and the one person who'll make this hell for Ian.

I cover my short pause by shaking his hand. "Kira. Nice to meet you."

Paul gets up. "You, too. Coffee?" He walks over to a little cabinet with a coffee thermos and cups.

"Yes, please." Not as good as Chai, but I need something to hold onto. "What happened to your friend? If you don't mind sharing?" *So we can get to the drives.*

He pours two cups and sits across from me. Ian and Dimitri stay silent on the other end, their breathing a steady rhythm in my ear.

Paul sips his coffee and sets the cup back down. A drop spills over, leaving a smudge as he pushes the cup aside. "We were both sixteen at the time, and I think he—his name was Ian—had his license for maybe six months when he crashed."

I gasp—and so does Ian.

Hearing Ian's name in past tense makes my stomach turn.

Paul's expression turns bitter. "Yeah, right? Way too young. He was a responsible driver, I'd say. Young, but responsible. No drinking, no drugs, no nothing. It was in the middle of winter when he crashed into a tree. The car went up in flames. Took us over four hours to put it out. I've never seen a car fire that intense since." He slides his cup back and forth, leaving more smudges on the table.

Ian and I reach the same question simultaneously. "Why—" whispers Ian, as I ask Walters. "Wait, you were there?"

"Yep. Junior member at our Volunteer Fire Department. Ian's death was maybe my third or fourth call during my training."

Oh, hell. Poor Paul. Knowing the person dying and burning in there is your friend… gruesome.

By now I don't have to act anymore, I genuinely feel sorry for him. "That must have been horrible. Did you know right away it was him?" I keep my voice soft, and I'm though I hate pushing further, I need to work this angle.

Paul pinches his lips together. "Yeah. It was his car, and there were hard drives scattered around it. Ian never went anywhere without at least one computer. Biggest geek I know." A dry laugh escapes him. "The world would've been better a better place with him. He was brilliant. Full of ideas."

He sighs. "Eventually we got the fire out, and the coroner pulled out something I wouldn't have recognized as a human if it hadn't been for the remains of his favorite leather jacket." He pauses. "That's when I lost it."

Yeah, no kidding.

I catch up on Ian's faint whisper. "I'm so sorry, Paul... I didn't know..." The raw pain in his voice makes my eyes well up. Why did he have to make the mics so darn sensitive?

I take a desperate gulp of my coffee. The sadness pouring from Ian and Paul's unresolved grief makes me want to curl up somewhere and cry. I thought I understood Ian's nightmares and guilt, but being caught between his voice in my ear and Paul's pain in front of me shows both sides of the tragedy, and neither is bearable.

Deep breath. Mission. Information. "What happened to—"

"I had nightmares for months. Still get them. Tell that to your readers. When I joined the police, it was partly because of him. I needed answers—everything was left hanging. To me, none of it added up. A clean guy, careful driver, a fire much worse than normal, and a body more unrecognizable than any burn victim I've seen since."

Oops.

Apparently, the Secret Service's coverup wasn't so perfect after all. How can I spin this? "So, if they never really figured out what happened, what about the car and all the stuff you said was scattered around—discs or something? Wouldn't that be evidence?"

"Correct. What's left of the car is in an evidence impound somewhere, and everything else was in our local evidence locker... until recently."

Hold up. Until recently? "What do you mean?"

Paul grimaces, fidgeting with his cup. "Part of it got released about four months ago. There wasn't much left anyway, most computers, drives and discs all melted. Disintegrated. Only two of the hard drives survived, scratched and damaged, but at least not melted. The ones that got thrown clear during impact, you know? I took them to the Donckers—his parents. As… I don't know, something to remember Ian by. He lived for that stuff, and his parents had nothing left of it… seemed right."

All three of us come to the same conclusion at the same time.

One: Some hard drives survived.

Two: Ian's parents have or had them.

Three: There's the connection we were looking for.

"Shit," says Dimitri.

"Oh, no," breathes Ian.

Crap, I think, but say instead: "That's really thoughtful of you. I'm sure they appreciated it." I stop myself from adding the usual platitudes about losing a child—Ian's still listening, his breathing too fast. No need to twist the knife.

Paul gets up, grabs a paper towel and wipes away the coffee smears. "You'd think so. The Donckers had a pretty bad break-in a couple of weeks after I dropped them off. Not much taken— besides the hard drives and some cash. Funny thing is, I was so glad I had given them away when I did, because we had our own break-in at the evidence locker. Somebody set fire to it. I would have been furious had the drives survived Ian's wreck only to get destroyed right before I wanted to give them to his parents."

"Wait, the evidence locker was broken—"

A screech pierces my ear—*screams, a loud bang, another scream, this time muffled*—

Ian.

With a short gasp, my hand flies up to my ear. What—

More chaos, multiple voices, Ian's ragged breathing and muffled screaming, more shouting and—

Dimitri, at the top of his voice. "Whizkid—report! Report! REPORT!"

One more strangled scream—

145

Silence.

No response.

Then, one blood-curdling howl—and nothing.

My throat constricts.

What—

Paul tilts his head. "Everything okay? You don't look good."

I wheeze on my next breath.

Dimitri, again, words clipped between breaths. *Running.* "Trouble, abort! I repeat: abort! Retreat! *Trouble, abort and retreat!*"

The room starts spinning.

Something went wrong.

Abort and retreat.

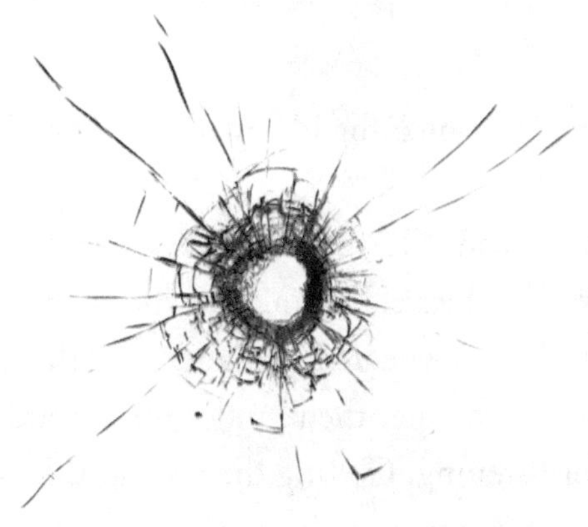

CHAPTER FOURTEEN

Unexpected

"Kira?" Paul gets up and walks around the table. "You really don't look well. Do you need anything?" He squats down, hand on my shoulder. "Want to lie down?"

Want to—

My heart threatens to break out of my chest. My ears ring with a deafening volume.

Want to—

No.

I shake my head to clear it.

Abort and retreat.

I stand up so fast the chair crashes backward. "I… Asthma. Stress induced. Inhaler in the car. Excuse me." I try to squeeze past Paul.

He shoots his hand out and holds me by the arm. "Not so fast, I don't want you to collapse. I can get it. Where are you parked?"

Crap. He's too nice for his own good, or for mine, in this case.

I shake my head. "Thanks, I'm okay, just hate when I feel it coming." I add a wheeze. "Thank you for your help, but need to cut it short today." I wheeze again and open the door.

Paul holds it for me, then guides me toward the exit. "No, thank you for listening. Getting the human side of accidents out there matters. If you want to finish the interview on another day, feel free, okay?" He hands me a business card.

I stare at it. Such a mundane gesture when everything's falling apart.

Abort and retreat.

I take it and shove it in my back pocket.

"Thank you." Wheeze, wheeze.

Paul raises his hands. "Of course. A pleasure meeting you, Kira." He gives me a genuine warm smile that I return.

"You too, Paul."

My knees wobble as I leave the building, but at least the fresh air helps to clear my head.

Slowly now. Can't run yet, can't run yet…

Around the corner.

That's I bolt. Am I glad the brace is gone, or I'd never manage this speed.

Thank you, near-photographic memory, thank you for the map of downtown Little Springs burned into my mind. I sprint around two corners, until I reach a park.

Perfect.

I duck behind a tree, strip off my jacket and turn it inside out. Instead of black leather, it's now an off-white parachute material.

I pull a grey beanie out of its pocket, put it on, and stuff all my hair under it.

Quick scan… Good. No witnesses to my transformation.

Heart still racing I emerge from the trees and head toward the downtown shopping district.

Busy streets equal good cover, but they work both ways. I'll have to stay alert for anyone on my heels. Staying calm is hard. *Hard.* Every instinct screams to run straight to the extraction point, but if I did, I'd make myself an easy and obvious target.

I wish Dimitri would say something, but he's maintaining radio silence, and so am I.

Ian.

What happened? Is he okay? What were those sounds?

Occasionally, I pick up Dimitri breathing or background noise, but nothing from Ian, and it freaks me out.

Five blocks, two lefts and three rights later, I enter the designated bookstore. I browse casually while making my way to the back, then slip out into a courtyard. I take a seat by a little fountain, pretending to play with the water while keeping a watchful eye on the door. After three minutes, I'm sure. No tail.

Still no word from Ian or Dimitri.

Not panicking has never been harder.

I dry my hands on my pants, cross the courtyard, and cut through another store to reach the street.

After two more turns, I'm nearly at the extraction point. No car. No Ian. My heart plummets. Where is he?

A hand covers my mouth as I'm being yanked backwards against a hard chest. "Shh."

Dimitri.

Hell, he nearly gave me a heart attack.

He releases my mouth once he's sure I recognized him.

I blow out a heavy puff off air. "Dim—"

He shakes his head and lays his finger across his lips. Quiet.

I snap my mouth shut, another wave of adrenaline hitting my blood stream.

With a pointed glance at me he reaches for his ear and pulls out the little speaker. He drops it onto the ground and grinds his heel into it until nothing but tech dust is left of it.

Oh.

Not good. So not good.

With shaking fingers I do as he did. It feels strange to be cut off from Ian, but if he could use the com, he already would've. Dimitri is right. Whatever happened, the little device could compromise us further.

Dimitri takes me by the shoulder and guides me forward.

Neither of us speaks as we stick to back alleys and shadows. Twice we turn to face a wall, pretending to look at something on Dimitri's phone.

I'm running on autopilot.

Eventually, we reach our hotel's street. I want to sigh a breath of relief, but Dimitri steers me past the hotel and into a coffee shop within view of it. He picks a table near but not directly in front of the window and pushes me into a seat.

"Sit. Stay." He presses on my shoulders, emphasizing *stay*.

Completely unnecessary. My knees shake—no, my whole body trembles like I was freezing.

Cold. It's so cold here.

A minute later, he returns with a hot chocolate for me and something else for him. No food, but my churning stomach couldn't handle it anyway.

Dimitri unzips his jacket half-way and retrieves the RSWB-pen. He activates it and scans our surroundings. Despite the precautions, he doesn't say a single word until he hides his lips behind his cup.

"Job well done," he says calmly, as if there was nothing else we needed to discuss more urgently than my performance at the police station.

I grab my mug with shaking hands, nearly spilling. "What happened? Where is Ian?" My voice quivers.

Dimitri's expression hardens. He pinches his lip together and grabs the cup so tight, his knuckles turn white. A wonder that thing isn't getting pulverized by the pressure.

None of this behavior is reassuring in any way.

Despair floods me. "What is it, Dimitri?"

"He's gone. I made it in time to see the car speed off—two people in the back, one driver, looked like Ian unconscious in the passenger's seat." He nods his chin over to the hotel. "I'm assuming we're compromised, but I don't know how badly. We both got out clean. Now we need to determine if we can return to home base or not." He jerks his head at the hotel.

That's why we're here. Watching for tails.

My stomach roils from the one sip of hot chocolate. "Who took him? What do we do?" Fear courses through my veins, coiling in my gut.

Dimitri loosens his death grip on that poor cup. "I don't have answers yet, but we *will* figure it out. They won't hurt him, they want something from him. Our job is to find out what that is and who they are. Then nothing will stop us from getting him back. Am I right?"

He covers my trembling hand on my mug with his.

Protected.

Big brother's got my back.

"Yes," I say, steel entering my voice, "and they won't know

what hit them."

We stay and observe the hotel.

After an hour, Dimitri refreshes our drinks. We stay quiet, for several reasons. One, the pen only lasts a couple of minutes anyway, two, we have work to do, and three, most of all I don't know what to say. I'm too worried about Ian.

I can process all of this logically, but I can't allow myself to truly *think* about him. Still my mind wanders, imagining where he might be, hoping he isn't injured, hoping he knows we're safe. I do my best to keep my face even and calm, but a couple of tears escape anyway.

And Dimitri notices.

After a second hour, he gets up and returns with a double chocolate muffin. "Eat. A wise man once said cake helps."

I manage a weak laugh. Ian's words from graduation day. Another tear falls, but then I take a bite of the muffin, and it grounds me enough to regain some control.

Dimitri monitors our room's video feed, hallway cameras, and hotel lobby through his phone. Our security precautions worked out well for us. We have eyes everywhere.

I can't stand watching Dimitri work, while I'm sitting here, doing nothing besides thinking. I need to get my hands on our computer, and start tracking Ian. *I need to find him.*

Finally, when we're sure nobody followed us and our hotel isn't compromised, we carefully make our way back to our room.

Exhausted, I collapse onto the bed Ian had called dibs for only a mere three hours ago.

Three hours—and everything has changed.

I bury my nose into the covers, desperate for a little bit of his spring soap scent, but nothing's left.

Surprisingly the tears don't come this time.

The pain runs too deep for that.

Instead, I squeeze my eyes shut, dig my fingers into the sheets and focus on simple things, like breathing.

Ian.

My heart breaks at the thought of him hurt somewhere.

Dimitri sits beside me and lays a hand on my shoulder.

And it helps.

I gradually relax my fingers and release my death grip on the blankets. Breathing gets easier. Not by much, but enough that I can sit up again. "Thanks," I mumble.

He hands me a Kleenex. Huh. Much more perceptive than I gave him credit for.

After a gentle pat on my back he rises. Message received: Time is of the essence, and thanks to our precautions, we've wasted enough.

Agreed. So, I wipe my eyes, blow my nose, and power up our mobile command unit, i.e., Ian's laptop, and sign in. My first move is checking the tracking program. I pull up the frequency that tracks Ian and—nothing.

My stomach drops.

I close the program and restart it.

Still nothing.

I reboot the computer, then re-open the program.

Nothing.

I check Dimitri's and my frequency: We're two clearly visible dots on a map of Little Springs, Washington.

My throat constricts.

Not good.

If we can't track Ian, how are we supposed to find him? "Dimitri, Ian's tracker… it's gone." My voice is raw. Weak.

Dimitri looks up from his video surveillance feed. His brows draw together and lines form on his forehead. "Gone? It's implanted—"

"I know." My arm throbs at the memory of the injection. "But not anymore."

Our exchanged glance speaks volumes. They removed Ian's tracker. They *knew* he had a tracker.

I swallow the sharp spike of panic and force myself to focus. *Think*, for crying out loud!

Maybe I can track the car then.

I crack my knuckles and type away. In less than three minutes, I'm hacked into the city's traffic surveillance program, piggybacking off their feed.

Police station. There's me.

Other intersections. No.

City Hall. No.

School. No.

Another intersec—

There.

My heart makes a silly little jump when I spot Ian's intersection. "Got you," I whisper at it. I access its file and rewind to the time of Ian's abduction and—

Static.

"What the…?"

I forward again to normal video feed.

I rewind to the time of the abduction and get static.

I rewind further: Normal video feed.

"Bastards," I mutter. They killed the video feed during the grab. No way this was a spontaneous kidnapping. This was definitely planned. *Well* planned.

But how good can they be? One camera out doesn't mean they're invisible.

Like a maniac, I click through traffic cam after traffic cam. There must be a nice red-light camera catching me a mug shot of the driver. There must be *something* that tells me where the car went.

No such luck.

Our car is nowhere to be found.

I check all of them around the time of the abduction, and nothing. A short burst of static here and there for a couple of seconds, but no car.

I slam my fist into the mattress so hard Dimitri looks up from his work in surprise. "They played us," I whisper. "They knew, and they played us. I can't find the car—"

Click.

Of course.

Absence of evidence is not the evidence of absence.

I may not be able to get a visual, but I can get a route. I grab a pen and paper, mapping out the static bursts chronologically. First hit: Ian's abduction site. Last hit: their exit route. North

Yes. Much better. Game on.

I crack my knuckles once more and look for the next public cameras on the freeway. It takes me several hours to hack into all those systems and find what I'm looking for. It's like searching for breadcrumbs in a very dark forest. Poor Hansel and Gretel would've never found anybody anywhere under those conditions. Initially, I'm not sure I'm going to find anything, but I'm betting the kidnappers think they're clever enough to keep using the same technique.

They're surgical about it—hacking just enough to cover their tracks without triggering larger alarm systems. They're good.

But so am I.

Finally, after what feels like forever, I have a location. The static trail ends here, suggesting they've stopped. I access a US Government satellite and zoom in to the location. We're *this* close to finding Ian.

"Dimitri." I wave him over from his research. "This is it. I need your military eyes on this."

The satellite image sharpens into focus: rural terrain, their car abandoned in an empty dirt field. Are they still in it? After so many hours?

Dimitri leans closer, expression darkening. "Zoom into here a bit more." He points to some marks in the ground.

His jaw tightens. "They switched to a helicopter." He balls his hand into a fist.

No. They couldn't have outmaneuvered us.

But they did.

I close my eyes as my stomach twists into knots.

We've lost Ian.

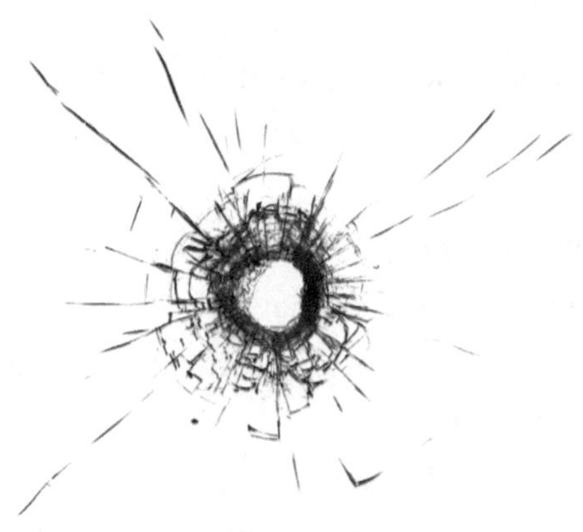

CHAPTER FIFTEEN

Nice to Meet You Two

My heart skips a painful beat.

We lost Ian.

"No," I whisper hoarsely. "That can't be." I shake my head against the sharp spike of fear lodged in my throat.

It can't be.

There must be *something*.

We can't have been outsmarted so completely.

Damn it, with my IQ, I should be able to figure this out! Ian would know exactly what to do—but Ian isn't here, and that's the problem.

I collapse back onto the bed and curl into a ball. I'm exhausted, drained, a physical and mental wreck, but there's no way I could sleep, despite the sun having gone down hours ago.

My body and mind are wrung out, but I can't rest. Won't rest. I owe it to Ian to give it everything I have. And although I never met them, I owe his parents to keep them safe too. Who knows what—

Now, wait a second.

I snap my eyes open.

His parents. Of course. That's it!

I bolt upright, hope surging through my veins. "Dimitri. Let me run something by you."

Dimitri turns on his bed to face me. "Shoot."

I smooth my shirt, organizing my thoughts. "Remember when we thought the blackmail was meant to separate Ian from me, and I might be the target? We were on to something, just not what we thought. They wanted to get Ian away from PRICS, but it was the wrong conclusion. Nobody was after *me*, they were after Ian. Right from the start."

Dimitri cocks an eyebrow. I have his attention.

"Here's what I'm thinking. Someone knows about Ian's high school Torpedo program and its location in the police locker. That's our leak—somebody high-ranked with serious security clearance, access to top secret files—or else they wouldn't know about Ian, his tracker, or Torpedo. They try to grab Torpedo from the locker, but it's gone because Paul gave it to Ian's parents already. So they break into the Donckers' house, steal the drives plus some cash to mask their true purpose for the break-in. They work with Torpedo, hit a wall, and realize they need its creator. They need Ian. Through the leak they get more info about him and plan to draw him out with the blackmail when they threaten his parents. See where this is going?"

Dimitri nods slowly, gaze glued to mine.

"We played right into their hands. Coming to Little Springs was *exactly* what they wanted, though our reasons were different. We were tracking Torpedo, which we only found thanks to

Sneaker—a code so classified, even our leak didn't know about it. They couldn't know we discovered Torpedo's theft, but they had us mapped out well enough to grab Ian. Our leak fed them our every move. That's our biggest enemy right now."

I look at Dimitri. It makes sense. It does.

He cocks his head. "What makes you think the people who tried to blackmail Ian into coming out here are the ones who stole Torpedo? Could still be separate events."

I point at him. "Fair question, but think about it. These kidnappers hacked city surveillance with serious skill. What are the odds of *two* tech-savvy groups targeting us at the same time? It fits too well to be a coincidence."

There are tons of holes in my theory, but it's the first one we got. And yup, just like that, I connected the Dark Unit with Ian's Blackmail. And Ian's abduction.

Which leads to one conclusion.

"Dimitri, the helicopter could've taken them anywhere. We need names and faces if we want to find Ian. And I know how we can get them."

I brace myself. He's not going to like this.

"Ian, he installed a security system at his parents' house with facial recognition and print readers. We need that break-in data."

I take a deep breath.

"I have to visit Ian's parents."

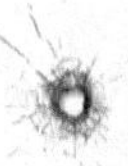

"Keep on walking, Trouble. Almost there." It sounds odd hearing Dimitri's calm baritone calling me Trouble when it's not at the White House. That's Ian's nickname for me.

As it is I'm sure Dimitri would agree the name is appropriate.

He's not a happy camper today.

Not at all.

Let's just say he wasn't exactly thrilled with my plan.

We pulled out one man short of the mission already, no need to repeat that.

It's too dangerous. His parents could still be under surveillance.

But eventually, logic won out.

Still, he's keeping me on a tight leash, not letting me out of his sight, not that I expected that.

I reach the Donckers' house shortly after nine thirty in the morning, grateful for my thick coat and gloves on this freezing day.

Their home is charming—two stories instead of the nieghborhood's usual one, rich wood tones, abundant greenery. It radiates warmth. I can picture Ian growing up here, playing in the yard. On his laptop, naturally. A small smile tugs at my lips, but before the emotions can turn on me and tear me up, I hurry up the stairs of the porch and ring the bell.

The lead ball in my stomach gets a bit heavier.

I can do this. I have to.

After about twenty seconds, the lock clicks. Ian's mom opens the door, and the resemblance to her son is striking.

"Yes?" Her smile is warm, open, and so much like Ian's, it hurts.

I extend my hand. "Mrs. Donckers? Hi, my name is Kira Sanderson, a college student working on an article for our paper, and… you know…" I stare at the ground and bite my lip. How do you tell somebody you want to talk to them about their dead son?

She saves me from fumbling further. Her face lights up. "Ah, you must be the one writing about teenage car accidents, aren't you? Paul mentioned you stopped by the station yesterday but had to leave early. He thought you might come by." She winks. "Come on in, let's talk."

I'm stunned.

She doesn't even know me. I'm here to bug her about her son's death, and she's the friendliest person I can imagine. Now I see where Ian got his generous spirit.

I follow her inside. "Thank you very much, Mrs. Donckers, I really appreciate it. Hopefully it'll make a difference for the students." I take off my gloves and stuff them in my jacket's pockets before sliding out of the jacket too and handing it to her when she reaches for it.

"Call me Teresa, Sweetie, and it's our pleasure. If we can spare other parents what we went through…" She takes my coat, a shadow dropping over her face. There's the pain I was sure I was going to see eventually.

She leads the way toward the living room. The inside of their house is equally cute as the outside, nicely decorated, comfy. Traces of Ian are everywhere—framed certificated from science fairs and spelling bees, glimpses of family photos. It's as if he's still alive, except nothing dates past sixteen.

We enter the living room, where somebody is sitting on the couch, hidden behind a newspaper.

"Honey, this is Kira from the school paper Paul mentioned. Kira, my husband Hank."

At the sounds of his wife's voice, Ian's dad lowers the newspaper—and my heart stops. The blackmail photo didn't do him justice. He looks *exactly* like Ian.

Those same bright green eyes, that same warmth creeping in when he looks at me. The only difference is a dimness Ian's never had. Still, the resemblance is so striking, a pang of longing slices through me. An emotional punch to the stomach.

"Trouble?" Dimitri's voice in my ear startles me back to reality. Right. Respond.

I clear my throat. "Wonderful to meet you, Hank. I was just telling Teresa I hope I'm not imposing. This story could really help people."

Hank nods. He points to one of the chairs around the coffee table. "I think it's a great idea. Told Teresa so yesterday after Paul called."

Somehow, after just minutes with the Donckers, I feel like I've known them forever. Maybe it's because I know their son. His mannerisms, his expressions… they're all here.

I take a big breath. "I… I want to say how sorry I am for your loss. I know it's been several years, but still… I'm really, really sorry." I pour all my genuine empathy into the words, thinking of Ian's nightmares, his guilt. In a way, I also apologize for him.

"Thank you, sweetie," Teresa says. "Five and a half years next month. It gets easier, but not a day goes by without thinking of him. Without one of us crying."

Oh my goodness.

She looks as lost as Ian did seeing that blackmail picture. I want nothing more than to hug her, to tell her everything's fine. But of course I can't.

I need to steer the conversation toward the drives, carefully. "Paul told me what happened. Would you mind sharing your perspective?" Better to start gently and see where it leads us.

Ian's parents exchange a quick glance, before Hank begins with a sigh.

"It was a normal night. Ian was heading to this computer club—he was brilliant with technology, got that from Teresa." He winks at his wife and she returns it. Cute.

"You know how you replay those last conversations? What

did you say, what did he say? Did he know how much we love him? I think from that point of view we were lucky, if that word even applies. We were both home that night. I used to work at the local police station, Paul might have told you, but I was off that day. Before Ian left, we all had dinner together, and in retrospect, it was almost as if he knew something was going to happen." He pauses shortly, pushing the newspaper onto the table, then leans back into the cushion again.

Wait, first the Secret Service screws up evidence destruction by not burning everything, and now Ian drops hints?

Hank continues. "We had such a great dinner. We talked much longer than we usually do, about old family vacations, his first visit to the dentist—let me tell you, that one did not go well—how school was going. It was like reviewing his whole life. We laughed, we had a great time, and it was the perfect final conversation. We're both very thankful for it each and every day. That's what people should know and understand. You never know when it is going to be the last time you talk to your loved one. Imagine if we'd had a fight." He shudders.

My heart warms. Ian planned it perfectly. He couldn't be there to comfort them, but he knew they would find comfort in knowing how much he loved them, and how loved he had felt. A good-bye note without writing one. Well done.

Teresa takes over, her voice controlled and quiet. "Hank is right. We needed something to remember Ian by, and that helped a lot. You know, we kept everything in his room the way it was, but he took all of his computer equipment the night he died, so it looked much emptier than it normally would have."

"You kept his room the way it was?" It's been over five years. I'd have expected an office conversion, but I underestimated their attachment to everything Ian.

Teresa nods, cheeks reddening. "We've been recently thinking about letting go, but we're having a hard time with it. Everything has a memory attached to it, and if he knew we gave away his spaceship collection…" She looks to the ceiling as if to apologize for having these thoughts.

I can't help laughing. "He already had a spaceship collection back then?" So typical Ian. Teresa looks at me quizzically and I realize my mistake. "At sixteen?" I quickly add.

They both smile knowingly.

Dimitri's warning grunt in my earpiece reminds me I almost screwed up. Well, yeah, thank you, I got it.

"Come on," Hank says, "we'll show you."

Upstairs, Hank leads us to a corner room. Stepping inside is like stepping into who Ian was, although it's clear he was always like Ian. Had somebody shown me ten teenage boy rooms, I would've known in an instant this was his.

At least twenty starship models hover from nearly invisible strings, creating an illusion of flight. The walls not covered with overflowing bookshelves display posters that make my heart do a little happy flip: Einstein with one of his most famous quotes: "I have no special talent. I am only passionately curious." A "Wanted—dead *and* alive" poster looking for Schrödinger's cat. Also, a bunch of Star Trek, Star Wars, and Dr. Who artwork.

Besides that, there's only a small bed in one corner, and a massive, oddly bare desk in front of the window.

Yup. This is undeniably Ian's space.

Seeing his childhood room feels more intimate than the little kiss he gave me. This was his true heart, his sanctuary.

The kiss, we both know, wasn't real.

I clear my throat and step forward to look around. "He had *that* model of the USS Defiant? These are incredibly rare." I tap one of the spaceships.

Teresa and Hank exchange glances before she retrieves a pair of scissors from Ian's desk. "If you'd like it, it's yours, Kira. Anyone who recognizes it will treasure it properly."

I don't know what to say. "Oh no, I couldn't possibly—it's seriously a cool little ship—but I can't accept it."

"Yes, you can." Hank insists, taking the scissors and snipping the string. "We're learning to let go. Better you have it than risk losing it to another burglar like we did a few weeks back." His face turns red and his jaw hardens.

There's my opening. "Burglar? You're kidding me. What did they steal?"

Teresa takes the spaceship model out of her husband's hands and dusts it off with a Kleenex as Hank points to the windows. "Came in here, ransacked Ian's room for two hard drives, then grabbed some cash from our bedroom. That's all." His voice drops to a low whisper. "But those two drives were all we had left. We hadn't even looked at them yet."

Because they barely got them from Paul.

Teresa sighs and looks at the starship again. A small chuckle comes from her throat. "You know, we were both so mad and disappointed, we decided it's unhealthy to cling. So here you go, have fun with it." She hands me the Defiant. "Though Ian almost had the burglar though, from beyond the grave." She looks at Hank, pride shining from her eyes.

My skin tingles. I have a feeling I know where the conversation is going.

Hank's tension eases as he chuckles, pointing to the window. "All windows in this house, all exterior doorknobs, and the doorbell are supersensitive fingerprint scanners. It doesn't matter which entry point you choose, Ian's system captures the prints and runs it against the police's database. Unfortunately for us, this idiot hasn't been fingerprinted by the police yet, but if he ever does, we will ID him."

So Ian wasn't exaggerating. "Seriously?" I have no problem sounding amazed and astonished at all. "How… I mean, it must all be connected somehow, automated, networked… how did he do it?"

Please show me the computer, please show me the computer, please show me the computer.

Hank winks conspiratorially. I like him. He's so very much like Ian. "You're quite the tech person yourself, aren't you? I'll show you. But don't tell any burglars, or I'll come and get you—you rang the doorbell after all. We have your prints."

For a heart-stopping moment, the panic is there—the panic that I just got fingerprinted, because my fingerprints are *so* in the police database. If the system accesses an up-to-date database, then the Donckers will discover they just hosted the First Daughter.

Oh, wait: Gloves. Phew. Close call. Damn Ian's paranoia.

Hank lifts Ian's mattress, revealing an array of drives and lights.

"Wow." I take a step closer.

This is it, don't screw it up, Forrester.

I pretend to fidget with my ring, but in truth give Sneaker a half turn to activate it. Kneeling, I place my hand on one of the drives, as if to examine it. "He built that himself? He really was a smart guy. I've never seen anything like it." I keep my hand steady, waiting. Any moment now…

"Right you are," Hank answers. "He probably would've made good money selling it, but all specs and plans are lost now. We just maintain it with updates."

"Updates?"

"Yeah. Ian set up some kind of subscription before he died. We don't really understand it, but we get occasional emails with files to install, and it works perfectly."

I fight back a smile. Ian. Of course he signed them up—with himself. I have absolutely no doubt he's sending them the updates to keep the system going.

Sneaker vibrates.

Got it!

Let's hope present-day Ian's programming can crack past-Ian's security and paranoia.

I stand and look at both Ian's parents. "Your son must've been a really cool guy."

It's both my signal to Dimitri and the absolute truth.

Pride illuminates their faces. "Thank you, sweetie. I hope we could help you a little bit with the human aspect of teenage driving accidents."

I return their smile. "More than you know."

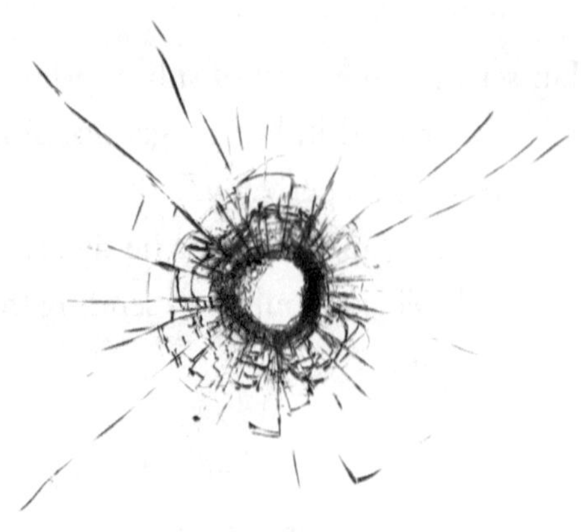

CHAPTER SIXTEEN
Katharina

On my way back to the meeting point, I'm psyched.

Psyched that I got to meet Ian's parents; psyched it actually worked and Sneaker did its job and hopefully grabbed up all the clues my heart desires. I'm flying high on the success of this latest mission—until I get to the intersection where Ian was kidnapped.

I crash onto the hard ground of reality.

What if I overplayed my game, and this doesn't work? Then we're SOL. Completely.

My gaze drifts down the street to where Ian's car was parked.

How fast must they have been, in broad daylight and in the middle of the street? Somebody could easily have seen—

Wait.

An electronics store sits one building over from Ian's last known location—and an electronics store means camera surveillance.

Adrenaline rushes through my body. They might've caught a full-frontal of the kidnappers. Even if Sneaker can't crack past-Ian's security, they could have what we need.

My decision is made in a heartbeat. It's worth checking out.

"Mulberry Road," I murmur, pretending to read the street sign. Dimitri knows better.

And he doesn't like it. "Trouble, stay on the road. No diversions. Stay on the road." His command voice is impressive, but I ignore it. This lead is too good to pass up.

The store is barely half a block away—and there they are: two security cameras aimed right at the street. Oh, happy day. Now I just need access.

"Solomon's," I announce for Dimitri's benefit.

"Negative, Trouble. Return to base. Repeat, negative. Do not divert."

I open the door to the store. Honestly, he needs to relax. It's a store, my goodness.

"I said *do not divert!*"

I wince at his volume. That man can yell. But I still ignore him—have to, with the clerk approaching.

"Hello, how are you?" He's maybe forty, greying, and somebody should tell him he shouldn't be wearing those brown corduroy pants to work anymore.

I smile at him. "Hi, fine. Yourself?"

He nods. "Fine. What can I help you with today?"

Dimitri's breathing quickens in my ear. Running. I don't have much time. His yelling makes it difficult to focus though. "Abort! Return to base, Katha—Trouble! Return to base!"

I gesture outside. "I was hoping you could help me with something. My car was stolen from across there yesterday" —I point—"and the police can't find anything. I was wondering if I could please check your security footage? It was my first car, from my dad." I deploy my full helpless-girl arsenal: wide eyes, worried brow, trembling lip.

The clerk looks sympathetic to my loss. "Oh no, this is usually such a safe area. I'll have to warn customers. Sorry about your car, but the street feed isn't saved, it gets overwritten every twelve hours. Everything from yesterday during the day was overwritten last night. Nothing's left." He gives me an apologetic one-shoulder shrug.

Crap.

Disappointment washes over me. Too good to be true.

I'm about to thank him when the door bursts open, nearly ripping off its bells.

Dimitri.

Store clerk jumps, and so do I.

Dimitri storms in as if he owned this place, ignoring the clerk completely until he stands in front of me. Correction, until he *towers* over me. He's making good use of his height and stature. Even behind the sunglasses I feel the fury radiating from him. *"Kommst du mit oder muss ich dich tragen?"*

Are you coming or do I need to carry you?

Crap.

If he's switched to foreign languages, he's mad. More than mad.

"I'm coming," I mumble, not even attempting German. No reason to go all protective on me, it's not like I was doing anything risky.

Dimitri grabs my hand and pulls me out of the store.

And down the street.

And around a corner.

I'm practically jogging to keep up, and keep up I must—I doubt he'd stop if I fell.

"Dimi—Elroy! Stop! Ouch! Elroy, stop, you're hurting me!" I try prying his fingers loose with my free hand, but it's futile—it's Dimitri, after all.

And Dimitri doesn't stop.

He yanks me from public view into back alleys, never loosening the death grip on my hand, never slowing down. Sensation in my fingers is gone, and if he continues at this rate, I'm not sure if I'll still have a hand when we're at the hotel.

Another attempt to free myself. "Elroy, you're hurting me, stop! Ouch!" Useless. Dimitri is locked in.

Thirty meters farther ahead, he pauses to check the alley and clear the turn.

I try again, but it's like playing tug-of-war with a boulder, I'm getting nowhere.

Anger surges. Time to snap him out of it, so I do the only thing I can: I kick him full force into his shin. "Let go, you asshole, you're hurting me!" I hope it hurt, and I hope it leaves a bruise. Payback for the bruises I'll have on my wrist—

Dimitri freezes.

"What did you say?" His voice is deadly quiet, he doesn't even turn.

Crap.

"Uhh, let go, *please?*" Maybe insulting him wasn't my smartest idea.

He drops my hand, and finally—finally—blood flow returns. I massage my crushed digits. Dang, the tips are blue already. Pretty optimistic nothing's broken, but—

Dimitri raises his hands in front of his face, staring at them like they're alien things.

That's concerning enough, but add the fact that both of his hands are shaking while he mouths something in Russian… yeah, my annoyance is gone and worry steps in. Great.

"Dimitri?" I take a careful step closer and lay a hand onto one of his quivering ones. "Hey. What's going on?"

One-Mississippi, two-Mississippi, three-Mississippi, four—

He turns his head slowly. Oh boy. His face is drained of all color, like he might collapse.

And *boom*, my priorities have shifted.

Dimitri is not okay.

I don't care that we're in the middle of a small alleyway and trying to get to home base as quickly as possible. I'm pretty sure we weren't being followed. I need to make sure Dimitri is all right.

"Hey." I gently tug at his arm. "Come here." I pull him closer, until I have him in a hug.

That's a first, me hugging Dimitri. Probably even Dimitri hugging anybody. After all, this is Dimitri. He doesn't really invite hugging.

Still, I wrap my arms around his chest, since I can't reach around his neck. I squeeze a bit and press my face into his chest.

"I'm sorry. I didn't mean it. You were hurting me and didn't stop and I got angry. I'm sorry, Dimitri."

Like in slow motion, he inches both arms around me and hugs me back, gentler than I thought possible, given the fact that Ian's warning *easy on her, Dimitri* never helped during Krav class.

"Katharina," he whispers ever so faintly.

Katharina—like he tried to call me earlier.

Awkwardly I pat his back—well, his kidneys, probably. "Want to talk about it?" I break away from the hug. Behind us is the windowless wall of a house, so I gently push him there, and to my surprise, he comes with me. He still doesn't look any better. I turn him around so his back is to the wall, reach up to his shoulders, and press down on them.

"Sit. Stay." And that's what Dimitri does.

I check our surroundings. Wall at our backs, wall to a backyard opposite from us. Can't talk too loud, somebody could be in there. Otherwise, it's an unremarkable alleyway without hiding places for unwelcome visitors. We're good.

I sit on the ground next to a very quiet and pale Dimitri.

One of us needs to get this started, so I playfully bump my shoulder into him. "You want to tell me why you've been so tense lately? I mean, besides the mission and Ian getting kidnapped?" Another bump. "I need you at a hundred percent, Dimitri. I can't deal with you not talking to me, I mean, less than normal." He's not known for his monologues.

Dimitri turns his head toward me at sloth-speed and takes off his sunglasses, his light blue eyes full of grief and pain.

I link my arm through his. "I'm listening."

Dimitri takes a deep breath. "I had a sister. She was about your age when she died."

Oh, crap. No further explanation needed. The past always resurfaces at the worst moments.

"Katharina?"

He nods with visible effort. "She was a year younger than me. She… looked a lot like you do now in your disguise, but with a bigger nose." He taps the tip of my nose, and I appreciate his attempt at lightening the mood. That explains why he stared at me so often.

"What happened?"

He takes my hand, the one he almost squished off, and turns it in his. "She was killed because she had the wrong boyfriend."

What?

I can't have heard that right.

Dimitri stares straight ahead, lost in the memory, voice barely a whisper. "Her boyfriend was African-American, a nice guy, Shavone. I liked him. Didn't even need to threaten to treat her right. One night, Mom asked me to take them out since they were underage and I had just turned eighteen."

I try picturing teenage-Dimitri and fail. He must've been born serious and adult.

His voice is full of sorrow. "We went to the pier, had food, and a good time. It got late, people went home, and eventually so did we. But we didn't make it far. Eight neo-Nazis blocked our way. They surrounded us, started shoving Shavone around. I knew they were a problem. Drunk. They were eight, we were three. They attacked him, and I barely got him out of there. I was decent at fighting then, but the odds were bad. I yelled at Katharina to follow me when I carried Shavone, and..." He clenches his free hand. "...and I expected her to follow. I *needed* her to follow. Only once I had Shavone safe in the ice cream shop, I realized she hadn't come with us."

He squeezes his eyes shut. "Typical for her. Not listening. Thinking she could handle it. I sprinted back. Only thirty seconds, if at all, and I was maybe gone for a minute before I came back, but they already had her on the floor, trying to strip her. She was screaming, fighting, cursing them. Such a fighter, never giving up. I charged in, knocked one guy out, threw another one off the pier, but they kept coming. More than eight now—fifteen plus. All having 'fun' with us. They—"

He pauses for a second. "Five or six held me down. I was fighting with everything I got, but I couldn't break free. Katharina... was on the floor, and they weren't trying to undress her anymore. Just kicking her, stomping on her chest, her stomach, her head, calling her a… well, using a hateful racial slur. Over ten people. She never stood a chance."

Silence falls between us.

I can picture it vividly, and I wish I couldn't. The story of Katharina's death explains why Dimitri is Dimitri. Strong, unemotional, insisting on safety and protocols. Because all of that went wrong on the day Katharina died.

I rest my head on his shoulder. "Dimitri… I'm so sorry, I didn't know."

"Nobody does, besides Ian. It's been such a long time, and I have dealt with it. But seeing you look so much like her… and then you diverted from protocol and I lost eyes on you…" He blows out a big puff of air through pursed lips. "It took me back to the night she died."

"Did the police ever get them?"

"All of them. Nobody helped me or her during the fight, but people at least called 911 and recorded the whole thing. None of the attackers made it off the pier, they arrested every single one of them."

He locks his ice-blue eyes with mine. "Alix, it's why I became a bodyguard. I couldn't protect her, and I didn't want to let anybody else get hurt like this." He covers my hand on his arm with his. "I couldn't save my sister, but I need to protect you. We've already lost Ian, please don't make me have to search for you too."

His eyes shine with worry. Regret. Loneliness. Determination. Maybe even a certain warmth that's always been there, hidden behind his sunglasses.

I hug his arm tighter, settling against his shoulder. "Don't worry. History won't repeat. And if anything happened, I know you'd always get me out of whatever situation it is, Dimitri. Thank you for that."

He and Ian are my safest harbors. Ian with his brilliant mind and wits, and Dimitri with his strength and skills. With them, or at least one of them around, I'm never truly afraid.

Dimitri rests his head against mine, and we sit in silence until we both feel strong enough to stand.

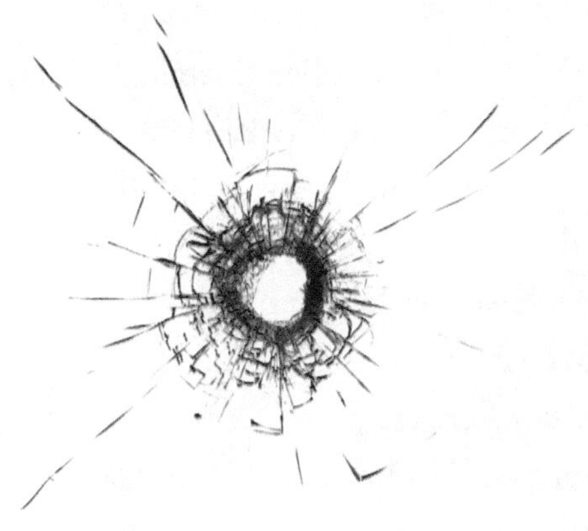

CHAPTER SEVENTEEN
Puzzle

Dimitri returns to his normal stoic self quickly, and I've never been so relieved to see him grumpy again.

Finding such deep cracks in his armor they still can burst open scares me. Yes, everybody has a breaking point—and I just found Dimitri's. The helplessness of not being able to rescue his sister paired with a heavy dose of survivor's guilt… no wonder he keeps all of that hidden behind dark sunglasses.

Back at the hotel, I throw myself into work. Every hour matters. The longer Ian is a hostage… yeah. The chances of survival sink with every hour.

I don't want to think about that.

Sneaker. Priorities.

I infiltrate the Donckers' system, and thanks to Sneaker I don't fall into any of high school-Ian's traps. And hel-lo data. There it is. Every touch of a doorknob, window, or the bell, all neatly recorded, and, if identified, matched with that person's ID.

I scroll through. Teresa, Hank, a couple of regulars…

Where is the date of the break-in? If there's nothing here, we're screwed.

Then we'll have lost Ian for good.

I scroll faster.

He's fine, he's fine, he's fine.

We have to get Ian back. *I* have to get him back. Failure is not an option.

As if that thought was all I needed: "Yes!" I pump a fist.

The right timestamp. With prints. *And* a mug shot. Jackpot!

Dimitri looks up from the list he's putting together. "What?"

I beam. "I've got him! Give me one second…" A quick copy and paste later the FBI database rattles away, doing its thing.

Dear system, please find something. Please make it easy for us, for once.

Ping!

"Yes!" My next victory punch to the air nearly clocks Dimitri.

As fast as I can I scan over the information, adrenaline surging. "Nice! Possible facial match, no definite one on his prints though."

Dimitri scoots closer to look at the screen as I double click the attached file. "Sergey Mostoroff, thirty-four, no felonies, no jail time, known hacker, but never caught. Says here he works with—" *Gah.* I hate it when I'm right. "The Dark Unit."

Great.

Now it's official: The Dark Unit has Ian.

As expected.

What were the odds of two hacker groups targeting us simultaneously? Still, seeing my theory proven doesn't feel as good as it should.

Because now it's real, and that complicates things.

Dimitri punches the mattress. "I'd hoped for amateurs, a small splinter group, unorganized, easy to take down. With the Dark Unit we need to proceed with extreme caution. The one advantage we have, is that I'm sure Ian is still alive. They need him."

I choke back my shock. While his assessment of Ian's survival is reassuring, I'd taken it for granted. Dimitri hadn't. My blood pressure plummets as implications hit.

We have a serious problem.

"Dimitri… Remember the Dark Unit's recent government site attacks? They weren't showing off, they were practicing. Those hacks were trial runs with minor government sites, to see if and how they could get in. They improved with and learned from every hack, and finally got Torpedo to work for them, somewhat at least. MU was supposed to be their masterpiece, and Torpedo was supposed to get them in, but they didn't expect Sneaker. Sneaker kicked them out, and now they needed the only person able to outsmart Sneaker again—Ian."

It makes sense. Ian couldn't make sense out of the frequent seemingly random and minor hack attacks. They were training strikes for the MU hack. The question is, what do they want from MU?

Dimitri taps Sergey Mostoroff's photo. "Dig deeper. Use the government facial recognition if needed and track his movement." He gets up from my bed and returns to the desk, continuing his work.

I sigh, crack my knuckles, and delve into Mostoroff's life. First hit: a helicopter pilot's license. Perfect. Another puzzle piece confirming his involvement. Now off the facial rec—No, wait. A helicopter needs to refuel, right? He can't land at any gas station, there are only so many options for a helicopter to get gas. Okay then. I hack into the closest three airports' security logs.

Apparently, this heli runs on air alone. Nothing in the first three airports.

I'm onto something though, I feel it in my bones. All airports in the State of Washington? Nope, neither. Either their flight was a skip and a hop, or so long they didn't even refuel in Washington. Oregon? Nothing. Idaho? Nothing. Montana, in case they flew across the little pointy part of Idaho and straight into Montana? Still nothing.

Gah. Next idea. What if they tried to be tricky? They could've stolen kerosene from firefighter stations with stationed helicopters. I check—and nothing. That must mean they stayed close, but it doesn't make sense. Why fly if you could drive?

I squeeze my eyes shut. Where could they've gone? Can't go west, and I checked the neighboring— Ugh, wait, no: I know what they did! They stayed in the US, I'm pretty sure of it—only not where and how I expected. I call up a different site.

"Sorry, Canadians," I mumble as I hack into their airport security. Something about international hacking feels worse than domestic even with PRICS authorization.

Adrenaline gives my heartbeat wings as I scan over their data. Show me, show me, come on… Yes! A helicopter refuel matching the timeframe of Ian's kidnapping. My fingers shake, missing the keys several times as I pull up the visual.

I barely catch the laptop from falling when I jump off the bed. "I found them! British Columbia, baby!"

Dimitri appears instantly, studying my screenshot. "A Bell 430. Range about 350 nautical miles max, depending on—"

I'm already typing, using his information. *Longer range. Airport security feeds. Snapshots. FBI database. Correlate.*

With a starting point and range the next fuel stop is much

easier to extrapolate. But then… nothing. Sweat drips down my neck. If they didn't refuel again, their final destination must be within half their tank's range, assuming they want to be able to fly back without running out of fuel. That narrows it to the western Canadian provinces, or, if they're staying in the States, as I suspected before…

Alaska.

I switch to the satellite feeds.

Search, scan, search, scan, search—gosh, this thing is slow and sluggish today—*search, scan*—hah! There they are! There, in the middle of a green, lush landscape of trees, grass, rocks and lots of other plants I don't have a clue about, sits a black-and-red Bell 430 Helicopter next to a small cabin in the center of a clearing.

That's where Ian is.

I yank my shaking fingers off the keyboard as if burned. "There! The middle of nowhere in Alaska!" My heart cramps. That's where Ian is.

Dimitri reaches for the laptop and turns it for a better view.

Relief floods through me as my lungs remember how to work. We found Ian. From here on, it should be easy-peasy, it's not like they're holding him in Fort Knox. It's only a matter of time until we have him back. His kidnappers won't stand a chance when—

"Zoom out, please." Dimitri narrows his eyes.

"Say when."

"When." He tilts the screen and points at it. "There. Ohlsson Air Force Base, about a hundred kilometers out. Then there, a small facility about forty miles out. See? On top of the mountain. Probably part of Ohlsson Base and their SERE program— survival, evasion, resistance and escape training," he adds, catching my confused expression. "Usually deserted, unless there's an active drill. Fact is, the Dark Unit is alone out there…

but I don't like it." Dimitri stabs his finger at the screen.

"Why?" I like everything about this hut. That there's nobody around who could be their friend instead of ours. That it's small. That it's easy to take down. Easy to keep under surveillance. Easy to get Ian out.

"Do me a favor. Zoom in and do a thermal scan of the cabin."

A thermal scan in the freezing—ah, okay. It'll give us an overview how many warm bodies we have.

"Sure." I enter a couple of command codes and the satellite obeys.

Only I wish it hadn't.

Because there's not a single heat signature inside the small, easy-to-take-down cabin.

Nope.

Not a single one.

That's because they're all in the maze.

All seven kidnappers and one Ian.

They're all in an *underground* maze, spread out over an area ten times as big as the cabin and at least fifteen meters underground.

Rescuing Ian just became a tad more complicated.

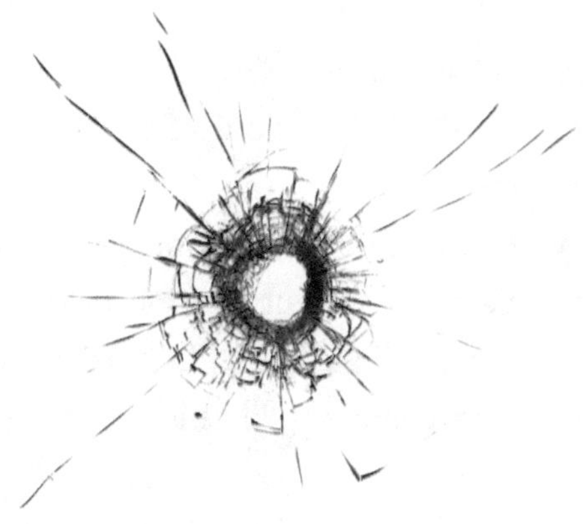

CHAPTER EIGHTEEN
Backup

My lungs forget how to breathe again. "How are we going to get him out of there?" A freakin' underground maze? Really? Who does stuff like that? Hiding in the middle of nowhere in Alaska should be safe enough, darn it, no need to go underground!

Dimitri stays quiet while staring at the screen, as if he could read the answers off it.

I blow a puff of air passed pursed lips. Yes, it's a set-back, but we can handle it. Must handle it. Must focus. Must figure this one out. "Okay. Okay. Problem-solving. We can do this. Totally. It's a group of hackers, how badass can they be, right? Right?" I mean, desk jockeys. Not Rambos. I hope. "So we could maybe, I don't know, somehow draw them out of their maze, set up a trap, and while you take care of them, I go in—"

"Absolutely not."

I whip around. "Huh?"

"Not going to happen, Alix."

I narrow my eyes. "What now? The trap? We have to get them out somehow, and—"

"I meant you joining the extraction." His light blue gaze falls onto mine with a serious intensity: he means it.

But so do I. "Oh, hell to the no, Dimitri! Of course I'm part of this! We started it together we'll finish it together! Ian needs—"

"Alix."

Nu-uh. "Ian needs both of us to get out of there alive, and he needs us as soon as possible, or—"

"Alix."

"Or he could lose his worth to them and then—"

"Alix!" Dimitri lays both hands on my shoulders and gives me a slight shake. "Please don't take this the wrong way, but you're going to stay behind on this one. Non-negotiable."

Stay behind? "I can't stay behind, Dimitri. I have to be there."

"No, you don't."

Funny how my genius IQ stumbles over three little words. Four, if you count the contraction. "But I do."

Dimitri sighs and sits on the bed next to me. "I can't take you into a hostage retrieval."

"Because I'm the president's daughter?" I want to scream, I want to rage, but all that comes out is a pitiful, faint whisper.

"That, and because you're seventeen."

"Oh, come on, I'm trained—"

"No, stop it. I know you're trained, but not for this. They may be hackers, but they're grown men, presumably. Your Krav Maga is solid, but we haven't covered multiple attacker scenarios yet, I wouldn't take you. I can't free Ian and watch out for you at the same time."

Ouch. Dimitri's last sentence is a stab to my bleeding heart. My next breath comes out shaky. "I can't abandon him, Dimitri." I can't. It's *Ian* we're talking about, I can't step back and sit this one out! If anything went wrong, I'd blame myself—*oh*. Heat invades my cheeks. Okay, I get it. If anything went wrong, Dimitri would blame himself too. Yes. *Yes*, I do see where he's coming from. Doesn't mean I have to like it. "I want to help, Dimitri."

"And you will. I need your input planning this, but then… Then you'll sit this one out."

Sitting it out—wait. "Dimitri, I can't sit it out. I—"

"You will."

"No, really." I twist my body toward him. "I can't sit it out, at least not the way you want me to. What are you going to do? Send me home? Alone? You're not going to do that. Drop me off? You're losing precious time. Leave me here—or anywhere, really—alone? Again, you're not going to leave the president's daughter unsupervised. So really, your only option is to take me." My heart beats a frantic *thump-thump* against my ribcage. He must see reason. I can be backup, I can—

A heartbeat passes as our gazes lock. "You might have a point."

My jaw drops. "I do?"

The smallest smile tugs on the corners of his lips. "You do. We have a problem. Two, actually. One is timing, you're right. With every hour lost, the likelihood of Ian's survival drops. Two is manpower. Under normal circumstances, I wouldn't think about going in alone, but these aren't normal circumstances." He taps his finger against the laptop's screen.

"No," I whisper, "they're not."

"I can't call for backup without possibly alerting the mole, and if that happened, we're not only risking Ian, but also risking you."

"And you." I rock into him.

"True, but not my main priority. Anyway. Agreed. This is a very vexing conundrum. I can't call for backup, which means I have to go in alone, and that means, I also can't leave you anywhere, so you'll have to come with me. But"—he points at me—"don't think you're going to come with me into the maze. I'll figure something out."

My hands clench around the laptop. Okay. At least he won't leave me behind. At least I'm going to be *there*, with Ian, when Dimitri frees him.

He clears his throat. "And I also have to notify your father."

What? Excuse me, *what*? I groan. "Seriously? That's not necessary, he—"

"He gave us clear parameters, which obviously have changed. I have to notify your father."

The bed turns into quicksand under me. He can't notify Dad. Can't, can't, can't, because… "If you brief Dad about this, you know what he's going to say, right?" *Bring my daughter home. Call backup. Don't risk my daughter for* him.

Dimitri nods once. "There is a distinct possibility he's going to order us home."

Distinct possibility—it's inevitable! And it'll cost Ian his life.

Nausea churns inside my gut. I grip Dimitri's forearm. "We can't tell him then. We can't."

"Alix—"

"No, listen. One, he's in Germany for the summit. I won't be able to reach him. That means I'll have to call Waterhouse or Lane, and no offense to either, I'm not talking about a highly-classified rescue mission with anybody, especially not over a possibly compromised satellite phone."

Dimitri presses his lips into a thin line. I got him there. Holding up two fingers, I continue. "Two, simple risk assessment, we're more likely to come home with a dead body if we don't act quickly. We call, we have to bring me home, we won't get Ian out alive. We don't call, but go in ourselves, he survives." Most likely, at least.

"But you—"

I throw up my arms. "I'll be sitting in a tree or wherever you put me, safe and out of view, Dimitri! Whatever you want, as long as we don't waste time we don't have! I'll be safe, I won't go off on my own or—"

He cuts an eye at me. "Vice-president. *Hint-hint.*"

Ugh. "Yes. Point taken, but also lesson learned. All I ask is that we give Ian a chance. Because if we call Dad, that chance will be gone." I balance the computer on my lap and fold both hands together. "Please, Dimitri. We can't lose Ian!"

Dimitri's gaze drills into mine, and for a moment all hope dwindles away. This is Dimitri. He goes by the book. He may have written it, actually.

But, to my complete and utter surprise, he nods. "Ask forgiveness later instead of permission first?"

Hope surges back. "Yes. Yes, definitely! I'll take the blame or whatever Dad wants to dish out when he hears about it." Phew. Big breath. Another one. "And now that that's clarified, let's talk about the obvious and no offense to you either, but they outnumber us—outnumber you—and they have all the advantages in their hands. How are we—?"

Dimitri switches to tactical mode and takes the laptop off my lap. "I don't believe in no-win scenarios."

"But—"

"No *but*. This isn't over till it's over, and it hasn't even begun." He pauses, staring at the thermal scan. "Three rooms, all connected to a central hallway. Only one way into the underground maze." He points to the single-room cabin. "I assume it's secured and under surveillance, via camera or manpower. Once I'm in, I should be able to use their inexperience to my advantage."

I take a deep breath. "But still—"

"No *buts*. I told you. Here. Eight people. Seven kidnappers and one motionless person. This is Ian."

My heart goes out to the motionless figure. It hurts for him. Aches. Worries. What have they done to him? Sedated? Hurt? How badly?

"This is curious though." He taps an especially bright room.

Well, with that one I can help. I think. "See? That's why you need me. That's a heater, that's why the signature is so bright. It's Alaska. They need some kind of heat source." I tap a finger against my lower lip. "But why do their signatures drop off and vanish when they enter the small room across from it?" As if on command, one of the kidnappers enters said room and— *zzzing*—vanishes off screen.

Dimitri shrugs. "Must be shielded. Thicker isolation. Don't know. Doesn't matter."

"Agreed. What matters is, how would you get Ian out?" Alone. Without support or proper back-up besides me. And let's be honest, at this point, I'm not quite sure whether I count or not.

A spark of mischief lights up in Dimitri's eyes.

"We smoke them out."

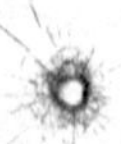

The next three hours come and go in the blink of an eye.

Dimitri is the man. He organizes surplus gear for our trek through Alaska—or better, for *his* trek, through part of it.

He organizes a helicopter to fly us there, and why, yes—of course he has a helicopter license. It's Dimitri. Duh.

He calls his contacts and orders three cigars, whatever that is, I'm pretty sure he's not talking about tobacco.

Long story short, he's on a roll, a one-man pseudo-007, the Daniel Craig version, rugged and tough. Me, I'm the… uhh, sidekick. Not the Bond girl. The brainy professor, who panics when things get tough. That would be me.

"That should do it," Dimitri says, lifting the backpack up with one hand, checking its weight. "You're packed?"

Well, since I'm not the one taking assault supplies and weapons, mine was a tad easier to assemble. I tap the satchel next to me. "Computer, collapsible satellite dish and tech basics for Alaska connectivity. That's kind of it."

He nods. "Very well. Wheels up will be in one hour. I suggest you rest until then. I'll go and freshen up." Dimitri grabs a towel and shower gel and vanishes into the bathroom.

Problem is, the moment our flurry of activities to rescue Ian ceases, the fear is back. The worry. The doubt, if I made the right call not screaming at the top of my lungs for reinforcements.

The plan seems solid: fly us in, literally under the radar, in case the Dark Unit has an uplink to a surveillance satellite, land outside visual range, Dimitri hikes in, while I monitor from the helicopter. Quote-unquote simple extraction.

That's what he *says* is the plan. What he *expects* is something completely else. I saw what he packed, and I wouldn't exactly call it confidence-inspiring: a heavy-duty medical kit. A sleep sack. Ratchet straps.

He expects serious injuries—beyond Band-Aids. The sleep sack and ratchet straps... they're for the double-worst-case scenario. Ian can't walk, Dimitri can't carry him. Then Dimitri would stuff him into the camouflage sleeping bag, hoist him into a tree, and strap him in place to a thick branch to keep him out of view until we can retrieve him.

So yeah, Dimitri is assuming Ian is going to look bad, and probably expecting not to be in much better shape himself when he's done. I'm not kidding, it physically hurts to think about that.

About ten minutes into my horror-visions grim scenarios Dimitri emerges from the bathroom... and my mouth drops open.

Not because he's only clad in a towel wrapped around his hips.

Not because he's shirtless.

Not because he's even more defined than I expected, strong muscles bulging under his skin and threatening to burst out.

None of that is why I'm staring.

It's because of the scars: Dark, crisscrossing scars all over his back, chest, abdomen, and his sides.

Dozens.

Some are short, some are longer, but all of them are old and well-healed.

"Dimitri..." My voice fails. What happened? Maybe I should politely pretend I didn't notice them, but he knew I would see the scars when he came into the room like that.

Dimitri rummages through his bag. "A mission, years back. Didn't go as planned." He finds a shirt and straightens up.

I'm on my knees on the bed. "Not as planned? You have at least—"

"Thirty-two on the back, twenty-three front." His tone is

distant, detached.

I can't believe it. What kind of person did that to him? "I don't know what to say—"

He turns, offering a faint smile. He pushes me down until my butt hits the heels of my feet. "There's a lesson here. Things can go wrong, Alix. Easily. Missions are fluid, and parameters change. If something goes wrong, you follow my orders exactly and to the point—even if they contradict what I said before. On mission, I'm in charge. Clear?"

Without his sunglasses, his eyes hold a vulnerability I'm not used to. They're open, like a window to a soul he usually keeps locked up.

"Clear?" he repeats.

"Yes." *Crystal.*

"Good. Because this is *not* a game. Lives depend on us."

He squeezes my shoulders and steps away, leaving me alone to my rising nausea.

Lives depend on us.

Ian's life.

And ours as well.

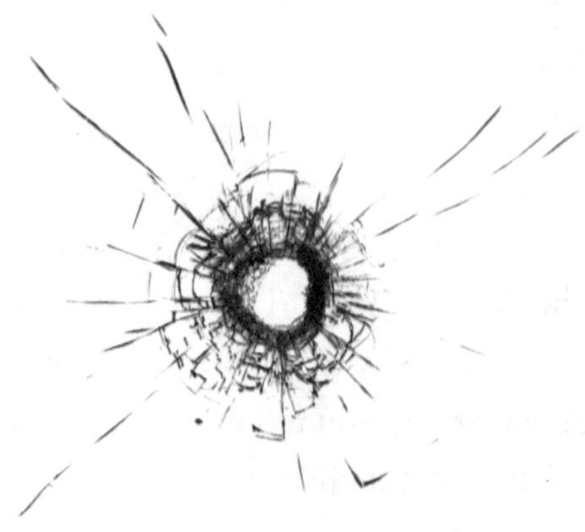

CHAPTER NINETEEN
Landed

"After you." Dimitri holds the helicopter door.

Why, thank you. Elroy McMonahan is even more polite than Dimitri normally is—or it could be because the rent-a-chopper company's employee is still lingering, in case Dimitri has more questions.

Which he doesn't.

He'd probably fly circles around the other pilot. Blindfolded.

I nod a thanks, climb in and fish for the headphones hanging off the headrest. Dimitri briefed me well. I know what to expect.

Dimitri takes his seat and closes the door, strapping himself in before throwing a sideways glance at me. "Ready? No second thoughts?"

About what?

Flying in a helicopter?

Breaking out Ian?

Neither is as harmless as I'd like it to be. In my opinion,

helicopters are out to kill you, and the Dark Unit… yeah, might be out for the same. I flash a fake smile. "Nope. I'm as ready as can be." If I say it often enough, I might believe it.

His lips quirk. "Okay then." He begins the start-up sequence, and the noise becomes deafening, no matter the earphones.

We lift off a minute or two later, and I wish I hadn't eaten.

My stomach drops to my knees like during a roller coaster ride.

Boy. Way bumpier than in the Air Force One. "Gosh, this is—" I snap my mouth shut.

"What?" Dimitri's voice comes through the headset.

"Nothing." The spoiled First Daughter wanted to complain about the rough ride until she remembered Ian would probably love to exchange his current situation even for the most uncomfortable helicopter ride.

Yeah. That shuts me up for the next hour or two.

Last thing I did before leaving was check on his heat signature: Still in the same position. Still a warm core, which means… well, he isn't dead. But he wasn't moving either.

I force a dry swallow down my throat. The view is spectacular, but it doesn't register. In my mind, I'm with Ian. Only when it gets dark and Dimitri keeps us closer to the ground than he normally would to avoid detection by radar… that's when I close my eyes and try to focus on something else.

It's not working all that well.

We land once to refuel, right on time.

After that short stop, we don't speak a single word. Dimitri focuses on flying in the dark, I focus on the rescue mission. On Ian.

I miss him.

"Ten minutes to destination." Dimitri's calm voice breaks

through the relative silence, making me jump. How he can be so collected, I don't know. The second I understand what Dimitri said, my palms instantly slick with sweat, my heart hurts with every beat, and a gut-wrenching feeling that I'd rather not have is taking over the pit of my stomach.

Who's the newbie?

Me.

Without a doubt.

Dimitri sets us down behind a small hill about two miles away from the cabin. Over the last two hours or so, the landscape—what I could see of it—has transformed into pristine wilderness. This is nature pure. Rolling hills draped in knee-high grass and scattered bushes. It would look beautiful during the day, and even now, the moon bathes everything in a silvery light.

Once the heli powers down, we jump out. My goodness, Alaska is cold indeed. I'm glad I'm well prepared in my thermals, thick jacket and boots—said the girl who's going to stay comfy inside the helicopter. Dimitri grabs his backpack and retrieves something from its front pocket. "I have a little gift for you." He holds a tactical holster and gun out to me.

Uhh, that was not mentioned in our previous discussions. Not even remotely.

"No, thank you," I squeak and take a step back. "I already have a knife." A knife Dimitri insisted I strap around my right lower calf. Everybody in the wilderness should carry one, he said, and although I'm going to stay behind, I see his point. He didn't say anything about a gun though, and I don't want it. If I carry one, it means I might have to use it. Shooting targets down in the Eagle's Lair is one thing, shooting at people a completely different one.

Dimitri ignores me and secures the holster anyway, wrapping

it around my hip and thigh. "Precautionary. I carry several weapons, and it would be neglectful of me to leave you without any means to defend yourself. You're a good shot, Alix. Shoot to disable, if you can—but if anything goes wrong and it is your life or theirs, you take theirs." He fastens the last snap around my thigh and looks up at my face, the light blue eyes reflecting the moonlight like a mirror.

He means it: *You take theirs.*

Well, yes, or rather, no—I don't want to get shot, or even be shot *at*. Been there, done that. But I also don't want to shoot or have to shoot at anybody either.

But I'm playing with the big kids tonight, and Dimitri explained the rules to me.

He rests his hand on my shoulder. "It's a last resort. Best case, you won't need it. But if things go wrong, do what you have to, and listen to what I told you."

I count off my fingers. "Stay in the chopper. Keep your eyes open. When in doubt, hide, and I don't dare follow you." That was a quote. Kind of.

"Correct." Dimitri rubs his knuckles over my head. "Now hop back into that helicopter, Trouble, before you freeze out here." He all but stuffs me into the cabin and hands me ears and a mic. "Remember to keep an eye out for me. As soon as you see me come back, you power up the engine like I showed you."

I push the speaker in my ear and affix the mic Band Aid to my throat. Look at that, still sticks despite the cold sweat building up on my skin. "Can do," I whisper hoarsely.

Dimitri gives me a thumbs up. "Be good."

I close my eyes, take a deep breath, and release it slowly. "No worries. I will be."

"I know." He rubs my head again, then turns to leave.

"Dimitri!" I pull him back by his sleeve, and before he has time to protest, into a hug. "Watch out for yourself, okay? And bring Ian back." My voice breaks at the end. Darn emotions.

His chest rises in a silent sigh. "I will get him out, Alix. I will."

And with that, he melts into the darkness.

The first five minutes of waiting are easy.

I power on the laptop and set up the small, portable satellite dish. Might as well be productive.

The second five minutes of waiting are a little bit annoying, mainly because I can't focus after I hear the short *blip* that tells me Dimitri is out of comm range. Takes me five times to log into the network, although I could swear I typed the password correctly. And once I'm in, I can't make up my mind what I want to check on.

Which brings me to the third five minutes of waiting: they suck. Majorly.

Okay, Forrester, pull yourself together. There's nothing you can do—which is exactly my problem. I blow a raspberry at myself and crack my knuckles. Focus. I should be well-informed when they come back, not sitting here like a nervous wreck. Bit pathetic, really.

I force my sluggish laptop to obey my orders. Looks like I'm not the only one with performance issues today, or it's because of the subpar connection thanks to my improvised uplink. Once I get what I wanted though…

I whistle through my teeth. "Dang you, Dark Unit." They pulled off another hack. This time, their stunt got them into all of the previously hacked sites simultaneously. Oh, and as a bonus, they added a graphic of twenty dead monkeys and a fallen Humpty Dumpty. It's a pretty gruesome image, zombie movie-style.

What annoys me most about it though is the countdown. *Tic-toc-tic-toc.* Thirty-two hours, twenty-two minutes and fifteen, fourteen, thirteen seconds. Oo-kay… what is that ticking down—

The screen flickers once.

Twice.

What the—

That's not my connection.

It's the laptop, and that shouldn't happen.

All of a sudden it's warm in here, way too warm.

It's nothing. It's absolutely nothing—

My fingers fly over the keyboard as I check the configs. The firewalls are up, everything's been updated and checked, I'm just delusional and paranoid, it's noth—

"Shit!" I yank my hands off the keyboard like it burned me. "Shit, shit, shit!"

Something's making the CPU work a lot harder than it should be. I pull up the task manager and check for what's pegging the processor. Crap! A packet sniffer. A freakin', stupid sniffer running in the background and spying on us. Repeat: *spying* on *us.*

A messy, icky lump builds in my stomach. This is bad. Bad-bad. The next breath comes in wheezy. I have thirty more seconds to stay under the radar, if at all. But to be honest, at this point detection doesn't matter.

Because this thing has been here, running quietly in the background and collecting data for who knows how long.

The lump grows and swallows my heart. Whoever did this,

knows.

They *know.*

Everything I typed, maybe even everything we talked about, depending on the sniffer, they know.

Which only allows for one conclusion: our mission is compromised.

For all I know, Dimitri is walking into a trap.

Breathe.

In and out.

In and out.

In and—

With all the willpower I have, I force the uprising panic down. Prioritize, Forrester!

Twenty more seconds, if at all.

I type, diving into the config. Even if they've spoofed their IP address, I should be able to track—

Holy freakin' cow.

I slam the laptop's lid shut and tear the power pack off the portable satellite dish.

Nothing but my harsh breathing echoes through the silence.

Can't be. Really, can't be. Must've been wrong.

But I know I wasn't.

The sniffer… Granted, for more details I'd need more time, but this is enough. The sniffer tracked back to the White House.

The *White House.*

Somebody was spying on us from *inside the White House.*

How they got it onto our laptop is anybody's guess.

I dive to the side to reach for the satellite phone, never minding the laptop sliding off my lap and falling to the ground with a cracking sound. Ain't touching that thing anymore.

My pulse kicks into overdrive as I hammer the key

combination into the phone I memorized almost a year ago.

After two rings a female voice picks up. "2-1-3-0."

"112-3-19."

No comment or acknowledgement follows, only the clicking as I get connected. Come on, come on, faster! This is too big to wait, I need help, I need Dad to know. He's the only one I can trust—

"Situation room. Lane here."

A spike of adrenaline shoots through my veins. Wait—Lane? Why—

"Hello? Lane here."

Dang it. "Uh, Brandon, hi. This is Alix."

"Alix!" His voice warms, then dims. "Have you landed alrea—what? Huh?" The last two words sound softer, like he turned away from the receiver. "No, it's Alix." Pause. "Yes, Alix *Forrester*." Geez. How many girls named Alix call on a secure line? I pick up on somebody else's voice in the background talking back to Lane. Deep, bad-tempered. Waterhouse.

Well, Dad did say they were backup, but doesn't mean I want to—or should—talk to either of them. "Brandon, I was wondering if you could connect me to my dad—"

Rustling, an outraged "Hey!", then Waterhouse's cold voice: "What's gone wrong?"

Oh, heck. Not what I need. "I need to talk to my dad—"

His voice is icy. "Your father is not available. What. Has. Gone. Wrong?"

Actually, I wouldn't know where to start. "I would need to talk to Dad—"

"The president is in the middle of summit meetings, Missy, which is why you're transferred to us. Meaning, he is un-a-vailable." He stretches every syllable of the last word. "So, what is it? Police didn't have anything it their locker, and now you're off chasing some other ghost? Don't you think it's about time you bring this back home?"

That annoying, arrogant son of a—

Wait.

A hot flush shoots down my body. *Police didn't have anything in their locker.* My heart picks up speed. How does he know the police locker was empty? We never filed that report.

What if… it's ridiculous, but what if… What if *Waterhouse* truly is the leak? I mean, for reals? 'Cause I've been there—accusing a high-ranking politician. I was right the last time, but come on, how likely is it that two…?

Waterhouse. It sounds insane, but… The perfect cover. A distinguished career in the FBI, above suspicion. He knows all our missions, he knows about Ian and has access to his files, and he was the one who added another guard at MU screwing with our mission there. Plus, he hates us. Maybe it's revenge. Maybe he's bitter about Ian taking over most of PRICS. Or maybe it's something else, who knows.

And to top it off, he is the head of the FBI Cybersafety Department—who better to plant a sniffer? *And* the fact that he never took anything the Dark Unit hacked serious? Yeah, because it plays into his hands!

Damn it, it could be possi—heck! I facepalm myself. "Of course!" Waterhouse held our laptop—in the Oval Office! He looked at the data! He could've easily opened the door for the sniffer!

Sweat builds up on my forehead. This is big either way. Me suspecting him is big enough, but if I'm right… If I'm right, I have to be careful.

Time to improvise. Apologetic voice, on. "You are right. I

apologize. I shouldn't bother you or my dad. It won't happen again."

"Sure hope so." Waterhouse grunts. "Please don't get yourself killed, will ya? It would be a hell of a lot of paperwork for me to go through."

How touching. "Don't worry, I won't."

And I hang up.

Holey freakin' moley! Breathing is weird, it doesn't bring any oxygen to my brain.

What do I do now? Can't reach Dad. Can't get backup for Dimitri. If Waterhouse knew we were on his heels, then I'm right, and most likely Dimitri is walking into a trap—or at least into a cabin with very prepared hackers. What do I—

Movement on my right, a small streak of red illuminated by the moon.

Training kicks in as I duck. Ever so carefully, I lift my head and scan the area where I saw the red. There! Again!

A jacket. A guy, a guy in a red jacket sneaking through the bushes toward the helicopter. Something about him strikes me as familiar, but it's tough to tell. He's still about fifty meters out, taking his sweet time hiding behind one tree and then another, waiting. Does he know I'm here? Does he not?

And does it matter? I can't become the next hostage.

Only one solution. Only one option.

With trembling fingers I disable the automatic ceiling light, then open the door just enough for me to slip through on the opposite side from the man. Rather than risk noise, I keep it ajar.

I duck and dart across the clearing into the tree line, staying low in the shadows, gaze locked on red jacket.

The man is standing still behind a tree, observing the helicopter.

Did he see me?

Did he—
He sneaks forward, ignoring me on his right.
Good.
As fast as I can while keeping quiet, I ghost from tree to tree. Thank you, mossy stuff on the ground, for muffling my steps. I sneak forward until I'm a good fifty meters behind the man. Then, I run.

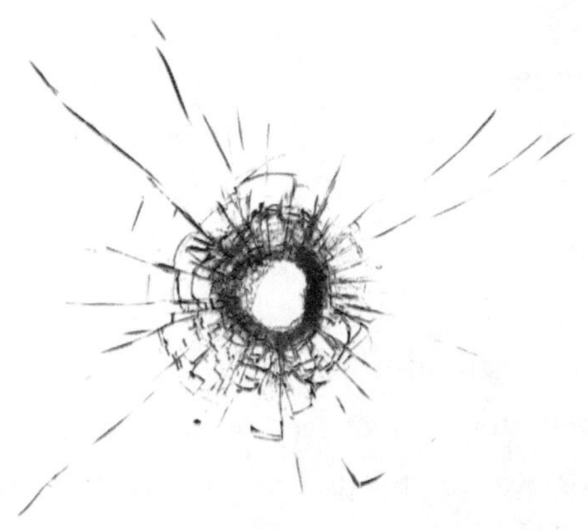

CHAPTER TWENTY
Maze

Once I have some distance between me and the heli, I pick up speed and dash through bushes, weaving between trees, vaulting roots, ducking branches and stumbling over stumps.

Moonlight guides my path, but that advantage is not exclusive to me. If I can see, so can he. As it is, I'm hoping I'm too far away for him to spot or hear me.

A mile in, my breathing gets raspy. Despite the stitch stabbing my side, I push on. Every second counts. If I ever get my hands around Waterhouse's neck… Well, they didn't teach me Krav Maga for a nothing.

Takes me about fifteen minutes to get to the area I recognize from the satellite scans—and there's Dimitri's backpack, hidden the way he taught me to.

He's here. I skid to a halt, my heart beating at an unhealthy pace of at least two-hundred BPM. My breathing sounds like a steam train to me.

"Dimitri, come in. Dimitri—" Static, nothing else.

Dang it. What do I do? Do I go in—

I tiptoe closer to the clearing, careful. Smack in the middle of the clearing sits the cabin, the Dark Unit's helicopter about a hundred meters behind it.

Somewhere in the maze deep beneath my feet, they've got Ian tied to a chair, waiting for us. Somewhere down there, Dimitri is fighting for him.

If he is still alive.

I hug my elbows.

No. He is alive. They both are.

Only one way to go. I drop my right hand to my hip and the holster Dimitri insisted I wear. Gosh, I'm nauseous.

But I don't have a choice.

I do a quick scan of the area in front of me before I step out into the open.

Everything is quiet.

BOOM!

I leap back behind cover, stifling a yelp. A figure bursts from the cabin—six pursuers on his heels. He spins mid-stride, firing.

Dimitri! It's Dimitri! Alive!

But maybe not much longer.

BOOM! BOOM! BOOM!

One drops, five keep on coming.

He turns, and—

Click—he's empty.

He curses, then sprints at full speed toward the woods on the other side of the cabin.

Bile rises. What the heck happened down there that Dimitri is out of ammo?

The men chase after Dimitri, screaming, cursing.

Then, silence.

And my decision is made.

Blood roars in my ears as I dart across the clearing. Really, what other choice is there?

Ian wouldn't hesitate, so neither do I.

I'm halfway to the cabin when—

An explosion shatters the night. A fireball the size of a three-story house paints the night orange, and it's coming right from—

"The heli!" Damn them! A black cloud of smoke rises up into the sky. I don't need night vision goggles for this. It's clear as day thanks to the moonlight. "They blew up our ride," I whisper.

A choked, cut-off gasp in my ear—

"Dimitri?" I slap my hand over the speaker pushed into my ear canal. "Dimitri?" No response. Still. "In case you can hear me, we've been compromised! They know we're here! The heli is… gone." My gaze drifts over the orange skies in the distance while I count to five, waiting for a reply. Nothing. "I'll try to get Ian, you keep them away from the cabin."

No time to worry about escape now. One problem at a time.

Heart stuttering, I tiptoe into the cabin and squeeze myself against the wall. All five kidnappers followed Dimitri. I should be fine, but better safe than sorry. The acrid smoke stings my eyes. Ugh, Dimitri's smoke bombs.

From what I can see through the stinging smoke and darkness, the cabin looks like we expected from the heat scans. Small, sparsely furnished, with only the outline of a table, two chairs, and a bed visible in the far corner.

Where's the—There! The trapdoor to the maze! I don't have any time to focus on my heart skipping a couple of beats. It's now or never. After gulping down another lungful of moderately fresh air, I descend the narrow and steep stairs into the smoky darkness.

Once down, I press my back against the wall. Wait, Forrester. Easy. The smoke burns and stings in my eyes as much as in my throat. And that's with some of that stuff escaping through the open trapdoor. The only tiny bit of light comes in from there, but it isn't much. I bet taking out the lights is part of Dimitri's assault tactic—because he definitely packed night vision goggles for himself. Would be great to have some myself—

Coughing.

Wheezing.

Ian!

Ian, wheezing from the full dose of the acidic smoke.

Everybody fled and left the prisoner behind.

His gasping grows more desperate, each breath accompanied by a harsh stridor.

The need to get to him overrules all the nervousness and fear that had its grip on me ever since the helicopter touched down in Alaska.

He's here. He's *alive.*

I have to make sure he stays that way.

Like Ian and Dimitri taught me, I keep my back to the wall and all my senses on receive. Overturned furniture clutters the hallway. Empty ammo shells cover the ground. Not good. No way this is all Dimitri's ammo. This is from the Dark Unit fighting back.

Yeah, they were warned alright.

I pass the first room—empty.

Good. Fingers crossed my luck holds.

Sweat builds up under my jacket.

Ian coughs again, more violent, and my throat burns with every breath. But it's doable. Diluted.

Almost there.

I turn right to where the coughing's coming from—and freeze.

I found Ian.

But I didn't expect him to look like *this*.

Whatever the Dark Unit wants from him, they want it badly.

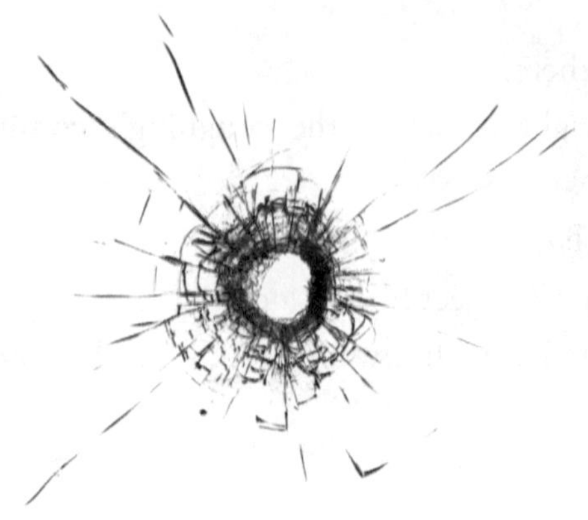

CHAPTER TWENTY-ONE
Surprise

I an.

I clamp my hand over my mouth to silence my scream.

Ian.

He slumps in his chair, and if they hadn't tied him to it, he'd fall off. There's barely any tension left in his body. Can't say if he's conscious or not, he looks out of it. His shirt and shoes are gone, but all that, I only register peripherally.

I'm rooted to the spot because his stomach, sides, and what I can see of his back are covered in blue and purple bruises, some grotesquely swollen. Dried blood cakes his right deltoid where they carved out his tracker. At least now I know how the Dark Unit found out about it. Damn Waterhouse.

Nausea builds up powered by sheer horror. To hurt him like that—that's not quote-unquote *just* a beating. That's torture.

Ian coughs violently, wheezing with every breath, and I unfreeze.

Priorities, Alix.

I sprint across the room.

"Ian, it's me!" No reaction. No sign he heard me at all.

What.

Have.

They.

Done.

Ian's face is a map of violence: split lip, left eye swollen shut in shades of purple and black, a fresh cut slashing above his eyebrow. That's not what terrifies me—it's his vacant stare. No recognition No response.

Drugged.

As we feared.

Rage coils into a burning ball of lava inside my stomach.

The Dark Unit will pay for this.

But first things first. Time to get him out of here as fast as possible. *A distorted grunt, a cut off curse, hissing static—*

Dimitri! He must be closer again, which could be our salvation or our doom, depending on whether he's alone or not.

"Dimitri, I'm with Ian. He's alive, but drugged." I keep it brief as I step in front of Ian and lean over him, checking his restraints.

Rope.

Thank whomever for small mercies. Cuffs would've been annoying.

Thanks, Dimitri, for insisting I carry a knife. I take it out of its sheath, reach even farther over Ian, and cut into the rope. The first strand gives without any effect on Ian, but once I cut the second one, he pitches forward into me.

"Ugh," I grunt. I brace against him with all my body weight, or else he'd take us both down. While holding him steady, I slide the knife away, then guide Ian down to the floor. Careful. Controlled.

Thanks to the draft of air flushing out most of the smoke, Ian's breathing is easier, but his eyes remain vacant. He's still not showing any reaction at all. No way I can get him out of here like this.

"Crap, crap, crap." Dimitri could've carried Ian like a sack of flour. Me? Not going to happen. Unresponsive like this he—

Wait. If the Dark Unit gave him something to keep him quiet, wouldn't they use something they could counteract when they needed Ian? He's of no use to them like this.

Which means, they might have an antidote *somewhere*.

Hope surges. I bite my lower lip. Where would—

There—the desk in the corner! As good a place as any to start. I lunge for it and yank open the first drawer with enough force to rattle the whole thing.

Please let me be right. If Ian gave them already what they wanted, they might've knocked him out without an antidote, but if—

My gaze falls onto the open laptop sitting on the desk, a single word catching my attention: Forrester.

Then: *Forrester's G20-speech @ 7pm, MET.*

Ice crystallizes in my veins. Not good.

The Dark Unit and my dad should not be mentioned in the same sentence. What do they care about that speech? A chill spider-walks down my back. Whatever it means, it isn't—

Ian coughs and wheezes.

Damn it, no time!

Improvising. There! A ratty old backpack gapes open on the desk like an invitation. Thank you, sir. I slam the laptop closed and shove it in, my jittery hands missing the opening twice.

Okay, focus. Ian. Antidote. *Please.*

I yank open the first drawer some more.

Paperclips, scotch tape, scissors. Nope.

I wrench open the second drawer so hard it nearly comes off its track.

Syringes, alcohol pads, medication bottles.

Much better. Now we're talking.

I scan over the labels, looking for one that'll help me to get Ian back to normal.

There: Rohypnol.

Of course. The perfect drug to make him talk and keep him cooperative.

And right next to it, another vial: *Flumazenil.*

The weight of a truck-sized boulder falls off my shoulders. Thank you, Fate, for the Dark Unit acting reasonable for once.

The smoke has thinned to ghostly ribbons now, making each breath less of a battle—for me, but especially for Ian. He's been marinating in this stuff for longer than me.

So speed it up, Forrester! My hands are way too sweaty and jittery already as I assemble the syringe and draw up the medication. Never have I been happier to be a physician's daughter, good in all things science, and PRICS-trained.

More static bursts through my ear piece, punctuated by harsh breathing and what sounds like—no, that can't be pain. Not from Dimitri.

I force down the acid churning in my gut and sprint back to Ian. "Sorry, Ian."

That's all the warning he gets before I ram the needle through his bloody jeans and into his thigh. At this point, infection-control is a luxury we can't afford.

He doesn't even flinch, and this shot, it hurts. Shows how out of it he is.

I throw the empty syringe across the room.

Okay.

Okay.

A few minutes, and he should be back to normal.

Except, we don't have a couple of minutes.

A muffled scream, a gunshot—

The acid inside my stomach burns up into my throat.

Time's up.

Decision made for me, I grab Ian's arms and heave with everything I got, combining strength and leverage. The meds must be starting to work, because he manages to stay upright, his arm draped across my shoulders like dead weight.

Not perfect, but I'll take it.

One step forward as I adjust my grip on his hip—

"Little Alix Forrester. Making my day."

The metallic click of a gun being cocked freezes the blood in my veins.

"Turn around, sweetheart. Slowly." The man coughs out a nasty laugh. "Or you're dead."

I go still as a statue.

My blood pressure bottoms out, leaving my brain scrambling for oxygen.

Oh, crap, oh crap, *oh crap.* Nobody's supposed to be here, they all ran after Dim—

"Any time now, sweetheart." His voice oozes false patience. "Figured the big oaf wouldn't be alone." The dry laugh morphs into steel. "*Now,* Alix."

My body reacts before my mind has completed the elimination process, Dimitri's tactical training kicking in on pure instinct. I pivot on my heels, the motion sweeping Ian between me and the gunman—using what I hope is his most valuable asset as my shield.

Yes. I'm using Ian as a shield to protect me.

Sorry, Ian.

The gunman chuckles. "Nice move. Doesn't matter to me. Use him all you want, you're not getting out of here. Neither of you are."

I risk a glance around Ian's shoulder. Tall. About six-three. Caucasian. Deceptively average-looking guy, except for one detail—the gun aimed dead-center at Ian's chest.

A knot lodges at the base of my throat. Every breath comes out raspy, forced.

Buy time. Think! "What do you want?"

I ease my right hand toward my hip, matching pace with a bead of sweat tickling down my spine.

His laugh comes empty, mechanical. "I heard you're a genius, Alix. You figure it out."

Blood rushes in my ears like a flash flood, threatening to drown me. How does he know? I'm classified. I mean, *Agent* Forrester is, so how—

My fingers brush the gun's grip.

Easy now.

The holster's snap releases with a soft betraying click.

Deep breath. Stalling. More stalling. "Then let's say the situation is a bit much for me." I wrap my fingers around the gun's grip. "What do you want with me and Ian?"

As if on cue, Ian stirs, taking some of his weight off me.

"Or let's say I don't want to play with a teenager here. Drop Donckers. Now." He aims low. "Or I'll shoot him in the leg first. Then you."

A pathetic squeak escapes my throat.

"Three."

Oh hell, I can't just give up—

"Two."

No mission is worth getting shot for. If this ever happens again, you abort.

"One, and—"

Commotion behind the gunman, fast steps—

Movement explodes behind him. Like an avenging angel, Dimitri appears out of the darkness and black fog, wielding a wooden panel overhead, muscles coiled for a devastating swing.

Maybe he made a noise, maybe I gave him away with a glance, but ultimately it doesn't matter.

The gunman whirls, snapping his weapon up to Dimitri's face.

My cry catches in my throat as, panel suspended uselessly high above, too far away to strike.

The gunman snarls, tightening his trigger finger around the trigger, and my world narrows to a single point of focus.

Training takes over. I draw the gun, clear Ian's shoulder—

And fire.

The shot thunders through the room, deafening me.

The recoil bucks against my one-handed grip, sending the barrel high. A bestial scream tears through the air, followed by a thunderous crack of wood meeting bone.

With a grunt, the gunman collapses on the spot, like a marionette with cut strings. Dimitri towers over him, panel raised for another strike. He looks like he's been through hell—outfit shredded, weapons stripped away. Hence, the panel.

Without missing a beat, Dimitri shoves the gunman's weapon into his own empty holster and secures the man's hands with cable ties, never minding the blood from the leg wound *I* gave him.

Nausea rises, be it from having shot somebody or because we're in deep.

Probably both.

Dimitri jumps up as soon as the gunman is secured, fury radiating off him.

"What happened to *you'll behave*, Alix? Why the hell are you here?" He jabs an angry finger at the ground, like an accusation.

"It was a trap, Dimitri! They knew we were coming. They were prepared, and—"

"Trust me, I've noticed." His words come out chopped. "Doesn't change you should've stayed at the—"

Nu-uh. "Couldn't. They found me. Had to run when a guy was coming straight for me. They blew up the helicopter." I grunt as Ian shifts his weight, still too weak to fully support himself.

A curse explodes from Dimitri. "Damn them!"

Agreed. I suck in a shallow breath. "What's the plan?" Because I don't have one.

Dimitri is in front of Ian and me in a heartbeat, checking Ian's pupils. "He's waking up. Can you get him out? Alone?"

I holster the gun, which should be easy to do, if it wasn't for my shaking hands. "Alone?"

Ian stirs against me, and I adjust my grip.

"Probably, but—"

Loud shouts erupt from the hallway behind us.

Dimitri whirls around, favoring his left side. What the hell happened to him?

Ian groans, his bare skin cool under my palms.

Running footsteps drum closer to our hiding spot.

Oh, crap.

Panic curls around me like an icy blanket, freezing me to the spot. Not even when I was tied to a chair knowing Dad was about to be killed did I have this sensation of utter helplessness. Back then at least I knew Ian and Dimitri were somewhere.

Now they're here with me, trapped, one wounded and weaponless, the other wounded and barely conscious.

Bang! Bang! Bang!

"Down!" Dimitri launches himself at us, driving Ian and me behind the wall beside the door just as bullets tear into the opposite wall, spraying wood and concrete. Ian's deadweight crashes into me, adding fresh bruises to the collection.

My breath catches.

Throat's too tight.

We're not getting out of this.

How could we?

All we wanted was Ian back with minimal casualties.

All they want is Ian—casualties be damned.

"They're going to kill us," I whisper, the sensitive microphone picking up on it nonetheless.

Bangbangbang! Bang! Bang!

More shots, more screaming. A bullet ricochets, but our wall holds. Are they firing blind? Holy cow—

Dimitri lays his hand on my knee. "They'll have to get through me to kill you. Won't happen." His eyes have lost some of their light, but none of their steel. "Five people. I shot one of them. When I give the word, you take Ian out the way you came in. No stops. No looking back. You take him, you get him out. Understood?"

My throat constricts, each breath a battle. My windpipe feels so tight, hardly any air is reaching my lungs.

Gunfire drowns out the multi-language cacophony of screams and yells from the hallway.

I force my chin down in a nod. "Okay. Okay. I can do that.

I think. I mean, yes, I can. But you—"

"I'm going to make sure you make it out." He squeezes my knee.

"Okay." Deep breath in. "Okay. Where do we meet?"

Dimitri hesitates a moment. "I'll… catch up to you. You keep going north."

Catch up to us? "How are you going to find us?"

He takes his hand off my knee and holds up a finger. "Not important now. Remember, do as I say. Follow my orders. Can you do that? This time, at least?" His voice is dead serious, a calm anchor in the storm of shouts and bullets around us.

One more deep breath. "Yes."

It's what I trained for—well, not quite, but ultimately, it was always a possibility.

A ghost of a smile plays behind his mask. "Mind if I use your gun?" He holds out his hand.

Do I mind? Not at all. One shot fired is one too many for me. I glance at the gunman lying on the floor. At least the puddle of blood isn't growing larger anymore. My bullet won't kill him, but it sure hurt him.

"It's better in your hands anyway." I drop it into his palm. It scared me. *I* scared me.

Dimitri checks both weapons, mine and the gunman's, counting ammo.

The hallway fire has slowed, but the men are still there, some taunting us and snickering. Guess they feel like they have the upper hand with us trapped in here, and they're right. We're in a crappy position.

Ian groans and sits up straighter—in slow motion, but still.

"Holy cow, Ian!" I catch him before he can fall forward and faceplant.

He's waking up! Finally, some good news. My eyes water up. "Ian. *Ian.* Hey. It's me, Alix! Can you hear me? Stay still, we're getting you out. Understand?" My voice wavers, but at least he stops fighting my grip.

He blinks quickly, hard. Takes a big, heaving breath, shakes his head and tears his eyes wide open. His gaze wanders until it finds me.

One-Mississippi.

Two-Mississippi.

Three—

Something lights up in those mesmerizing green eyes. "Alix," he slurs.

The antidote's working. A single tear runs down my cheek.

It's working!

Something is working!

"Yes, Ian. We need to run soon. Can you do that?" I squeeze his hand.

Ian's brows furrow. His brain hasn't reached full processing power yet, but eventually he nods. "Think so—"

"Come out with your hands up and we're not going to hurt you!" barks a man in the hallway.

Dimitri and I lock eyes. No way.

Dimitri's whisper barely registers. "Ready?"

"Ready." And strangely enough, I am.

Kind of.

We can get this done.

We *have* to get this done, there's no other option.

Dimitri holds out his fist and I bump it—comfort in small rituals. My heart squeezes. Everything's so surreal. Dimitri raises an eyebrow at me, a wordless check-in: *are you sure?*

I nod, and he acknowledges it with one small bump of his

shoulder into mine. Then, he gestures for me to get Ian up. I shoulder Ian's weight as he finds his feet, more alert now.

Dimitri leans against the wall, eyes closed, a gun in each hand. "On my command. Good luck." His eyes pop open and they're shooting fire. "Go!"

He rolls around the door, guns blazing, a one-man army protecting his friends.

And the fight is on.

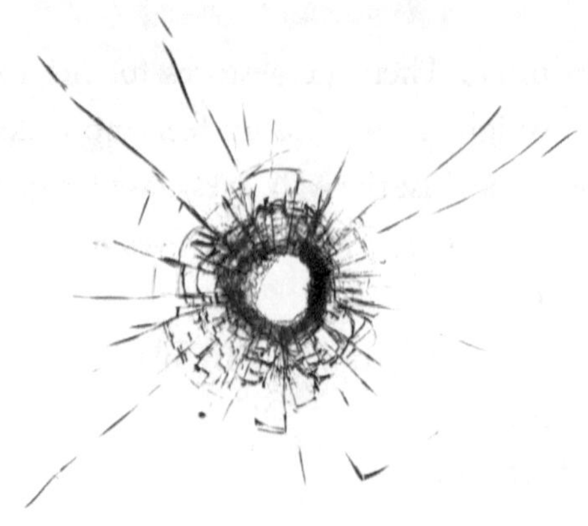

CHAPTER TWENTY-TWO
Topwards

Gunfire tears through the hallway. Bullets ricochet, their high whine painful to my ears. At least five voices scream through the chaos, punctuated by howls of pain and rage.

Dimitri's grunts crackle through my earpiece

I hold onto Ian so tightly my fingers dig into his skin. I'm hyperventilating, but who cares, at least I'm breathing.

The shooting and noise retreats deeper into the complex.

"Now!"

Dimitri! My green light!

I don't bother with a reply. No time to lose. "Come on, fast, fast, fast!" I drag Ian with me around the corner after a quick left-right scan down the hallway.

The smoke is thinner in the hallway than before, revealing two motionless bodies to our right. I can't tell if they're breathing or not, and maybe I don't want to know. Otherwise it's empty. Dimitri's distraction is working.

My training takes over as I hurry us through lingering whisps of smoke toward the stairs leading to freedom. Ian stumbles twice, but stays upright. Overall, he's getting better—and I couldn't do without that.

Behind us, the fighting intensifies again.

"Report," Dimitri barks through the comm.

Another burst of gunfire erupts, each shot like a dagger to my heart. Somebody laughs.

Crap.

"Not there yet—twenty meters plus stairs!"

Dimitri's cry of pain splits the air.

Double-crap.

I don't ask what's going on. Can't distract him. Instead, I focus on speed.

Another agonized sound tears from his throat, and I swear my soul splinters.

"Stairs. Come on, Ian! One foot at a time, help me, help me here!"

He lifts each foot like it's made of lead.

The sound of splintering furniture and rapid gunfire spurs me on. Adrenaline spikes, if that's still possible, bringing a wave of dizziness. "Ian, steps! Come on, *come on!*" I force him up the stairs, lungs burning.

A different kind of cry pierces my ear—and this time I can tell it's bad.

I freeze halfway up the stairs. "Dimitri!"

All I hear through the comm is his ragged breathing, his grunting… It's not hard to picture him wincing with every sound.

He's hurt. Badly.

Then comes a scream that will haunt my nightmares.

The blood inside my veins turns to ice. "Dimitri," I whisper.

The gunfire stops. Cruel laughter filters through my earpiece.

Dimitri is in trouble, no doubt about it. And he needs help, also no doubt about it.

I lower Ian to the stairs. Dimitri needs my help—

Boomboomboom! "Run, Alix! *Now!*"

My foot hovers mid-step on the stairs. Damn mind-reader—

A pained gasp. "Get Ian and yourself out! That's an order. Follow—" He chokes back pain. "Follow my order! *Now!*"

For one split second I'm about to ignore him. Maybe two split-seconds. That's how long it takes for reality to crash in. I'm alone, unarmed, against multiple heavily armed hostiles.

I'd be worse than useless.

I suck in a shallow, messy breath. I promised Dimitri I'd do what he says. That I'd follow orders.

And this was an order.

A hole opens in my chest, split wide open. I can't help him. With a heart heavy as a boulder, I turn on my heel and run back up to Ian. "Yes, sir!"

Tears stream down my face. Everything in me rebels about leaving Dimitri—we don't leave *anybody* behind. Neither of them would leave me! They'd always come back!

But today, I'm following orders.

I haul Ian up—and luckily for me, this time he's helping. We stumble out the trapdoor and into the night, where moonlight and stars paint the world in deceivingly peaceful silver. A coughing spell wracks my body with the first breath of truly fresh air.

Below, the shooting resumes. Dimitri's still fighting, but the sounds tell a grim story.

My harsh breath comes out choppy. "We're out of the cabin!" But I don't stop, I don't slow down. I drag Ian with me until we hit the tree line close to where Dimitri hid the backpack.

"C-cold," he stutters through clenched teeth.

Well, yes. It's cold, and he's barefoot and shirtless. The moment we reach the woods and the backpack, I lean him against a tree.

"Clear!" I call into the mic, slip out of my jacket and wrap it around Ian.

I push Ian farther back, scanning the area between us and the cabin. Weaponless or not, I want to see them coming. Nerves bubble inside of me. Dimitri...! Come on, come on out...!

"Acknowledged," Dimitri rasps through the comm.

Ian's teeth clatter. "Alix, what… where…?" He shakes his head and rubs his eyes. The cold night air is burning through the sedation's fog.

I allow myself one tiny moment of relief. Giving Ian a small smile feels good. "Rescue mission. Slightly improvised. Can you walk? Dimitri will catch up with us." I point to where I think north is.

His gaze drops to his bare feet, understanding dawning. "S-sure." He shrugs. "N-no other option."

That's when it hits me why he's undressed like this. The Dark Unit's insurance against escape through the Alaskan wilderness. Cruel—and effective.

"Backup?" Ian reaches for the sleeve of my thick sweater and tugs on it.

I shake my head. "None. And, uhh… our heli kind of blew up." It's really been a successful mission so far.

Ian's gaze flies to the Dark Unit's helicopter near the cabin. "D-doesn't matter. Dimitri c-can fly anything. And hot-wire it."

Despite the seriousness of our situation, my smile widens. Ian is back.

We got Ian back!

I turn to share the moment—when Dimitri's cry shatters the night. It deafens me through the earpiece, but even Ian jerks and gasps.

"Katha—" Coughing. "Alix! Tree line?" His voice is wrong. Weak.

"Positive," I press the comm deeper, straining to hear.

His response comes as a whisper: "Stay!"

Bang! Bang! Bang! Bang!

A rapid burst of gunfire—then an earth-shattering, deafening, deep *boom* that makes my skull vibrate. The ground trembles, the rumbling building to an eardrum-bursting crescendo.

"What—" Ian grips a tree as the earth begins to move.

Fifty meters ahead the ground yawns open.

The cabin folds in on itself in eerily slow motion, walls crumbling, roof collapsing, as it slides into the abyss. The clearing followed, swallowed by what was once the Dark Unit's underground maze—Ian's prison.

The helicopter pitches sideways, rotor blades screaming as they bend before it too vanishes into the void.

Fifteen seconds.

That's all it takes for everything—cabin, helicopter, clearing—to disappear into a gaping wound in the earth, filled with twisted metal and broken concrete.

Once the movement and downfall stops, it's quiet.

Dead quiet.

Numbness settles in my bones. This can't be real.

"Dimitri?" I ask into the silence, my heart beating like a drum.

No response.

Again: "Dimitri?"

Static.

Fuck.

I tap the mic on my throat. "Dimitri, come in! Come in! *Dimitri!*"

Nothing.

Nothing, nothing, *nothing.*

A wheezy breath leaves my throat and I squeeze my eyes shut tight. "Dimitri, *come on!* Say something! Dimitri!" I shout the last word—

Nothing.

My legs give out and I collapse to my knees.

Dawn breaks over the hills, painting the smoke from our destroyed helicopter in ghostly beauty.

But it doesn't change that Ian and I are staring at a grave.

Dimitri's grave.

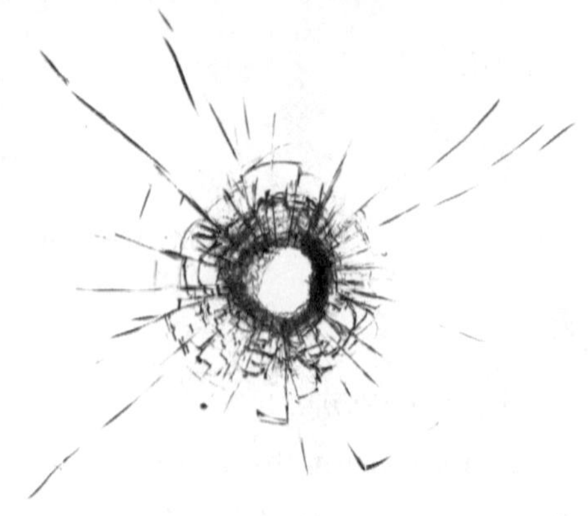

CHAPTER TWENTY-THREE
Back-Up Plan

"Dimitri…!"

The sound might leave my lips, or maybe it's just echoing in my head.

I can't say when the tears start coming, or when that messy ball of emotions finally bursts and drowns me in sorrow.

All I know is that Dimitri is down there.

Buried under tons of dirt, a house, and a helicopter.

"Dimitri…!" Just moments ago he was there, ordering me to get out—while he stayed behind.

And now he is gone.

No, not *gone*.

Dead.

Ian crumples beside me. "Dimitri's gift for us." His voice breaks. "He got us out."

He grips my hand and that little touch combined with the waves of grief radiating from him, shatters my last defense.

I throw myself into his arms. Hot tears stream down my face, but I'm not the only one crying. We cling to each other, holding tight, giving ourselves over to the raw anguish.

Dimitri is dead.

We weep until there's nothing left. Until I'm hollow.

Ian sniffs. "It's what he would have wanted, you know?" He pulls back slightly and wipes his eyes with the back of his hand. "Making sure we got out alive. That's all that mattered to him."

I nod. "We didn't turn into Katharina."

"He told you about his sister?"

I give him a faint smile through tears. "We had some time to bond."

"If he told you about Katharina… you were family to him. It is—" His voice catches. "—was his darkest secret. His deepest wound." He glides his hands down my arms and gives both of them a little squeeze before he lets go. "And speaking of… I know it feels wrong, but we have to move, or his sacrifice means nothing."

I glance at the black smoke still rising from behind the hill. "You're right. The guy who blew up our ride might still be out there. We need to be as far away from here as possible before he's back."

"Agreed." Ian sniffles.

Of course we can't stay, for many reasons, but abandoning Dimitri here feels like another betrayal. We shouldn't have to leave him here. Not even dead.

Inch by inch, like an old man, Ian stands, trying to avoid pinecones or broken twigs with his bare feet. "Give me a timeline. Distance to the helicopter, when it blew…" He steps from one foot onto the other. It must be freezing without shoes and shirt.

"Fifteen minutes as a sprint, my speed. That's when the heli exploded. Maybe another ten, fifteen minutes since then."

Ian rubs his arms against the cold. "So whoever did it might already be here."

"Or at least close. I doubt that person ran like I did."

He shifts from foot to foot. "Either way, we better contact the extraction team while putting some distance between us. I'm all for getting away from here as fast as possible, but I do have a small problem." He looks down at his bare feet.

Right.

But that's not our only problem. It gets worse. I swallow once to get rid of the sharp spike of panic in my throat. "Ian? The satellite phone… was in the helicopter."

The color drains from his face. "O-okay…" Pause. "What do we have, Trouble? Talk to me."

I close my eyes. "One sleep sack, ratchet straps, first aid kid, and if we're lucky, some food and water."

Translation: We're stranded in the Alaskan wilderness without equipment, backup, or communication, with a likely hostile on our heels.

Our next move will have to count, or we'll be in serious trouble within a few hours.

Survival of the fittest hits different when you're the prey.

We retreat deeper into the trees before taking stock.

Dimitri's backpack is perfectly packed for the rescue mission we planned.

It's less than ideal for the situation we're actually in.

Alas, we make do. No other choice.

Priority one: Ian's feet. Hiking barefoot is asking for disaster, so we improvise. The first aid kit's entire supply of elastic bandages is now wrapped around his feet. Makes him look like a mummy and won't keep him very warm, but it'll prevent immediate injury.

Speaking of warmth—our second concern. Wouldn't say that I'm exactly cozy in my thick fleece sweater, but at least I'm wearing thermals under my outfit. Add hiking and hopefully the sun coming out soon, and I should be fine—and I'm using that term loosely. *Fine* means I won't freeze. Won't be comfortable either, but that option is out the window, because Ian needs my jacket, or else he'd be bare-chested and frozen solid within the hour, no matter our hiking speed.

We prep in silence, racing against our two enemies: Mr. Hacker and Mrs. Hypothermia.

Ian secures the bandages with some more tape. "What are our options out here, Trouble? Nearest town?"

I shake my head. "Nothing. An Air Force Base about a hundred kilometers out." That's what Dimitri said, I think.

"Ouch. Too far." He points at his feet. "What else?"

I huff. "Nothing. We're smack in the middle of nowhere."

"Ouch, again. Did… did Dimitri give you any instructions? I mean, in case of…?"

"In case he didn't make it back?"

Ian nods, wide eyes meeting mine.

I swallow hard and drop my gaze. "No. Down in the maze, he said to head north, but—" The aerial view clicks into place. "There's a small facility or something. On top of one of the mountains. Dimitri said it was…" Dang, what did he say? I rack my brain. "A SERE-facility or something? About forty miles out?" If I remember correctly.

Ian blows a puff of air through pursed lips. "Forty miles…

An average speed of three miles per hour for hiking, minus rough terrain and bad equipment… it'll take us a good twelve hours. Minimum."

Probably more, if we're honest.

We're underprepared, under-equipped, and not in good shape. But choice isn't a luxury we have.

One last glance at the sinkhole. The Dark Unit's message is clear. I shoulder the backpack. Today, I'm the stronger one out of the two of us. "Better move."

"After you." Ian shoves his hands into the pockets—and cocks his head. "Wait, what—" He pulls out the little spaceship Hank and Teresa gave me.

Wonder, grief, and disbelief flicker across his face. His throat works. "Is… is this…?"

I nod. "From your parents. Your mom gave it to me." What do you tell somebody who hasn't seen his parents for years? They're fine? They miss you? Life goes on?

I settle for the truth. "I've never met more loving, level-headed parents than yours. Your room's untouched, and when I recognized the Defiant, they wanted me to have it. They're amazing, Ian."

He turns the model in his hands, looking so young, so much more vulnerable. Like a boy who lost his parents.

"Yeah, they are." He bites his lip. "They are." Clearing his throat, he shoves the little ship back into his pocket. "Now tell me why you went there, what you found, and what else happened since I was… gone."

I hold a couple of branches out of the way for him. "You know, the last thirty minutes were actually the most… enlightening."

"Why don't I like your phrasing?"

"What first? Start easy, with the Dark Unit's latest hack?" And then, for the grand finale, we'll get to who hacked *us*.

"Sure." Ian sounds less than thrilled. "Bring on the bad news."

Okay then. "Latest hack: all previously hacked sites. A dead Humpty-Dumpty crowned with twenty dead monkeys plus a countdown to tomorrow. Something is coming tomorrow, but I don't know what."

The sun paints nature in an Instagram-worthy reddish sheen.

Ian winces. "Not good. Countdown threats make me nervous. And I wonder how much of the information they wanted came from me. It's all fuzzy, thanks to the drugs. They kept asking about Torpedo—updates, improvements. They enhanced it themselves, it could break ninety-nine percent of firewalls now. Sneaker might be able to handle it, but I wouldn't bet on it." He steps over a fallen tree stump.

"I couldn't find out what they needed Torpedo for, but they needed it quickly. The Russian guys in that group were talking about something happening on the twenty-third. When is that, by the way?" He returns the favor and holds a couple of branches aside for me.

"Twenty-third? Tomorrow. Same as with the countdown."

He pauses to adjust his makeshift footwear. "Everything about this feels wrong. The Dark Unit has never been violent before, and now—kidnapping, gunfire, destroying our helicopter? It must be something big. Countdown threats always spell trouble. I wish I could've had a closer look at their computer. All I got was a castrated version to work on Torpedo's code, no internet, nothing."

Wait a second. "A closer look at their laptop, you mean? The one in your room on the desk?" The one I took and have in the backpack?

Ian raises an eyebrow. "Yeah, that one."

"You ask and receive." I swing the backpack down and pull out the laptop I snagged.

Ian's face lights up. "Nice, Trouble! Whoever trained you should get a recommendation."

My answering smile is part pride, part sadness. One of the people who trained me won't be around for any kind of recommendation.

Ian boots up the computer and rolls his eyes. "Seriously. Not password protected. And that from people in the hacker-business."

I peek over his side onto the screen. "Or they know whoever wants access, can hack into it." One glance up at Ian. "You could."

"True, but—" Ian's jaw drops. "Oh, hell."

He scans over the document I glimpsed earlier.

He scrolls down.

Types something.

Scrolls some more.

"What is it?" I stretch to see, but still can't make it out.

More scrolling, more typing—and then he stops and looks up from the laptop right at me, eyes wide.

His mouth closes once and opens again.

My heart sinks. I squeeze my eyes shut. "I don't want to know." Whatever he found, it can't be good, and we're already neck-deep in trouble. A bead of sweat trails down my spine despite the cold. I shiver. "On second thought, tell me."

Ian blows out a heavy puff of air. "Remember the first hacks we dealt with back at the White House? The ones displaying messages, and I thought they were warnings and Waterhouse thought I was nuts? Hate to say it, but I was right."

He closes the laptop, passing it back. "I have three puzzle pieces. Humpty Dumpty—the metaphor for a weapon used by the Government against their opponents. That's Torpedo—our program, stolen by them to be used against us. The *twenty* jumping monkeys, now all dead, and a countdown that comes into fruition tomorrow."

He sucks in his lower lip and pauses. "The document on their computer. Tomorrow is the G20 Summit. I cross-referenced it. The countdown aligns with your father's speech."

His gaze locks into mine. "Humpty Dumpty—our weaponized Torpedo—plus all this…" He nods at the laptop. Tomorrow the Dark Unit will use it to breach Sneaker, infiltrate MU, and—"

He stops.

"And what?" At this point I'm expecting the worst. "What am I missing?"

"The missile," Ian whispers. "Torpedo is going to crack a prototype American defense satellite and unleash a nuclear strike on the Berlin Reichstag during your father's speech."

His eyes are wide, haunted. "There will be no survivors."

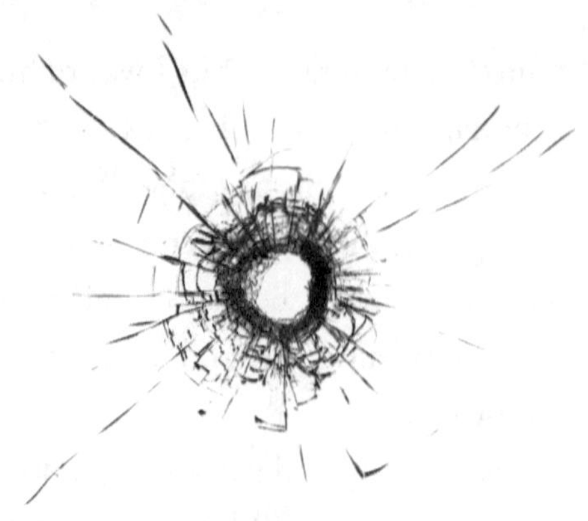

CHAPTER TWENTY-FOUR
Wilderness

Sweat trickles down my spine, despite the biting cold.

"No," I rasp, "that's impossible. Can't be. We don't have nuclear weapons up there, it violates every treaty we ever signed—"

Ian's laugh is bitter. "Want to time-travel back to the Cold War era and bring that up to President Johnson? Or Nixon? Maybe Ford? Whichever president green-lit this?"

Okay. Okay. Maybe we tried to keep one leg up against our enemies, but still—

A shiver runs down my back. "Even then, it can't be possible. The security protocols—"

"Security that Torpedo will slice through, especially after—" He leaves the rest unspoken. Especially after Ian modified it for them.

The silence that follows is deafening.

A nuclear missile.

Aimed at the Berlin Reichstag.

I don't need my PRICS-training to know what's going to happen. Destruction of a magnitude not seen since WWII. The first wave will perish in the blast. Others will fade slowly, poisoned by invisible death. Panic will spread like wildfire—a nuclear strike from space. They might blame Russia first, but when America's fingerprints surface… Neither they, the EU, nor NATO will stand idle while one of their own burns.

America is going to become the world's enemy.

And we'll have lit the match for World War III.

I wrap my arms around my body, trembling. Sweat freezes against my skin.

Ian rakes his fingers through his hair, wincing as he brushes across the purple-black bruises hidden at his hairline. "And we're trapped here, powerless—" He punches the air. "Damn it! Damn it, Trouble! We're watching World War Three unfold!"

My thoughts exactly.

Another punch at nothing. "Damn! If we were at PRICS, I could modify Sneaker as a defense, I could get things in motion, but from here…" His fury deflates like a punctured balloon. "Waterhouse is our only shot."

Leave it to me to pop that bubble of hope. "Yeah. About that. I'm pretty sure he's the mole."

"What?" Ian stops dead in his tracks. "Waterhouse? That's—"

I bump his shoulder, urging him forward. "Keep moving. I know it sounds crazy, but I'm pretty sure. Which brings me to the other bad news I wanted to tell you." As in, before we found out we're at the brink of a nuclear war. "I found a packet sniffer on our laptop. Didn't have much time, but I traced it to inside the White House."

Ian hisses through clenched teeth. "You're joking. Actually, you're not."

"Wish I was, but no. Then I remembered, Waterhouse handled our laptop during the White House briefing. He could've easily—"

"Breached our firewalls? Quite risky, under everybody's nose. Plus, he couldn't have known he'd get access to our laptop. Difficult to gamble on something like that."

"True, but if you were working for an international hacker group, wouldn't you be prepped for something like that? I mean, just in case? Mom always carries a fully-stocked medical kit in her car. Wouldn't a hacker be prepared for, well, a hacking opportunity?"

Ian guides us around a fallen tree trunk too massive to climb. "Okay, point taken. But Waterhouse as the mole... I'm not seeing it."

"Well, I didn't want to *jump to conclusions* either, but he gave himself away. He knew we came up empty-handed at the police locker—information only somebody involved would have. So I made an executive decision: neither he nor Lane, for that matter, got the full spiel of what Dimitri and I discovered." Gosh, it hurts saying his name. It *hurts*.

"What exactly did he say?"

"He said something along the lines of 'well, you didn't find anything in the locker', which we didn't."

I can practically hear Ian's mental gears grinding. "Not exactly smoking gun territory. You're connecting this to the unexpected guard at MU?"

"And his overall behavior."

Ian bounces on his toes to keep warm. "What did Dimitri say?"

A hot flush runs down my body. "Never got the chance to tell him." Because we were a little busy running from the Dark Unit.

Ian crosses his arms in front of his chest and rubs them. It's so cold, his breath comes out in little foggy puffs. "Waterhouse probably needled you because he enjoys being difficult. He's odd, but I never saw him as a mole or leak."

I pick up the pace, hoping for faster movement to combat the cold. "You're right about him being difficult. I call, he attacks me right away. Lane? He asks if we'd landed—"

The rest of the sentence dies in my throat. No, no, no—please no. Suddenly, my backpack weighs a ton, or maybe it's the crushing weight of my own stupidity. I double over, bracing against my knees. The backpack follows the siren call of gravity and knocks against my skull.

"Trouble!" Ian is by my side half a second later. "What's wrong?" He grabs me by the arm and tries to stand me up, but I can't yet.

Can't.

Need to wrap my mind around the fact that my emotions and prejudices got the best of me and overruled what Ian taught me: to listen and to use my brain.

"Trouble?" His grip on my arm steadies me, and boy, do I need it.

I meet his eyes—eyes I wanted to be filled with pride, not the disappointment I'm about to see. Guess I've got nobody to blame than myself for what's about to come. "It's not Waterhouse," I whisper. "Same theory, wrong suspect."

Ian cocks his head. "Meaning…?"

"Not Waterhouse, Ian. Brandon also handled the laptop in the Oval Office. He had *difficulties* with it, remember?" I use air quotes, because if I'm correct, those weren't difficulties. Or maybe they were, who knows how well the Dark Unit trained him, but he took that time to poke a hole into our firewall.

"I remember, but—"

I grasp his forearm. "When I called and wanted to speak to Dad, he asked if we had landed already. He couldn't have known that—unless they had access to the laptop. So, yes, the National Security Advisor is our leak."

He's why the Dark Unit was prepared for us.

He's why Dimitri is dead.

He's why WWIII looms on the horizon.

Ian grabs my hand, pulling me into step behind him. "You could be onto something. It fits. Clearance level high enough. Not been in the picture for too long. Knew about the mission to Little Springs, and yes, could've used the time with the laptop: Pull up a website the Dark Unit set up, drive-by infection with malware… Could have happened that way. But why would he— ugh, of course."

He stops and rolls his eyes. "Obvious. The abduction years ago. Either they turned him then, or they're still leveraging something. Maybe family. Yep, Lane is our guy." Another sigh escaped him. "We need to get the word out, Alix. We need to hurry up, make it to the facility on top of that mountain. If it's a military facility, they will have phones, internet, the whole shebang. Our first priority is warning— Trouble?"

Within a heartbeat, Ian is next to me, hands on my biceps, gliding his thumbs over my sweater. My eyes are open, but seeing nothing. Dimitri is gone, and Lane is about to murder Dad along with an unspeakable number of other people unless we can stop him. Each breath fights against an invisible weight crushing my chest that must be metaphorical, but feels very, very real. Maybe

Sam was right all along. I'm just a teenager playing spy. I can't do this.

Sam.

For the first time in days, I think of him—now that he's about to die in a nuclear blast on foreign soil. What does that say about me?

The universe's cruel joke: Sam might die because of me, proving my point I was never cut out for this.

Ian crouches to meet my gaze. "Trouble, we'll make it. The fight isn't over." He cups my face and draws it up.

I can't meet his eyes. I'm afraid he's going to see the tsunami threatening to drown me. My knees tremble as nausea floods my system, and all I want to do is rewind time and make it all undone, because right now I don't know if we can prevent the coming catastrophe.

It sure doesn't look that way right now.

A single tear escapes. Ian catches it mid-fall, swiping it away with his thumb.

Butterflies.

Thousands of completely inappropriate, annoying, stupid butterflies. I hate them. I hate them, because they feel so right, but their timing so completely inappropriate, it's ridiculous.

"Trouble?" Ian lets go of my face and steps back.

Ah, right. That, too.

All those cutesy, pretty butterflies die a fast and ugly death when I remember we won't lead anywhere, anyway. Ian didn't kiss me when he had the chance. No more interest. Moment's gone. Even if that wasn't the case, we're forbidden. Dead-end from the start.

Still, the temptation to give in and cry on Ian's shoulder is huge. I want to melt into him and let him hold me in a bubble where Dad's life and the world's fate don't rest on our shoulders. I want a moment of normal, where Dimitri is still around, and there isn't a gaping hole in my heart, missing him every second.

But I cannot surrender to that fantasy.

Ian is right, the fight is still on. We need to get going.

So I gather all my strength and guide Ian's hands off my face. "I'm okay. Just… a bit much over the last three days."

Ian gives me the look that says *really, that's it*, but drops it. "Okay. Then let's make this happen, Trouble."

He takes my hand and leads us toward the mountains. Our only hope.

Over the next hours the landscape transforms as we hike. Mini-forests give way to tundra-like bush. Two young brown bears play beside a lake to the left. Neither of us truly sees the breathtaking wilderness surrounding us.

In our minds, it's WWIII already.

Occasional sparks of joy flicker through me—*Ian is alive!*—but I suffocate them before they can bloom. It feels like betraying Dimitri's sacrifice to welcome any happiness about Ian.

It's messy.

So I pretend not to notice him holding my hand those first minutes. Or how my body gravitates toward his until we brush together. Or those freakin' butterflies taking flight at the slightest hint of his Ian-scent that's miraculously still there.

And every time I catch a glimpse of his battered face, I'm glad Dimitri took those bastards out. I hope he flipped them off before the end.

Once in a while, we check behind us, but nothing. Just

emptiness. Maybe fate threw us a bone and killed the guy who blew up our heli in the same explosion. Do I feel bad for wishing him dead? Maybe. But not enough to root for his survival.

The sun is high in the sky when Ian stops at a large rock formation. "Break time." His legs wobble as he settles onto a smaller rock, leaning against the dark boulder behind it, eyes falling shut.

I let the backpack slide down my arms and collapse beside him. "No complaints here." Both of us are exhausted. To my utter disappointment, the rocks are stone cold, literally. The sun doesn't pack enough power at this time of the year. Although it's high noon, it's still freezing cold.

After a couple of long breaths, Ian gestures toward the mountains. They seem a tiny bit closer to us compared to earlier. "Six hours to the base, I'd say. This here is our last break, because there's zero cover between here and there. Unlikely the Dark Unit's still trailing us, but assuming they aren't goes against training. They'd expect us to head up there." He nods toward the mountain.

Six more hours of hiking sounds brutal, but a nuclear strike on the Reichstag sounds worse, so yeah, hiking it is.

I rummage through the backpack. "Food." There isn't much since we didn't expect to be here for long, but at least there are rations. Emergency rations.

Ian's eyes light up. "Calories. I'd eat bark right now."

We nibble on the bars in silence and share the little water I have. No matter how long we stay, we will need refills for that. Maybe one of the streams, assuming it's bear-free.

Speaking of water, I dig through the backpack until I find what's left of the first-aid kit. "Let me see." There's not much I can do for his injuries, but that doesn't mean I shouldn't do it.

Who knows how long we're going to be stuck here. We need to be at our best.

I tear open an alcohol pad. "It's going to sting."

Ian's eyebrow arches. "Think I can handle it."

Right. Dark Unit torture survivor. "Never mind."

Carefully, I wipe away the dirt around his wound on his left eyebrow. Not too big. Healing. "No stitches needed." Why my voice is a whisper, I don't know.

I squeeze some antibiotic ointment out of the small packet, tracing the outline of his eyebrow to apply it.

Ian's gaze stays on me.

The. Entire. Time.

Keeping my face straight—keeping it from blushing, let's put it this way—is a challenge.

It's nearly impossible.

Especially when taking care of the cut on his lip.

His *lip*.

Guilt floods me as my gaze drops to his mouth. *Everything* about this feels forbidden: ghosting my finger over his lower lip to assess the wound, working in the antibiotic ointment. Imagining those lips—

I slam the breaks on that thought, but my heart's already racing at a speed about to give me a coronary, threatening to jump out of my chest and fist-bump Ian's, his pulse equally fast in the hollow of his neck.

The last time we were this close, Ian kissed me.

My nose. Fourth of July.

And then he and Dad erected a wall between us I can't overcome.

I straighten. "As good as new."

No point torturing myself.

Ian's gaze holds. "Thank you, Trouble."

I shake off that frustrating sensation of loss and pack everything back up. Not even five minutes later, we're moving again. We still have several hours of daylight we need to use before the night hits. Walking in an unknown terrain with moderately dangerous nightlife becomes too risky after dark. Shelter is a problem neither of us have mentioned, although I know Ian is worried about that too. After all, we share the same training.

The day drags, and we slow down considerably after a while. Ian limps, but he doesn't say anything. His makeshift shoes must be killing his feet.

Cold seeps into our bones. We're both more than exhausted.

We refill our water bottle at a stream, hoping it's amoeba-free.

Once or twice I think I hear something behind us, but see nothing when I check. Maybe the whole situation has me jumping at shadows. Time ticks away, and we're nowhere near the top of the mountain. Barely at the base.

Only a couple more hours, and not only Dimitri will have gotten killed, but also Dad and countless other people I don't know.

Ian stops. "Alix, look." He points skyward—at dark clouds hanging low and heavy. They writhe like living things, colors shifting from black to a stormy blue-grey.

"Rain." A storm. "Where to?" Our options are limited, but getting wet in these temperatures… best case: we slow to a crawl. Worst case: we die of hypothermia.

"Nothing here. Maybe the mountains will give us shelter." Ian leans forward and supports his weight on his knees.

Exhausted.

Me too.

But we don't have a choice—we haven't had a choice in a while now.

Silently we quicken our pace while keeping an eye out for shelter in trees, rock formations, anything. It's not like we have much energy left, but we push on. Ian's limp worsens, while I shuffle like an ancient crone, the backpack boring into my shoulders. Dimitri never intended for it to be carried for this long, no matter how light he thought he packed it.

The scenery changes again as we reach the foot of the mountain. Green yields to stone, and each step up the incline demands double the effort.

"Shelter. Soon." Ian pauses, gasping. "That rain is about to hit hard. Can't risk that climb in rain and darkness."

I agree with him. Night-climbing equals suicide, and we'll be even less helpful dead.

A flash splits the sky, thunder crashes, and the heavens unleash their fury.

I thought I knew rain from D.C., but this—this is biblical. Within seconds, we're soaked to the bone. Breathing becomes a challenge, because no matter how I turn my head, the air seems to be more H2O than O2. Water is everywhere. We're both gasping for air. One or two degrees colder and it would be coming down as snow. Sounds worse, but would be the better alternative: This way we're screwed. Wet and screwed.

Shelter.

We need something. *Anything!*

My muscles spasm uncontrollably, though I've lost all sensation. I'm numb from the wetness and cold, frozen to the bone.

The rain strikes like needles, hard and merciless as the wind whips it in our faces. Darkness envelops us, broken only by lightning's harsh illumination every few seconds.

The temperature hovers just above freezing, but not by much, and it doesn't matter. Between the water and the wind, hypothermia will kick in shortly.

Our chances for survival just plummeted.

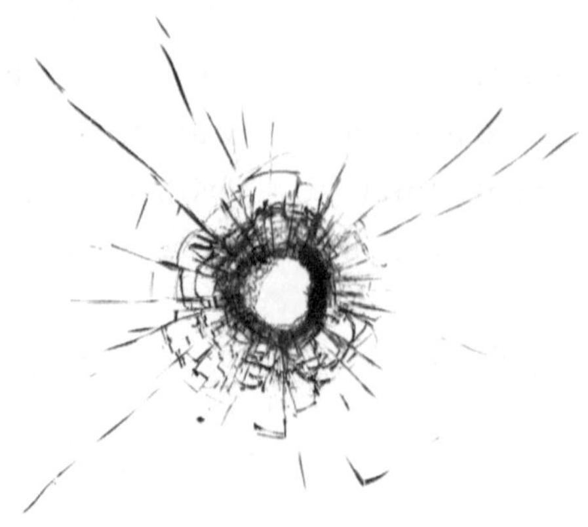

CHAPTER TWENTY-FIVE
Warming Up

With a loud roar the storm picks it up a notch.

Thunder.

Lightning.

Winds.

A violent gust slams into my chest and knocks me off my feet, like a schoolyard bully.

"Ian!" His name tears from my throat as gravity takes over and I tumble down the uneven slope, gravel worming under my layered sweaters, carving paths across my back. Nothing to grab, nothing to stop me—until my shoulder crashes into a rock, ripping a scream from me. But at least it stops my uncontrolled descent.

My head spins and my body hurts from head to toe—the parts that I'm still feeling, that is.

I groan and push myself up onto all fours.

Nothing broken.

Lightning shoots down from the sky, illuminating the rock formation in front of me. Wait, what—a cave!

"Ian!" I yell. "Over here, over here!"

I didn't need to bother. He's already coming, bent double against the wind.

He grabs me by the shoulders to help me up. "Are you okay?" he shouts over the storm. "That looked bad, Trouble!"

I shake my head and point to the gap—the gap that might save us tonight. "I'm fine. Look, a cave, if we're lucky," I shout back over the pounding rain. If the skies were angry at us, that's what they would sound like.

We're at the gap in less than a minute, pounding rain or not. Ian tries first—and lo and behold, he makes it inside. He sticks out his arm. "Backpack," he yells.

I pass it through, then squeeze through the tight opening into a blissfully dry little cave. Even the noise dampens to tolerable levels.

For a moment, we both stand rooted to the spot, panting, dripping water onto the ground, our teeth clattering. Every lightning bolt shooting through the darkness illuminates the inside of our cave.

It's tiny.

Whatever I thought a cave would look like, this isn't it.

Ian apparently came to the same conclusion. "Not big, but it'll do."

Not big is generous, really. It's claustrophobic. We can half-stand, barely fit shoulder to shoulder, and it's maybe three meters deep, but I don't mind that part. It means nothing is going to come up from behind to eat us Lord-of-the-Rings-style.

The best news is that the ground is relatively flat, scattered with dirt and leaves from previous tenants, but luckily, no rotten or half-eaten prey. Also, no current resident. Thank whomever for small favors.

Ian surveys our shelter between labored breaths. "That works for now. What's in the backpack we can use?"

I wipe the wet hair out of my face, fumbling for the zipper with my cold and numb fingers.

There.

I brush against something soft and fluffy—the vacuum-packed sleeping bag.

Ian's relief shows in the next lightning flash.

I don't feel the same.

Yes, it means warmth.

Dryness

But one bag

Two people.

Basic math tells me what's coming. My face blazes hot enough to lighten the cave. Ian and I are going to share a sleep sack.

Ian peels off his rain-plastered jacket. It clings to him like a second skin now that it's wet. "Okay. perfect spot for the sleeping bag right here, in the middle of the cave." He bends down and tests the ground. "No hard rocks, nicely cushioned. We've got to strip. Wet clothes will keep stealing body heat. Few hours of sleep, then—" He shudders. "—then back into the wet clothes, hope the storm is over, and hike on. And hope that we make it to the top to call for help before hypothermia wins."

Or before Berlin becomes ground zero.

Ian takes the sleep sack from me, frees it from its bag and spreads it out.

Me, I'm still processing.

This is happening.

Like, now.

The way he says it, so matter of factly, it makes perfect sense. But then… we're going to share a sleeping bag. Not wearing much.

Logically, it's sound. I'm so cold I can hardly move—besides my jaws, they're clattering up a storm. I'm not even hungry or thirsty or anything, I'm only cold. Cold and tired. So yes, warming up is our priority, but it's also a big, big deal.

To me.

Not him, clearly.

Another flash of lightning.

Ian's makeshift shoes are gone, so are his jeans.

Another flash.

Ian in black boxer briefs, the short illumination enough to show the extent of his bruising, but also to highlight his abs and chest muscles.

Cardiac arrest imminent.

I swallow dry, which is ironic, since everything's so wet.

Ian in underwear and one sleep sack, that's… that's…

Torture.

A new variety, but still torture.

Ian brushes past me, jacket in his hand. "Come on, Trouble, get those wet clothes off." He drapes the jacket across the entrance, like a curtain. One short moment of hesitation as he looks outside left to right, scanning the area before he shrugs and tugs the jacket around the gap as much as possible, using smaller stones and rocks to keep it in place.

The next bolt of lightning brings a softer light to the cave, but still enough to see Ian tip-toe to the sleep sack, arms wrapped around his chest and hands rubbing up and down his upper arms.

Somehow, I'm dizzy.

Thunder crashes through the night, and I jump.

Warming up. Right.

I'm pathetic. I can either make this a problem and freeze, or… Or I can pretend I'm a big girl and cool with this.

Okay then.

The sweaters peel off reluctantly, clinging like a second skin.

Boots—gone.

Socks, too.

Dang, it's even worse this way. It might be dry, but the ground is sucking the heat out of me in a heartbeat. I step on the part that's covered in dirt and leaves. Much better than the rocky, frozen surface near the entrance.

My fingers hover over the button of my jeans.

Deep breath.

One more, for good measure.

Pop.

The button's open.

Another flash of lightning throws light into our cave. I don't look at Ian, because if he is looking at me… I don't know if I could take off my pants.

One slide and push later and the pants are gone.

All that's left are panties and a bra—and they will stay. Period. With Sam, I didn't even get to this point, and we were together for months.

Rustling from the ground, teeth clattering. "This way, Trouble."

And dang it, I hesitate again.

Ugh.

It's no big deal.

Hypothermia is.

Keeping each other warm isn't.

And I could've shared a sleeping bag with Dimitri without any second thoughts. It's different with him.

Was different with him.

I swallow hard.

Priorities, Alix.

I tiptoe over to the sleep sack and Ian, feeling my way so I won't step on him.

He shifts. "Here." More rustling, and from what I can see, he holds the opening up for me to slide in.

In a rare display of grace, I slide in feet first, my back brushing against Ian's chest. As soon as I'm in, he seals the fabric tight around us, maximizing heat retention.

I'm sharing a sleeping bag with Ian.

My back and his front are connected in more places than I can count, and—

I clamp my eyes shut so tight it hurts.

And I feel every breath of his.

Every heartbeat.

Ian, like any good boy would, tucks his hands against his chest instead of draping them over me.

Because this is about warmth, nothing else.

His breath cascades down my neck, scorching my frozen skin. Goosebumps erupt everywhere, the kind that make me want to scream, the ones that go down all the way to my toes and through my stomach. Every time he shivers, the friction against my back is heaven and hell at the same time. I have to work to suppress the urge to push deeper into him to touch him with more of my body.

One minute, and nobody has said a word.

Two minutes.

Three.

Ian moves his legs, his icy feet brushing my calves, and I squeak. "Eek! Cold!"

Ian chuckles.

And somehow, this small sound—this small, light sound—it breaks me.

It unlocks everything I've banned from conscious thought and more. As if my mind had waited for me to be at my most vulnerable, it floods me with emotions and images, and it's not all about the impending doom of nuclear destruction. No, it starts much closer to home: Ian, abducted, his tortured screams in my earpiece. Dimitri, his panic for me, then our bonding. The fear of losing Ian. The agony of losing Dimitri. The guilt that I—we—survived, and he didn't.

The *guilt*.

My shoulders shake. I fight it, but it's a losing battle. Not even holding my breath works. My shoulders tremble anyway as tears escape past squeezed-shut eyelids and burn down my cheeks.

And alas, this bag is too small to hide anything.

Of course, Ian notices. He slides his hand up onto my trembling shoulder, then brushes his thumb in circles across my skin, hesitant at first, then soothing.

And boy, it breaks me open.

I should be stronger. I should be a teen-hero and power through, no matter the pain, the pressure, the *loss*—but I'm not. And even if I was, darn the movies, that stuff is unrealistic, because *this*, it hurts! *Everything* about it.

I cry into my hands, my body rubbing against Ian's. Can't exactly say that's calming me down. Teen-hero girl would turn around, and cry into his shoulder, no matter the lack of clothing. Clearly that's not me. I wish I had that kind of courage.

But I don't.

So I cry into my palms until Ian tugs on my shoulder.

"Come on. Turn around, Trouble," he whispers.

Turn around…!

Thunder crashes, lightning flares. Even the rain seems to crank it up.

"Come on…" He tugs on me one more time.

Maybe I'm not teen-hero girl, but I'm the girl who listens to what Ian says. Gathering all my courage, I make an awkward turn in the sleep sack and roll to face Ian.

He slides his hand from my shoulder to my cheek, tucking a strand of hair behind my ear. For a moment, his hand lingers, and it's heaven.

His deep, endless sigh cuts through the clashing thunder, over the pouring rain, over the pounding of my heart—and then he cradles the back of my head and draws me gently into his chest. His chin comes to rest on top of my head as he weaves his fingers through my hair.

I'm not cold anymore.

In fact, I'm burning.

While yes, I keep my hands in front of my chest, because hugging Ian like this would be way out of my league, I can't focus on anything else but how my cheek is pressed against his bare chest.

I can hear his heartbeat.

Du-dun, du-dun, du-dun, du-dun—faster than normal.

I breathe him in, and the butterflies soar. After everything he's been through, despite the literal beating he took, he still smells like Ian—like home.

"Trouble?" His throat vibrates against my head.

"Mh?"

"None of this is your fault." He massages some more. "Not Lane, not Dimitri. Especially not Dimitri. He knew the risks of this mission. If anybody's to blame, it's me for missing the patterns I should've seen. For modifying Torpedo." Bitterness edges his words.

I ball my hands into fists to keep them where they are. "Not your fault either," I whisper against his chest. "They drugged you, Ian. They beat you."

"Still doesn't change it was me who enabled Torpedo to release a nuclear weapon from our satellite."

Silence stretches.

Ian's chest rises sharply. "Dimitri … I've known him since I joined the Agency. We survived another mission that went horribly wrong, nearly as much as this. He nearly died then, and I know that while he obviously preferred to live, giving his life to protect his team is the way he'd choose to go." Another deep breath. "Doesn't mean I won't miss him like crazy."

I sniffle. "Me, too." And off to the truth… "I missed you too." Like crazy.

I pull back a little bit from his chest. Too intimate. Too close. Too tempting.

Ian's hand slips from my hair as he folds them between us, mirroring mine.

Another lightning flash. A small smile plays around his lips, and the way he looks at me, it turns the Alaskan chill into a sauna.

He takes my hands into his. "I missed you too. I was torn between hoping you'd come, and hoping you'd stay home where it's safe." He softly kneads my hands to warm them, the occasional knuckle brushing over my chest or bra.

I have a hard time focusing on anything else.

"You're still wearing Sneaker." He taps my ring.

Of course. My last connection to Ian. Removing it would mean giving up hope.

I bite my lower lip and shrug. "Oh, yeah. Difficult to get off, and I kind of got used to it."

Thunder crashes, and this one has me jump inside the sleeping bag.

Ian chuckles again. "We should sleep. Today was brutal, and tomorrow is going to be worse."

A shiver runs through me. Much worse, because our countdown is ticking on. I don't even want to think about that. He's right. We need strength to beat the clock. "Good night, Ian."

"Good night, Trouble," Ian says.

A moment later, his eyes are closed, and soon, his breathing turns more regular: Asleep.

Not me though.

Never me.

And how could I?

Ian still holds my hands, and this small contact is all it takes to keep me awake.

I'm pathetic, I know. Just like in his bedroom, where we had the perfect opportunity, nothing happened.

We're trapped in a freakin' sleeping bag together, basically naked—and nothing happens besides what friends would do, consoling each other with some innocent hand holding.

Lightning flashes, taunting me with a perfect snapshot of Ian. His usually messy hair even messier now, but somehow still perfect. Stubble from not shaving for three days gives him a rugged look. His new wounds, the split lip and cut above his eyebrow stir something deep inside.

I look down at his hands holding mine, and while it's too dark to see anything inside the sleeping bag, I know what his fingers look like: Long, elegant, and thin. Perfect for working a keyboard, but still surprisingly strong. Strong enough to give

Dimitri a shiner a week ago.

That thought makes me crack a weak smile. We were quite the team, the three of us. Whatever Ian and I will become now, it's going to be different. Someone will replace Dimitri, but nothing will be the same. This mission has changed us, tough to say in which way exactly.

The only thing that hasn't changed is the way I feel about Ian, the way I've felt for him for a while now, the way I never stopped feeling about him.

Hindsight is twenty-twenty, that much is clear.

I should take the hint and let it go. This stupid crush won't lead anywhere, I'm only setting myself up for humiliation.

But then… he's so close: His warmth, his breathing, his Ian-scent… I don't *want* to let go of my feelings for him. It's like a life vest keeping me afloat. A drug I can't get enough of. An addiction keeping me hooked no matter what Dad said, no matter what Waterhouse ordered. Pretending those feelings are gone means lying to everybody, most of all myself.

Yeah, hindsight is twenty-twenty.

So is introspection.

Even now, with him asleep and no connection besides the brotherly hand-holding, my body craves him in an unforgivable way.

And, well, because the darkness acts as a cover and Ian is sleeping, and because I will never get a chance like this again—or the nerve—now that he's asleep, I grant myself one little wish. Gathering all my courage I lean forward and brush my lips over the tip of his nose in the tiniest, most feather-like kiss possible.

Ian's eyes snap open like a switch was flipped.

Oh, *shoot.*

He wasn't asleep.

Crap, crap, *crap.*

I squeeze my eyes shut as embarrassment floods me like a tsunami. If I could, I'd run away from what I did, run from the feelings I put so openly on display because I thought it was safe.

Bullshit.

Ian withdraws his hands from mine, creating distance between us.

What have I done?

More thunder crashes, loud and scary, and I wish it would swallow me whole.

The next second both of Ian's hands cradle my face, burning through my skin. "Trouble?"

What—

He traces my cheekbones. "Trouble?"

My heart stumbles and regains its footing, but only barely so.

Another brush of his thumbs over my skin shoots electricity into every cell of my body, and my eyes fly open. I all but fall right into Ian's green gaze, so close, our noses separated by mere millimeters. His eyes hold a question, but also a spark I haven't seen in months.

"Ian?" My whisper barely exists. I turned into goo the moment his hands cupped my face.

The continuous caress of his thumbs is driving me insane. So gentle, so soft—so close. So, so *close.*

His gaze drops to my mouth. A muscle in his jaw twitches, he swallows hard—

"Screw it," he whispers—and closes the distance.

Moving with infinite slowness, giving me every chance to retreat, Ian touches his lips to mine.

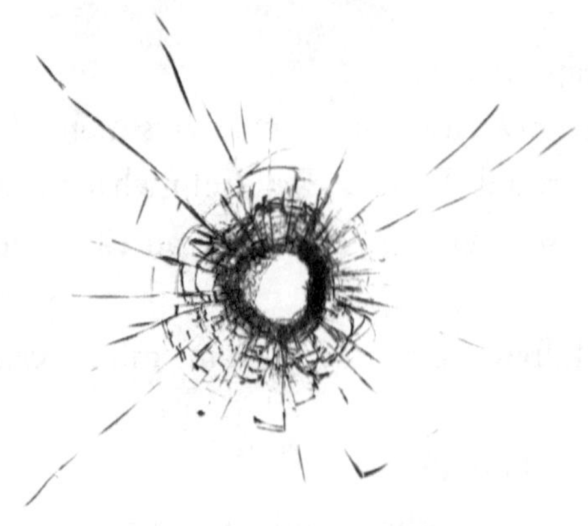

CHAPTER TWENTY-SIX

Crossed the Line

The instant our lips connect, something explodes inside me.

These aren't butterflies dancing. This is a wildfire raging, consuming everything from the start.

My whole body contracts in a spasm.

Ian.

Ian is kissing me.

His goatee tickles my lips, and I'm floating.

The universe shrinks to just us. Nothing exists beyond his touch, igniting every square inch of my skin, burning me where his body meets mine.

Ian.

I throw my arms around him—finally, finally!— like I wanted to do for so long and bury my fingers in his hair. A soft moan escapes him, and it tells me all I need to know.

He wants me.

And boy, do I want him.

I press closer, as close as I can without breaking the kiss. I need to feel him, to touch him, to be touched by him. Like the bottle had been opened and the genie escaped, there's no containing this.

Each touch, each kiss makes me crave more.

His breathing goes ragged as I gently nip his lower lip. It only takes a second and his tongue meets mine. My insides are on fire. How I could be cold less than thirty minutes ago I don't know, because this is pure and all-consuming heat and inferno.

There are no words.

One of his hands leaves my face and wraps around my waist, fingers digging into my skin, pulling me closer.

We align perfectly—chest to chest, stomach to stomach, legs to legs… so close, it's obvious he likes what we're doing.

So. Do. I.

I glide my hand over his spine, caressing and memorizing every muscle I touch on my way down. He shivers, another moan escaping.

I might combust spontaneously. Wouldn't be surprised.

Ian's feather-light touch down my back shoots pain and craving down my body.

I reach the small of his back and hesitate. The next step seems big—

Ian takes it easily: He trails his nails down my lower spine and across my left butt cheek—over the panties he bought for me in another lifetime.

Fire races through my veins, pooling low inside my core. Flames of desire lap at me in places I didn't know existed.

Ian's scent surrounds me, engulfs me, and makes me light-headed.

Ian's touch brings me to life.

Ian's taste.

Everything Ian.

It's too much and yet not enough.

"Trouble." It's a faint whisper against my mouth, one that comes with a surge of heat to all the interesting body parts. Bold beyond recognition, I wrap my upper leg over his hip and thigh, drawing us impossibly close. *Tight.*

We're connected everywhere. My softest spots and his hardest.

A deep moan leaves Ian's throat.

He rocks forward, meeting me where I burn for him. Where I want him. Where I need him. Two of his fingers slip under the hem of my panties, and I might pass out. Every touch is dragging an electric current over my body, leaving sparks.

Exquisite, agonizing sparks.

I press closer, feeling him respond. His body is firm and muscular where mine isn't, yet somehow we fit together perfectly. Sweat builds between us, skin sliding on skin.

Each kiss, each stroke of tongue comes with a roll of my hips against his. He shudders and flattens his palm onto my butt, stretching his fingers as if it took him all the restraint he had to keep his hand still.

With a small groan, he breaks the kiss, resting his forehead against mine.

Panting.

Hot breath mingling.

"Trouble?"

"Mh-hm?"

"We need to stop, or… I can't promise to behave."

Oh.

I think I know what that means.

For a moment, only our heavy breathing disturbs the silence. Even the thunder and lightning has quieted.

A kiss to my forehead. "But I'm bookmarking exactly this position. When we're back home… we'll pick up right here." I hear the smile as much as I feel it against my skin, and it lights me up. Not in the all-consuming heat of the last minutes, but in the steady warmth of something that has the chance to last.

"Sounds good," I whisper, trailing my hand up from his butt to his chest. His heart still thunders a wild rhythm in there. Like mine.

He gently pushes my leg off of his hip. "This too, or I can't make any promises." Ian chuckles and ever so softly kisses the corner of my mouth.

Time stretches as our heart beats slow and our breathing steadies.

Not cold anymore.

So far from cold.

"Trouble?" he murmurs after a while.

"Mh-hm?" I burrow into his chest.

He hesitates. "Don't take this wrong, but… we need to talk about this. About us." His throat works. "There are only two options, and… I'll understand whichever you choose."

My eyes pop open. "That sounds ominous."

Another kiss to my forehead. "It's complicated. We're complicated. Option one—and like I said, this is your choice. No judgement. I…" He releases a sigh so deep it makes my stomach clench. "Option one. Tonight was it. We call it a temporary lapse in sanity, keep it to ourselves, and when we're back home, everything's back to normal. Option—"

"Oh, hell no!" Proves intuition is not to be underestimated—

option one sucks. Majorly. "Not happening, Ian, forget about it!" I refuse to reduce this—us—into a dirty, forbidden one-night mistake. Nope.

Lightning reveals his wide smile. "Okay. Okay. Can't say I liked that option either, but… Option two is tough, Trouble. Really tough. The world's against us—"

"No, just Dad and Waterhouse—"

"And your father is not my biggest fan, because I'm your teacher—"

Dead wrong. "Which you are not, you're my superior officer—"

"Which I'm not. You graduated. Colleagues."

Silence.

Holy cow.

I graduated. I *graduated.* I don't know what to say, I'm stuck on this simple, but life-changing statement. Why didn't I think of it before? *Flabbergasted.* "You're not my superior anymore. I graduated." Dad's whole position-of-authority-legal problem: gone. Congrats to me—to us.

His lips twitch. "True that. One problem down." Another kiss for the tip of my nose. "About twenty more to go."

"Nu-uh. Maybe one, and I don't care about the age gap." Those couple of years, whatever.

Ian blows out a puff of air. "Well, let's ask your father. I'm sure he cares." He pulls me closer. "You're still underage."

I huff against his chest. Who cares? Seventeen and twenty-one. Soon eighteen and eventually twenty-two. Then nineteen and twenty-three. Then, meaningless. "Two months until I'm eighteen. Then we're legal—"

"We were always legal, except for the teacher-student thing. DC's age of consent is sixteen."

Right, though dating your student *is* illegal.

I shoot a mischievous grin up to him. "What about Alaska?"

Ian chuckles. "Sixteen. Still, won't matter to your father. He—"

"Don't underestimate him. We've come a long way. Plus, once I'm eighteen, it's not like he could order me around anymore." Not that he won't try, but still. I force in a deep, calming breath. "His problem was you being my teacher, which you're not. Dad wants me to be happy. He's going to be fine, Ian." And even if he wasn't, being with Ian feels *right*, consequences be damned.

He massages my scalp, messing through my hair. "I hope so," he whispers. "Because… I've been waiting for you a long time."

Whoa. I pull back, looking up at him. "You have?" And I was so sure—

He plays with my hair. "Since we met. Maybe even before, when I started working on your file." He kisses the tip of my nose.

A small, light laugh bubbles up. *Since we met.* "So, you don't think I'm your little sist—"

Oh.

Oh.

I roll my eyes so hard, it's a wonder they don't get stuck in the back of my skull. "You don't have a sister." For how long did Ian's assurance to Waterhouse bug me? *Alix reminds me of my little sister, sir.* It ripped the ground from under my feet and had me free-falling for far too long. And when I met his parents and saw their home—not a single picture of anybody other than them and Ian.

Did it register?

Nope. Because it wasn't important.

Shows how preoccupied I was, how single-focused on freeing

Ian.

His brows pull together. "A sister? No. Why do you— Oh. Waterhouse." He grimaces. "I was trying to save what could be saved. Waterhouse never remembers anybody's personal lives, he just doesn't care enough. If he'd removed me from your training… I don't know how I'd have handled it."

So much swings in his words, so much. Months of longing, of denial. Of feelings—for me.

I let go of a long breath. "If he'd removed you, I would have quit." On the spot.

"No matter I saw you as *my sister?*" He gives my hair a teasing tug.

I chuckle. "No. I was in way too deep already. Better to have you as my big brother, than not at all."

He peeks up at me from under his lashes. "Believe me, none of my feelings for you were—are—brotherly. I think I made that clear on Fourth of July. I told you, in another life…"

Yeah. In another life Fourth of July would've ended differently.

And everything after as well.

I swallow hard. "I've been an ass." Really have. "To Sam. To you. I wasn't strong enough to go against the grain, and I convinced myself I wanted Sam, because I *always* wanted Sam. And you, you were—"

"Shh." He twirls my hair around his finger. "No explanation needed, Trouble. We wouldn't have worked out four months ago. Everything's different now. Things have changed since then. Your father knows about PRICS now. We're equals, not teacher and student anymore. We—"

"Why didn't you ask me to wait?" I blink into the near-complete darkness. "You could've asked me to wait for you until graduation. I would've." And I would've clung to that beacon of hope like a lifeline.

"It wouldn't have been fair to ask that of you. Not with everything that had been going on, not with Sam being so perfect for you. Your first kiss. Your age. Clearly in love with you. As painful as it was, seeing you happy was more important than seeing you with me." A faint roll of thunder underscores the sadness seeping through his words.

I snuggle closer, pressing a soft kiss to his chest. Maybe those four years matter more than I thought. Ian kept his head on straight, while I was—still am—the hormone-driven teenager. "I'm sorry, Ian." Words Sam needs to hear, too.

"Don't be. Nobody said love was simple."

Love.

Whoa.

I pull myself closer. If I could, I'd crawl into him. *Love.* His scent is everywhere, his skin soft, warm—hot—and his heart beating a cha-cha-rhythm next to my ear.

Mine matches its rhythm.

Love.

I sneak a hand over his side onto his back and squeeze until I can't tell where my body ends and his starts. "Don't let go," I whisper. "Don't let go."

Ian curls his body around mine. "I won't, Trouble. Never."

Good.

We stay tangled together until sleep claims us, and even then we don't move apart. We never let go.

And despite today's horror and tomorrow's looming threat, I sleep more peacefully than I have in months.

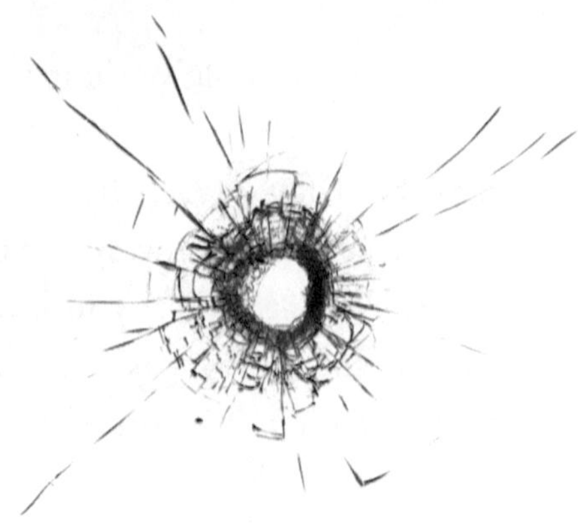

CHAPTER TWENTY-SEVEN
Highest High, Lowest Low

I wake up in Ian's arms.

My fingers are spread out on his chest, his heart beating against my palm from below, steady and strong. A very calming beat.

This must be heaven.

Then: *Dimitri. The Dark Unit. Dad's speech.*

The next breath catches. No, not heaven—a time-out from hell.

Ian stirs and stretches. He weaves his finger in-between mine, resting both of our hands on his chest.

"Good morning, Trouble." His lips brush my forehead.

A wave of warmth flutters through me. Last night *was real.* We *are real.* "Good morning, Ian." I *so* need a nickname for him.

As he turns to face me, the same mischievous glint from last night dances in his eyes. He cups my cheek, fingers grazing through my hair behind my ear, and as slowly as yesterday he brings his lips to mine.

Savoring me.

His goatee and stubble rasp against my skin, adding delicious friction to the softness of his kiss.

It takes less than a second and I'm lost in his touch, lost in Ian.

Unfortunately, it doesn't take long before he pulls back and leans his forehead against mine. "I could stay here forever, but…"

I kiss his nose. "I know." Our time-out is over. On the other side of Ian's improvised jacket-curtain, birdsong announces approaching dawn, and soon it'll be safe to hike on—wet clothes and all.

Heavy silence hovers for a moment.

"We have to reach the top and warn them, Ian."

We must. We must warn them, we—

"We will. We will make it in time, and Waterhouse will have his best men on it. Torpedo doesn't stand a chance."

Silence speaks volumes.

Neither of us says what both of us are thinking. Waterhouse's best man is currently lying in a cave in the arms of his Commander-in-Chief's daughter. And Torpedo has outsmarted Waterhouse's entire team so far, why would now be different?

Ian draws me into his chest for an eternal moment before he zips the sleeping bag open.

Cold.

Damn, it's cold!

Goosebumps break out all over my body as the freezing air bites every exposed square inch of skin like a hungry beast out for a snack.

I was right when I woke up. A time-out from hell, now expired.

Obviously.

Forcing on wet, dirty, almost frozen clothes is hell.

Re-wrapping Ian's feet in what's left of the bandages is hell.

Taking off into the near-darkness with the world's fate on our shoulders is hell.

For the first couple of minutes, we climb cautiously. It's still mostly dark and doesn't quite qualify as dawn yet, but as light creeps in, we speed up.

The moment the sun breaks through over the horizon is pure salvation. The temperature rises no more than a couple of degrees, but it makes all the difference. We're lucky it's above freezing—barely—or we'd be even worse off.

Worse. Har-har. Good one. Wet clothing in almost-freezing temperatures is the fastest way to hypothermia.

Out of breath, I pause to rub my hands together, blowing onto them. My breath comes out in white puffs. I stomp my feet to warm them up, gaze trailing down the part of the mountain we've already hiked. Pretty spectacular view, especially with the sun bathing everything into orange-red light, the tundra—

Wait.

I squint.

Is that…?

A blue-red dot, moving in our direction?

"Ian. Ian, look—over there." I point downslope. So much for fate watching out for us and killing him in the explosion. Kind of disappointing, actually.

Ian halts and turns.

And swears. "Damn it! Crap!" He punches the air. "Move, Trouble, faster! We've got to speed it up." He grabs the sleeve of my sweater and tugs. "So much for a clean get-away. He's one of the Russian guys from the cabin. I recognize the awful jacket.

Sergey something."

Sergey? Now I know why he looked familiar at the helicopter. "Mostoroff," I rasp between two labored breaths.

"Huh?"

"Sergey Mostoroff. He's the one who broke into your parents' house and stole your hard drive." Not that knowing his name makes a difference.

Ian throws another look back. "I thought I saw something last night. A flash below. Could've been him, could've been gunfire. Better to assume he's armed and keep our distance."

"How long?" I ask, scrambling to match his pace.

"How long until he gets to us?" Another backward glance. "Thirty minutes max if we stopped moving. Depends on his condition. Right now we're not exactly at peak performance either." Between wet clothes and bone-deep exhaustion.

Thirty minutes.

Thirty minutes that we must keep between him and us, or else.

Even if he doesn't have a gun, I don't want a fistfight. Going out on a limb, I'd say a weak and injured Ian plus a newbie to Krav Maga won't stand a chance against a determined terrorist, no matter if he's a desk-jockey or not.

So we hike. We climb.

After ten minutes, both of us shiver and shake, despite the strenuous workout of our ascent.

After ten more minutes, my fingers lose sensation.

After another five, when I dare to look back, Mostoroff is still there, and worse. "I think he's gaining."

Ian pauses briefly. "Crap. Yes, you're right." He resumes climbing. The slope's transformed from hike-able to near-vertical. Once or twice, we have to use our hands to help us up, but thankfully it's not sheer rock face.

I'm not good at rock walls.

"Once we're up, we'll break in however necessary. First priority is calling Waterhouse." Ian sounds hoarse. Wheezy.

And then we'd only have one problem at hand—Mostoroff—instead of two, Mostoroff and a nuclear missile.

We speed it up.

The top of the mountain is at least another hour.

At least.

And I don't need exact data on our relative speeds to do the math: It's going to be a close call.

Dad's speech is at 4:00 p.m. local time, which means it's at 7:00 a.m. Alaskan time. It's not even 5:00 a.m. now, so theoretically we should be good.

Theoretically.

That's assuming we do get into that building, we do get word out, and somebody does have the skills to hack Torpedo.

Plan B, evacuating Berlin…

Yeah. Too late already.

I bite my cheek and push harder, almost slipping on loose gravel.

Ten minutes later, we have to stop and catch our breaths.

"Damn exhaustion," Ian wheezes. But there's nothing we can do, besides power through.

And on we climb.

The wind is so strong at this point, it cuts through my two sweaters like they're tissue. Ice crusts Ian's jacket, probably mine, too—if I had the energy to look.

Another hundred meters have passed.

Can't go much faster.

My jeans fight me with every move, crackling as if they'd

shatter when I bend my knees. The last time I felt my feet was down in the sleeping bag, but I'm sure it must be worse for Ian in his makeshift shoes.

Another hundred meters.

Every step drags, every movement is so agonizingly slow.

Ian shakes his head. "The Russian is closing in on us. If he's using the same gun he had down at the cabin, it has a reach of a maximum of a hundred meters. With this wind and assuming he didn't have any sniper training, he'll need to be much closer to hit us."

That's reassuring—until the implication hits. "You're assuming he *is* going to catch up with us, aren't you?" Why else calculate weapon's range?

Ian climbs on, movements sluggish and slow. "I can't promise you he won't," he mutters.

An icy knot of fear takes hold of my heart. We have to be faster.

But that's easier said than done. The terrain fights us every step along the way. This is not a hike anymore, it's a climb. My fingers bleed from countless rock cuts.

We are slow.

So. Damn. Slow.

Our level of exhaustion is climbing to new nights, no pun intended.

Another stop.

Another minute wasted gulping air, waiting for oxygen to reach screaming muscles.

Ian's breath turns ragged, wheezy, and mine isn't much better.

The summit's close, but we're not doing well on time. Definitely behind schedule. And what if we can't break in fast enough? Or if there's no way to call for help.

Can't go there. Can't let the fear of failure paralyze me.

I scan below. No Russian guy.

The icy knot inside my heart melts a little. Would it be wrong to hope he fell and broke his neck?

As if Karma heard me, my foot slips.

I yelp out, and only my death-grip on the ledge saves me from a fall.

"Trouble!" Ian whirls around.

"I'm fine!" I pull up, finding footing. "Go." Even this one word comes out slurred. My body and lips move like molasses. Sluggish. So sluggish.

I'd laugh if I could. A year ago, I wouldn't have made it through fifty meters of this. Not with my wheelchair, my immobile leg, the splint, and the crutches. I've come this far, literally and figuratively, because Ian fixed me.

I need to keep going.

Failure is not an option, and neither is giving up.

Ten minutes more.

Heavy breaths, slow movements, wide eyes.

The cold barely registers now. Can't feel anything. I don't feel my body either. I have to watch my feet to place them where I want them. There is absolutely no feedback from any of my body parts as to what they're doing at any given moment. I can't *tell* if my hand is holding on to something, I have to *look*.

Ian doesn't fare much better. His eyes are glassy, he gasps for air and he's shaking so badly from the cold, he looks like he is having a seizure.

The moment we reach the top of the mountain is pure ecstasy.

We did it.

The climb is over.

We did it.

And no sign of Mostoroff.

Thank you, Fate.

I glance at my watch. Crap. I take it back, no thanks to Fate. "Ian," I croak. "We've only got fifteen minutes." Fifteen minutes until doomsday. We were too slow. Too weak.

Ian's face loses all color, but still, he schleps himself forward, bent over like an old man, arms wrapped around his chest. "Then we've got to make this the fastest break and entry into a military facility ever. We can still warn them."

The unspoken truth hangs between us: until we get connected to somebody at the White House who can deal with this, and until they get their A-team together to fight off Torpedo's attack on MU…

Meaning, we can warn them, but there's no guarantee Waterhouse's men will be able to stop Torpedo within this short time.

We might already be too late.

Fifteen minutes.

"Come on, Trouble. Faster," Ian rasps. He takes me by the sleeve and tugs me after him toward the small building another hundred meters away on the middle of the plateau. But hey—at least it's a distance bridged horizontally, not vertically.

I force my frozen limbs into some cruel resemblance of a jog. *Zombie-jog.* "Not what I imagined," I croak. Grey exterior. Not big. Square. Couple of windows with blinds or curtains closed, no door, so we're probably at the side or back of this thing.

Ian picks up a rock the size of a baby's head, and maybe it's my imagination, but it feels like his speed slows down with the added weight. We're running on empty.

"Outpost. Basic emergency supplies for cold weather

training. Get them equipped and out the door again."

Supplies sound promising.

Ian readies the rock. "Once we're in, priority is a phone line. Second priority is a weapon and keeping Mostoroff away."

"Got it." I double over, hands on my knees. My heart's racing at twice the regular speed, maybe more. Exhaustion plus altitude. Not my forte. Add apocalyptic pressure…

With one big throw, Ian sends the rock flying. Never have I thought the sound of a shattering window could be this satisfying. He clears the remaining shards with a stick. "Ok. Safe to climb in. Come on."

He waves me over and helps me through. I hit the ground and tumble forward, too numb to compensate for shifts in balance. Ian follows stat.

"Time?" His voice comes out as a distorted wheeze as he rushes past me into the room.

"Twelve minutes." It has to be enough, it has to be enough, it has to—

"Find weapons, Trouble!" Ian limps straight to the desk by the larger windows on the left. Desk means phone. Question is, what can I use? Only one room, and not much bigger than Ian's office in the Lair, but looks more like a small gymnasium. Not the sturdiest building. Linoleum floors, white walls and ceiling, cold neon lights high up. Right side is nothing but lockers, cabinets, and other means of storage. Farther in the back—well, actually, the front, since it's close to the door—it looks like a medical cart and gurney against a window, and that's about it.

But it could be empty as long as it features a phone, and I'd still love it. No wind. Mercifully warmer. A *phone*.

I stagger toward the first cabinets. Locked. Labeled *cleaning supplies*. Ugh. On to the next.

Locked. *Spare supplies.* Useless.

On the other side of the room, Ian lets go of a small *whoop.* "Phone! Yes!"

Next locker. *Insulated clothing.* And why-the-f is it locked, too? Who steals from a mountain top? Come on!

Next one. *Jager skis.* Freakin' locked—not that I think a ski would be great to defend against Mostoroff, but at the moment I'd take it.

Across the room, Ian has switched into command mode. "2-2-4-0." He's going for Waterhouse directly.

One glance at my watch comes with a sting through my heart. "Eleven minutes!"

Next locker. Freakin' locked. I give it a frustrated shove.

Ian paces, phone pressed to his ear. "Come on, come on, come—Mr. Waterhouse, Donckers. No time. The Dark Unit is planning to hack MU and into one of our... *defense* satellites. They'll—what?"

Next locker. *Emergency rations.* Tempting, but not helping. And locked. *Gah!*

Ian halts. "No, stop. No time. Listen—" Pause. "No, listen—" Another pause, followed by a frustrated grunt. "No, you have to—stop it, sir, and *listen*, damn it!" He punches the air. "The Dark Unit is about to release a nuclear missile from one of *our* satellites and fire it onto the Berlin Reichstag during the president's speech. I need—"

One more locker. *Medical supplies.* "Damn it." I ball a fist and release it. My gaze jumps through the room. I can spend my time trying every drawer, locker, or cabinet, but with my current experience, it's safe to assume they're all locked. What else can I use—

Ian barks into the phone. "Who is on that? Whom do you

have? Make sure they—" He bites his lower lip as his fingers curl. "No! Not—my goodness, is there nobody—" He punches the air again, his gaze racing around the room, searching for— "Never mind. Alix. Laptop!" He rips the Ethernet cable out of the desktop computer under the desk.

Lapto—oh! The trophy I brought from the maze! I zombie-sprint to the desk facing the window, slipping it out of my backpack on the way there and ripping it open.

There. "Ian." I thrust the laptop at him. "Ten minutes."

He nods while booting up. "Yes. No, not you, sir. Put Wildason and Ayala on conference call, I can talk them through—just *do it!*" He jabs a finger at the phone, turning on the speaker. "I have a laptop with internet access here. We have ten minutes left, look at that freakin' countdown! I need them to help me, or else we will be too late!"

Oh, crap. Oh, crap, oh crap! Ten minutes to stop a hack? It took Waterhouse's team half a day to clear the hacked DMV site.

"Ian?" An unfamiliar voice crackles through the speaker, the volume and distortion a pain in my ears. *"What are we doing?"*

Ian cracks his knuckles. "You reinforce Sneaker's walls. I'll hit Torpedo with all I've got. It can't be successful controlling the satellite."

Okay. Okay. We're on it, there's hope. They strengthen the launch control's defensive wall, while Ian goes for the kill. If anybody can outsmart Torpedo, it's—

Boom!

Wood splinters as a bullet rips through the door's lock.

Ian's and my eyes pop wide and our heads whip over to the right: Mostoroff. He's here.

He's coming in.

The door handle rattles back and forth—but the door doesn't

open. Yet.

My pulse kicks into overdrive. "Shoot." It comes out as a wheeze.

Ian's gaze darts between the door and me, then through the room. "Alix, I want you to stay close. Hide. I'll take care—"

Crackle, crackle. "Hide what?" it screams from the speaker.

Ian flinches. "What? No, Ayala, not you. Focus on—" And with that his attention is on the problem at hand—the *more pressing* problem at hand, all things considered.

Which leaves our second priority to me: Mostoroff.

Boom! A second shot—and this time light pierces through a hole where the lock used to be.

Training takes over. I sprint toward the door as instinct screams retreat. Logic counters with a risk assessment as the panic inside my stomach curls tighter and grows a spine. My hands ball to fists. No weapon, but I can distract Mostoroff. Buy Ian time. Buy Dad time.

"Alix! No, come—"

"Ian, Torpedo isn't backing down—"

He emits a defeated groan. "Damn it! Check the firewall—"

Yeah. This is my job. Ian's got his to take care of.

A muffled grunt comes from the outside, then cracking and splintering as the door flies open and slams into the wall.

No time to think, no time to analyze.

A burly silhouette blocks the rising sun—gun aimed straight at me. Momentum and adrenaline keep me moving. *Shit.* I'm wide open, without cover—

"Wildason? Timer?"

"Eight-fifteen, Ian."

Ian curses. "Okay, crank it up. I need you to—"

Mostoroff pivots, pointing the gun at Ian.

His mistake.

Like Ian said, this guy's a desk jockey, not a trained assassin. Those precious one or two seconds he takes to aim, I catch up with him.

Ian, distracted by the noise, glances over his shoulder—at the gun. At me. His eyes widen as he realizes what I'm about to do. "Trouble! No!"

Can't have him focused on anything else but the missile. "I got this!"

I reach, grab his wrist with one hand a split-second before wrapping my fingers around the muzzle of the gun. With a quick pull and push motion I've redirected the line of fire off Ian—

Boom!

The slide bites my skin. I yelp out, but don't let go.

I got this. I can keep Ian safe.

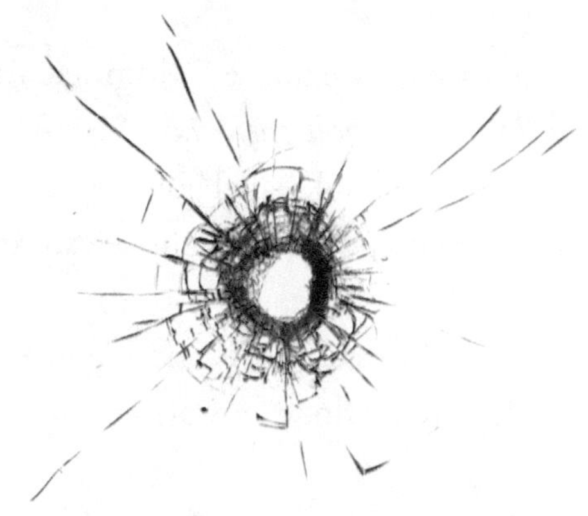

CHAPTER TWENTY-EIGHT
Blackhawk

Time freezes for a heartbeat as my mind goes blank

Mostoroff staggers backward, wrestling for control of the gun. My paralysis shatters as higher brain functions collide with pure panic.

Adrenaline kicks my body into overdrive, bringing crystal mental clarity: protect Ian, keep the gun away. Ian is the priority. Ian is Berlin's only chance. Dad's only chance.

A primal roar tears from my throat, and it comes way more naturally than I thought it would. Mostoroff yanks on the gun with all his strength, but I keep my elbows tight to my body. He pulls the gun, he pulls on me. I'm not letting that line of fire come anywhere near Ian!

With a frustrated grunt Mostoroff digs his heels in and drives his bodyweight back. We stumble out the door—

"Alix!" The clatter of a chair toppling backward comes from behind. *Ian.*

Fast steps approach, as panicked, distorted voices from the speakerphone. *"Ian? Can't keep them out! We need—"*

Crap, crap, crap, I— "Ian! Stay! I got this!" Because Ian needs to fight Torpedo. And I need to fight Mostoroff. "Priorities! Seriously!"

Ian's approaching footsteps stop, and I ignore the hefty curse he spits to the side as relief floods my system. *I've got this.*

Kind of.

"You little—" Spittle flies from Mostoroff's mouth.

Got to get that gun.

Unfortunately, the moment I try to break the gun out of his grip is the moment Mostoroff realizes he has a free hand available for strikes.

With an animalistic roar he rams his left fist into my temple.

I grunt, I stumble—but I hold on to the gun. Letting go means I'm dead, means that Ian is dead, and then—

Mostoroff seizes my hair and rips my head back.

Ow! Pain explodes along my scalp.

A chopped off growl leaves his throat as he tries to overpower my locked joints. My cervical spine screams from the unnatural angle, and my mind joins the chorus: I'm losing. My elbows will give in eventually, and then—

Time to act.

I have one shot at this—yikes, bad phrasing.

Like during training, Alix! Just like during training!

My knees buckle as he forces my body to bend backward. It's now or never—

Before I'm losing control of the gun I keep my elbows in close to my body, rotate my body toward him and force the weapon in the same direction while pulling on his wrist.

Crack!

Mostoroff's shriek pierces the air as his trigger finger breaks.

"Countdown's dropped to three-thirty!" shouts the voice on the phone.

Ouch. To both.

His grip in my hair vanishes, and I'm back in business. Before he can recover, I wrench the gun free from his useless, broken finger, and step back.

I got the gun! I—

Mostoroff swings his leg up and over, foot connecting with my hand and tearing the gun from my grip.

Crap!

It clunks to the ground a good three meters away, half-buried in-between grass and bushes. The pain in my hand doesn't register. Only the gun counts. I dive forward—

Too slow.

Mostoroff snares me behind, arms crushing around my torso like an iron vise. "You're an annoying little thing." A whiff of old sweat assaults my senses.

The gun lies there, taunting—

Nervous, near-panic chatter spills from the speaker. Ian's replies come muffled, fat with tension.

"I'll deal with you later." He tries to swing me around and dump me to the ground, but hell to the no—ain't gonna happen! I hook my right leg behind Mostoroff's and anchor my body to his, while attacking the hands across my torso with all I've got. One finger is broken already, and I can make it hurt more!

A hoarse howl rewards my assault. "Bitch!"

He tries to swing me, but I'm no beginner.

"Asshole!" I ram my head back, going for teeth, but finding shoulder.

"Bit—" He stumbles back two steps, me in his arms.

"Fuck!" Ian's curse brings bile up to my throat.

I thrash wildly—left, right, right, left again—each hit finding Mostoroff's solid shoulders. But I don't stop. Every movement weakens his hold and keeps him from the gun. If he's busy with me, he isn't busy with Ian. So yeah. I howl, I kick, I go ballistic.

I might not defeat an adult man, but I'm not giving up, not with Dad's life on the line, Ian's, countless others'! I'll buy Ian as much time as I can.

I tighten the leg hooked behind Mostoroff's—and *boom*, I drive my other heel up and into his groin with all the force I can muster.

Mostoroff emits a grunting choke. "You little—" Like a switch flicked, he lets go of me.

The speakerphone crackles. *"Two minutes. Ian, only two—"*

I hit the ground running and bolt for the gun. Just keep Mostoroff away for two lousy min—

I make it exactly two meters.

Mostoroff hits me like a freight train and tackles me, driving me into the frozen ground. My lungs empty as his weight crushes down. I stretch, the gun *right freakin' there*, and still out of reach. He crashes his elbow in the back of my head, my skull bouncing off the dirt.

Mostoroff shifts to grab the weapon, but I'm quicker. The instant his weight lifts, I flip onto my back and drive my fist into his face.

You're welcome, ass!

He jerks, the moment where he thought he could go for the gun gone. Growling, he focuses on the immediate threat—me.

My defense snaps up—thanks for months of training—barely deflecting his punch. But that's where luck runs dry.

Mostoroff wraps his fingers around my throat.

And squeezes to kill.

I lose it. Rational thought goes poof as pure survival instinct kicks in.

I buck my hips and twist my body, throwing every ounce of strength I can squeeze from my exhausted muscles into breaking free. I swing my legs, I wiggle—

Mostoroff grunts.

But doesn't loosen his grip on my throat.

Sweat breaks out from every pore as my body exhausts its reserves. The need for air becomes overwhelming, but I can't get him off of me. I fight like a madwoman. I throw everything I have into this. I *must*. I kick and thrash—forward, backward, it doesn't matter as long as I don't hold still, as long as I don't give up. My knees hit his back without much of an effect, but I don't give up. I won't back down. Somewhere in the Berlin Reichstag, Dad is preparing for his speech. Straightening his tie. Going over his notes one final time. I'm. Not. Giving. Up.

But I'm getting weaker. *Dizzy.* Lungs are burning.

A low rumbling rises up from somewhere below us, rumbling so deep it vibrates in my chest.

Mostoroff cocks his head as the noise picks up in intensity—

And I take this one split-second of distraction.

With the last bit of strength I have left in me, I buck my hips and pluck at the hands around my throat, targeting his broken side first. With a surprised grunt, Mostoroff loses his balance and flies forward. I twist, rolling on top between his legs, and ram my fist into his face with as much power as my oxygen-deprived muscles can muster. Mostoroff's head snaps back and hits the ground. His eyes roll into their sockets, his arms drop—and on instinct, I dive to the side and out from between his legs, reach for the gun—

Mostoroff jerks and pushes off, trying to scoot for the

weapon—

Not on my watch.

My fingers close around cold steel, drawing it from the grass.

Yes!

As I scramble up to standing I tap the gun's magazine and rack the slide. It's jammed—

Mostoroff works himself up to standing.

Crap, crap, stay down! I back away from him. "Stay where you are," I shout over the deafening *whopwhopwhop*-noise growing closer. The wind has turned into a small storm, pelting us with debris, but I stand strong, gun in my hand and aimed at the man who hurt Ian. Who wanted to kill us.

"You bitch!" Blood streams from Mostoroff's broken nose. He lurches forward—

"Stay!" My gun—well, *his* gun—is up and aimed at him. I really, really don't want to shoot him, but I will if I have to.

Mostoroff roars at the top of his lungs as he charges me, arms outstretched—

I fire—and nothing!

A panicked scream tears from my throat—the slide, dammit, it's jammed, I—

The noise cranks it up to ear-splitting—

Bang! Bang!

Mostoroff yelps out in pain and drops to the ground a mere meter in front of me. I scramble backward as he clutches both hands to the back of his left thigh. Blood oozes between his fingers—

For a moment, I don't understand. What—

Clouds part as a helicopter rises from below the plateau's edge, its rotor blades unleashing a storm worthy of hell around us. It tears on my sweaters, rips my hair free, and steals the scream right from my lips.

The helicopter slides over the ridge, hovering before us, and there, in the open door, holding on to a handle with one hand and aiming a gun at Mostorroff—

I blink hard.

No. It can't be.

Five men in military fatigues jump out, weapons drawn. They yell something that's impossible to hear while they run toward us. For a split second, panic swells. They're not thinking I'm the bad guy, are they?

But no, they're not. Four soldiers swarm Mostoroff, securing him on the ground none too gently while the fifth signals over to the helicopter.

My breath comes out choppy. My temple hurts, where Mostoroff hit me, maybe that's why I'm so slow in uptake.

Mostoroff isn't a problem anymore. Help came. Help—

The heli touches down about twenty meters in front of me, and finally, *finally*, the wind dies down.

Movement catches my attention. The soldier with the gun, who shot Mostoroff, lowers himself from the chopper, slowly, like he was in pain.

I blink against the sun.

He's huge.

Covered in bandages.

In torn black clothing.

With… sunglasses on his nose.

The gun in my hand shakes.

No. Impossible.

It can't be.

And yet…

"Dimitri," I whisper.

Dimitri.
Dimitri!
Dimitri is alive!

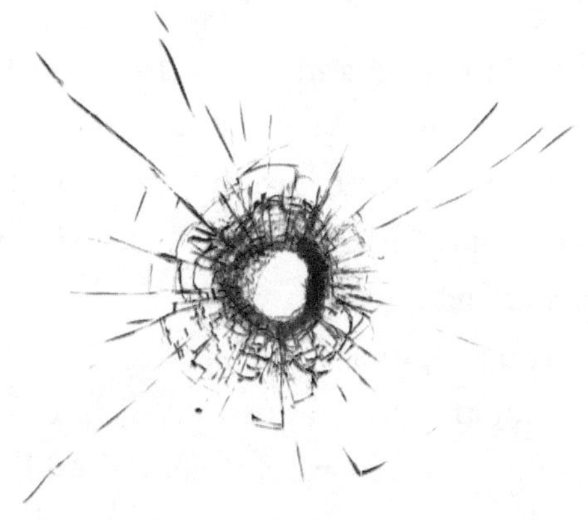

CHAPTER TWENTY-NINE
Eighteen Seconds

"Dimitri!" The cry tears from my throat as I thrust the gun, barrel down, at the nearest soldier.

Dimitri.

I run, my feet flying over stones and leaves, covering those few precious meters in record time, until I crash into him with desperate force.

I wrap my arms around his waist as far as they will reach and bury my face against his chest. "You're alive!" Dimitri is alive! *We* are alive!

He tightens his embrace and rests his chin on top of my head. "And just in time, it appears."

In time. My body goes rigid. Not so sure about that.

I pull back, breaking his hold. "Dimitri—Ian! He's inside, the Dark Unit is trying to—"

One sharp nod and he releases me. "What can I do?"

Good question. Time blurs. How long does it take to almost

choke somebody to death and then get overwhelmed? Probably more than two minutes. "Pray." Bile rises as I grab Dimitri's sleeve and drag him with me into the building. "Ian, what—"

I freeze so abruptly that Dimitri collides with me, sending me stumbling forward another two steps.

It doesn't really register.

Ian slumps at the desk, arms folded, head buried between them. The laptop sits askew, as if shoved aside in frustration. Nothing but white noise hisses from the phone's speaker.

This is what defeat looks like.

All strength leaves my body. "No," I whisper. No. It can't be. It can't have happened. I can't be standing here, whole and breathing, when moments ago, a nuclear missile was fired onto the Berlin Reichstag. When moments ago, Dad died. When countless others—

Ian's shoulders heave. He releases one explosive breath and rocks back into the chair, shoving both hands through his hair.

A fissure splits my chest, fracturing through my body into my soul. Too late. We were too—

Dimitri sidesteps me. "Ian."

As if tasered, Ian jerks. He launches from his chair, spinning to face us, eyes wide, mouth agape. "Dimitri?"

"The very same."

Ian takes one hesitant step forward. "What… How…?"

Dimitri shrugs. "Got a few tricks up my sleeve." He nods at the laptop. "Care to elaborate?"

It takes Ian two blinks to catch up with Dimitri. "Oh. *That.*" He twists, nudging the laptop to display its screen.

00:00:18

The countdown froze at zero hours, zero minutes, and eighteen seconds.

Eighteen freakin' seconds between us and nuclear devastation.

Ian did it.

A ragged breath escapes me as my knees threaten to buckle.

Ian did it. *We* did it. Dad's alive. Dad's safe, and so is Berlin.

A low chuckle breaks free from Ian. "Spot on, eh?"

"That's how we work best."

"True."

Something passes between them—and then Ian crashes into Dimitri's arms beside me. One of them sneaks an arm out of the hug and pulls me in, squishing me in-between the two guys who mean the world to me.

For the next ten seconds, nothing matters besides this.

Dimitri.

Ian.

Me.

Us.

The dizziness is gone.

The nausea.

The light-headedness.

I lift my face from the shoulder it's pressed against. "We did it," I whisper. Teamwork. PRICS-style.

Nobody will get killed by a nuclear missile.

Dimitri is alive.

We have Ian back.

Ian nods. A shy grin pops up on his face. "We did it." He tilts his head to the side, loosening his hug around Dimitri's waist. None of us reach higher, and Ian isn't small. Emotion storms in his eyes as his gaze flickers back to me and locks with mine. "We did it." He tugs until I release Dimitri. "You took care of Mostoroff."

Kind of. "I had help." Without Dimitri…

Ian sweeps his thumb across the back of my hands. "Not when I saw you attacking him. I died about a thousand deaths when you went for him."

"But if I hadn't, he would've killed you, and then those thousand deaths would've been real." And many, many more.

"True." It's a hoarse whisper. "Doesn't change that letting you face him was the hardest choice I've ever made." His gaze holds everything I've been longing for this past year, and more.

With a little pang, all the painful knots of worry in my stomach detangle and unfurl into something else, something more powerful. Headier. Deeper.

I throw myself into his arms, ignoring Dimitri—the witness to my *inappropriate behavior.*

Ian locks his arms around me like steel. One hand tangles in my hair, the other clutches at my sweaters.

"We did it," he whispers against my ear, pulling back just enough to look into my eyes.

Heat blooms in my chest.

Everybody's safe, and Ian and I—

A mischievous smile tugs on the corners of his mouth.

Then, his lips find mine.

Ian and I, we're together. Life is good.

Dimitri mutters, "About time," but I can't be sure. My world has narrowed to Ian alone.

Ian and a future that's safe.

Thanks to us.

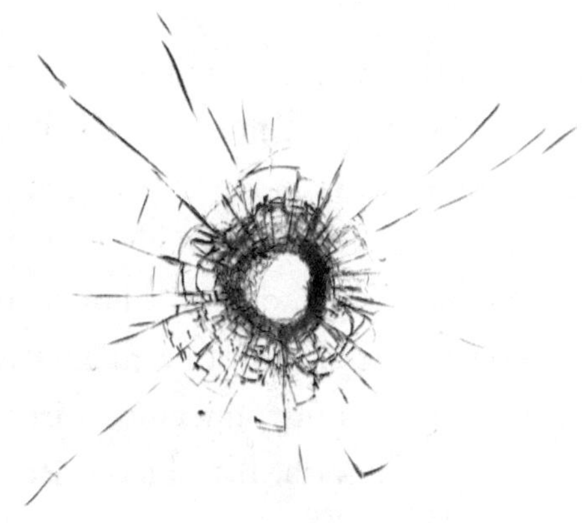

CHAPTER THIRTY
Top Secret

Eventually, we're ready to leave the mountaintop. Mostoroff is tied into a neat package and stuffed into the helicopter. Ian has developed quite the interest in a cell phone he took from him. While Ian updates Waterhouse, Dimitri nails a blanket over the two broken windows to at least keep some of the elements out until it can be repaired. I do feel sorry for the damage we caused, but then, not really.

Dimitri waves for us to follow and leads us to the big Air Force helicopter.

Ian takes me by the hand and whistles through his teeth. "A Blackhawk. I want to hear *that* story."

Dimitri helps me inside. "You will. In time." Meaning, nobody here has clearance to hear the whole story.

The half-hour flight to Ohlsson Air Force Base passes in a blur. A pair of MPs meet the helicopter upon landing and escort us straight to the Medical Wing.

At this point, a little bit of sensation has started creeping back to my hands and legs, but not much. I'm still more wobbling than walking, and so is Ian. Even Dimitri, who avoided our deep-freeze experience, moves with less than his usual grace.

We all must look straight out of a horror movie as we're zombie-walking across the tarmac toward the medical facility: wrapped in blankets, hair untidy, unkempt, dirty and worn out, and in desperate need of a wash. Blood has dried in rust-colored patches on Ian and Dimitri's skin, all of us are beaten up, our clothes mudded, caked and torn. We're quite the sight to behold.

The medical team, hardened by military service, doesn't even bat an eye at us. Walking wounded usually make it—it's the ones arriving on stretchers that worry them.

Modesty is out the window as we're placed in three beds next to each other, and nurses work on us from all sides, cutting our clothes off, taking our vitals, checking our wounds. The only few minutes the curtains are drawn between the three of us is when we're butt naked. After the nurses have taken care of our wounds, they hand us Air Force-issued underwear, and the flight surgeon, Dr. Myers, examines us. Prescribes pain meds. Antibiotics. Whatnot.

When the curtains part again, we're all sporting matching-green underwear, cleaned up but still looking like we've been through hell. Dimitri's torso has become an artist's palette of bruises, his breathing shallow and stilted... broken ribs, I'd say.

And cuts.

Knife cuts on his arms and sides.

He'll have new scars to add to the ones already on him, but at least he's alive to tell the tale.

On my other side, Ian is equally pale and crappy looking. The little spaceship stands sentinel on his nightstand, rescued from the jacket before they stripped us down. He's shaved, his goatee as perfect as before this whole ordeal. The wound where they dug out his tracker looks even more savage now that he's clean.

At one point, the combination of exhaustion and blissful warmth knocks me out and I fall asleep. When I wake up again, the flurry of activity around the three of us has settled into nightshift quiet. Dim lights illuminate the three empty beds across from us, the curtains still drawn back.

Ian.

Following an impulse, I slip from beneath my blanket. The cold floor bites at my bare feet, but compared to the last days, this is nothing.

I pad over to his bed. Ian lies still, breathing regular. Asleep. Dang it, I—

Without opening his eyes, he lifts up his blanket in a silent invitation.

Should've known. Always alert.

I slide in beside him, curling against his shoulder. He wraps his arms around me as he tugs the blanket around my back as far as he can reach.

Home.

His lips gently touch my forehead. "Hey," he whispers.

"Hey," I whisper back to him. This feels natural. Not awkward, not forced. Normal. Not like any of the insecurities and questions I had with Sam.

I don't want to think about Sam right now.

The medical wing doors crash open, lights flooding the room as boot steps thunder in.

Dr. Myers, the flight surgeon, hurries past the group of people barging in like they own this place. "Colonel, they need rest—"

"They rested long enough," one of them—the colonel?—grumps.

Ian smoothly extricates his arm from under my head, sitting up as five uniformed men approach. A stern-faced officer in his fifties fixes us with a narrow-eyed stare.

Ian clears his throat. "Lieutenant Colonel Cooley, an honor. Jason Miller, White House Teaching Staff. We're grateful for the rescue."

Yes, it says "Cooley" on his fatigues, but knowing Ian's OCD-like preparation for missions, I wouldn't put it past him to read up on all military bases around the States, to be prepared. And since he's using his alias like up in the helicopter, Colonel Cooley—or some of his men—is not ranked high enough to know about PRICS.

Cooley draws himself up to his full, impressive height. Dimitri-sized. Tall.

He harrumphs. "White House Teaching Staff? And that gives you authority to commandeer one of my helicopters with an override code?" He throws an angry glare at Dimitri. "And since when does the Air Force One divert to my base for a personal pick-up? I expect answers, Mr. Miller."

Well, I can help with that. I mean, the president's daughter can. I raise my hand. "That would be my doing, sir. Alix Forrester, the president's daughter."

The atmosphere in the room shifts.

Cooley's expression remains carved in stone as he meets my gaze.

One-Mississippi.

Two-Mississippi.

Three—

"Out. Everybody out. I need the room." He doesn't take his

eyes off me.

The other soldiers and Dr. Myers file out without any questions. Military hierarchy.

Once the door clicks shut, Colonel Cooley drags a chair from the table and plants himself in front of Ian's bed.

Dimitri rises from his bed to join us, perching on the corner on Ian's bed next to me. We huddle together like three kids at story time, me nestled between the guys.

Cooley heaves a sigh, arms crossed. "You want to tell me what really happened? Military override code? That's not standard bodyguard knowledge. Hiking in freezing Alaska as unprepared as you were when we pulled you out? Not very smart, and doesn't sound like a school project either. The president's daughter, her teacher and a bodyguard arriving beaten and bloody? Also not standard, and what you'd expect from a hiking tour. The president's daughter in her teacher's bed? Well, things surely have changed since my kids went to school."

My face burns tomato-red, but Ian takes over before I can say anything.

"No sir, nothing of this follows protocol, but all of it is sanctioned." He folds his hands on top of the blanket. "Unfortunately, that's all I can tell you. Order 336, subsection two. I'm really sorry about that and I wish we could repay you with more than unanswered questions, but our hands are tied."

Silence stretches between us.

Cooley's scrutiny bounces from Ian to me, then Dimitri, before settling back on me. The stern military commander melts away, replaced by something paternal. "These two treating you right?"

"Yes, sir. Couldn't ask for better." The words come easily weighted with truth.

Cooley nods once. "Good. While you gentlemen might not fall under my command, I can make your stay here pleasant or decidedly less so. This young lady just earned you the former." He gives me a quick little wink and smile that I return. I appreciate the concern, unnecessary as it may be.

Cooley gets up and returns the chair to the table. "Air Force One's making a detour on its way back from Germany. Landing at 0400 hours, and we're giving them a proper reception. Everybody out on the tarmac, unless Dr. Myers declares you unfit."

"That won't happen. Thank you, sir," Ian states with quiet confidence.

Ten seconds later, Cooley is gone. The moment the door closes behind him, we release our collective breath.

Ian nudges my ribs playfully. "Look who scored us first-class transportation. Air Force One, not too shabby." His grin is infectious.

"Right?" Gotta say I like that too. I can't wait to see Dad. He needs to know everything—and I mean *everything*. I need to talk to him as an agent and member of PRICS and tell him every detail about the mission, from beginning to end, including my screw-ups. I need to get that off my chest.

But even more, I need to talk to him as his daughter and tell him every detail about the mission that won't be in the official report, including Ian. He was so worried about me when Sam and I broke up, he's going to be happy to know Ian's there for me now.

Can't wait to see his face when he hears the news.

Dimitri is about to get up off Ian's bed, but Ian holds him by the sleeve. "Stay. Report time."

He falls back onto the edge of the mattress, sending tremors through the bed.

Ian reaches over to his nightstand and turns on the radio, a clear sign we are going to talk business. No RSWB-pen here, unfortunately.

As soon as Rihanna's voice fills the air, Ian spreads out his arms. "Okay. How the heck did you pull that one off?" He shakes his head slowly.

Dimitri lifts an eyebrow. Thanks to all those bruises on his face, he looks more dangerous than cool, those light, piercing eyes adding their part. "Diligent preparation, astute observational powers, exceptional marksmanship, and a whole lot of luck." The corners of his mouth slightly curl upwards.

Ian buddy-punches Dimitri into the shoulder. "Got a lot of things to say to you, but one has priority: Thank you. We wouldn't be here without you."

He holds out a hand and Dimitri takes it. For a moment, neither of them moves—a moment frozen in time, eyes locked in wordless communication.

"Thank you," Ian whispers again, emotion catching in his throat.

"Unnecessary. You know that." Dimitri's voice carries equal weight.

Goosebumps prickle up my skin from the raw honesty passing between them. Something is passing between them, something I don't—

Ian clears his throat. "Still. And seriously, I need to know how you pulled that off. I need details before the president arrives. Bring me up to speed."

Ian weaves his fingers through mine, attention still on Dimitri. Normal. Casual. I love it.

Dimitri's lips inch up a tad more. "Another day at the office, Ian." He shifts his weight. "It didn't take me long to realize your kidnappers were warned. No hacker group should be this well prepared for an armed attack." He points to the knife cuts on his body. "Once the two of you were out of the cabin and safe, I didn't have many options left. No weapons. Injured. No way out of the maze. So… I blew up the cabin."

"You *what*?" I mean, yes, something big must've happened to make the entire cabin fold in on itself, but what the hell?

Dimitri shrugs. "Only way out. I took shelter in their walk-in safe—that was the room where the readings dropped off."

"The room with the heater next to it," I whisper.

Dimitri nods. "Their *gas-powered* heater. Boom." His fingers imitate a gun.

Ian gapes. "Hell of a gamble, Dima. Chain reaction, explosion through the heating system bringing down everything…" He shakes his head.

"Got rattled some."

Some.

Right.

"Digging out took time. No supplies, injured, and you two gone—had to move fast. Jogged to the nearest Air Force Base." He indicates our surroundings with a casual gesture.

He jogged *here*.

"You jogged—" I can't do the math. The distance staggers me. "All the way here? That took you—"

"Twelve hours, cross-country. Drank from a stream. Couldn't rest, because if I did—"

"Hypothermia. Exhaustion."

"Correct."

And I thought we'd had it rough.

Dimitri cracks his neck. "Triggered their perimeter alarm deliberately. Once the response team arrived, requested their CO, used the override code. Alix's tracker led us to you. The rest you know."

Un-be-freakin'-lievable.

Dimitri is a machine. He weathered that same storm. Granted, he didn't have to climb up a steep mountain, but still. His whole summary sounds like a series of action movie highlights strung together. How he could pull this off is still a mystery to me, despite his explanations.

If the odds fight you, you fight harder. Lesson learned. Thank you, Dimitri.

Ian falls back into his cushions, stunned. "Dima, that's… unbelievable. Even for you."

Dimitri gets up. "I may have said that before, but I don't believe in no-win scenarios." He winks—actually winks—at us and walks back over to his bed. "But even this machine needs sleep." He tugs himself in and turns on his side, effectively ending the debrief.

Story time is over.

"Good idea." Ian taps my shoulder.

I get the hint, nestle against him, tracing the veins mapping his hands. One of his fingernails is black and blue, the skin on his usually soft hands much rougher than normal. We were so lucky to have come out alive.

So darn lucky.

The whole last week is one distorted blur, and while part of me can't wait for my dad to come and pick us up, I don't want this to end, this us-against-the-world-thing.

I lift one of Ian's hands up and kiss it, a soft brush of my lips against his skin. His head is so close to mine, I can feel him smile before he kisses my neck near my spine, sending sparks and goosebumps all the way down my body.

No, in *this* time out I could stay forever.

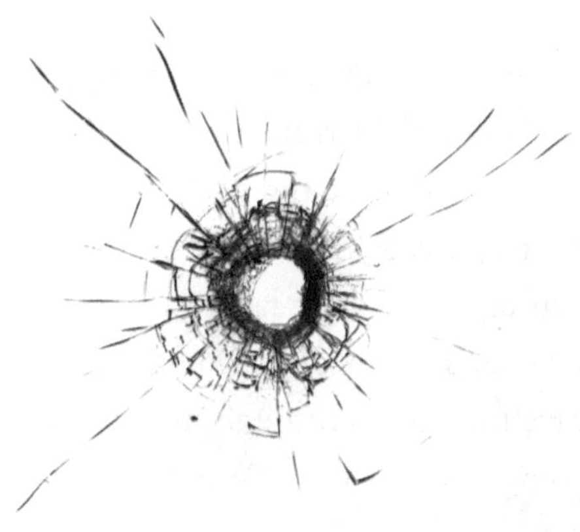

CHAPTER THIRTY-ONE
Daddy

Several hours later, we're outfitted in pristine military fatigues. Never knew fresh-washed clothing could hold such an appeal.

The tarmac gleams under floodlights, the pre-dawn air crisp, but we're neither wet nor half as exhausted as the last day, so I don't think either of us mind.

The red carpet is out, quite literally, flanked by precise rows of personnel. Lt. Colonel Cooley heads the formation with his command staff, followed by Ian, myself, and Dimitri. The rest of the airmen stand at parade rest across from us, their uniforms immaculate.

Three lights pierce the darkness—one red, one green, one white landing light—growing larger until Air Force One descends majestically onto the runway.

Have I mentioned I love AF-1? I do. Especially today.

I'm not only happy to see the white and blue on its outer hull, but to be the daughter of the man who flies it. Well, not literally, Dad has enough trouble getting a car through thick traffic, but figuratively. I'm proud to be the daughter of a man who tries to make this country, this world, a better place.

I straighten my spine and glance at Ian. He's grown paler in the last hour or so. The upcoming briefing with the president, I assume. I weave my fingers through his, and squeeze his hand.

We're going to be fine. Whatever comes next, we've weathered worse.

Air Force One taxis into position in front of us, engines winding down. Shadows move behind the windows as the gangway descends. Two Secret Service agents take their positions, and then Dad appears.

"*Ten hut!*" The Colonel's shout shutters the dawn stillness. With a sound like clapping thunder, the whole battalion snaps to attention, eyes straight ahead.

Dad doesn't waste any time with ceremony.

No waving down, no show for the non-existing cameras. He hurries down the gangway, trailed by Oliver Brooks, his chief of staff.

And Jenna Altman, the press secretary.

And Yoshi Nagakawa, the deputy chief of staff.

Oops.

Not a quick pick-up.

"Damage control," Ian whispers next to me.

Indeed. When word leaks of the president's daughter's detour to Ohlsson Air Force Base—it needs to be airtight. Politics, with a classified twist.

Dad exchanges salutes with the Colonel. "Colonel Cooley."

"Mr. President, sir. An honor to have you on Base."

"The honor is all mine, Colonel. Thank you for picking up

my daughter from her ill-advised hiking expedition. Her teacher and I will be discussing appropriate field trip locations." He and the Colonel shake hands.

"Our pleasure, Mr. President. At your service, any time. Please let me introduce my staff to you."

My dad nods and Cooley introduces him to the officers standing next to him. They exchange a few pleasantries, and then Dad's gaze falls onto Ian and me.

And onto our joined hands.

Dad is smooth, he always was. I'm sure Ian doesn't even notice it—or maybe he does, it's Ian, after all—but I see the tightening around Dad's mouth like under a spotlight. The slight narrowing of his eyes. Could be a suppressed smile, or a suppressed I'm-going-to-rip-her-head-off. When he's in public mode, I can't tell.

Then Dad holds out his hand to Ian. "Mr. Miller, welcome back. Next time, a more adequate destination for a hiking trip, perhaps?" The smile is diplomatic, but let's not kid ourselves, that's for show. We hear the underlying message as clear as day: don't get her in trouble again like this, my friend.

Ian clears his throat as he takes my dad's hand. "Yes, sir. And thank you for picking us up." His grip tightens around my hand.

Then Dad's attention shifts to me. "Alix." He opens his arms, and that's all I need to fly into him.

This.

This I missed for all last year.

Dad and me, in the same corner.

He angles us away from Cooley and the others. "Everything okay? Are you all right?"

I hide my mouth in his shoulder. "Yes. We're fine. And I'm sorry about this, but we had no choice. Things… happened. I'll explain later." The words tumble out, a promise and a confession.

"You're here. That's what matters. We'll sort out the rest." He releases me to greet Dimitri with the same carefully crafted story about hiking safety.

Dimitri takes it in stride. It's showtime, after all.

While my dad makes his way down the red carpet toward the base, the rest of his staff follows. Oliver, Altman, Nagakawa… and then, as the last person, looking sharp in his suit, Sam.

Sam.

His face carved from stone, eyes fixed ahead, deliberately unseeing.

The rejection stings, deserved or not.

My fingers clamp around Ian's so hard I might break something, but minutes later the entourage disappears into the base. We say our thanks to the medical team before boarding AF-1.

Twenty minutes later, Dad walks into our little room. "Alix, Mr. Miller, Dimitri. My office." Not a request. An order.

"You too, Sam," he adds in a more quiet tone when he sees Sam in the hallway.

Sam's jaw drops. "Y-yes, sir."

We trail Dad to his office like ducklings. A strange déjà vu hits me the moment he settles behind his desk, coffee steaming before him.

"Sit." Dad points to the chairs in front of his desk. "You too, Sam."

Dimitri stays by the door, and I try to keep my nerves sitting between Ian and Sam, my current and my ex-boyfriend.

Things sure have changed over the last days.

Dad takes a deliberate sip of coffee. "Report, please."

"Of course." Ian leans forward, shoulders squared, and for the next ten minutes, he tells our story from the last time we sat in here, right after planting Sneaker at MU.

He doesn't spare any details, which… well, makes my dad swallow hard a couple of times. Once we get to the point of Ian's abduction, I take over.

I walk him through Ian's parents, the scavenger hunt for clues, freeing Ian.

Losing Dimitri.

The words catch in my throat—his survival doesn't erase the ache.

Dad swirls the coffee in his cup. "Lane?"

Yeah, Lane. I sit up straighter. "I should've picked up on it sooner. I thought it was Waterhouse. His behavior was odd, while Lane… well, he played the concerned citizen perfectly, only it was his game plan to stay under the radar. Ian figured it out right away."

I glance at Ian, who takes his cue. "The lines weren't that clear cut, sir. I know Waterhouse very well, but if I didn't, everything Alix told me he did would've made me suspicious, too. But by now, we have concrete proof it was Lane, not only a suspicion. We retrieved this from our gunman."

Dad's eyebrows shoot up. "Gunman?"

Yeah, we hadn't really mentioned Mostoroff yet.

Ian holds up the phone, wincing. "Getting to that part, sir. Anyway, this here contains Lane's private cell number with several texts from him—one revealing our Little Springs destination, another sent to him with instructions on how to open the door to packet sniffers to infiltrate our software."

Click-click, access one of their websites, malware sneaks in. They'd dumbed it down for a non-tech like Lane. Can't really beat myself up for missing Lane's act in the Oval Office, but when he gave himself away during the phone call… I should've known. I should've listened, but I was too focused on getting my prejudices about Waterhouse confirmed.

Listening to what I hear was the *first* thing Ian taught me on my very first day of being a PRICS Agent, and I still can't pull it off. Still. Can't. Pull. It. Off.

Dad's jaw ticks. "I would still like to hear about the gunman. As in, now."

"It's less dramatic than it sounds, Dad." He never even got to aim it at me. With intention to shoot, at least.

"Really. Then by all means, enlighten me."

I exhale slowly. Somebody has to tell him I willingly charged Mostoroff head-on. Might as well be me. But I don't have to make a big deal out of it. I know Dad.

"Mostoroff, one of the hackers, followed us. After destroying our heli, he guessed we were heading to the mountain facility. He caught up with us when Ian was cyber-fighting the Dark Unit, so I… I kept him busy."

The silence stretches.

"You kept him busy."

My face burns bright red like a sundown on Hawaii.

"I distracted him to keep him from shooting Ian."

"And he had a gun—"

"That never pointed at me, Dad! I'm trained, I kind of know what I'm doing." Emphasis on *kind of.* "In fact, I took the gun from him."

Dimitri clears his throat. "Correct, sir. When I arrived, Alix had disarmed Mostoroff and had the situation under control."

Thanks, Dimitri, for leaving out the part where I needed the heli's distraction to not get choked to death and Dimitri to shoot Mostoroff, but anyway. I give my dad a pointed glance. See?

Dad's jaw works hard on the next sip of coffee. "Can we tie Mostoroff to any other members of the Dark Unit?"

Ian nods. "I believe so, sir. We have ample information on his cell."

"Good. I want the Dark Unit eliminated."

Pause.

His gaze pins me. "I'm wondering. How did you manage the night in these temperatures without any fire in the cave?"

Uhh.

Might've skipped over a couple of completely unnecessary details there…

"Sleeping bags." I swipe a strand of hair out of my face. Once more. And again. "Dimitri packed sleeping bags for us." *Please don't ask how many bags, please don't ask.*

Dad's gaze slides from Ian to me and back, then over to Dimitri, and lastly to Sam.

One more sip of coffee.

He sets the cup down with a soft clink.

A vein pops at his temple.

Then a frown flickers across his face, there and gone. A short nod. "Exceptional work, team. Needless to say that me, my staff, and most of Germany are deep in your debt. You averted a disaster, no matter how close the call. On the upside, this incident will help me decommission that satellite, or at least disarm it. The cold war's behind us." He rises in one fluid motion straightening his jacket.

"I still need detailed debriefings from each of you. Ian, Dimitri, the classroom. Alix, Sam, I'm sure you can find topics to discuss until I return."

Without another look at me, he strides around his desk and out the door, Ian and Dimitri following stat.

Then the door closes, and I'm alone with Sam.

Uhm.

Not what I'm prepared for.

I keep my gaze down on the spotless floors.

Neither of us moves.

Neither of us says a word.

I don't think either of us breathes.

Ridiculous. I've faced down a mad Russian, I should be stronger than that.

Deep breath. "Sam—"

"Alix—" he says at the same time, and we both smile.

I turn on my chair and face him. "Hey."

"Hey." It's a sad reply.

Okay then, big girl panties. Time for courage. "Sam, I need to apologize. For keeping PRICS secret—though orders tied my hands there. For my behavior, how I treated you. I truly—"

He holds up a hand. "Stop Please. *I'm* the one who needs to apologize, Alix. I behaved like an idiot. I…" He plays with a button on his suit jacket, twirling it left and right between his fingers. "Don't really know where to start, so… the beginning, I guess. Alix, I told you, I… I've liked you for a while. Then your dad takes me aside and tells me to keep my hands to myself. Shocker right there. I mean, *your dad!* The Senator. Presidential candidate." He shudders. "I hated it, but what was I supposed to do? And then, when he talked to me again and said that if you were interested, I'd have his blessing…" His mouth closes and opens, and closes again. A sigh escapes. He looks up at me, eyes sad. "It should've been perfect. It should've been a green light, a home run. Only it wasn't."

Oh. "I get it," I whisper and swipe that same errant strand of hair behind my ear. "Pressure." Don't I know it.

A sad smile joins the sad look. "Yeah. Your dad expected me to be with you. Watched me. Encouraged me. So did my dad, by the way. And… it screwed with my head. I wanted to be with you for so long that when it finally happened, I was so afraid of making mistakes that all I did *was make mistakes*. I was terrified. Terrified I'd do something wrong, terrified to act, and terrified not to act. Terrified you would like someone else more than me, terrified your dad would fire me if we ever broke up. So I guess… I kept you at a distance right from the start."

His raw honesty cuts deep. "That's what it felt like," I whisper. That's what it felt like, me always trying to reach Sam, and never quite getting there. Rejected from the start.

Sam drops his gaze to his hands. "I know. I pushed you away and hurt you every time. That was me bracing myself for the heartache I knew would come." He laughs out harsh. "And it did come, only I brought it on myself."

There's no way around it, I have to come clean. "Not just you, Sam. I wasn't innocent either." I force myself to sit up straight and look at him. He deserves that much. "To continue where you left off, it was the same for me… with Dad. You were always his favorite. The night Dad and I had the fight before dinner, he called me out about Ian. Nothing was going on, but he told me in clear terms Ian was forbidden. *You* weren't." I wait for my words to take root.

Sam swallows hard. "A setup."

"Sort of. It's not as if I hadn't wanted to be with you, Sam. Really. I crushed on you a while ago, you know that, and when we were finally together, it was fulfilling that dream."

He tilts his head. "I hear a *but* coming."

I shove my hands under my thighs. Not easy, the next part. "Yeah. Jason. Ian. I… In the beginning, it was a crush. Stupid.

School-girly. But… it grew into something real, even with him keeping things professional." I don't want Sam to think it's Ian's fault, because it isn't. The responsibility is mine, and mine alone.

I curl my fingers under my thighs. "With PRICS, I always had to prioritize. Work came first, and you came second. And yes, while I can blame PRICS, I also… I wanted to be with Ian, Sam. Maybe subconsciously, but I wanted to be with him. And…" Boy, this sucks. "And if we hadn't had my dad and Waterhouse against us, we'd have gotten together sooner." On July Fourth. Without a doubt.

Silence.

Sam falls back into his chair. "You're together. Ian and you." Not a question. A statement.

I blush and nod. "It kind of happened over the last days." But it was a long time coming.

Pause.

"So when I pushed you away, I pushed you right into him." He gives a dry laugh. "You know, I wish I had a better reason why I behaved like an ass when you told me about PRICS, but in the end, it wasn't only that suddenly Ian and even you were way cooler than I was, it was also that I… *I* wanted to be the cool guy in the West Wing for you, not somebody else. Come on—a *secret* branch of the Secret Service? How am I going to beat that?" He lifts his hands, palms up. "No chance! I was jealous already even without that, from day one. Ian is nice, don't get me wrong, but he was with you way more than I was. When you told me it wasn't just school… I couldn't keep it together." He gives me a faint smile. "I'm sorry how this all played out."

My eyes widen. "You're apologizing to me?"

He shrugs. "Yeah. Because I think we had a shot. We *would've* had a shot, if things… had been different. I was scared. Jealous.

You were scared, and then—"

"In love with another guy," I whisper. "I'm sorry, Sam. I truly am." Our eyes lock, and the sadness wafting through the room cranks it up another notch. We would've had a shot, if… Yeah. *If.*

Sam loosens the tie around his neck. "Alix?"

"Yeah?"

"Friends?"

Surprise flickers through me. I don't have to think about it. "Of course!" He's offering me what I thought I lost, what I thought I destroyed.

I'm not losing Sam for good. We're still friends, and we were better as friends anyway.

Both of us jump out of our chairs like pulled up on strings. We fall into each other's arms, and boy, does it feel good.

Whole.

"I missed this," I whisper into his chest.

"Me, too," he whispers back.

We hold on to each other for a long time, slowly rocking back and forth. A couple of butterflies flutter up when his butterscotch-scent hits my nose, but they're weak. I guess I'll always love Sam, in a way. It's a different love than for Ian; that much I know now. Ian's love gives me wings and makes me stronger. Sam's warmed me up and kept me afloat, but it didn't reach the heights Ian's does. With Ian, I can fly.

Eventually, we pull apart.

Sam chuckles. "You know what? Your dad called me into this office on our way to Germany. He showed me reports from your missions, pictures and other stuff. Got a pretty good verbal beating for behaving like I did. And I deserved it. It opened my eyes. So I guess I'm tagging on another apology. I'm sorry I didn't believe in you."

The honesty in his words makes me stand taller, although… "Yeah, well, didn't always work out that smoothly during this mission. And, by the way"—I lift both hands in defense—"I didn't tell Dad anything about what you said. You know how he is." And despite that it's a bit embarrassing that he gave my ex-boyfriend a talking down, I love, love, *love* that he's got my back.

Sam laughs, and it is great to hear. "I know. I also know my boss slash your dad." He winks at me.

The door opens without a knock. Well, it is my dad's office after all. With one glance, he assesses the situation. "Good, so this is taken care of, too. Thank you, Sam."

Sam hears the dismissal as clearly as I do. "Thank you, Mr. President."

He throws me a questioning look, but still leaves.

Dad pours himself another cup of coffee from a thermos. Something's off. His shoulders are so square, the seams of his jacket are close to bursting, and somehow… somehow the silence is heavy.

I didn't do—

Oh.

The gunman. Crap.

I suck in my lower lip.

I'm going to get chewed out for attacking an armed man by myself. After the July fourth-sniper Dad's *grounded for life-*warning about risking my life for others seemed playful, but then … this is Dad.

And I deserve it. Like so much else.

I take a deep breath and brace myself for what's to come.

Dad's shoulders heave up once. He turns around, and I… I nearly step back.

I haven't seen this look since… since before I saved his life. Since the VP got arrested.

A muscle in his jaw pops, and he delivers the deathblow. "One. You are leaving PRICS. Two. Whatever is going on between you and Ian ends now."

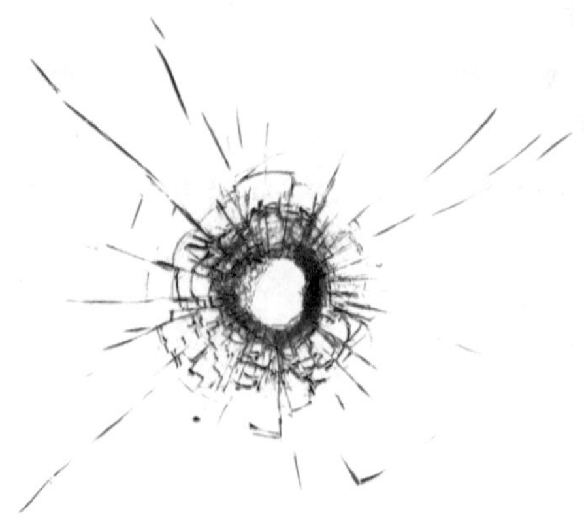

CHAPTER THIRTY-TWO
Dismissed

My jaw drops to the floor. "What?" I heard that wrong. He didn't say that, he—

"You heard me right the first time, Alix! Don't make me say it again."

A knife to the heart couldn't hurt any more. "What?" My voice rises. "You can't do that, you promised!" After the VP incident—more power to us, less to Waterhouse, and even if not, PRICS is independent from the president, he can't—

Coffee sloshes as Dad sets his cup down. "Don't underestimate me, Alix. I'll find a way to remove you from PRICS, even if I have to dismantle the whole organization. You will not, I repeat, you will *not* work for them anymore. Period."

The knife in my heart gets twisted and pushed deeper. "You can't do that." My mind is stuck in repetitive mode. He can't do that. PRCIS is off his access, he doesn't have the authority to—

"I'll find a way if I think it's necessary to protect my

daughter."

This isn't real. We're not talking about this, and not in this tone.

I shake my head. "To *protect* me? *Ian* is the one who trained me and gave me the skills to defend myself! *He's* the one who helped me through the roughest year of my life, so if you ask me, he's doing a darn fine job of protecting me!" I'm all but screaming at Dad, but at least my voice doesn't hold the same shake to it as my hands.

Whatever is going on between you and Ian, it ends now.

No.

No, no, *no*.

Dad raises a cool eyebrow. "That's not what I meant and you know it. Don't pretend I'm stupid. *Two* sleeping bags, really?"

"Oh." I deflate a little.

"Yes, *oh* indeed." He takes a sip of his coffee, lips pressed white. "Trust me, this is not a conversation I want—here, now, or ever—but if he got you pregnant—"

"Dad!" Oh my god, Dad didn't think Ian and I—

"If he got you pregnant or touches you in any inappropriate way ever again, his career in the FBI is over." He takes another sip of his coffee. At this rate, not much is going to be left in a minute or so.

My mind is a swirling mess of chaos, a Gordian knot of emotions, all twisted, knitted together and screwed up. He can't separate me from Ian—he *can't*.

"Dad," I start again. Focus, Alix. Focus! "Dad, it's not like this. Nothing happened—"

He interrupts me, a scowl on his face. "Again, Alix. I'm not stupid."

And suddenly I'm back where we were a year ago.

The cool, distant and disappointed dad.

The daughter who wants to do right for him.

It's the same helplessness, the same paralysis, the same fear.

But *I'm* not the same anymore.

Not by a long shot.

Anger coils inside my core. "Well, Dad, maybe you are. No, my turn," I interrupt him before he can protest. "First of all, it's not *your* decision to make whom I'm falling in love with. I'm happy to hear your suggestions and guidance, but that's all it's ever going to be. Second, how can you ask me if he got me pregnant? I don't even know where to start!" I take two steps back. I can't be next to him, I need distance. "That question alone implies a stupidity on my part that's insulting. Two people are part of getting somebody pregnant, and believe me, I know how that works, Mom has been all over me with her talks since I was ten!"

Another step back, or I might do something I'd later regret. My hands are curled into fists, my heart races a marathon inside my chest.

I. Am. Mad.

"That you don't trust me to have the good judgement to *not* sleep with Ian while we've barely escaped the Dark Unit, while on the run, and while being hunted by a mad Russian is even more insulting. Do you think that little of me? You should know me better."

I take a step forward. "*You should know me better.*"

Dad stays silent, observing me like an animal in the zoo.

My heart drops into the chasm that has opened between us. Deep breath. I've got to save this… somehow. "Dad, please… PRICS is what I want to do. And you didn't have a problem with Sam, so please don't have a problem with Ian either. It didn't work out between Sam and me, but with Ian… it's already different. *Please*, Dad."

Something flares in his eyes. "Something is different? *Something is different?* Well, you're right with that, Alix! First, he's your teacher, your superior officer—"

"He is not my teacher! You know that very well! It's his alibi, and just FYI, I graduated, and he's not my—"

"Whatever you want to call it in your situation! I don't really care! You will not, and I repeat, *not* start a relationship with the man whom I should trust to keep you safe!" He jabs an angry finger toward the hallways in the general direction of our classroom. "And second, you will not be in a relationship with a man that much older than—"

"Sam is older than me!" Hell, everybody is older than me!

"I don't care," Dad yells. "I don't give a damn! That was Sam, and Ian isn't! He's your teacher *and* he is too old for you! This ends *now!*" He slices his thumb in a cutting-motion across his throat.

For a moment, only his heavy breathing fills the room.

My heart seizes and shatters into a million pieces. "Dad—" A mere whisper he doesn't even hear.

He looks at me.

Cold.

Detached.

"This is how it's going to be. Consider yourself lucky I'm not sending you to the boarding school, but unfortunately, I don't trust you enough at the moment to let you move away from my supervision."

"Wha—"

He holds up a hand. "In addition, I will give it my best to shut PRICS down. This nonsense ends now. I realize there might be a bureaucratic battle, so until PRICS is terminated and Donckers is off the premises, you're not going to be in a room alone with him ever, under no circumstances. I spoke to Dimitri already, the order is given." He lifts his index finger in warning. "Any inappropriate conduct will have consequences. I don't know if you would call it a break-up already, but if so, then that's what's going to happen. You are going to break up with Ian, and any refusal or evidence to the contrary will get you both in trouble."

He tugs his suit jacket straight. "You're dismissed."

I'm dismissed.

Dismissed.

Like a sleepwalker, I turn to the door, finding the knob blindly. What the Russian couldn't accomplish on the mountain, what the VP failed to do last year, Dad managed in under five minutes.

I might still have a heartbeat, but I'm dead inside.

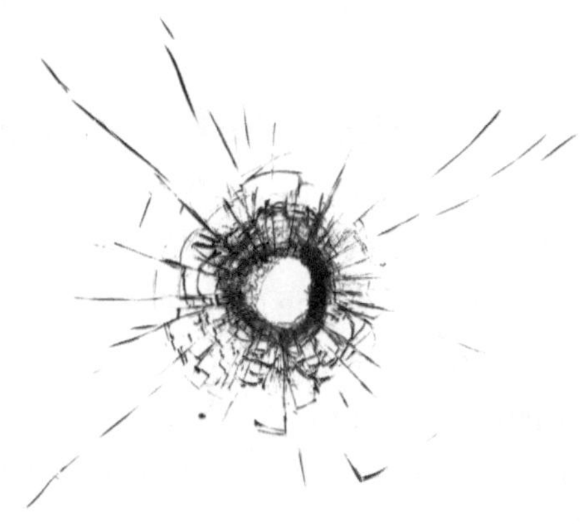

CHAPTER THIRTY-THREE
Reunited

Four weeks later, I'm standing at Reagan National Airport, Terminal B, arrival level, dressed in a similar suit-style uniform as Dimitri, complete with a chauffeur's hat and sunglasses.

I tug on the collar. Scratchy.

A crowd of people passes us, all looking weary from the flight, all with suitcases or at least bigger carry-ons, but none of them the people I'm waiting for. Judging by their seats on the plane, they're probably going to be among the last passengers to leave, so it might be another couple of minutes.

Fine by me. I don't get out that often, so it's a treat to mingle without people recognizing me. Thank you, chauffeur's uniform and visor cap. Despite my hair being back to its normal pseudo-blonde, I'm pretty positive no one's going to recognize me as the president's daughter.

Which suits me perfectly, given how I feel about Dad right

319

now.

I lift the sign I'm holding a bit higher, just in case. I don't want to start out this premier by screwing something up—again. This is a big deal. A really big deal. It's a regulation that needed to be broken and changed a long time ago from my point of view, and that's what Waterhouse did.

One of these days, I'm going to bake him a cake or something. Since the Alaska mission he's had our backs in *every* aspect, and I don't even count the memo for Jenna Altman to brief the public on my *long-planned hiking trip with unfortunate consequences due to unforeseeable changes in weather*. That one was an easy and necessary explanation after my little excursion became public. I'm talking more about supporting Ian and me in everything PRICS.

We're not shutting down PRICS, but not for lack of trying on my dad's part. That must've been one heck of a conversation Waterhouse had with him. Never have I seen Dad as steaming mad as after that meeting. Well, only fair, because I'm also steaming mad. Still.

Luckily, we didn't need his presidential approval for the change of *this* policy either. Waterhouse still let Dad know, common courtesy and all, but I don't have a clue what he thought about it. We don't talk that much these days.

While the change in statute went through quickly, getting *this* set up took us a while, screw the NSA and their precautions. We couldn't make mistakes on the home run. Finding the right backstory, arranging and planning the raffle, notifying the *winners*… it took care and caution, especially after having dealt with a leak.

After Lane's arrest, everyone in the White House, and I mean everyone, got vetted again, and even more thoroughly than the first time. No more leaks for us. Lane was enough. I do feel sorry for him though. The Dark Unit had a pretty good grip on him and his family. They got to him when he was abducted in the line of duty all those years ago, and kept the pressure on him. His family is now in a witness protection program, but Brandon won't join them for a while, unless he gets out of jail early—as in under twenty years.

Dimitri straightens up. My clue. I scan over the masses and hold my sign up higher: *Donckers—WhizKid Tours*

And there they are.

A woman with the same smile as her son, and a man who looks just like him.

Hank sees us first and points us out to Teresa. They pull their overnight trolley over to us. Dimitri's turn.

"Mr. and Mrs. Donckers? Welcome to Washington DC, and congratulations on winning the raffle. My colleague and I will take care of your luggage and get you checked in at the hotel. Follow us, please."

They shake hands while I busy myself with the luggage.

Not yet.

The glances Hank shoots at me are enough at this point. Should've known. Ex-cop. Plus, Ian's gotta have gotten his observational skills from someone.

While Dimitri opens the limousine's door for the Donckers, I load the luggage into the trunk and close it.

Showtime.

I slide into the rear and take a seat opposite of Ian's parents, my back toward Dimitri and the front.

Dimitri pulls out into traffic, I buckle in… and then take my cap off. And my sunglasses.

Hank tilts his head and Teresa gasps in surprise. "Kira?"

I wave. "Hey, Teresa, hey, Hank. Good to see you again." It *is* good to see them again. I like those two.

"What a surprise. You moved here?" Teresa asks. "Straight to DC from Little Springs, that must be nice."

And that's where the critical part starts. "Yes and no. I've been in Washington DC for a while, I was more… traveling through Little Springs when we met."

Both their browns furrow.

Time to rip the Band-Aid off.

Band-Aid number one, that is.

"I have to come clean a little bit. My name isn't Kira, and I don't, or didn't, go to the Little Springs College. I—"

"You're the president's kid. Forrester's girl." Hank. Ex-cop, like I said.

I give an acknowledging nod. "Correct. I'm Alix. Nice to meet you, officially now."

They exchange glances. "Wait—why is the president's daughter working as a chauffeur for a tour of the White House that we won?" Teresa shakes her head.

"Because this isn't what it seems to be. Something else is going on, and I bet it has to do with why you were at our house, asking about Ian. Doesn't it?" Hank cocks an eyebrow at me.

Credit where credit is due. "You're right. At the moment, I can't tell you much more besides that it'll be worth the confusion. I need you to trust me, and if you can't do that, then at least bear with me for another five minutes. Please."

Another glance, and Teresa holds out her hand to the middle of the seat for Hank to take. "Yes, we can. Don't mind the old grump here." She lifts up their entwined hands.

We reach the White House perimeter and Dimitri circles us into the parking garage. It's the middle of the day, so it's pretty full, at least down to a certain sub-level. Dimitri keeps going down in circles until we hit the tenth sub-level. Could have been the ninth. I always get confused.

I point a thumb behind myself in the direction we're driving. "As a heads-up, please don't worry about what happens next. Remember Ian's invention, the holographic wall he was supposed to present at a science fair? Well, this is it."

Dimitri speeds up and aims for the wall.

No way we can go in slowly and minimize the shock for the Donckers. Too crowded.

Like me on that fateful day a year ago, Hank and Teresa expect to crash into the wall.

Their eyes widen, their mouths open, their grip on the other one's hand tightens—and with a little squeal by Teresa and an *hmph*-sound by Hank, we break through the wall.

Dimitri hits the brakes, the sudden deceleration throwing us all into our seat belts.

Hank's face splits into a wide grin. "It works! I always knew it would! He spent so much time on it—I *knew* it!" He lifts Teresa's hand to his mouth and kisses it. "I *knew* it."

The look they share, this proud, yet happy look… Definitely about time we're getting rid of this charade, and before they start wondering why the White House has their dead son's technology installed.

Band-Aid number two is about to come off.

I unbuckle myself and get out first.

The limousine came to a standstill right in front of the traffic cones. Dimitri was so precise, he didn't even add new skid marks to the wood floor. Mad skills.

The Lair is even tidier than normally. And homey-er. We got some water bottles for the table, some flowers…

"Please have a seat, I'll be back in a minute." I guide Hank and Teresa to the couch, and they automatically grab a water bottle when sitting down. Something to hold on to. I know how that feels.

Dimitri takes position in his usual corner, and I palm my way into the adjacent surveillance room. I want to spare Ian's parents the whole mysterious *they're here*-announcement I went through almost a year ago. Ian had been sitting in this very office, well knowing I had just arrived, like he knows his parents are here now.

I close the door behind me. The room is tiny, but filled to the brim with monitors on the walls and on every desk surface. Keyboards, phones, radio—from here we can access every surveillance item we need to.

Stiff like a statue, Ian stands in front of the screen showing his parents on the couch. No sound, but not because we don't have it, but because Ian chooses not to listen in.

I wrap my arms around his chest. "They're doing fine. They *will* be doing fine."

A strangled breath escapes his throat as he buries his face between my shoulder and neck. His heart hammers inside his chest so hard it almost bruises mine in the process. This is tough on him, but it's been that way since the day he quote-unquote died.

I rock him back and forth a little bit, and he lets go of a desperate sigh.

"Am I doing the right thing? What if I'm making things worse? This knowledge can be dangerous."

We've been over this countless times.

"They were in danger the moment Lane leaked your information. We're giving them the tools to fight back.

Knowledge is power, and this knowledge will help them." I drop a kiss onto his cheek.

Ian pulls away a little to look at me. "What if they get mad? If they can't handle it? I'll lose them all over again." His eyes plead with me, asking for a promise I can't make.

I take both of his hands in mine. "They will be *fine. You* will be fine. Your parents are smart and strong. They will get it."

I hope.

He gives me a faint smile in return. "And everything else… We still keep secret, right?"

I don't need to ask what he's talking about. A sad necessity with an overprotective dad. "Yes. Everything else… we'll have to keep secret."

Like to my dad and the rest of the world, Ian and I will be either colleagues, or teacher and student. Not a couple.

"I wish it wasn't so," he whispers, his hands gripping the fabric of my shirt as he draws me closer again.

I swallow hard. "Me, too," I whisper back. As it is, every touch, every hug, basically every thought I have about Ian, is violating Dad's orders—and orders they were, despite the fact that he can't *officially* order either of us three around.

Let's say the definition of *not alone together* has been stretched a little bit over the last weeks.

I squeeze Ian's hands once more and then let go. "Ready?"

The more we drag it out, the tougher it's going to be.

Ian nods.

I go ahead, open the door, and step through first. Behind me, Ian takes and releases a deep breath and then follows me into his office.

Hank and Teresa are talking to each other in soft voices, not even looking in our direction. I step aside. My part in this is over for now.

Ian stands still for another two seconds, and when he speaks, he sounds much younger than he actually is. "Mom? Dad?"

Boom.

Like a bomb dropped, both his parents jerk.

For a moment, Hank freezes in mid-motion, while Teresa's head whips up and over to where Ian's voice came from. Her hand flies up to cover her mouth, but she can't suppress the little yelp when she sees Ian.

She gropes blindly for Hank's hand. They both look like they've seen a ghost, and somehow they have. It's been five and a half years since they buried Ian.

Ian takes one little step into the room and hesitates.

Insecure. Afraid. Not like the man who turns into a ninja when he steps onto the mat, but then, this is different.

"Hey… It's really me." He tries a shy grin, and for Teresa, it's all she needs.

She launches off the couch, and Ian meets her halfway. They collide in a crushing embrace, both crying. A moment later, Hank is there, carefully stretching out a hand to touch Ian's shoulder.

"Ian," he whispers.

Ian looks up from his mother's embrace. "Dad," he whispers back through tears.

He opens up the embrace, and Hank falls into it.

All three hug, cry, and hold on to each other for dear life. Ian is squished so tightly in-between his parents, I don't know how he manages to breathe.

At one point, he lifts his gaze and locks it with mine.

His face is wet from tears, but the anxiety and fear are gone, replaced with love and happiness.

The intensity of the emotion reflecting in it makes me blush, but he won't look away.

We don't need any words.

I blow a little silent kiss over to him.

Same here, Ian.

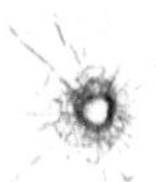

The reunited Donckers family takes a long time until they can let go of each other.

I bring Kleenex and water, then change into regular clothing and out of the chauffeur's uniform and run to the cafeteria to get some cake and cookies.

Eventually, everybody sits around the coffee table. I get out of my corner seat. "I should leave and—"

Ian catches my hand. "Stay. Please." A quick hidden brush of his thumb over the back of my hand, and I fall right back into the cushions. Okay, privacy is overrated for family reunions anyway.

Besides… this is the hard part. The coming clean.

The confessing that Ian did this willingly to them.

Hank is the one to start. His police senses must've been going crazy since I picked them up from the airport. He gestures around the room. "Now, tell us how you got into this mess. What is this, and why are you not—"

"Why am I not dead?"

It sounds wrong hearing Ian say that, and Hank flinches when he nods. "Yes."

Ian takes a sip of water and tells the story of the last five years of his life.

His recruitment, the staged accident by the NSA, training, his work at the FBI and then at the Secret Service and PRICS.

When he gets to the fake accident, Teresa cries and Hank drapes an arm around her.

Ian gets the story out matter-of-factly and without apologies. When he's done, Hank blows out a breath through pursed lips. "That's… quite the story." He looks over to me. "So if I understand it correctly, Ian is training you as a spy of sorts. Was that why you came to Little Springs the other day?"

I exchange a glance with Ian. My part to tell the tale. Ian's poor parents are not being spared a thing today.

I try to go lightly on the whole kidnapping story and especially certain gruesome details, but I guess they can imagine how badly the Dark Unit beat and injured Ian. Teresa is white, and Hank doesn't look too well either.

Silence hovers when I'm done.

Hank looks from me to Ian and back. He glides a hand through his hair, and now I know where Ian has that gesture from. "I… I don't know what to say. I want to be mad at you for leaving us like that, I really do."

Ian bites his lip and drops his gaze. Exactly what he was afraid of. Losing them all over.

"But when you tell the story, it all makes sense. For every step, I understand why you did what you did. Do I like it? Heck, no! Am I going to ruin seeing my son again by accusing him of cruelty or hurting us? No. You made your decisions, and we all had to live with the consequences. Not only us, but you even more. You had to live with knowing how much you hurt us, and I think that's punishment enough."

He shakes his head and huffs. "I would still like to know how recruiting minors like this can be legal, but—"

"It's complicated," Ian and I say in unison, and break out in a grin. Neat.

Teresa and Hank burst out laughing, all the emotional load of the last minutes gone.

For the next four hours, we sit and talk. I get us some more cake and cookies from the cafeteria after the first batch vanishes within minutes. Ian shows off his drink dispenser with bioelectric signal detection to his parents, and when Teresa doesn't ask a question, Hank does, and if he doesn't, it's her turn again.

When everybody is getting up to leave, Teresa hugs Ian firmly. "You're still going to be here tomorrow, aren't you?" She says it lightly, but can't hide the worry in her tone

Ian hugs her back. "I am, Mom. I really am."

He guides them both to the limousine, and a minute later, Dimitri has backed them through the holographic wall and out of the Lair.

It's as quiet as a tomb in Ian's office.

Teresa's perfume and Hank's aftershave still hang in the air, the only reminder this afternoon truly happened. Finally, it feels like we're on an upwards slope again, despite my dad's shitty behavior.

Yup.

Upwards and onwards, by all means.

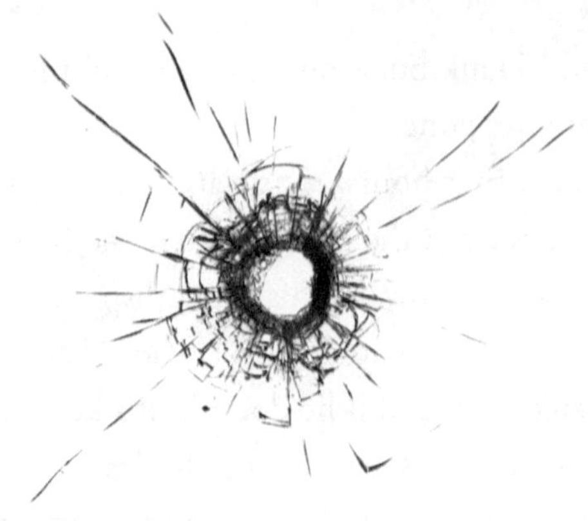

CHAPTER THIRTY-FOUR

Against Orders

Dimitri pushes his chair back. "I'll be... using the bathroom."

He stands up from Ian's small dinner table, face an unreadable mask, although I'm pretty sure I know what he's thinking.

Something along the lines of *you better not get caught*, because if we did... it's his head as well as ours.

Needless to say, Ian and I owe Dimitri big for, uhh, his weak bladder, and of course for turning a blind eye.

Also needless to say, we know we're walking a line here. A fine line. One wrong move, and Dad—

I swallow my last bite of dinner. We won't make a wrong move. And Dad brought this on himself. We could've talked like adults. We could've come up with guidelines, rules. It's not as if we would've made our relationship public anyway—that would've been rather messy.

Pictures of the First Daughter and her boyfriend?

Oh look, isn't that Ian Donckers, who died five years ago?

So no, not a good idea.

And I get it. He's my dad, he's worried. But besides that, we're back to square one—trust issues, daddy-daughter issues—I can't deal with him accepting Sam and rejecting Ian. Double-standard.

The door closes behind Dimitri and Ian gets up. "Give me a second. Right back."

Hurry back. Those precious seconds alone together come far and in-between, I don't want to lose a single one of them.

I take a sip of my water and lean into my chair, casting a glance out of Ian's fake window. For tonight, he chose the same view he had from his childhood room at home, and I like it. I don't want to see mountains and snow anytime soon, but I like Little Springs and Ian's old home. It's cute. Birds are flying by, cars come into the street and find parking right away, and the sun is creeping down behind the woods in the distance.

At some point, we'll have to go back there. I still have Paul's business card—

A pop-up window appears over the view of Little Springs. *Warning. Republican Senator accusing President of fraud during election. Warning.*

"Uhh… Ian?" I yell into the room. A pop-up warning. Should've known Ian's never off work.

"Yep?" His voice comes back muffled from the bedroom.

"There's a warning popping up here. You wanna have a look at it?"

A moment later, he comes out of his room, keeping the door behind him ajar. "Republican Senator… huh. Well. Nothing that needs our immediate attention. We'll deal with it first thing tomorrow. Now, we've got other stuff to do." He makes a wave-slide motion and the pop up vanishes, leaving the view of an undisturbed Little Springs.

Tomorrow? It's not *that* late, we could still look through whatever data we have now. It's a waste of our Dimitri-free time, but still. "I don't mind. Pull the info up here, so we don't have to go upstairs." I point to the fake window.

"Nope."

"Nope?" That doesn't sound like Ian.

"Nope," he repeats and comes over to me. "Close your eyes, Trouble."

Close my—

I squeak as Ian lifts me out of my chair and holds me tight to his chest. Out of reflex, my arms go around his neck, but I still can't let it go. "But what if it's important?"

Ian chuckles in my ear. "If it was important, we'd have sirens."

Oh. Of course.

So, well, I focus on more important things, like Ian's gentle but firm hold of me. His spring soap scent. He has *something* planned, and my mind plays out a couple of scenarios quite vividly. Tingling shoots down all the way to my toes.

A door opens—and my heart stumbles over its own feet. The bedroom.

Ian is *carrying* me to his *bedroom*.

It takes all my willpower to keep my eyes closed and appear totally cool.

Because I'm not.

Not cool at all.

Nope.

My body is made out of flames where Ian touches me. Burning, sizzling flames. I suck in my lower lip and bite it. I need pain to keep me grounded, or—

Ever so slowly, Ian lowers me down into something soft. His bed.

Dimitri-free minutes FTW. No offense, Dima.

"Keep your eyes closed, Trouble."

I do. I really do, but it's hard work.

The mattress dips next to me. There he is.

I work on a dry swallow.

"Open your eyes, Trouble."

I obey—

—and I fall right into the universe.

Saturn, to be precise.

The pitch-black darkness around us stretches Ian's room to infinity, or at least to the sixth planet of our solar system. The projection moves, bringing Saturn's rings into view. Smaller and larger pieces of rock and ice float through Ian's room as we move through the rings, one by one.

It's beautiful.

Mesmerizing.

And the best... "You remembered," I whisper. He remembered I asked him if he could do Saturn.

"Of course," Ian breathes into my ear. He inches a hand up my shirt to come to rest on my stomach. "Do you still want to talk about pop-up warnings?" His fingers curl across my skin, leaving burn marks in their wake.

"Hell, no." I shake my head. Never in my life has politics been more unappealing than now.

"Good." Ian trails soft little kisses down my cheek toward my mouth.

I grab his shirt with one hand and his hair with the other. The fingers on my stomach circle around my belly button, and slowly, slowly, *slowly* creep up until his thumb grazes underneath my bra.

My back arches off the mattress and into Ian.

There is this one split second before we kiss, when our eyes lock and I can see all the way down to his soul.

And it's beautiful.

Raw.

Mine.

Our lips meet, and the universe around me loses focus, turning into a multitude of colors and sensations.

Pop-up warnings can wait.

Ian and I will be there to face them tomorrow.

About the Author

Micky O'Brady is a pediatrician-turned-writer living in beautiful, dry Southern California with her husband and two critters (one son, one dog). Her award-winning YA thrillers and sci-fi novels blend action, romance, and the kind of adventures she wishes she'd had as a teen.

Time Warped—the opener to her sci-fi romance trilogy—recently swept the 2025 Outstanding Creator Awards, claiming First Place in Time Travel / Alternate Reality / Multiverse, Science Fiction, Speculative Fiction, and Best World-Building, while fan-favorite Captain Kieran Wildason walked off with the coveted "Hottest Character" title. Her 2024 release Playing with #Fire captured Best Fiction Book of the Year and dominated seven categories at the same awards, and CRISPR—CRIS PARR continued her winning streak with honors at the 2025 Feathered Quill Awards. All three novels were also American Writing Awards finalists, adding to her rapidly growing shelf of accolades.

When she isn't up at around 3 a.m. (with a cup of tea, Earl Grey, hot) drafting stories she can't get out of her head, she can be found at a martial arts dojo, though maybe not at 3 a.m. She holds a second-degree black belt in both, Krav Maga and Judo, and is convinced every girl should know how to kick some butt.

Micky remains a firm believer in the healing powers of Nutella eaten straight from the glass and in the magic that can happen on a rainy day, as long as there are fuzzy socks and a cup of hot tea involved.

Before diving into YA fiction, Micky published several academic works including a doctoral thesis, medical articles, and a book on emergency communication. None of them are as fun to read as her YA novels though.

Through Snowy Wings Publishing, Micky has released an impressive collection of YA fiction, including "The President's Daughter" series (THE PRESIDENT'S DAUGHTER and its sequel TRIAL BY ICE, originally published by Curiosity Quills), the "Time Warped" sci-fi romance trilogy (TIME WARPED, TIME BOUND, and TIMED OUT), the award-winning sci-fi romance BETWEEN WORLDS, the multi-award-winning PLAYING WITH #FIRE, and the standalone novels ANGEL DOWN, 33 DEGREES, and the acclaimed CRISPR--CRIS PARR. All titles are available on Amazon and at mickyobrady.com.